(Continued on next page . . .)

D1397617

ANVIL OF THE SUN

"Groell may have created a pair strong
enough to rival Nick and Nora Charles or
Fafrhd and the Grey Mouser. . . . A lively,
swashbuckling air. . . . The well-drawn
main characters are surrounded by a strong,
individualized supporting cast. . . . Highly
recommended."   —*Starlog*

"An engaging, high-spirited romp through a
world full of color and excitement."
                          —Paula Volsky, author of
                          The White Tribunal

"Plenty of likable characters, and the
lighthearted tone and fast pace keep things
fun."   —*Locus*

CAULDRON OF INIQUITY

The Third Book of The Cloak and Dagger

ANNE LESLEY GROELL

A ROC BOOK

ROC
Published by New American Library, a division of
Penguin Putnam Inc., 375 Hudson Street,
New York, New York 10014, U.S.A.
Penguin Books Ltd, 27 Wrights Lane,
London W8 5TZ, England
Penguin Books Australia Ltd, Ringwood,
Victoria, Australia
Penguin Books Canada Ltd, 10 Alcorn Avenue,
Toronto, Ontario, Canada M4V 3B2
Penguin Books (N.Z.) Ltd, 182–190 Wairau Road,
Auckland 10, New Zealand

Penguin Books Ltd, Registered Offices:
Harmondsworth, Middlesex, England

First published by Roc, an imprint of New American Library,
a division of Penguin Putnam Inc.

First Printing, December 1999
10 9 8 7 6 5 4 3 2 1

Copyright © Anne Lesley Groell, 1999
All rights reserved

Cover art by Allan Pollack

 REGISTERED TRADEMARK—MARCA REGISTRADA

Printed in the United States of America

This one belongs to Kay,
for keeping the faith.

ACKNOWLEDGMENTS

To Joseph and Marjorie Groell, for continued love, support, and the hotel room in Athens that started this whole thing. To my cast, for being mostly obliging. (No, Absalom, you will *not* be getting your own series!) To the editorial pre-production players—Lizzie Bancroft, Miriam Ashley-Ross, Jenni Smith, and Stephen Dooley—for beating me and this book mostly into shape; to Jen Heddle for expertly completing the job; and to Laura Anne Gilman for giving her (and me) the chance. All remaining mistakes are mine alone. To the sharpest eye in the east, Felicia Browell, for proofing. To Andrew Dansby, for gifting his middle name to a burned-out druggie. To Kay McCauley, for drinks, gossip, and enduring belief. To Pat LoBrutto, Juliet Combes, Evelyn Cainto, Chris Artis, and Jamie Warren-Youll, for being the bestest bunch of colleagues a gal can have—and for keeping me sane at work. To the Upper West Side Posse—Diana Gill and Jaime Levine—for movies and drinks and keeping me sane at home. To Ben Kremer, Sarah Strasser, and Simon Taylor for distracting me over the ether. To the roomies—Natalie Mai, Sonja Srinivasan, and Stuart Ruggles—for the parties, and for tolerating the occasional (?) late nights of writing and loud music.

Viva La Sequined Donkey!

PROLOGUE

"Saul Soleneides, my dear old friend; how delightful!" Owen DeVeris beamed at the face projected in his crystal. "I didn't expect to hear from you again quite so soon. You're looking well, as always."

"As are you, my friend. As are you."

"Oh." The Guildmaster sighed. "No. I'm looking old. And feeling older. To be honest, I don't know how you do it, looking like a man only half your age. It must be the wages of sin."

His companion chuckled, raven eyes glinting out of a face still taut and smooth despite its sixty-odd years. It was, Owen reflected—running swollen, arthritic fingers through the thinning strands of his own white locks—quite blatantly unfair. No matter how many suns rose and set, Saul Soleneides barely seemed to change. He still held himself like a man twenty years his junior, his body lithe and supple, his movements unfettered and ripe with that animal grace Owen remembered so clearly from their youth. Even his hair remained thick and lustrous, bearing that same tight Konastan curl. And the faint dusting of silver that dimmed its strands from purest raven to a deep iron grey only served to add maturity to a face which otherwise might have looked far too naive, too guileless, to belong to the shrewdest businessman this side of the Belapharion.

Boyish and beautiful—with features so fine they were almost feminine and dimples that popped whenever he smiled—it was a look that had plagued Saul during his youth. Yet instead of senescing, he had settled, his features firming into a classic middle age that left him looking handsome and competent, and as sleek as a rich illusion club owner could appear.

Those dimples were still as much in evidence, however, as he grinned and replied, "As I recall, what you do is not entirely legal either, my friend."

Owen chuckled, acknowledging the truth of this with a nod. They were, neither of them, running quite on the side of the law; but they each, in their way, did good. In his position as master of the Hestian Guild—the largest collection of assassins, bodyguards, and spies yet assembled—Owen De-Veris weeded out society's cancers. And Saul Soleneides used the profits of his rather nefarious industry to become one of the biggest philanthropists in all of Konasta.

It was no wonder they had become such friends in the days of their youth at Ceylonde University.

"So," Owen said, folding his arms and settling back more comfortably in his chair, his feet propped casually on the studied clutter of his desk. He was aware of the odd picture he must be creating in Saul's crystal: a strange, foreshortened figure, all boots, with a small, tip-tilted head. "How long *has* it been?"

"Too long, and not long enough," his companion answered cryptically. "How did you get on, last month, with that information I gave you?"

"Very well, thank you." Owen brought his feet back down and leaned forward, studying his friend's visage intently. "This isn't a pleasure call, is it?"

"Lovely as it is to talk to you, no. Not entirely."

"Hmm. What's happened?"

"Someone's put out a contract on me, I suspect. The first two attempts were fairly inept and easily countered, but I may not be so lucky the next time. Especially since I swore on my mother's grave that I would let my two best bodyguards go to Phykoros in two weeks, and I hate breaking a promise. Therefore, I was wondering if I could have one or two of your more minor operatives to fill the gap—any that you can spare, of course—just to keep an eye on things until my regular pair returns and all this nonsense blows over."

"And what makes you think it's likely to blow over?"

"I don't see why it shouldn't. Even rogue assassins charge a nominal fee, and if the Telos family is behind this, as I suspect, they are bound to be running out of money soon. Especially if you put an end to Papa Telos' dealings?"

This latter rose as a question, and Owen smiled. He still didn't know how Saul had twigged to his identity during their University days, or guessed that the classes Owen was taking were not quite what they appeared, but when the man had confronted his then-roommate, Owen had been too surprised to deny the charges. And from that base of mutual trust they had built a friendship, and from there a partnership—for the fledgling Wolf had been integral in helping Saul seize the reins of his family business when his parents had died. Their combined schemes had catapulted the youngest Soleneides to the peak of his profession. In return, the Konastan had done certain favors for the Guildmaster—including determining for him, upon occasion, the names of some of the minor players in the Dreamsmoke arena.

Owen supposed that his friend's connections as owner and manager of the infamous Cauldron of Iniquity—as well as a whole string of lesser-known clubs—did not extend to garnering the name of the master supplier, but every shred of information counted. The Dreamsmoke trade was, in Owen's opinion, one of the most reprehensible in all Konasta, responsible for the wreckage of many promising young lives—one of his own top operatives among them. And as Guildmaster and Varia's *de facto* conscience, he felt duty-bound to eliminate it.

What he wanted was the master supplier; in the meantime, he'd settle for as many minor dealers as Saul could finger.

Certainly Sauron Telos had been no exception: a slimy, two-bit player it had been a pleasure to eliminate. He said as much to Saul, adding, "The Stiletto took him down—and, in addition, made certain none of his family would ever resume the business again."

"Yes, I believe I did hear something to that effect. The Stiletto struck quite a terror into their collective hearts . . . or so it's rumored."

The Guildmaster grimaced. "The Stiletto can be useful upon occasion. But she does have her own . . . unique methods."

"Including torture and chaining people in basements for weeks on end?"

The Guildmaster arched an eyebrow. "More rumors?"

"Yes. Why? Are they correct?"

"How should I know?" Owen answered blithely. "As I've told you, operatives are on their own from the moment they receive their assignments to the moment they complete them. I have no idea how the Stiletto achieves her effect." It was no less than the truth, but with the Stiletto, he simply didn't want to know. She was subtle, ruthless, and efficient—as sly, quick, and deadly as her namesake— and he had a feeling her methods would leave even him shaken. But she got the job done, and that was what counted, for even in the Guild there were certain assignments that demanded that kind of touch, much as he might personally deplore it. And there was no denying that the Stiletto was the best at what she did.

"Still," Saul continued, "with Sauron out of the picture— and the Dreamsmoke trade out of the family—they're bound to be feeling somewhat resentful toward the man who informed against them."

"And how do they even know it's you?"

"They must," Owen's companion answered logically. "Who else would have motive to kill me?"

The Guildmaster nodded; that was no less than the truth. Most of Konasta depended upon Saul for their livelihood; it was in their best interest to keep him alive.

"Besides," his friend added, "you forget how prevalent the rumor net is in Konasta—especially around the illusion clubs."

"True enough. Very well, then; I'll get you a team. If you don't mind one that's still in training . . ."

"Not in the least. It's just a bodyguard position, after all; nothing strenuous. Probably more like a vacation, considering what the weather must be like in dear old Ceylonde at this time of year. And that's one thing I certainly don't miss! Tell me, has it started snowing, yet?"

"What do you think?"

"I think you need to journey to Konasta along with your operatives. It's no wonder you can't hold a knife anymore;

your joints have all frozen! Well, never mind. I trust you to do what's best."

"More fool you," Owen quipped. "I'll send you the Cloak and Dagger: one of my most promising pairs, but still in want of a little . . . tempering. A bodyguard position should be just the thing."

"Perfect. I can pay, of course."

"Nonsense, I owe you. Besides, it was my urging that got you into this mess to begin with."

"And what else am I supposed to do when one of those cursed dealers inadvertently reveals himself other than contact my old friend Wolf? I deplore the Dreamsmoke trade as much as you do; it keeps people out of my clubs. No, I'd say we were in this equally, old chum—but thanks for the waiver, nonetheless."

"Anything for a Soleneides," the Guildmaster replied, and cued off the crystal. Then, raising his voice, he bellowed for the man who was at once his assistant, mage, and strong right hand. "Vander! Get me Vera, would you?"

Three hours later, the Hawk was seated in his private sitting room, scowling at him across a small expanse of sodden carpet. She had made rather a point of shaking out her snowy cloak, and already the residue was beginning to steam in the heat. Her cheeks were pink from the cold, her nose and ear-tips red, and she blew rather pointedly on her hands as he gestured her to sit.

"Well?" she demanded tartly, crossing damp, booted feet. "What is so urgent that you called me out in the teeth of this inclement weather—and just as I was ready to leave this forsaken country, no less?"

He grinned and handed her a mug of hot mulled cider: one of two that Vander had brought him. She wrapped her hands around the thick pottery cup and took a deep pull. When he sensed that she had thawed enough to be civil, he responded, "Absalom's returned, I take it?"

The frown crept back over her features. "I hate it when you do that."

"Do what?"

"Answer a question with a question." Obviously she was not as warm as he had imagined. "Yes, if you must know,

Absalom has returned, and faster than I expected. I swear sometimes that man can control the weather—because otherwise how he got a ship to carry him through the Narrows at this time of year is beyond me!"

"Well, he probably didn't go *through* the Narrows," Owen temporized, "but rather across them to Haarkonis, and then caught a coach and six from there. Ships do make that hop in the winter, you know."

"Honestly, Owen, stop destroying a perfectly good theory." But she grinned for the first time since she had entered the room, and announced, "They found it, you know."

"Found what?"

"Black-naphtha. In Arrhyndon."

"Gracious." Owen's voice was mild. "Then there's definitely going to be a war with Montrechet come spring."

"It certainly looks that way. But it also looks as though Arrhyndon is going to win, thanks in part to my niece." The Cloak and Dagger's last assignment had been in Arrhyndon and, three months later, Vera was still defending their actions to her Guildmaster. Granted the job had gone rather spectacularly sour, but it hadn't been as awful as some first jobs Owen had witnessed—Vera's included. It was just that she felt responsible, having brought them to his attention in the first place.

"Mmm," he said. "And speaking of your niece . . . Do you think she and that partner of hers are ready for a new assignment?"

"Always. Why? Have you found one they might actually be able to handle?"

"I might have. How does a bodyguard position sound?"

"Suitably innocuous. Where?"

"Konasta."

"You dog!" Owen laughed. He knew how Vera Radineaux loved that part of the world, though to be honest he didn't know how she could. It always reminded him too poignantly of Nick. "What's the assignment?"

He related his discussion with Saul, and at the end of it she snorted.

"Under contract, eh? Poor old bastard—though I suppose it was inevitable. How many dealers has he handed you?"

"Somewhere around two dozen."

"And still no leads on the master criminal?"

Owen flushed. "Well, he is trying . . ."

"I know that. He's trying, you're trying; we're all trying. To no avail. And doesn't that make you even the slightest bit suspicious?"

"You honestly don't think *he's* responsible?" Owen exclaimed. "Vera, I know you don't approve of his livelihood, but . . ."

"There's no need to treat me like a child just because I'm acting like one." The Hawk smiled wryly. "No, I don't approve of your friend's business. I think the illusion clubs are a needless indulgence of a depraved society. But as long as there's a chance to bring down the Dreamsmoke trade, I'll take what I'm given. No matter the source."

He was silent for a moment. "You're thinking of Nick, aren't you?" he asked at last.

"Nick? I'm thinking of all the Nicks. Of all the poor bastards who threw their lives away on an illusory escape only to find they could no longer return. The Lammergeier—Varia help him—wasn't the first victim of the Dreamsmoke trade, nor will he be the last."

"Still," Owen mused, "I don't see how you can stand Konasta, knowing what happened . . ."

"Blast it, Owen, what happened to Nick is tragic, but that was Nick's fault, not Konasta's. Besides, I've had more good times in Konasta than I've had bad, so why let one tragedy color the picture? Shall you tell Jen about the job, or shall I?"

"When will you be seeing her?"

"I'm leaving for Bergaetta tonight. Jen and Thibault are down there already, enjoying their winter break. Or at least Jen is, because Eduardo just announced his retirement, leaving poor dear Thibault without a steward. He is frantically interviewing replacements now. Jen, of course, trailed along to offer moral support."

"By which we are to translate: 'lounging about doing nothing'?" Owen grinned. "Well, I suppose she deserves it."

"She and Thibault both. They've been studying hard this past semester, and Jen, for one, has been on her best behavior since Arrhyndon. I think it's time you let them have another crack at the action."

"Which is precisely what I intend to do. So, how long until you reach Bergaetta?"

"With Absalom along?" She chuckled. "Record time, I'm certain. So if you think Saul can wait an extra five or six days, I'll deliver the message myself. And if they need more information, they can contact you through Absalom."

"Good. Then we're set?"

"Apart from one thing."

He raised an eyebrow.

"Me," she clarified.

"You?"

"Do you think I'm about to let them muck around down there unsupervised? Especially after what happened the last time?"

"Then you admit it was a disaster?"

"I admit it was a first job," she countered firmly.

"Well," he acknowledged, "I suppose it couldn't hurt. But how can you expect them to be independent if you are forever supervising?"

She wrinkled her nose at him. "For one thing, I am not 'forever supervising.' I let them go a full five weeks the last time without intervention."

"How very magnanimous of you."

She grinned. "Second, if we do our jobs correctly, they'll never even know I'm there. What do you say, Owen? How about if, for a moderate fee, I sniff around the Dreamsmoke trade for a while and see if I can't locate our master distributor?"

"That sounds all very well and good, but what constitutes a 'moderate' fee? And who is going to pay it?"

"Why you are, of course. And as for the amount . . ."

Folding her arms complacently, she settled down for some earnest bargaining.

1

Thibault's twenty-first birthday passed quietly and without fanfare, sandwiched between two exams and a paper, but that was the way he preferred it. The expectations of social festival had always seemed ridiculous to him, as if it mattered to the world that, on such and such a day, he had joined it. And to those few who did care, it would mark no more than the occasion for a lot of useless fuss. If there was one thing Thibault hated, it was being the center of attention—especially if he felt he had done nothing in particular to deserve it. Such as being born, which seemed to him an awfully passive act. So he had kept resolutely silent, informing neither Jen nor Vera, and if there was nonetheless some quiet part of him that felt regret, he ignored it assiduously.

Better, he told himself sternly, that Jen should ignore his coming of age because she never knew than because—in some rare moment of absorption or single-mindedness—she forgot. It had been exam time, after all, and she was in her usual frenzy of last-minute cramming and self-flagellation, rushing about Vera's Ceylonde manor with ink on her cheeks and her hair all askew. No, best simply not to give her the choice.

Besides, it hadn't worked out that badly. As a result of his labors, he had received top marks in all his classes. And he had his house, to boot.

His house. He still loved to think it, even after all these months.

His house.

His job.

His independent income.

Despite everything, it was worth it.

Smoothing down his ruffled hair, he let a faint smile curve his lips as he surveyed the gracious proportions of Harriet Delacourte's Bergaetta mansion—*his* Bergaetta mansion, he reminded himself—and reflected that this wasn't such a bad way to spend the holidays. Ceylonde had been buried under increasingly heavy snows by the time he and Jen had packed their trunks and departed, yet here the air was mild, the days longer.

And despite its many aggravations, this was a truly lovely afternoon. The sun slanted in through the balcony's wrought-iron railings, casting an intricate pattern of shadow and light across the blond wood floors, while outside the windows, the splendor of Bergaetta fell away to the half-moon curve of the bay, still as blue and sparkling as a finely cut sapphire. Paper-wrapped lanterns, extinguished for now, hung in ropes from the eaves, and a lone cabbage rose from one of the potted bushes Jen had recently seen fit to purchase brushed softly against the glass, filling the room with the indefinable scent of summer.

Sighing and stretching, muscles creaking and joints popping in protest, Thibault levered his six foot four inch frame from the chair and opened the pane, reaching for that one tantalizing bloom. He brushed his fingers over the petals, marveling at the gradations of color from orange to yellow that were veined in among the pink, then snapped the stem.

The flower fell graciously into his hand.

"What are you doing?" Jen demanded from behind him. He could chart her progress by the tripping of her heels, the sharp, staccato taps indicative of careful grooming. "Don't tell me you're violating my chosen bushes already?"

He grinned and turned. As expected, she was stylishly arrayed in a gown of sprigged muslin, her chestnut hair drawn up in a smooth twist, her feet encased in heeled boots. She had obviously been out shopping again.

"Ah, but for a good cause," he responded, bowing faintly. "For you, my lady." And he extended the rose like an offering.

"Why, thank you, Thib. How sweet." Flinging her reticule onto a nearby chair, she accepted the bloom with a smile, tucking it behind one ear. "So, how goes the search?"

He grimaced ruefully, and ran impatient fingers through his hair. "Dreadful, of course. What else?"

She chuckled. "Poor baby. Tell me all." And settling down onto the nearest settee, she patted the cushion beside her invitingly. With a sigh, Thibault complied, reflecting that Jen had become a lot more tactile since he had acquired the Bergaetta mansion and started—reluctantly—acting the lord. Almost as if she had a stake in his coming success, or perhaps simply because she felt that blasted social gap between them closing.

As if inheriting a mansion and three hundred marks a month had in any way altered the essential Thibault, the same lad who had grown up in a two-room cottage mere yards from her aunt's imperial manor. As if it meant her basic feelings toward him had in any way altered. He was still her best friend and stalwart companion; she was still the center of his heart and existence. Being alone with her like this, in this grand dwelling, was a subtle torture—bittersweet and irreplaceable.

She looped a hand through his elbow and patted his arm, inviting confidence. He covered her fingers briefly with his own, then heaved another, greatly exaggerated sigh. "What's to tell? I swear those last three candidates were sizing up the furnishings. One even seemed to have an unhealthy interest in the silver!"

"That bad?"

He nodded, but actually it was worse. What, he wondered, had ever led him to believe he could pull this off, aping the aristocrat? At the first sign of trouble, all his careful delusions had deflated like a punctured balloon, leaving him helpless and stranded.

After all, how hard could it be to find a steward?

The news certainly hadn't prostrated him when Eduardo had related it, a little before the semester's conclusion. In truth, he had expected it. Harriet Delacourte's steward was well into his seventies, too old to be running a house for a vital young master. Not to mention that his mistress' death had left him a very rich man indeed. So he had written to Thibault, deferentially laying out his reasons for retirement, kindly offering to stay on until his replacement was procured and trained.

Not a bad bit of business, all told. Thibault had graciously acceded to the former, and gratefully agreed to the latter, promising to come down and supervise the interviews once the term ended. Now he was beginning to understand Ruairi NaBlaine's annoyance when Jen had cost him *his* steward at the end of their last assignment.

It was a cursed chancy business, hiring a man you could trust with your house and your honor—and in some cases, Thibault thought wryly, your identity—on the basis of half an hour's acquaintance. Perhaps aristocrats born and bred were accustomed to it, but it cost him nearly all his composure not to run shrieking in a panic every time some new candidate arrived.

Maybe if he leaked word about his affiliation with the Hestian Guild, all these candidates would think twice about coming back and robbing him blind. He was still too new to the idea of possessions to know anything about guarding them properly.

He said as much to Jen, who merely pursed her lips and frowned. "Now, Thibault, you know you can't go boasting about the Guild. That would only get us both in more trouble than I care to contemplate."

"But I thought you liked trouble," he replied, with a tiny smile. "Besides, I was only kidding. In part."

She grinned.

"How do you aristocrats manage it?" he continued. "Is there some sort of inbred instinct that I'm lacking?"

"How in blazes should I know?" she responded blithely. "I've never had to hire a steward. But if I did, I'd probably just muddle through the same as you."

"Thanks for the vote of confidence. Your faith in me is overwhelming."

She laughed at his dry tone, and rested a hand boldly against his thigh; he couldn't help the faint quickening of his pulse at the contact, which rode a little too high to be purely casual. Curse her for knowing his weaknesses. Curse him for letting her use them. He stifled a gasp as her hand stroked impertinently upwards, though her teasing expression showed nothing more than a playful desire to unhinge him.

But, "On the contrary," she said, more seriously than he

expected. "My faith in you is the one thing I can rely on. You'll find the perfect steward, I guarantee it. And you'll know it the moment you set eyes on him. You just haven't found the right candidate yet."

"Mmm," he answered, unconvinced. "But thanks anyway." And, greatly daring, he cupped a hand against her cheek.

She removed her hand from his leg, then, and stood: a precise, deliberate movement. "Do you know what I bought today?" she said, suddenly halfway across the room.

"What?"

She turned to face him, her face split by an incandescent grin. An incandescent *smug* grin, he amended. "Two Mepharstan carpets, a gorgeous crystal chandelier for Absalom to work his magerie on, and a kitchen full of pots and pans."

"Oh, Jen, you didn't! For one thing, I like the house the way it is . . ."

"Nonsense. It's far too plain."

"And for another . . . Who the blazes is going to use all those pots and pans? You?"

"Varia forfend. You'll have to hire yourself a cook, too, I suppose."

"Jen . . ."

"What? Oh, come on, Thib, don't look at me like that. It's a great house, but it wants some fixing. And you certainly can't afford to do that on three hundred marks a month."

The subtle scorn in her voice goaded him into asking, "And how am I expected to repay you?"

"Repay me?" She sounded horrified. "We're partners, Thib. What's mine is yours, and"—she grinned—"what's yours is mine. Besides, I like this a lot better than Ceylonde in the winter." She was silent for a moment, then added, rather plaintively, "So, do you think Owen will ever give us another job? It's been over three months, and I've been very good . . ."

"Excessively so. And I'm sure he'll find us something. Isn't Vera due today? Perhaps she'll bring word."

"Yes, dear Vera. Perhaps she will." Jen brightened, and came to stand behind him, reaching up to ruffle his hair. "You look knackered, love. Shall I fetch us tea?"

"Please, but don't hurry. I have one more candidate coming, and I think I just heard the bell."

And indeed, scant moments later, Eduardo tapped deferentially against the panels and poked his head around the corner. "Another one, sir," he said. "Shall I . . ."

"Yes, show him in," Thibault said wearily, stretching like a cat. "Oh, and Eduardo?"

"Yes?"

"Any good?"

Harriet's steward rolled his eyes and disappeared, leaving Thibault to the disheartening prospect of another less than successful interview.

It was all too ridiculously domestic, Jen reflected as she laid out tea cakes and boiled water—the total extent of her culinary skills. She had changed into a far more practical gown and her feet were bare against the cool tile of the kitchen floor, yet still Rafiq was hovering anxiously, clearly distressed to see his not-quite mistress sullying her hands with such a menial task. But, truth to tell, she enjoyed it. It was almost like being grown up at last, keeping house with a beloved life-mate. Except that the life-mate was none other than Thibault—her best friend, partner, and strong right hand—and this house, comfortable as it was, no more than a play house, worlds away from the vast Radineaux mansion in which she had been raised and which she would inherit in a little over two years.

Besides, they were the Cloak and the Dagger—fledgling assassins in the Hestian Guild—with a lifetime of adventure stretching before them. What could be better than that? Certainly something as mundane as domesticity ran a pale second.

But nonetheless, it was fun to pretend, if only for a moment. Her recent sojourn with Ruairi NaBlaine on Arrhyndon's wild eastern coast had shattered any number of illusions, not the least of them that love—true love—was not always the trap she had once envisioned it. With the right person, it was possible to share your life without losing your identity, and a tiny, almost unacknowledged, corner of her heart had begun to yearn for that sort of stability and caring. For a place where she could finally put down the roots of her desultory soul.

And if, in the darkest part of the night, her mind put a familiar cast to that mystery lover—a shadowy amalgam of strength and stability, capped by a lackadaisical grin—it was something she stubbornly refused to acknowledge.

She had always been good at denial.

And so she contented herself with puttering about Thibault's new house, fixing tea and rearranging furniture—every so often immersing herself in an orgy of shopping from which she returned laden with barrels and boxes and potted rose bushes, all part of her well-meaning quest to provide him with a house of which he needn't be ashamed.

Harriet Delacourte may have been an aristocrat, but she was an elderly one, obviously unaccustomed to the style in which a true aristocratic dwelling must be maintained. And if Thibault was ever to enter her world and host elaborate parties for the flowers of Lusanian society, then he would need to possess more than the equivalent of a sea-side villa with rattan furniture and no obvious marks of wealth or social stature.

Jen, with her status and breeding—and a considerable allowance of her own—was the perfect one to rectify that. Who knew better how aristocrats lived? It was the least she could do, and she was particularly proud of today's acquisitions: the vibrant carpets of blue, green, and dusky rose; the dripping fall of the crystal chandelier. Before making tea, she had recruited Rafiq's help in laying down the rugs, and had the chandelier out and waiting for Absalom's arrival.

Already, the place looked better. Thibault had, after all, claimed a brief acquaintance with the prince; Jen was determined to secure a royal presence at their table. And should she succeed, the man simply had to feel at home.

She paused for a moment in her meticulous arrangement of the tea tray, puzzled by her seeming obsession with royalty. Usually, she cared not a whit for such things, but she soon decided it was Thibault that prompted it. Her poor, loyal Thibault who had passed his childhood in a two-room cottage. Who had spent his nights in little more than a pile of straw, heaped in the loft above the storeroom. Who had been forced to earn his living in the Carpenters' Guild until Jen had been released from her hated schooling. Who, curse it, had paid his dues and now deserved the best the world had to offer. Princes and all.

"Are you *sure* I can't help you with that, Domina?" Rafiq asked again nervously, interrupting the tumble of her thoughts.

"Yes, quite sure. I . . ." She glanced down at the tray, only to discover that, in her distraction, she had piled the tea cakes at least one layer too high and that the whole structure now threatened to topple. Hastily, she stuffed four into her mouth. "I . . . umph"—she swallowed hastily—"I have everything well under control. And I also have, as I have told you, a perfectly good name. It's Jen. So please knock off that Domina nonsense and use it."

"Yes, Do . . . that is, Domina Jen."

The Dagger grimaced. She supposed it was as good a concession as she was likely to get from the raw young suhdabhar.

She heard the back door open and shut as Eduardo ushered the latest candidate from the portal, and she padded across to the kitchen window, pressing her nose to the glass. The lanky, stooped figure who disappeared through the arch at the end of the stableyard, spectacles perched precariously on the tip of his nose, looked more like a scholar than a steward—clearly ill-equipped to deal with a household of up-and-coming assassins.

Poor Thibault.

Maybe Vera would have some solution when she arrived.

Returning to the counter with a chuckle, Jen hefted the tea tray—oblivious to Rafiq's squawk of protest—and nudged the kitchen door open with one bare toe. Then she padded decisively down the hall, across the vibrant spread of the new carpet, leaving the servant little choice but to trail helplessly in her wake.

2

Gideon Gilvaray was taking out the trash. It was, Aubrey Dunning reflected, something that his compatriot did very well indeed—despite the odd contrast such an endeavor created. Gideon Gilvaray, the Golden Boy. Gideon Gilvaray, the paragon of mortal existence. Gideon Gilvaray, whose hair shone with a light rivaling the sun and whose ice-green eyes were as cool and mesmerizing as two bits of milky jade. Whose fine, almost boyish features bore the stamp of innocence and charm, saved from softness only by the firm sweep of jaw; the precise, classic descent of nose; the aristocratic arch of cheekbones.

No one, seeing him on the street or in the clubs, would picture him thus, knee deep in the wreckage of what had once been a man. And yet from his expression, which relayed nothing but an obscure kind of amusement, he might have been filing papers or even sweeping a dusty floor.

The Golden Boy, indeed.

"Tarnation, what is it, Aubrey?" the paragon now declared, dropping a loop of bluish intestine into the gaping cavity whence it had emerged. "Don't tell me you're going squeamish after all these years?"

"Varia forfend," his companion answered. "But still . . . doesn't it make you think?"

"About what? Life and death? Don't be ridiculous, Aubrey. This man was nothing more than a common criminal, due for execution in a week or two, anyway. At least now he makes a little money for his country."

"I suppose."

Gideon shoveled a few more spongy bits into the hollow between the splayed ribs, then said, "What?"

Aubrey sighed. "It's just . . . who would do this?" And he gestured about him helplessly.

Gideon laughed. "Who? Any one of our rich clients who is willing to pay. We offer the fulfillment of fantasies, Aubrey, not judgment. You know the prices Saul charges. If they're willing to pay, we're willing to oblige them."

"Mmm." Aubrey grimaced; he supposed it was true. He had seen any number of things in the years since he and Gideon had been handling the day-to-day management of the Cauldron of Iniquity, Konasta's largest and most famous illusion club, but he had never been able to credit the seeming nonchalance with which Gideon embraced every aspect of his position.

Truth to tell, most of the time Aubrey didn't care, either. What the rich did with their perversions—and their cash— was of no concern to him. But every so often the extremes got to him. Such as now, standing in a room awash with blood, its walls spattered in a whimsical pattern that seemed more reminiscent of a child's painting than the brutal ending of a life.

It was a simple room at the best of times, sparsely furnished—for what need had the grander illusion clubs of luxurious extras when the staff mages could turn even the plainest chamber into a sumptuous den, tailored precisely to their clients' needs? Ordinarily the walls were a greying white, somewhat in need of repainting, the floors scuffed and bare. The iron bedstead had clearly seen better days, and the couch, while still plump and firm, was gradually fading to a uniform drabness.

In contrast, the corpse—with its bright shades of crimson peeling back on occasion to reveal the stark whiteness of bone—looked about as out of place as a prince in a pigpen. Not that bodies were any surprise in these back rooms. Quite the contrary. The illusion clubs offered many levels of reality. In the glittering front rooms, which were as far as most people penetrated, the mages' spells rotated by the week with staggering displays of imaginative ingenuity. One week, the bar and dance floor might be swallowed beneath the sea, with weird attenuated creatures swimming between the patrons; the next, it might be a city in the clouds. Or a forest. Or the harem of one of the eastern potentates.

And for the vast majority, that was enough: providing a salacious escape into the exotic or unattainable.

For others—with more money to spare, or more needs to be met—there was a hired stable of whores: all the better for the fact that the mages could cast upon them any appearance. And no longer limited to the young and beautiful, the clubs could select for skill rather than style; for willingness rather than winsomeness. Choosing the women had always been Gideon's favorite part of the job, and even Aubrey had to admit it wasn't a bad perk. Although he did rely more heavily on the mage's help when bedding some of the more unattractive prospects.

Gideon, though . . . Gideon didn't seem to care. How old, how plain; it was all the same to him. Maybe because he was more integral in testing the limits, in searching out those who would venture into the muddy waters of perversion. And in the illusion game, there was more demand for things out of the ordinary, things that no one would admit to while wearing their own face or identity. Such as the revenge fantasies—the hankering for bloodshed and violence—which led to the existence of rooms such as these.

Of course, it was all highly illegal, and publicly frowned upon by the relevant authorities. Though, when enough money was involved, that frowning was entirely irrelevant. Which meant that all the larger clubs had secret back-back rooms in which influential types could slaughter in effigy their own worst enemies. Where would-be killers could practice their art or simply still the bloodlust for a space. And at least (or so the argument went) it got them off the streets and thus spared innocent lives.

The result was that, for an exorbitant price, the Konastan government filtered a small percentage of their doomed criminals into the clubs so that, for an even more exorbitant price, they could die at the hands of the desirous. It was all very clandestine and sordid, with neither side publicly acknowledging that such practices occurred. Which was why people like Gideon and Aubrey existed, to facilitate the transfers and tidy up the messes. Which was why people like Gideon and Aubrey got paid so highly, and why Aubrey ordinarily didn't care what these people did to each other.

But every so often it went beyond the usual stabbing or strangling. Every so often, the victim was filleted like a salmon: ribs spread back like wings, extremities covered with a thousand meticulous lacerations, eyes removed and mouth stretched into a rictus of horror that spoke of intense and prolonged suffering.

Death not for therapy but simply for the sheer joy of the thing.

It was no wonder Saul Soleneides left the daily administration of the Cauldron to his associates.

Aubrey's stomach knotted yet again as Gideon placidly deposited the mutilated body on a cloth, then proceeded to roll the whole thing into a bundle; there was, Aubrey noticed, a speck of blood high on his companion's right cheek. "There, I think that's most of it," he said. "I'll go dispose of the man. Do you mind mopping up?"

With a faint sigh, Aubrey shook his head. Then, realizing his companion had turned his back, added, "No. Gideon . . . What did he do? This criminal of yours?"

"Robbed one of the magistrates, I believe. And you know how it is. Caught four times, and . . ." Gideon rotated, grinning, and ran a finger graphically across his throat. His aureate curls caught the light, momentarily encasing his head in a golden nimbus.

"Four robberies," Aubrey responded. "Hardly deserving of *that*." And he indicated the canvas-swathed burden slung casually over his companion's shoulder.

Gideon arched an eyebrow. "What are you saying, that life is supposed to be fair? Wake up and smell the effluvia, Aubrey! Now, you'd better get that mess sponged up. We have a meeting with the boss in an hour."

Saul Soleneides ushered them into his office with his usual good cheer and a rakish flash of dimples. "Gideon; Aubrey. Come in! Have a seat. What can I get you?"

"Brandy, please," his Golden Boy responded, sinking into one of the plush armchairs and casually crossing his outstretched legs at the ankle.

"Aubrey?"

The latter grimaced. He could still smell the metallic after-odor of blood on the soles of his boots. "The same."

"Bad day?" Saul inquired, offering them each a glass in turn.

"About average." Gideon yawned. "That new girl had me up half of last night."

Saul's eyes twinkled, obsidian to Gideon's jade. "Literally, I take it?"

"Most of the time, yes. I think she'll do rather well. Quite a high pain threshold."

"Good, good. What is it, Aubrey?"

"We got another one today."

"Another what?"

"Mutilated body," Gideon answered for him. "He thinks it's the same client."

"Shall we report him?" Aubrey added.

"Why? What's he paying?"

"Two thousand."

Saul chuckled. "Tarnation. For that price, he can *eat* the body! Aubrey?"

"What?"

"Have you heard any reports of similarly mutilated bodies in the news?"

"No . . ."

"Then stop worrying. Better he kill one of ours than an innocent. How much did we pay the prisons for the victim?"

"Five hundred," Gideon answered.

"By Varia, a bargain at any price! Will a hundred of that fifteen hundred mark profit help ease that intermittent conscience of yours, Dunning?"

"Most likely."

"Well, then."

"What about me?" Gideon inquired, plaintively.

"You? You have no conscience. And you enjoy it far too much. But in the interests of equity . . . Don't let it be said that I don't take care of my employees. One hundred each. And if I didn't love you boys so much, I'd begrudge losing so much of my earnings into your pockets. Now, what have we got lined up for next week?"

"Well, the Palace theme proved so popular at the Cauldron that several of the lesser clubs with rotating displays are bastardizing it for the coming week," Aubrey responded.

"Wonderful. And the Cauldron itself? What have you been discussing with the mages?"

"Well, since we are never ones to let complacency linger," Gideon answered, "we were thinking of going to rather the opposite extreme."

"A kind of slum theme," Aubrey added. "What do you think?"

"Brilliant. Implement it. And the take for the week?"

Aubrey took out his notebook and he flipped to the relevant pages. "Eleven thousand for the Cauldron, eight-five for the subsidiaries."

"And minus operating expenses?"

"Five and two."

"Seven thousand?" Saul gave a great shout of laughter. "Not a bad week, indeed! That thousand for public works is certainly going to make less of a dent than usual. Good work, boys. In fact, I'm feeling enormously expansive. Throw another five hundred into the widow and orphan's fund this week."

"Munificence in bounty?" Gideon said.

"Quite!" And their employer rubbed his hands together, as if polishing the debated marks. He grinned at his Golden Boy, who smiled back.

"So," Gideon asked. "Anything else?"

Their boss sobered. "There was another attempt, today," he said. "Poison. Most unsubtle. Poor Cavan took it quite ill."

"Your suhdabhar?"

"Yes. I'd always suspected he had a dishonest streak to him, and it seems I was right. Apparently, he'd been in the habit of sneaking food off my table. Fortunately for me, as it happens." Then his eyes momentarily went hard. "Though Lucinda was supposed to be surveying the food preparation in the first place, now that I come to think of it; I shall have to take that girl to task."

"And Cavan?" Gideon asked wryly. "Will he make it?"

"What do you care?"

"For the boy? Not a whit. For the poison? A great deal. After all, if you die, I'm out an employer. And a cursed good one, at that."

"Gracious. I'd be flattered if I didn't think it was completely in your self-interest to serve me."

Gideon grinned then, his whole face flaring to life like a magelight. One look like that, Aubrey thought, and the gullible would follow him to perdition and back. Saul was beaming like a fond old uncle, and even Aubrey himself wasn't entirely unaffected. "That transparent, am I?" Gideon said. "Well, I'll be hanged."

"I doubt it. However"—Saul grimaced—"it wasn't a bad attempt for a rogue assassin. Cavan still might not make it."

"Curse it, Saul," Aubrey inserted. "And you're letting Avram and Lucinda go to Phykoros? What are you planning to do about this?"

"Why, hire some Guild bodyguards for the interim."

There was a long, pregnant silence.

"Blast it," Gideon burst out eventually. "Are you sure that's wise? What if they . . ."

"What? Stumble onto something they're not supposed to?" Saul raised an eyebrow. "Little chance of that. I made sure to finagle Owen's most junior team. They'll be too overwhelmed to do much more than keep me safe. Leaving all of us free for higher pursuits."

"But . . ."

"But what? Owen DeVeris owes me. And besides, he's an honorable man. He'll do as I asked. He trusts me to train his people."

"In what?" Aubrey asked sarcastically. "Morality?"

"So he still doesn't know?" Gideon added.

"Know what?" Saul smiled cruelly. "Owen DeVeris is a fond, blind old man who puts too much faith in old acquaintances. Believe me, I have our revered Guildmaster eating out of my hand. He'll send me my junior assassins— by deadline, I have no doubt—and then we can get on with our lives. But Gideon . . ."

"Yes?"

"Keep an eye on them, nonetheless. I didn't get where I am by being stupid. If they show any signs of nosing about the truth, divert them; I don't care how. And Aubrey, that goes for you, too. Understood?"

And when they both nodded, Saul beamed benevolently and sent them off to face yet another week in the Cauldron of Iniquity.

3

Jen and Thibault were squabbling playfully over their tea—something to do with interior decor—when Jen heard the chiming of the downstairs bell. Instantly, she propelled herself off the sofa and ran to the windows, flinging them open. Then, darting onto the balcony, she folded herself almost double over the railings, peering down into the street. Below, as expected, bobbed the twin dark heads that were her aunt and Absalom. A hired hansom was just pulling away, leaving a small spattering of luggage on the sidewalk. Jen had never understood how her aunt could travel with so little baggage. She never seemed to require more than one small box.

"Ahoy, there," Jen called, attracting their attention by waving one hand gaily over the railing. Her bare toes poked out from beneath the wrought iron vines. "Welcome to summer!"

Two faces turned up at her greeting. Absalom, still in his rugged guise, grinned at her, but Vera's dark eyes held a certain reproof. "More like early fall, I'd say," her aunt answered. "Good afternoon, Jenny. Forgetting your dignity already, I see." And her knowing gaze swept over Jen's threadbare gown, her bare feet, and the thick plait of hair that swung casually over the railing. "Whatever will the neighbors think?"

Jen flushed and straightened, shaking crumbs from the folds of her skirt. Her aunt, as usual, was correct. For all her desire to establish Thibault as a person of reckoning, here she was, in an unguarded instant, annihilating all her careful cover.

How typical.

"Is that Vera?" she heard Thibault ask from behind her,

and an instant later her partner joined her on the balcony, resting his elbows on the railing and looking, in his casually elegant clothes and prodigious height, every inch the lordling. "Hello, Vera. Absalom. Welcome to Bergaetta. Eduardo will be right down to show you in."

And indeed, an instant later, the aged steward eased the door open, ushering the pair inside. Rafiq, darting out in his wake, collected the bags.

Jen heaved a regretful sigh and rested her cheek briefly against her partner's shoulder. "I'm sorry, Thib."

"Whatever for?" The Cloak draped an arm across her shoulders. "Come, let's welcome our first guests."

Vera had never set foot in Thibault's Bergaetta mansion, but she could see Jen's touches from the moment she entered. A gracious entry hall, awash with light which streamed in through the frosted panels of the door and the two decorative windows set to either side, was marred by the spread of a priceless Mepharstan, utterly at odds with the chamber's otherwise starkly elegant lines. Blond wood floors and a straight rise of polished blond wood stairs; beveled mirror set with the coathooks along one wall; two rattan sofas strewn with silver-green cushions, bore no relation to that expanse of wildly patterned carpet. Nor, likewise, to the tiered crystal chandelier that was hooked over the bannister, obviously awaiting installation.

With a faint sigh, Vera regarded the elegant spray of brass and fluted glass which now graced the ceiling. She definitely would have to speak to the girl.

At Eduardo's urging, she mounted the stairs—only to find a similar problem reigning in the main body of the house. What should have been a continuous sweep of light and air, room merging into room with a kind of organic grace and symmetry, was likewise interrupted by an even larger and more priceless Mepharstan which sought to create divisions where none were necessary.

"Well, what do you think?" Jenny demanded, tripping out of a back room to meet her. "Not bad, huh?" She had, Vera noticed, donned shoes, and pinned up her braid.

"Quite attractive, actually," the Hawk answered. "However . . . This is yours, I take it?" And she gestured at the carpet.

"Yes. Gorgeous, isn't it?"

"Exquisite. Except that it looks positively horrendous in its current setting."

Jen stared at her for a moment, then scowled. "That's your opinion."

"Mmm. Not just mine, I suspect." Vera exchanged a knowing look with her niece's partner. "Hello, Thibault. How have you been keeping?"

With an amused twinkle in his unassuming brown eyes, the Cloak enfolded her in one of his all-engulfing hugs. How he could have grown so tall with Sylvaine so tiny, she would never know.

He dropped a quick kiss on her cheek as he released her, saying, "Far worse than appearances suggest, I suspect. Hello, Absalom. Do either of you know any good stewards?"

Vera grinned. "Nary a one."

"Is the search going that badly?" Absalom added.

Thibault tugged briefly at his hair. "You have no idea! But, enough about my problems. Come in; make yourselves at home. Rafiq will take your things. Vera, you'll have the rose room; Absalom, the blue." As the servant disappeared, Vera couldn't help but smile. She could tell by the quirk in Thibault's lips that he was enjoying his new position immensely—even if he didn't know quite what to make of it. She exchanged a look with Jen.

"Quite the grand master, isn't he?" her niece agreed, hugging her partner's arm proudly.

Thibault went bright red. "And how was your journey?" he inquired.

Vera looked pointedly at Absalom, who smiled and said, "No cause for complaint. Or so I've been told."

"Well, then." Jen looked about expectantly. "Does anyone care for tea?"

"Tea?" The Hawk chuckled. "My gracious, how very domestic of you."

"I know. Positively revolting, isn't it?"

"So, what news from Ceylonde?" Jen asked later as cups

and cakes were dispensed. "I'm sorry, but the tea seems to have gone a little cold in the interim. Shall I . . ."

"No need," Absalom inserted, heating the cooling beverage with a casual word. Then, as Jen gaped, he added, "Just one of the many small services a mage can provide."

"Tarnation. Handy to have around, aren't you?"

"A million useful tools in one." Absalom bowed faintly. "I take it you want me to ensorcel that chandelier downstairs?"

Vera cut off the Dagger's response, saying, "Oh, for Varia's sake, don't put that monstrosity up! Promise me, Jenny."

"Why not? It's a lovely piece."

"And as inappropriate as the carpets. Please."

Thibault grinned.

"You're on her side, aren't you?" Jen accused.

The Cloak just shrugged. "I do love the rose bushes. And I'm sure the pots and pans will come in handy . . ."

Jen looked from one to the other, then flung up her hands in disgust. "Very well, you win. I'll put it in my own house when I'm of age. And Absalom . . ."

"You have but to ask."

"Thank you. At least one person respects me. So, what's my reward for complying?"

Her aunt arched an eyebrow. "How about a job?"

"What sort of job?"

"An Owen sort of job. The little so-and-so summoned me into his office—in the teeth of a snowstorm, I might add—just as we were departing. It seems one of his oldest friends requires a little bodyguarding."

"Why?" Thibault asked.

"Where?" Jen inquired.

"Konasta, you little minx," Vera responded, addressing the more pleasant question.

"Bully!" the girl exclaimed, clapping her hands. "Tell Owen I love him."

"Tell him yourself; Absalom's here."

"True. Great stars, Konasta! Did you hear that, Thib?"

"My hearing is quite equal to yours, I assure you," her partner responded dryly. "Vera?"

The Hawk couldn't quite keep the disgust out of her voice as she replied. "Your employer is the owner of one of the most famous—or perhaps I should say infamous—illusion clubs in all of Konasta: the Cauldron of Iniquity."

"I've heard of that," Jen said.

"Don't tell me you're impressed."

"Well . . ."

"What's the job?" Thibault persisted.

This time Vera addressed herself directly to him. "Saul Soleneides is an old school friend of Owen's who has been periodically feeding our Guildmaster information about the Dreamsmoke trade. Information designed to help eliminate it. Now it seems that the family of one of the dealers he fingered is out for revenge, hiring a rogue assassin to eliminate their betrayer. And with his two regular bodyguards about to leave on vacation, Saul naturally felt that his time would be better spent if someone else took over the job of worrying about his safety until they return. Owen has volunteered you two."

"For pay?" Jen inquired.

"Of course. Five hundred apiece, same as last time; you're still in training, after all. Acceptable?"

"Come on, Vera, you know the money's no issue."

"Then why did you ask about it?"

"Because even I don't work for free." Then a knowing look appeared in Jen's eyes and she asked, "What will you be doing during all this?"

"Me?" Vera feigned innocence. "What makes you think I'm involved?"

"Because you love Konasta and you hate the Smoketraders," Jen answered. "Reason enough?"

"Not this time," Vera lied. "This one's yours alone."

"Really?"

"Yes; lucky you."

Vera was aware that latter sounded unaccountably sour, and therefore wasn't surprised when Thibault asked, "Why? What's the matter? Why do you object to this?"

Vera remained silent.

"Actually, I think it should be rather fun," Jen said. "I've always wanted to see one of the illusion clubs."

"Oh?" Vera responded tartly.

Confronted with three sets of eyes—two curious, one subtly accusing—Jen scowled. "Well, why not? What's the matter with you, Vera? Why don't you want us to take this job?"

Vera exhaled gustily. But, "What you do with your time is entirely your own business," she conceded.

"And if it were your job?"

"Fortunately, that's not my decision. You know I respect Owen's friendship and values. If he feels this job is worthwhile, that's enough for me. But personally . . . I deplore it. I deplore the illusion clubs, and I deplore the idea of guarding the life of someone who perpetrates those excesses. No matter how good a friend of the Guildmaster he is, nor how many good uses Owen claims he puts his profits to."

"And why is that?" Jen retorted. "After all, the clubs provide a valuable social release. Without their presence, everything they contain could well spill over into everyday life."

The Hawk snorted. "Don't be naive, Jenny. You're just swallowing the standard tripe. That's what everyone says: keep the excesses off the streets. Well, look about you. What makes Konasta so special? Why isn't Bergaetta stewing in a pit of corruption without illusion clubs? Why is it Konasta alone that requires such release?"

"What, like there's not any revelry here? Or prostitution? That the illusion clubs put it all under one roof doesn't make them inherently evil."

"No?"

"What's that supposed to mean?"

"That you're young, Jenny. You haven't seen what giving people latitude like that will lead to!"

"And you have?"

Vera was silent again. She had never told Jen about Nick Navarin, nor about those shadowed years of her life, and she doubted she ever would.

"Curse it, Vera," the Dagger continued, "by that token you're in favor of curtailing people's basic liberties—telling them what they can and can't do with their private time— and that's no better than consigning them to live in a dictatorship!"

"Is it? What are laws, after all, Jenny? Do you really

think that people should be allowed to steal and murder all in the name of personal freedom?"

"Hang it, that's different—and you know it! The illusion clubs don't impinge on anyone else's liberties."

"Don't they?"

"Now, children," Absalom inserted, finally entering the discussion. "This is clearly not something you are going to resolve in one afternoon, and it strikes me that we have more important things to determine than whether the illusion clubs are morally viable."

"They're not," Vera grumbled.

"And who makes you the arbiter?" Jen retorted.

"Children," said Absalom more sharply, and the sudden, spontaneous thumping of the tea table against the floor shocked them both into silence.

"Does the furniture usually move about by itself when he's excited?" Jen muttered in an undertone to Vera.

"How should I know? I try to keep on his good side wherever possible."

"Now," Absalom continued, ignoring them, "no one questions that our revered Cloak and Dagger must undertake this assignment. Correct?"

"Yes . . ."

"Well, that obviously means that preparations must be made to get them underway as quickly as possible. Which, in turn, leaves us with another problem."

They all regarded him curiously.

"Thibault, my lad," the mage concluded, "do you have any idea what you're going to do about a steward?"

The Cloak groaned and smacked his forehead. "Blast it all to perdition . . ."

"Umm, excuse me?" Rafiq poked his head around the doorframe. "I've taken care of the rooms. Is there anything else that needs doing?"

Vera could almost see the light of calculation coming on behind Thibault's eyes. "Actually, I can think of one thing. How about becoming my new steward?" And at the lad's look of baffled incomprehension, he added, "I'm in deadly earnest, Rafiq; it's the perfect solution. What do you say?"

Vera exchanged a look with Absalom, who was looking

quite smugly satisfied. "You knew all along, didn't you?" she accused.

"And you didn't?" Her companion grinned. "Ah, for the wisdom of advancing years."

The Hawk just scowled. "Speak for yourself," she said. "I am *not* old."

4

It took almost the full twelve hours leading up to their departure for Thibault to convince Rafiq of his earnestness, but eventually he prevailed, and his new steward seemed delighted by the position. Granted, it was somewhat of a sinecure—the master, after all, would rarely be home, and how challenging could that be?—but Thibault supposed it was nonetheless an honor to jump straight into a job of that caliber without fulfilling all the requisite antecedents.

Eduardo, obviously a stickler for the social niceties, seemed torn between relief and disapproval. Clearly he would not have to wait around for Rafiq to be trained; equally clearly, he took exception to the elevation of one so young and callow.

Thibault couldn't have cared less. In fact, he would later wonder why it had taken him so long to reach the obvious conclusion. For even as the immanence of their departure sent him into a frenzy of last-minute preparations, Rafiq proved eminently level-headed, placidly locating items that Thibault had misplaced, preparing tea and simple meals with a relief that spoke volumes about having Jen out from underfoot.

Of course, there were other details to attend to. The matter of a cook, for one. Vera and Absalom had gratefully accepted Thibault's offer to stay on in Bergaetta, enjoying the milder climate, and someone would have to feed them. Moreover, with Rafiq as steward, someone else would have to take over the duties as suhdabhar and general dogsbody.

But Rafiq just shrugged off most of these concerns. "I have a cousin," he said, "who would be delighted to come in occasionally to cook. And with only two people in residence . . . Well, I'm used to tidying up. I don't expect they'll think any less of me if I undertake both jobs for a while. At least until your situation settles down a bit."

"Bless you, Rafiq," Thibault had declared, seizing his new steward's hands and pumping them warmly. "I knew I made the right choice. Now, what do I pay you?"

At that, the staggeringly competent Rafiq had stumbled into silence. "I . . . I don't know. Whatever you feel like paying me, I suppose."

"Honestly, Rafiq, I have no idea what the range even is! What does Eduardo receive?"

"Somewhere in the hundreds, I believe. But he has been with the estate for almost forty years. That's way too high for someone of my stature."

"So what do you suggest?"

"Fifty?" Rafiq said tentatively.

"Fifty a week?" Thibault nodded decisively. "Done."

There was a long moment of silence. Then, "A *week*?" Rafiq managed, his voice rising in a horrified squeak. "I was thinking more in terms of months."

"Fifty a *month*?" It was now Thibault's turn for indignant horror. "Gracious; I had no idea! But still . . . Seventy-five, and not a mark less. Otherwise, I'd feel crawlingly guilty. Acceptable?"

Rafiq looked pale. "Eminently. But please . . ."

"Yes?"

"Don't tell anyone. I don't think they'd ever forgive me!"

Thibault chuckled and clapped the lad on the shoulder. "Nonsense. Between my absent-mindedness and Jenny's shenanigans, you'll have more than earned it. Now, about your cousin's salary . . ."

But Jen had solved that particular problem, arriving scant seconds later with a large purse which she dumped unceremoniously into Rafiq's hands before Thibault could protest. "Here," she said. "For household expenses. That should last a few months, at least. And let me know when you need more."

Rafiq peered into the purse, and Thibault could see his face go paler still at the sight of all that gold.

"Don't you . . . I mean, aren't you even worried that I

might just abscond with all these marks?" the lad hazarded at last, in a small voice.

"Not in the least," the Dagger countered cheerfully. "I know Thibault, and he would never choose a dishonest steward."

"I . . . well . . . Thank you, Domina."

"Ah, yes, there's that little matter, too, isn't there? Now that you're official, it strikes me that there's even less need of this 'Domina' nonsense than before. You can either call me Jen or, if you prefer, Jenifleur—though I do think that latter is a bit excessive, don't you?"

"Yes . . . Jenifleur," Rafiq managed uneasily.

Thibault grinned. But after she had departed, he turned to his flustered steward and said, "Don't fret yourself about Jen. She can be a bit much at times, I know, but she does grow on you. And she means well."

So everything was settled, and a day later Jen and Thibault were ensconced in a flurry of last-minute activity as the hired hansom was loaded and the final farewells were said.

"You'll be fine here without us?" Thibault asked anxiously.

The Hawk just smiled and patted his cheek. "Absalom and I have been out on our own for many years, and I think we're both adult enough to survive a few weeks without a chaperone."

To his mortification, Thibault went bright red. He had never really thought of Vera and Absalom in that light before. They both seemed too perfectly—self-contained, he supposed—to be involved in something of that nature. Besides, the man was a mage—and Thibault couldn't quite desist in thinking that somehow lifted him above the earthly plane.

Still, he supposed it could be possible.

"I didn't mean . . ." he stammered, but Vera merely chuckled, her very matter-of-factness allaying his doubts.

"Of course you didn't. I was only teasing. And we won't disrupt your household, I promise. Rafiq will scarcely even know we're here." The mischievous twinkle that appeared in her eyes made Thibault glance at her rather more sharply than he intended, but before he could frame a query the look was gone, leaving him convinced he had simply imagined it.

"We'll be fine, really," Vera repeated, then called, in a more carrying voice, "Jenny, slow down. You're going to do yourself an injury in your haste!" And indeed, Jen was dashing from house to hansom and back in a frenzy of seemingly pointless activity, bearing nothing that her partner could see. "Goodness knows," the Hawk added in an undertone, "just what that girl thinks she's up to. You two have barely enough baggage for one trip, and I should know. I helped her pack it."

Thibault grinned. "Whatever would we do without you, Vera?"

"Doubtless be traveling twice as laden. Honestly, the things she seemed convinced were dire necessities . . ." And the Hawk shook her head, letting her voice trail off. "Quite absurd. I made her leave them all behind." Then, turning, she added, "Jenny, are you quite done?"

"Yes, Auntie, I think so," the girl returned, flashing a too-innocent smile in her direction.

"And whose is this?" Absalom inquired, scooping up a tiny pouch that had fallen abandoned to the pavement.

"What?" Vera asked curiously, reaching for it. Jen, Thibault noticed, started guiltily, so he merely said smoothly, "Mine. Sorry, Absalom," and pocketed the thing before Vera could intercept it.

Jenny flashed him a grateful smile which he countered with a stern glance, raising a querying eyebrow in return. She just shrugged, unrepentant.

"Is everything ready?" Vera said at last.

"I think . . . Oh, one last thing!" And Jen dashed again for the house.

Vera sighed as she disappeared. "I think you're in for trouble, my lad." Then, with a sudden smile, she added, "However, I have been waiting for just such an opportunity to give you a little something I had commissioned in Ceylonde." And she drew out one of the most beautiful daggers Thibault had ever seen, with a sheen like purest silver and a razor's edge, dense with the aqueous ripples of much-folded steel. The sheath was of sturdy leather and the hilt elaborately tooled—elegant without being gaudy. There were no flashy jewels or ostentation, just a simple lozenge, engraved on both sides with an antlered stag's head.

And, best of all, it didn't disappear into his grip but rather molded to his hand as if it had been made for it—which he supposed it had.

"Vera, it's lovely," he breathed. "Is this really for me?"

"For you, on your twenty-first birthday," she confirmed. "I suppose I should have gotten you a cloak rather than the dagger, but I simply couldn't resist."

"Then you remembered?"

"What, your birthday? Don't be an idiot, lad! I didn't live next to Sylvaine all those years for nothing. And I would have given it to you earlier, only I didn't think you wanted all that fuss. Not to mention that bloody, temperamental artist of a smith didn't have it ready in time!"

He laughed and lightly touched the stag's head. "What is this?"

To his surprise, Vera looked almost embarrassed. "It's what you remind me of, my dear. Tall and proud; noble and wild. Carry it well, Thibault; I can't tell you how proud I am of you."

He felt a betraying prickle of tears in his eyes and fought for composure. "I . . ."

"However"—Vera was abruptly brisk—"you might not want to show it to Jen just yet, because she's not getting hers for a little over two years."

Thibault grinned, and hugged her. "I'll take it under advisement. And thank you, Vera. It means a lot to me."

"And me. I'm glad Jenny's got you. Good luck, Thibault—and remember, trust in your instincts as much as Jenny's. They're every bit as reliable—and sometimes even more so, I suspect. Especially where men are concerned."

As if in response, Jenny emerged from the house as unburdened as she had entered. "Uck, mushy stuff," she teased, and flung her arms about her aunt while Thibault quietly slid the sheathed dagger into his pocket. "Wish me luck, Vera," she said.

"Luck," Vera answered, embracing her.

Then, skipping away, Jen came to a skidding halt before Absalom. "Oh, and Absalom . . . While we're at it, do you think you could manage to renew that contraception spell for me?"

Thibault groaned.

"And what kind of mischief are you expecting to get into this time?" Vera demanded.

"Oh, no concrete expectations. But better to be safe than sorry, eh, Auntie?" She paused long enough to let Absalom lay a light hand on her abdomen, then whirled away, spinning the mage in a half circle and dropping a kiss on his cheek as she released him.

"I never trust her when she calls me Auntie," Vera growled, turning to regard her niece as she settled herself demurely in the hansom. "She's up to something, I know it."

"Are you coming, Thibault?" the minx called, for all the world as if her frantic activities had not been the ones delaying them for the past ten minutes.

Thibault, though, was staring at Absalom. "Was that it? Was that the spell?"

"Quite. I could, of course, have included all that ceremonial nonsense, but I figured we were both beyond that. Not to mention lacking the time if you are to catch that ship of yours."

Thibault chuckled. "Ah, how quickly illusions are destroyed! Goodbye, then, Absalom. Take care of yourself." He gripped the mage's hand firmly.

"And you, as well, lad."

He started to turn toward the carriage.

"Thibault . . ." Vera called.

"Yes?"

"One last thing. Don't let the illusion clubs overwhelm you. They can be quite seductive on the outside, but someone has to see below the surface. And I trust your clear sight and judgment. Don't let Jenny's prejudices blind you."

"Vera . . ."

"No, Thibault. I'm not trying to divide you, or denigrate your partner. I just want you to remember what I said. It could be important."

"All right. I . . ."

"Hurry, Thibault, or we're going to miss our tide!" his partner trilled from inside the coach.

The Cloak heaved a sigh, turning at last to regard his steward. "Rafiq, will you be all right? Is there anything else I've forgotten?"

"If there is," the lad answered calmly, "I'll handle it when it arises. Go on, don't miss your boat. Everything here will be fine."

"Fine," Thibault echoed weakly. He touched the hilt of the dagger in his pocket, then added more firmly, "Fine. Yes, of course it will be fine. Whatever am I thinking? Thanks again, Rafiq, for managing my life so well; I knew I made the right choice." He set a foot to the sill of the hansom, ready to spring in, when a sudden, last-minute thought occurred to him. "Oh, and Rafiq?"

"Yes?"

He leaned out of the cab, gesturing his steward closer. Then, when he was certain Jenny couldn't overhear him, he whispered, "Do me a favor and take up those rugs while we're gone."

Once they were firmly settled in the hansom and clattering toward the quay, Jenny turned to her partner with a frown. "What was all that about?" she demanded.

"What?"

"That. With Rafiq."

"Oh." Thibault flushed slightly. "That was nothing."

She could tell instantly that he was lying. And, convinced it had something to do with her, she was about to elaborate when he suddenly drew a small suede pouch from his pocket.

"And what, may I ask, is this?" he demanded, dangling it before her.

She grimaced and tried to grab it, but he swung it deftly out of her reach. The jouncing of the cab and her own abortive snatch sent her tumbling against him, her legs across his lap and her face buried somewhere in the hollow of his shoulder.

Furious at her betraying flush, she pushed herself upright, aware of a taunting warmth in the pit of her belly. But whether that was due to Thibault's presence or the residual effects of Absalom's spell, she really couldn't say.

Thibault, meanwhile, had opened the pouch and spilled its contents across his lap, his big, deft fingers sorting among the vials. "I thought I recognized this. It's your poison kit, isn't it?"

She tossed back her hair and met his eyes defiantly. "And what of it?"

"Why didn't you want Vera to see it?"

"Because my revered aunt said I wouldn't need poisons on a bodyguard mission."

"And?" He grinned, and once again she felt a return of that annoying flush.

"I begged to differ," she snapped.

He laughed then, scooping the contents back into the pouch. He drew it shut, and returned it to her with a flourish. "Yes, Vera did say that she tried to . . . well, shall we say, *restrain* your packing?"

"Indeed she did, the witch! She expected me to go off without the most essential of items."

"And?" her partner countered.

"Honestly, Thibault, do you really think I'd let her get away with that sort of control? Every single item she eliminated, I put right back. What else do you think all that last-minute frenzy was about?"

"Oh, no, Jenny, you didn't! How?"

She knew her voice was filled with a certain smug triumph, but she couldn't help it; it was too perfect. "Didn't you even wonder why the seat cushion was a little lumpy?"

"Tarnation! Jenny . . ."

"One by one, under my skirts," she confessed. "Now, get up. You're sitting on my second best outfit." And grabbing the strap, she pulled herself upright against the sway of the hansom, shaking a generous carry-all from under her gown. Then, hauling a bemused Thibault to his feet, she upended the cushion and began retrieving a multiplicity of items from the various corners of the cab—including another carry-all, her make-up bag, and at least two wigs—stuffing them somewhat chaotically into the bags.

Thibault, clinging to the strap, was practically folded double with laughter, but then, at six foot four, he couldn't very well stand up inside the carriage anyway.

Eventually, restoring the cushion, she allowed him to take his seat again, and proudly patted the two bulging bags which reigned at her side. An instant later, the hired cab pulled up to the quay, and the looming bulk of the trading vessel that would carry them east to Konasta. It was, Jen was pleased to note, a good sight grander than the ship which had previously borne them east to Ashkharon, and with a sudden lift of spirits she skipped up the gangplank—leaving Thibault, as usual, to pay off the driver and collect their remaining luggage.

At last, she thought, they were underway again. And adventure awaited!

5

"And just what do you think you're doing?" Rafiq demanded three days later, clinging desperately to the window of the hansom as if he could hold it back by sheer force of will.

"I told you," Vera replied calmly from inside. "Leaving."

"But I thought the master said . . ."

"That we were free to stay and enjoy his hospitality—and yours. Which we have. Immensely. But now we're off. Aren't we, Absalom?"

"Whatever you say," the mage answered placidly.

Vera nudged him.

"Yes, yes," he amended. "We are most definitely leaving. And thank you so much for everything, Rafiq."

"But . . ."

"Yes. Take a holiday, or something, Rafiq," Vera added. "Goodness knows, you've earned it."

"I . . ."

"Good-bye, then." Vera rapped imperiously on the roof of the hansom. The cab lurched into motion, shedding the baffled steward like overripe fruit.

"That wasn't very nice," Absalom chided, but there was a trace of a smile in his voice.

"Perhaps not, but it needed doing. He's a sweet lad, but entirely too earnest. Determined to do his best by his master as he sees it. Including holding us hostage, if that suits."

"Come now, Vera, you're exaggerating. Besides, he's new at his job. He'll grow out of it in time."

"Either that, or Jenny will give him the what-for." She leaned back against the fading cushions with a sigh. "Well, I profoundly hope you're right. But for now the problem's behind us—and we, too, have a ship to catch."

"Do we have everything we need?" the mage inquired puckishly. "Your luggage did seem a little light . . ."

"Experience," Vera responded. "And we do indeed have everything—save for that amulet you crafted against illusion, which has unaccountably disappeared. I could really have used that."

"Not to worry. You are here with the source. I'll craft you another."

"For how much?" Vera teased, recalling their meeting. "Twenty-five? Or was it thirty?"

"Thirty. Although, as I remember, you bargained me down to fifteen. However, I'll give you this one for free— if you promise not to tell anyone. It'll ruin my reputation if word gets out I've gone soft."

"Reputation? What reputation?"

"You have a point," he admitted. He leaned back against the cushions. "You really shouldn't be doing this, you know."

"What?" Vera was indignant. "I have a perfectly legitimate job to perform."

"One that you bullied the Guildmaster into granting you, and don't you dare try to pretend otherwise! I am infinitely wise to you, my lady."

"Dearest Absalom." She chuckled and squeezed his hand. "Whatever would I do without you?"

For the briefest of instants his form wavered, and the scruffy mage with the filthy half-beard and single eye whom she had met in the Nhuras bazaar half a year earlier leered back at her.

She dropped the hand that had momentarily become a lump of fused, scarred flesh and yelped, "Quit it, will you? Someone might see you." But he had already reverted to the rugged, dark-eyed paragon whose looks so distracted and disturbed her. In truth, she had expected to become inured to that particular incarnation months ago, and was always a little startled to discover she hadn't.

The mage just grinned and, as usual, changed the subject. "Nice work, getting us a ship so quickly. I thought there wasn't a vessel bound for Konasta for another week after your niece and her partner departed. Who did you bribe?"

"No one." Vera smiled. "Just pulled in a favor with a friend."

It had been pure luck, she supposed—either that or fate—to encounter her sometime lover Kharman Black haunting the Bergaetta docks. He had put in for supplies before shipping to Mepharsta, and had been only too pleased to add an unscheduled drop in Konasta. Not to mention offering free passage for herself and a companion—although admittedly his face had fallen a bit when she disclosed the latter.

"What, competition?" he had said cheerfully, but nonetheless with a certain query in his bluff, dark eyes.

"Only a friend, I assure you. You know my heart belongs to you, Captain Black."

He gave a shout of laughter. "I know no such thing, you absurd woman! But it is always a pleasure having my own dear Leonie on board."

"Oh, and about that?" She beckoned him closer and approached her lips to his ear. "You might want to call me Vera, this time."

He turned, then, his face bare inches from her own, his black eyes dancing. His raven hair and beard were as wild and untamed as she'd remembered. "Oh? And why is that? What is it you really do, Malle Varis?"

"Oh." She grinned. "I could tell you, but then I'd have to kill you. And what fun would that be?"

"Mmm." He nodded. "Guild, right? Never mind, you don't have to answer that. I always suspected there was more to you than met the eye. How many cabins will you be requiring?"

"How many do you think?" she answered, slyly.

"Well, a man can always hope . . ."

"Indeed he can. And I'd give you ample proof of my intentions if we weren't standing in the middle of such a crowded street."

"Then," he said, engulfing her fingers in his gentle, calloused grip, his touch still able to thrill her, "I'll look forward to a time when we are not so much in the public view."

"As will I," she responded. And, remembering, she

grinned quietly to herself as the hansom rattled towards
the quay and the looming bulk of the *Belapharion Traveler.*

"You're up to something," Absalom said. "I don't trust
that look. Who is this friend of yours?"

"A ship's captain," Vera responded.

"A lover?"

"What difference does that make? He's offered to carry
us to Konasta for free."

"Indeed?" Absalom frowned. "Does he know who you
are?"

"Not entirely, no. The last time we met, he thought I
was a failed schoolteacher named Leonie Varis."

"And this time?"

"I just told him to call me 'Vera.' "

The mage raised an eyebrow. "Do you really think
that's wise?"

"Honestly, Absalom," the Hawk retorted, rather sharply,
"I survived perfectly well in this profession for almost
twenty years without you. Have a little faith in my abilities.
And my judgment. Believe me, Kharman Black is one of
the good ones."

"Oh, yes. I see. His name positively inspires confidence."

"Absalom! I refuse to take you on this mission if you
don't behave."

"Yes, my dear. Whatever you say," the mage responded,
with such a complete lack of obedience that Vera was
tempted to throttle him. "Quite a nice day we're having,
isn't it? Very mild weather. Nice sun. Well, well, the cab
seems to have stopped." With one deft motion, he slid
down the pane and leaned his head out the window, observ-
ing, "Ah, yes. We appear to have arrived; I think I can see
our ship now. Oh, and your captain. My, my. Quite a bear
of a man, isn't he? With a marked piratical demeanor. Just
needs an eyepatch to complete the image. And perhaps a
mangy parrot. Yes, most inspiring of confidence. Truly, my
dear, I commend your tastes. Ahoy, there; Black! Are you
Captain Black?" The mage flapped one hand flamboyantly
out the window.

Vera did hit him then, but she was laughing too hard to
give any real impetus to the blow.

Captain Black, meanwhile, had approached the hansom,

resting his brawny forearms in the open window. He winked at Vera, then turned his attention to Absalom. "And you must be Leonie—I mean, Vera's—friend . . ."

"Epheziel," the mage put in without hesitation.

"Absalom," she hissed, poking him. "Behave!"

He turned an unrepentant grin her way.

"I'm sorry, Kharman," she said. "I can't think what's gotten into my companion. He's usually more civilized than this; I think he's just annoyed because I cut his vacation short. And call him Absalom—no matter what he tells you."

"Absalom," Black said. "Welcome. I'm delighted to offer my ship to any friend of Leonie's."

"My thanks." The mage smiled brilliantly and offered his hand, and Vera did a sharp double-take because her companion had just lost twenty years off his age.

"We'll be with you in a moment, Kharman," she said sweetly, and slammed the window shut. "What's the matter with you?" she demanded. "Are you . . ." An appalling thought occurred. "Are you *jealous*?"

"Good gracious, no!" her companion responded, with convincing horror.

"Well? What, then?"

"I just . . ."

"What?"

"Well . . . The next time you plan on turning my life upside down, at least give me a few hours warning!" he said in a rush.

Vera laughed and pounded him on the shoulder. "I knew it! I knew you were upset that I'd destroyed your vacation." Then, sobering, she added, "Look, Absalom, I know how hard you've been working in Arrhyndon with Jeremy, and I know you wanted a few days to recover, but I have a bad feeling about this job. I need to keep an eye on Jenny. And I'd rather have you with me, but if you really want to stay behind, I'll understand."

"And what fun would that be?" her companion answered. "No, Konasta it is. And I'm sorry for my bad humor. I'll behave, I promise."

"Good; thank you."

"But did you have to tell that man my real name?"

Vera's eyebrows winged upward at the plaintive note in

the mage's voice, but all she said was, firmly, "If it is your real name. Besides, I, for one, refuse to spend the entire voyage calling you Epheziel!" And with Absalom's rich chuckle echoing in her ears, she paid off the driver and collected their scant belongings, following Kharman Black onto the ship.

Though she couldn't help hoping, as Absalom trailed her up the gangplank, that this job would go a good sight better than the last time the *Belapharion Traveler* carried her off to foreign ports.

Her second voyage across the Belapharion passed both more slowly and more quickly than Jen had anticipated. Without the terror at her aunt's predicament which had stretched every hour into an eternity seven months back, the days seemed to pass with an unremarkable sameness. Yet without all the additional worries and high-jinks that had occupied her on that initial voyage, it was amazing how long a few weeks could seem when passing at their normal, unhurried span.

Could she really have become jaded that quickly?

But then it was only a bodyguard position, a mere bread-and-butter trial assignment to ensure that she had learned her lesson—hardly anything to challenge her. If she could just get through it without succumbing to terminal boredom—although a few illicit jaunts into the illusion clubs might help—then perhaps Owen would start giving them the real jobs again.

"Odd, isn't it?" she said to Thibault on one occasion, as they leaned against the railing and watched the restless water streaming by below. "Don't you feel like we're starting all over again? Back to the beginning, as it were?"

Her partner shuddered. "I sincerely hope not. *That* little adventure was an unmitigated disaster. Vera imprisoned, Pehndon mucking things up . . ."

"What, like our second adventure was a raving success?"

A glum silence reigned. Then Thibault added, "Well, at least this time we're legitimate."

"We were the last time, too. In Arrhyndon."

"Ah, but that was a first assignment," her partner countered, "and therefore doesn't count. Right?"

"Well . . ."

"I mean, even Vera mucked *hers* up."

"Mmm." Jen wrinkled her nose. Then, "Did she ever tell you what happened?"

"No."

"Me, either. But I think it's something to do with the illusion clubs."

"Why?"

"Because. Didn't you notice how adamant she was about them? There's something about the clubs she doesn't like, doesn't trust. Like they left some kind of horrendous impression on her. And how many times in her life has Vera fouled up? I think the two are related."

"You could be right," Thibault agreed, obviously remembering Vera's last words. Jen knew she hadn't been meant to hear them, but she had, and they rankled. Blindness, indeed. Granted Thibault was her trusted partner, but Vera was her aunt, and the remark had seemed distressingly like favoritism to her, placing her firmly on the losing end.

It made her more determined than ever to visit the clubs and discover the truth.

Thibault, seeing her frown, asked, "What's the matter?" Then, "Oh, blast. You heard, didn't you? What Vera said?"

Jen nodded reluctantly.

"I'm sure she didn't mean it. Or, at least, not as it sounded. Like you said, it was probably just her reaction to a first job gone awry."

"Yes, of course. Thanks."

But what neither of them acknowledged was why Owen would send a raw recruit straight into the jaws of the infamous illusion clubs. Unless, of course, it was another favor for Soleneides. Which might explain Vera's antipathy to the man.

Well, soon enough they would be in Konasta, and then they would see who was right and who was wrong. At least it would give Jen something more to do than simply bodyguarding.

She gazed back down at the waves as if she could see the miles flowing away between herself and her goal, and her lips curved in a small, secret smile.

6

The *Xanthippe* docked at Ephanon, the port capital of Konasta, on a grim, grey afternoon. A faint mist hovered over
the surface of the water like cotton batting, and no doubt
had wound up the serpentine streets earlier that morning,
bandaging them in the same ghostly gauze that had muted
the swells of the inner islands as the ship navigated through
the narrow channel that was the inlet to Ephanon Bay.

Jen found herself oddly disillusioned. She had expected
tropical islands set like milky jewels into the sweep of sea
and sky. She had expected sun and sand and leaping fishes.
Decadent luxury set shoulder to shoulder with squalling
penury, in that odd yet vital mix that was rumored to be
so uniquely Konastan. She had never expected this alien
landscape, chill and forbidding, with slate-grey waters lapping turgidly beneath a steely sky.

A faint, dispirited drizzle leaked onto her upturned face
as the ship nudged against the quay.

To her untrained senses, the city stank of fish and poverty, the voices of the dockhands sullen and muted beneath
the dripping clouds. The temperature was as mild as it had
been in Bergaetta—as befitted the more southern lati-
tudes—but it seemed that, even here, winter was making
itself felt. A line of carriages, gilt paint flaking, huddled
under filthy tarpaulins, and the horses drooped and snorted.
The dim, yellow plash of magelights did little to brighten
the rutted pavements, and if the splendor of the illusion
clubs held any sway over the ragged tiers of buildings which
straggled up the inclined streets, it was not one which Jen
could discern.

Even the palace, resting high on its pinnacle, seemed less

grand than tawdry, its pillared bulk misty and indistinct among the low-hanging clouds.

The Dagger sighed and ran a finger along the sodden wood of the deck railing. It was hardly a propitious omen for the success of their assignment.

"Not quite what you expected, is it?" Thibault said softly from beside her, and she grimaced.

"Not by half. Whatever does Vera see in this place, I wonder?"

"It probably looks a deuced sight better in the sunlight."

"As do most things," Jen acknowledged. "Hang and blast. You didn't think to bring an umbrella, did you?"

"No, but I don't think we need worry. It seems we are being met."

Startled, she glanced out over the docks. A tall gentleman with a large black umbrella was peering at them intently, and in response to her tentative smile he raised a hand, hastening toward the gangplank. She had, in the course of duty, told Owen the name of their ship, but she had never expected their employer to meet them.

Yet if this wasn't the lord and master of the most powerful illusion club in all of Konasta, then she was a jellied chicken. He palpably exuded power as he strode across the damp pier, and everywhere an awed buzzing seemed to radiate from his presence. Dockhands scraped and smiled, or pounded him on the shoulders with jovial familiarity, and for each he had some word or gesture—a handful of copper bits here, a shared joke or chuckle there. And when he finally arrived at the vessel's side and grinned up at Jen, she felt the whole day lift and brighten.

Seeing him thus arrayed, she could easily credit the sway he held among the people of Konasta. What she couldn't credit was that he was Owen's contemporary; that he had once shared a university lodging with the crippled, crabbed master of the Guild. Surely there had to be some mistake, for this man's hair was barely grey. Instead, it was thick, dark and lustrous, with a tight, springing curl. And his eyes were dark as a magpie's, brimming with mischief as if he knew some remarkable secret which he wasn't telling but which would nonetheless delight the hearer should he choose to relate it. He had dimples like a lad, and must, in his youth, have been a tearing beauty—there was, Jen decided, no other word for it. Even now, he moved like a boy, all fluidity and zeal.

"Jen and Thibault, I presume?" he said, and even his voice had a depth and texture that would make most men's pale.

"Indeed," Jen responded, shooting a surreptitious glance at her partner to see if he, too, had fallen under the spell. But Thibault's face was smooth and impassive as a statue's, revealing nothing.

"Well, then." Their host rubbed his hands together. "You'll pardon the familiarity, but Owen has told me so much about you that I feel I know you already. You're his two most promising protégés, he tells me. And you must call me Saul, of course. Have you much baggage?"

"No . . ."

"Perfect. For reasons too complicated to explain right now, I am unable to offer you the hospitality of a carriage. So, perforce, we must walk. However—come down, come down; and welcome to Ephanon—it's not far, and it is quite a lovely day. Such a wonderful release from all that beastly heat, don't you find? Much as I love Konasta, I do have to admit that day after day of unmitigated sunshine can be a little dire."

Jen exchanged an amused smile with her partner as they descended the gangplank.

"Oh, quite," he continued cheerfully, "I know just what you're thinking. The old man's gone completely daft in his dotage." He laughed and hailed one of the crewmen. "Petros, lad, bring down my guests' baggage, won't you? And where's . . . Ah, there you are, Rafellus, you old scoundrel; I didn't think you'd miss a chance to greet your best customer! I was delighted to hear that my friends took passage with you. You treated them well, I trust?"

"No complaints that I've heard," the captain of the *Xanthippe* responded.

"Indeed, not," Jen agreed. "A most pleasant voyage."

"My thanks. I have that shipment of Magjorcan spices you expressed an interest in, Saul."

"Tomorrow, my friend; tomorrow. Come by the office

and we'll talk business. But for now, we need to get these two out of the damp."

By now, courtesy of Petros, their small complement of baggage had arrived. While Jen claimed her two special packs, Thibault shouldered the rest of the burden, then gazed expectantly at their employer.

"Quite," Soleneides declared. "See you tomorrow, Rafellus."

"I look forward to it."

Then, with a sweep of his hand, Saul raised his umbrella and collected his new employees beneath its capacious spread.

"You wouldn't believe the variety of goods I have to haul in daily to satisfy my customers," he informed them cheerfully. "You'd think, by the way they ate and drank, that tomorrow was a completely uncertain proposition!"

"You do a lot of business down here, then?" Jen asked.

"Not usually, no. They mostly come to me. But our Harbormaster is cursed efficient and keeps track of all the docking ships with remarkable accuracy, earning my eternal gratitude, for I am far too dependent on their trade. Without supplies, you see, the clubs shut down. And without exotic supplies, a club's market edge is annihilated. But that, parenthetically, is how I knew exactly when and where to meet you. After all, I couldn't leave an occasion like this to chance." He winked and smiled, flashing those perfect dimples.

Jen laughed. "It sounds like Hestia should start hiring Harbormasters."

"Well, it takes some people longer to find wisdom than others," Saul conceded, as they wound up one of the narrow, rutted lanes that led away from the wharf; it was bordered on either side by a clutter of tumble-down houses. "But I believe you'll like Konasta. Ephanon has a spirit and character all its own which I think you'll enjoy. And hopefully—Good afternoon, Stannos—you'll have time to visit some of the islands before you return for the start of your term."

"We passed some of the inner islands today," Jen volunteered.

"Ah, but not quite at their best this morning, were they?

I know what it's like when the fog rolls in over the harbor; they must have been barely visible."

"It was a bit thick," Jen admitted.

"Well, that's not seeing the islands. To truly see the islands—Fine weather we're having, Jehan. What a truly remarkable hat!—you really must wait until spring. Summer, now that's too blasted hot. But spring . . ." Saul let his voice trail off wistfully, and Jen grinned. "However, winter will do if that's all you have. And I don't expect you to be busy with me for long; the Telos money is bound to run out sooner or later, and Avram and Lucinda should be back in a month. Owen filled you in on the situation, I take it?"

"The barest minimum," Thibault responded, "but, yes."

"Mmm. Well, that'll do for now. Still—Did you get that fish I sent you, Stabia? Ah, delightful. No, thank *you*—remind me when you leave to at least book you passage to Phykoros. We have clubs on a lot of the lesser islands, but Phykoros is by far the most beautiful, as well as the most popular. And due to overwhelming demand, we established a smaller version of the Cauldron there, which we jokingly call the Kettle. You've heard of the Cauldron, I take it?"

"Of course," Jen answered.

"Well—Good day, Marcus—it was the first club I ever opened, and it still remains my best. In fact, your very own Guildmaster helped me establish it, and I still feel he has a stake in the place—whether he wants to acknowledge it or not. Gideon will have to show the two of you around some evening."

Jen could barely suppress a smirk of triumph. "Who's Gideon?"

"Gideon Gilvaray, one of my two loyal associates. Also known as the Golden Boy."

"And the other? What is he known as?"

Saul looked momentarily blank. "Aubrey, usually. That's his name: Aubrey Dunning."

The callousness of his tone took Jen slightly aback. Obviously, Aubrey wasn't the favored one; she felt obscurely sorry for him.

"Still," Saul continued, "they're good lads, and you'll—oops. Quick, duck! I simply don't feel up to seeing Micah this morning." And he tipped the umbrella hastily over their faces, practically clipping Thibault's forehead in the process.

"Great bloody blazes," Jen exclaimed when he unveiled them. "Do you know *everyone*?"

Their employer chuckled. "Very probably, I'm afraid. After all, I do have a reputation to maintain. There, now, what do you think of that?"

The streets had been widening as they walked, the houses gradually growing grander, and now the lane burgeoned into a broad court containing a small garden, an elaborately carved fountain, and three magnificent townhouses with windows and balconies equally as generous as their Lusanian counterparts, if somewhat less ornate.

"Why, it's lovely!" she exclaimed.

"Is this where you live?" Thibault inquired.

"Not quite. As I said, I have a reputation to maintain— and the houses get grander the closer you approach the Summit. But I just wanted to show you that Ephanon does have its moments of glory. Beyond this is Sentenniel Street, which circumscribes the Summit and which is where all the markets congregate, not to mention the illusion clubs. We'll be passing the Cauldron shortly, and I live not far above that. You're not getting tired, I trust?"

Jen and Thibault hastened to reassure him, and a few streets later the avenue widened into a vast commercial district which would, Jen suspected, have been truly bustling were it not for the weather. As it was, it was hardly deserted, and ratty canvases had been erected in impromptu awnings over a wide variety of shops ranging from butcheries to jewelers, the perfumed elite rubbing elbows with fishwives and laborers. A vast dome, glittering with dancing magelights and with clouds of smoke steaming up from around its broad base, loomed over the squat spread of emporiums and markets. Above it all was the palace, barely visible beyond the rocky slopes of the Summit.

"Tarnation, is that building *burning*?" Jen gasped, pointing to the smoking dome.

"That?" Saul chuckled. "Far from it. That, in all its glory, is the Cauldron of Iniquity. Impressive, no?"

Jen exchanged a look with Thibault. Up close, it was

even gaudier than the most ostentatious of the mages'
dwellings, dancing with magical fires that gave off no smoke
or heat—except, of course, for that huge, signature billow
which announced the club's identity to even the most illiter-
ate of patrons. For those slightly more educated, a sparkling
curlicue of script arched above the doors, spelling out the
name.

But for all its ostentation, it was a solidly imposing building with heavily columned porticoes and broad, iron-grated
windows. Not to mention the huge swell of that gilded
dome.

"Over there," Saul informed them, pointing to a spired
monstrosity of Gothic proportions, like some castle displaced from the depths of the northern woodlands, "is the
Bear's Den, owned by my arch-rival, Micah Thaddeus—the
man whose dubious company I just delivered you from."
His puckish grin took the sting out of his words, though he
added, "Bloody dreadful name; bloody derivative club.
And that, there?" He pointed to another club that was
shaped rather like a galleon, complete with roof-mounted
topsails. "That's another one of mine. I call it the Rogue's
Gallery. Clever, no?"

Jen smiled, her eyes scanning the glitter like the rawest
of tourists, seeing in the vast buildings the symbol of promise they represented to an indigent population. The hope
and possibility of the many gaming tables, at which fortunes
could be made and broken. The glory of the vast, glowing
portals behind which, in exchange for a minimal entrance
fee (the main profits were made elsewhere entirely, which
was precisely the point), rich and poor alike could momentarily enter a world of fantasy and invention unlike anything they could otherwise experience. They were the great
levers of man, these clubs, masked behind the elaborate
facades which seemed to elevate all. It was no wonder they
were so infernally popular.

Once again, Jen found herself questioning Vera's intense
dislike of the places, which now seemed to her to fulfill the
most vital of social functions.

"Impressive, indeed," she said to Saul. "You must be
very proud."

"Oh, I am. Trust me. Very proud, indeed." His eyes twinkled. "Now, if you'll just come this way . . ."

And ducking up a small alley, they turned three more corners and emerged into an even larger and more impressive courtyard, this time fronted by a single grand manor. Further, by some trick of the winding lanes, the din of Sentenniel Street was muted as if it had never been, leaving only the gentle plashing from the large central fountain.

"Now this," Saul said grandly, "is House Soleneides. Pardon the deception, but . . . Slyly in the back door we go. All part of your cover, you understand; your designated position in my household. I hope you don't mind." He blithely led them around the sides of the mansion and into a back alley draped with laundry lines like any of the poorer streets.

"Yes, that is one thing I don't understand," Thibault said.

"What?"

"Precisely what our designated position in your household *is*."

Saul looked startled. "You mean Owen didn't tell you?"

"Tell us what?" Jen demanded.

"Avram and Lucinda, my regular bodyguards, always disguised themselves as part of the house staff to avoid calling any unnecessary attention to themselves. So I'm telling everyone I got you two from the local employment agency to replace them."

"But . . ." Jen faltered, seized by a growing sense of doom. "We won't actually be *working* in the house, will we?"

Their employer looked scandalized. "Of course you will. What kind of cover would it be otherwise?"

7

Jen was still in shock; Thibault was certain. For one thing, she was acting entirely too meek—and Jen was never meek unless she had been stunned virtually senseless. And for another, there was that tell-tale slackness to her jaw, the faint pinched frown between her eyes, which spoke of her desire to be reasonable, considered—offset by the rising tide of fury in her eyes.

He watched as the two impulses battled, wondering which would win. With Jen, you never knew. And then, eventually, her lips snapped together in a hard, tight line, shutting back the angry words. She would listen to their employer—let him explain his reasoning, though she might not like it—and Thibault drew a silent breath of relief.

Still, he was infinitely aware that, if he so much as smiled, she would kill him.

"I've found Avram and Lucinda's replacements," Saul called cheerfully into the depths of the house, and in response to his words a motherly looking woman dressed all in black—the housekeeper, Thibault supposed—appeared from around a nearby corner. She had greying hair, as tightly curled as Saul's, and a brisk, no-nonsense demeanor which made Thibault instantly feel they were in capable hands.

"Gracious, so you have," the woman announced, eyeing Thibault's prodigious height. He smiled rather ruefully back. "He should do nicely. Who's the other?"

"His wife. Two for the price of one, as it were," Saul informed her cheerfully, and Thibault could feel Jen stiffen at his side. Hastily, he draped an arm around her shoulders, giving her a sharp warning squeeze. The smile she forced out in response was so hard and precise it could have cut glass.

Fortunately, the woman seemed not to notice.

"She's a bit greener than her husband," Saul added, "but still willing to pull her weight in exchange for the chance to live in our oh-so-gorgeous country. You can put her to work between the kitchens and the cleaning staff, like Lucinda. And the lad will double as my suhdabhar. Especially since Cavan encountered that bit of bad meat."

"Yes, the poor darling. The house seems so empty without him. Shall I . . . ?" The woman held out a hand as if to lead them away, but Saul shook his head.

"Not yet. I want to talk to them both in my study first, to explain how things work around here and to work out the messy little details of their salary. But I'll call you soon enough."

"Very well." And the housekeeper trotted away.

"Sorry about that," Saul said in an undertone. "I honestly didn't expect to spring this all on you so quickly, but . . ."

"Needs must," Thibault answered dryly, since Jen didn't seem to be responding. "And it's quite all right."

"Good. Now"—and Saul opened a nearby door onto an expanse of wood-lined study, its walls paneled mostly with books—"come in and we'll talk." He shut the door behind them, muttered something that Thibault thought was "close," then settled himself behind his desk and gestured for Jen and Thibault to take up the two remaining seats. "First, and most importantly, what are your names to be?"

Jen looked startled. "I hadn't given it much thought," she said, in a halfway civil tone.

"And you, lad?"

Thibault shook his head.

"Well, we must have something. I've spoken to Owen enough to know his methods. Come, what will it be? And remember, not even Gideon and Aubrey, who know of your Guild affiliation, will be privy to your real names."

"Well, how about . . . Ty?" Thibault suggested.

"Short for Titan?" Saul grinned. "Fine. And you?"

"Gilyan?" Jen hazarded.

"Excellent. Oh, and sorry about that marriage thing, by the way. But one look at the two of you, and I knew I'd never be able to pass you off as siblings. You don't happen to be lovers, do you?"

"And what business is that of yours?" Jen snapped, giving rein to her anger at last. Thibault masked a smile.

"None, I suppose. I was only trying to sort out the sleeping arrangements. You'll have to share a room, of course. Do you want me to provide an extra pallet?"

Jen was still spluttering, so, "An extra pallet will be fine," Thibault supplied. "A long one, if possible."

"Not a problem."

"Thank you."

"You really expect me to do housework?" Jen demanded, indignantly.

"Well, of course!"

"But . . . I thought you needed bodyguards."

"I do. And Thibault—sorry, I mean, Ty—seems perfectly able to take over that role as my new suhdabhar. Not to mention being rather intimidatingly large. Wherever reasonable, I shall keep him firmly in sight. But, remember, the attempts on my life have not all been public ones. Someone also has to make sure that there are no nefarious traps set about the house, or that no one enters who shouldn't. The house is alarmed and shielded by magerie at night, but enough business is conducted here during the day that I can't afford that luxury continually. That's why I need you to split your time between the kitchens and the cleaning staff—the two places I could be most vulnerable. After all, Cavan did perish in that last attempt, and my family needs to be protected as much as I do. Which reminds me, I am far from the only one in this household. Also in residence are my son, Stavros; his wife, Lydea; and their son, Patroch." And there was something in his tone that told Thibault he didn't hold any of them in particularly high esteem.

Thibault cast a quick glance at Jen to see if she had noticed, but she was still too busy fuming. With a faint sigh, he caressed the knob of the stag's head dagger, which he had taken to carrying about in his pocket. As always, the gesture reassured him, carrying with it the memory of Vera's words: *tall and proud; noble and wild.* It had become almost a rite, shoring him up at those times when he most needed to be reminded of his strength and competence.

Which, when Jen was preoccupied, was far too frequently.

"My two safe areas are my offices—this one, and the one at the Cauldron—and I always activate the defences the moment I am inside. Thus you"—he turned to Thibault—"are free to amuse yourself as you choose while I am in either office, but I'll need you with me at all other times. We'll work out some sort of signal. And I'll enter you both into the house alarm system so you'll be recognized at night. Now I know it sounds like a lot," Saul added, "but you will be additionally compensated for the work. Not quite what Owen is paying you, but a viable servant's salary nonetheless. Twenty marks a week should be fair."

"But . . ." Thibault protested instinctively, remembering Rafiq's paltry seventy-five a month.

Jen's eyes shot daggers at him.

"I'm a rich man," Saul forestalled him, "and Konasta's wages are a sight higher than what you'll find in the rest of Varia. After all, even the servants must have enough to support the illusion clubs."

Thibault subsided into silence. He wondered if Saul was about to dismiss them when a knock came upon the door.

"Open," Saul murmured.

"Excuse me, sir." The housekeeper poked her head around the portal. "Sorry to disturb you, but Gideon and Aubrey are here, demanding to see you. I told them you were busy, but they didn't seem much inclined to patience."

"How typical. Very well; show them in. They can listen—and wait. It might do them good." Saul's voice was callous, but Thibault could tell he was secretly delighted. And, indeed, after his two associates had been ushered in, he beamed at them fondly. "Precisely on time, as always. Excellent. Come in, come in. Meet my newest helpers: the Cloak and the Dagger."

Thibault could see instantly why Gideon was called the Golden Boy. His curls shone like spun metal, almost seeming to rival the magelights. Nor was it the tight, fleecy curl of the Konastans, but rather the soft, looser fall of the northern climes—Haarkonis or Scandia, Thibault guessed. His eyes shone like two polished circlets of jade, inset with blackest jet, and his features were chiseled enough to rival the finest of classical statues. He was a man of extremes, this Gideon, with his ivory skin and luminescent smile—

almost as if everything he was and did were pushed to the limits of transcendence, giving him a superhuman air.

But if it was obvious why Gideon was the favored one, it was equally clear why Aubrey was not. In contrast to Gideon's beauty, the latter was altogether a tougher item. Both his hair and eyes were an indistinct shade of dark—not quite brown, not quite black—and his features were oddly unharmonious. If he ever had been handsome, it had long since been marred by a sullen expression that seemed to pull his face into perpetual lines—as if he were, at every moment, aware of Gideon's superiority and his own inability to match it.

Thibault glanced over at Jen, only to find her gazing at Gideon with the look of a starving man suddenly offered a seat at the lord's high table. It had been bad enough seeing her melt for Saul; it was even worse watching her liquefy for Gideon. All right, so the man was handsome. And undoubtedly magnetic. Even Thibault could feel the Golden Boy's charm operating on him as if it were magerie. But there was something about him that Thibault simply didn't trust.

But then again, the same could apply for any of Jen's conquests. He never liked them at first, no matter how virtuous they appeared.

With a silent sigh, he prepared once again to be proved wrong.

Saul cued them into the house alarm, then after a belated and inelegant introduction ("Oh, and did I forget to mention . . . ?") Alcina, the housekeeper, showed them to their room, hustling them along with a brisk efficiency which wasn't in the least affected by her voluble spate of chatter. But Jen had no conscious knowledge of what was said, nor even what grand chambers they passed in their perambulations, so lost was she in the endless cycle of her reflections. She had no idea whether to be pleased or dismayed at the course her life had taken.

To be a servant . . . That was intolerable. And yet . . . The job was not completely without its compensations. Compensations that came with jade-green eyes and sun-blond hair. Compensations that set her every nerve aquiver with possibility.

There was something—even now, she sensed it—reckless and dangerous about the Golden One. Something like the glitter of cat's eyes that momentarily held the mouse in thrall. Instinctively, she knew that she had never met anyone quite like Gideon Gilvaray, though she wasn't quite sure wherein the difference lay. Perhaps it was that, he alone of her acquaintances, stood at the height of his power, with his life mapped out precisely as determined and expected. Or perhaps it was something more nebulous still—a quality that arose, unbidden, from perfect beauty and confidence.

Whatever, it had dazzled her, lapping her in the luminosity of a smile which seemed to promise as much as it received.

Was it any wonder she had heard barely a scrap of conversation since?

However, she came down to earth with a bump as Alcina proudly ushered them into a dim, narrow little room which offered an unimpeded view of the back alley—laundry lines and all. The bricks of the opposite wall, yellow-grey with age and wear, were framed in all their pocked, chipped glory by a fall of dingy white curtains. The wood of the window frame was warped, admitting a faint, whistling tendril of breeze. There was a door to her left—too much to hope that it led to a bathroom—a rickety desk beneath the window, and an iron bedstead pushed into the far right corner. An equally rickety dressing table, complete with basin and ewer, was squeezed into the space between footboard and wall, and the mirror that hung above it was blotched and clouded with age and tarnish.

"The main bath's down the hall—with running water, no less," Alcina announced, as if it were some great miracle in modern design. But then, perhaps it was—at least among the serving classes. "And I do hope you shall be very comfortable here."

"Thank you," Thibault replied, with his usual charm. "I'm sure we shall be."

Jen managed a watery smile.

"I'll have your bags brought up in a moment, then once

you've had a chance to settle . . . come down and we'll put
you to work." She turned to Thibault with a twinkle. "I'm
sure the master has plenty of jobs lined up for you," she
said. Then, to Jen: "And Beroe can always use an extra
hand in the kitchens around this hour."

After she had departed, Jen leaned against the dingy
walls with a sigh, shutting her eyes against the sight.

"Come now," Thibault said cajolingly. "It's not that
bad . . ."

She opened her eyes again with a grimace. As expected,
the second door yielded nothing but a cramped, dark closet,
with a few hangers dangling impotently from the rod. There
was a chamber pot under the bed.

"This room is barely big enough for one," she declared.
"And they honestly expect us to share it?"

"It's no smaller than some of the inn chambers we've
occupied."

"Except for the bed. That's infinitely smaller." And Jen
flung herself onto the offending item, which creaked and
dipped sharply beneath her weight. "I guess I know where
you'll be sleeping."

"So do I, at that. Ah, Jenny. What happened to 'wither
go I'?"

"What do you mean?"

" 'The bed's big enough for both of us; what's good
enough for me is good enough for you,' " he quoted. Probably accurately; Jen couldn't remember her own words all
that clearly, but it sounded right enough.

She flushed. "Well, this time it isn't."

When Saul had first mentioned the joint quarters, she
had felt a certain surge of anticipation—not unmixed with
panic. But that was before she had encountered Gideon's
smile. Now she wished her solid, reliable partner, with his
clear, all-seeing eyes, about a thousand miles away. Or at
least in some other chamber where his disapproving gaze
wouldn't haunt her.

It was difficult enough carrying out an obsession without
having someone a perpetual witness to her folly. Especially
someone whose opinion she valued as highly as Thibault's.

It was, Jen thought with a grimace, going to be a very
long job indeed.

8

"Well, you'll be pleased to know that I've hired Avram and Lucinda's replacements at last, my dear," Saul said cheerfully, unfurling a napkin on his lap as the servants bustled about serving dinner, "so you won't have to experience a single day's break in your routine."

"Physical presence cannot substitute for competence," his companion responded sourly.

Saul just grinned.

Like the rest of his Ephanon manor, the dining hall was a grand affair, with long windows that overlooked the spread of the courtyard garden and, beyond, the island-speckled sea, though the latter was obscured by the winking lights of Sentenniel Street, and the smoking dome of the Cauldron, which somehow managed to rise into the exact center of the view. The dark cherrywood table was polished to a high gloss, mirroring the twinkle of the crystal chandelier and the magefires of the wall-mounted sconces, which had been exquisitely crafted into the form of flaming torches. Snowy mats marked the places of the four attendant diners, and between them reigned an elaborate branched candelabra, low enough not to impede their conversation.

Not that it really mattered, Thibault reflected. Kyrinne Lydea Soleneides looked tantamountly bored by the entire proceeding as she persisted, "Well? Are they competent?"

"Ask them yourself," Saul responded, and winked surreptitiously at Thibault. "One of them happens to be in the room at this very minute, looming over your left shoulder. His name's Ty. He'll be doing both Avram's and Cavan's jobs for now; if we like him, maybe we'll keep him on as Cavan's replacement."

Thibault kept his face deliberately bland as the Kyrinne's dark, impassive eyes swept him briefly and then returned to the contents of her soup bowl—which he had just ladled out, and which were obviously far more deserving of her interest.

"I've hired his wife, too—a lass named Gilyan—to work the kitchens and chambers until Lucinda returns," Saul added.

His daughter-in-law dipped her spoon fastidiously into the broth, sampled it, and—apparently finding it palatable—said, "And just what does this have to do with me?"

"Nothing whatsoever," Saul replied. "Except to serve as an intriguing piece of gossip."

"You must have a low opinion of my intelligence, then, if you think gossip of that nature would intrigue me."

"Varia forfend," Saul countered, though Thibault had the impression that his opinion of Lydea's intelligence was every bit as low as the lady had implied. "I merely meant that you shouldn't be surprised if you see new faces around the house."

"As if I would have noticed," his companion said scornfully, and Thibault couldn't help but agree. He had heard about the invisibility of servants in the grand manors, but he had never experienced it so directly before. Certainly Vera was no example; she treated her staff with the same consideration and respect she granted her friends. But to the three younger Soleneides, Thibault could as easily have been a piece of furniture or a patch of wallpaper for all the attention they paid him.

At least it gave him the opportunity to observe them, and he couldn't say that he was impressed with what he saw. Lydea herself, while undeniably beautiful, was cold and haughty, with a pinched face that seemed incapable of smiling, let alone of expressing any more tender emotions. But, judging from appearances, her husband would not have noticed the lack.

Amazing, Thibault thought, that this man was a Soleneides. A stolid man in his forties, Stavros Soleneides was everything his sire was not. He had not an ounce of his father's vitality or obvious sense of the absurd; Thibault wondered if the man had ever so much as laughed. Worse, he had the look of the self-righteously moral, as if he spent half his life in a state of high indignation.

Odd, that. Thibault would have assumed that the charming and voluble Saul should have made the best of fathers. Granted, his scatterbrained affability was more than part an act; no man could have risen so high with so ingenuous a persona. But, still . . . Life in the Soleneides household should have been fun, and he suddenly found himself wondering what had gone wrong.

Of course, it could merely have been a case of childhood rebellion: the son setting himself in opposition to the sire. But, by that token, young Patroch—Stavros' son—should have been the mirror of his grandsire, and that was clearly not the case. Although he had inherited the same delicate, almost feminine beauty that was so blurred in his sire, the perfect bow of his mouth was pulled into a sullen pout, the brilliant, thick-fringed eyes marred by an expression of world-weary discontent.

Thibault had never seen a more spoiled young man in his life.

"Is she pretty, this new maid?" he now inquired, his voice a tired whine.

"And what does it matter to you?" his mother countered tartly.

"I can't abide ugly servants. I don't know why you ever hired that Myrna creature, Grandfather. She really was most unappealing."

"As I recall," his father snapped, while Saul cast an apologetic glance at Thibault, "she was hired because she was a good worker. Which is more than I can say for you. I doubt you even know the meaning of the word!"

Patroch looked unconcerned. "So? It's the appearance of the thing that matters. What will guests think, to see such a vision opening the door?"

"Must this family be so blasted concerned with appearances?" Stavros flared. "First you with your nefarious clubs, Father, and now my son. Look what lessons he gains from your faith in illusions!"

Saul arched an eyebrow. "Patroch's life is his own," he replied. "As are the values he acquires, however you assume he came by them. And if you want to keep reviling the trade that kept a roof over your head for all the years of your childhood, go right ahead."

"Besides," Lydea added with a smirk, "if you're so concerned about appearances, Patroch, you should start by improving your own. How many times have I told you not to slurp your soup?"

The young man flushed an unbecoming magenta and clamped his mouth shut.

Thibault was almost glad when Lydea put down her spoon and pushed her plate away with a grimace, indicating the end to that particular course. Thibault hastily collected the bowl, and spent the next several minutes trotting between the dining room and kitchen, fetching plates and carrying tureens.

Jen, scowling in a drab, homespun dress, with her hair bound up in an untidy knot at the base of her neck, was seated at the large kitchen table, chopping vegetables with more passion than expertise. The rapid, silver flash of the knife—not to mention its taut, precise snicks—would have done credit to the most skilled of assassins. But the resultant, misshapen lumps of carrots and tomatoes which were piled before her and which occasionally flew off energetically across the tiles, had drawn the cook over with a frown.

"That's not a weapon," she said, plucking the blade from Jen's tight fingers. "Try wielding it with a little less enthusiasm in future. Here, Kore, why don't you take over? Gilyan, the pudding could use a stir."

Shoving a strand of hair behind her ear, Jen rose and surrendered her seat at the table, clearly reluctant to be parted from what was indeed a weapon. Wiping her hands forcefully down the front of her skirt, she marched up to the pot, seized the spoon, and began churning the pudding like butter.

Thibault, who was waiting for the meat to be sliced and laid out onto a platter, took the opportunity to approach his partner and supposed spouse, slipping his arms around her waist and drawing her briefly close.

"Easy, Jenny," he whispered, as she splattered pudding angrily up the sides of the pot. "You're overreacting."

"I hate you!" she spat, struggling against his embrace.

"No, you hate the job, and I don't blame you. But you

promised Owen to behave, so do it." And ducking his head, he surrendered to impulse and dropped a teasing kiss on the curve of her neck.

In return, she tromped viciously on his foot. But the furious motions of her spoon did slow, he noticed. Praise Varia that Owen's name still had the power to tame her.

Meat platter in hand, he returned to the dining room and began deftly tweaking slices onto the waiting plates.

"Do you know what I found in Patroch's room last night?" Lydea demanded.

"What was that?" Saul replied in some amusement, even as Patroch let out a howl of indignation.

"What were you doing in my room, Mother?"

"Well, obviously," she answered tartly, "checking up on you. Which seems to be required, considering what I found. A nice little stash of Dreamsmoke, Saul, secreted at the back of one of his drawers. Dreamsmoke!" Thibault started slightly at the revelation, almost delivering a slice of lamb straight onto Lydea's lap. Fortunately she didn't notice. "What, I ask you, is becoming of our youth today?"

"Oh, honestly, Mother," Patroch whined. "Everyone's doing it."

"Well, aren't you going to say anything to him?" Lydea persisted.

"Mmm." Saul frowned, then gazed levelly at Patroch. "You might not be aware, my boy, that I am currently being targeted by a rogue assassin because I recently turned a Dreamsmoke dealer in to the relevant authorities."

Patroch started visibly, then looked chastened, but his mother was not so sanguine.

"A rogue assassin?" she shrilled. "Shouldn't you hire some bodyguards or something? All our lives could be in danger!"

Saul glanced briefly over at Thibault, his eyes twinkling. "Nonsense, my dear. The only life in jeopardy is mine, and I didn't get as far as I did by countenancing rogue assassins. This is not the first attempt—nor, I suspect, will it be the last. I can guard easily against such ineptitude."

But Thibault noticed that his eyes hardened, no doubt remembering the one attack that had almost succeeded—

resulting in the dead suhdabhar. The one his regular body-guards had failed to foil.

Thibault was determined that he and Jen should not make the same mistake.

Quickly enough, however, Saul recovered himself and turned back to his grandson. "But you do see, my boy—my personal feelings on the drug aside—it does rather undermine my position to have a family member supporting a trade I actively try to discourage. Why don't you take up some other pastime instead? Like gambling?"

"Gambling?" Lydea shrieked.

"Honestly, Father, don't encourage him," Stavros said. "I seem to have survived my youth quite well without such pastimes."

"Ah, but then I was never completely convinced you had a youth to begin with."

"Just because I didn't hold with your profligate ways . . ."

"It's called having fun, my boy. And I don't see it did me any harm."

Lydea's mouth pursed. "I might have known I'd get no help from you. You're as bad as Patroch, what with your cigars and that revolting after-dinner liquor . . ."

"It's called brandy, my dear. And I must say my pleasure in it would be considerably enhanced if you didn't spend every evening denigrating it." Which, Thibault was convinced, was more than half the reason for Lydea's objection. "Now, no more Dreamsmoke, Patroch. Find something else to occupy you instead."

"Yes, Grandfather." The boy's eyes brightened. "I came up with an idea for a great new club . . ."

"Did you? That's nice."

"Don't you even want to hear about it?"

"What I want to hear about," Stavros interjected, "is how you can denigrate Dreamsmoke and yet countenance clubs that propagate a whole different set of offences!"

Saul looked amused. "The last time I checked, drinking and gambling were legal."

"By whose laws?"

"Konasta's, I believe."

"And isn't there a moral law? You, who claim to be so

concerned with public good, should at least understand that."

"And what sort of people would pay to attend the clubs you propound?" Saul scoffed. "My money has to come from somewhere."

"So you support ill to do good? Honestly, Father, you can't play both sides of the law against each other like that."

"Why not?" And before his son could answer, Saul added, "Don't split hairs, Stavros; you haven't the brains for it."

"Stop it, both of you," Lydea flared. "How I keep my sanity with what I have to endure in this household, I'll never know. My son on drugs, disreputable types in and out of here night and day . . ."

"And which particular disreputable types would you be referring to?" Saul queried, with an arch of eyebrow.

"Those business associates of yours, for one. That Aubrey is simply a horror—hasn't anyone ever taught the boy any manners? And as for Gideon . . ." She shivered. "I suppose he's pretty enough to look at, but there's something vaguely reptilian about him."

"Reptilian? Gideon? Honestly, my dear, I think you are overreacting. Besides, they are my associates, and I must do my proper duty by them."

"Blast them," Lydea spat. "I hope they're choking on their dinners."

But they weren't. In fact, they were sitting in a quiet corner of one of the upstairs balconies at the Cauldron, feasting on roast wild boar and rice—one of the specialities of the house that evening, in keeping with the newly modified decor. Aubrey had his back to the crowd, but Gideon, as usual, was surveying the house with a judicious eye, ensuring that everything was intact and functioning.

After five years as the de-facto head of one of the most powerful clubs in Konasta, Gideon would have thought that the novelty would wear off eventually. That he would become jaded to the nightly splendors. But this was his kingdom, the only thing he'd ever wanted. Being integral to its functioning exalted him as nothing else ever had. Not even his sessions with the Cauldron's hired whores, molding them to his tastes and dominion, had quite the same effect.

Who would have thought a rude child of the gutters could have risen so far? Except that, for Gideon, failure had never been an option.

The mages had outdone themselves tonight. Still, he surveyed the golden splendor with his standard expression of bored amusement that masked many a keener feeling and raised a negligent forkful of meat to his mouth. He chewed contemplatively for a moment, then said, "So, what do you think?"

"About what?" Aubrey responded. "The decor? Nice, as always."

The trouble with his associate, Gideon reflected, was that he had no appreciation of life's finer pleasures. Purely prosaic, that was Aubrey. Still, he supposed he could have had worse partners. Aubrey Dunning accepted the more extreme elements of Gideon's personality much as he accepted everything, with no more than a faintly disapproving scowl. Sometimes, Gideon thought, Aubrey would respond to fire, flood, and cataclysm with the same sullen, vaguely annoyed expression, as if it were merely another of life's quirks designed solely to inconvenience him.

"No, actually"—he grinned—"I was referring to our esteemed new colleagues, the Guild."

"Oh, that." Aubrey shrugged. "They seem awfully raw; I doubt they'll give us much trouble."

"Much? Try none. Did you see that girl's expression when she saw me?"

"Reverent, as always," Aubrey answered dryly.

"Precisely! I'll have that one eating out of my hand in no time."

"And how, exactly, are you planning to achieve that?"

"Why, cultivate her acquaintance, of course. She's not a bad looking thing, all told. A bit cocky, but . . . We all have our burdens to bear. I fully intend to keep her so occupied in her off-hours that she'll have no chance to go snooping around, should she feel so inclined. And I suppose you'd best do the same with the big one."

"I very much doubt I'm his type."

"Not unless you're his partner. But you'll manage." Gideon folded his arms. "Actually, I think this will be fun. I haven't played the decorous suitor in so long, it will almost be a challenge!"

"So, when do you start?"

"When better than the present? Finish your dinner, Aubrey. We've got work to do."

9

It was, Jen reflected, no more than she deserved. Thibault was right; she had been overreacting. But, by Varia, she was a lady, raised in true Hestian style and finished at the finest school in all Haarkonis. She was not designed to muck about in stuffy kitchens, where the steamy heat from fires and cookpots made her wilt like a stalk of old celery. Where vegetable peelers and wooden spoons left dents in her fingers. Where knives—humiliation of all humiliations—were wielded in ham-handed fists and used for the evisceration of no more than a few tomatoes or chickens.

She had been born for more than this.

The fact that she was clutching at the very trappings of aristocracy that she had once so reviled struck her as no more than vaguely ironic. Jen was nothing if not good at justification. But still, she couldn't help thinking, as Thibault departed, that Vera wouldn't balk at stirring a pot or chopping a few pieces of meat. As Vera saw it, every skill was vital, every task somehow meaningful. And no doubt she expected Jen to learn as much from Thibault's class as Thibault was to learn from Jen's.

And it was that, more than anything, that enabled her to school her face into a more docile expression and accept hasty orders from a woman her own mother wouldn't have acknowledged. And after a while she even found it enjoyable, secure in the knowledge that this was not the pinnacle of her existence. Unlike every other laborer in this house, she could return to a life of luxury and adventure. Granted the pudding had rather more lumps than expected, and the pieces of fruit she generated for garnish were so deformed as to be unusable, but so long as she treated it as another adventure, it really wasn't all that bad.

Until she realized that her duties didn't end with the meal. There were cauldrons to be scraped and dishes to be washed, utensils to be stowed and floors to be scrubbed—the kitchens restored to their pristine splendor so the whole cycle could begin again tomorrow. Then it ceased to be fun and simply became exhausting, and by the time Jen was released for the evening she was almost too weary to stand.

Briefly she debated stumbling up the back stairs to the room she shared with Thibault, but then decided that she couldn't stand company until she had a chance to unwind. Especially not if said company would be stifling a desire to laugh at her predicament, at the grand lady sunk so low. No, Thibault was the last thing she needed. Rather, she craved a quiet moment of beauty and solitude in which she could recapture the essential core of Jen apart from the guise of Gilyan. But where? And then she remembered the courtyard with its plants and fountains, now doubtless empty and lit by the faint sliver of the moon.

Surely no one would begrudge a servant a few spare moments in what was, essentially, a public place. Besides, it was late enough now that few would be abroad and, with the evening breezes sweeping off the water, it was bound to be cooler than the beastly kitchens. So she lingered behind the knot of dispersing servants, all discussing their evening jaunts and debating the merits of the various clubs, waiting for them to depart.

"The Den's running a special . . ."

"What about the Galleon?"

"It's two for one at the Cove tonight."

That apparently decided them, and they trooped riotously for the door, one of them—she couldn't remember which in the haze of her exhaustion—turning to call, "Are you coming, Gilyan?"

Jen shook her head and they vanished, leaving her marooned in the suddenly silent kitchens. Even the cook was gone, tidying the pantry and making lists for the morrow. And with the solitude came what could almost count as a resurgence of her native vitality. Releasing her hair from its bedraggled plait, Jen shook out the heavy mass, running her fingers through it several times to remove the worst of the tangles before rebraiding it. Then, shaking the crumbs from her skirts, she slipped quietly out the back door and around the side of the house.

The courtyard was as lovely as she imagined, wrapped in solitude and washed by a faint spill of moonlight. The fountain plashed quietly at its center, and each leaf-edge seemed limned with silver light. The glow of Sentenniel Street bled faintly over the horizon, reflecting off the arcing streams of water until they shone like mottled rainbows. The breeze was sweet and clean. And high above, beyond the lights and puffs of smoke from the dome of the Cauldron, the points of the stars shone bright and clear, discrete scintillas against the dark.

Leaning back against the cool stone of the house, Jen took several long, deep breaths and let the peace bleed into her, her world slowly returning to its accustomed dimensions. Each country, each city, had its own aroma, unique and unmistakable. Nova Castria stank of poverty; Ceylonde of refinement. Arrhyndon smelled of wilderness and freedom; Bergaetta of idle peace. Ashkharon of sage and dry bones, undercut with an indefinable taint of corruption. But Ephanon . . . Ephanon was wild, seductive and dangerous—a clutter of headstrong adjectives that made Jen want to throw all caution to the winds.

A betraying warmth began to build in the pit of her belly and, in retrospect, she wondered if it wasn't this that first alerted her to the man's presence. But as it was, lost in her musings, it took her several minutes to realize she wasn't alone. That a shadowy figure leaned casually against the lip of the fountain, regarding her, his contours distinguished mainly by the tip of his cigarette as it flared and died.

A trickle of smoke reached her, the tobacco undercut with the sweet, cloying odor of Dreamsmoke.

"Who is that?" she demanded.

"Who do you think it is?" came the amused answer as the figure detached itself and strolled her way. As it emerged from the shadow of the fountain and stood silhouetted against the bleed of multicolored lights from Sentenniel Street, the golden curls ignited like a halo.

"Gideon," she said.

"The same," he confirmed, and she let herself relax back

against the stone, her hand falling from the hilt of her hidden dagger.

"What are you doing out so late?"

He chuckled, his wicked, perfect features etched against the light. "It's still fearsomely early by Konastan standards, but just about what it looks like. Enjoying a quiet evening's stroll in the square." He drew deeply on his cigarette, the tip glowing, and when he exhaled the numinous cloud drifted up over the garden in lazy spirals. He shifted, then, the light flowing over his face like water, and she could see the faint, cynical twitch of his lips.

"Filthy habit, I know," he remarked, following her mesmerized eyes as they traced the drifting trail. "You want?" He extended the half-smoked fag.

Suddenly awkward, she shook her head, feeling all of three years old in the face of his casual sophistication. Even in repose, there was something magnetic about Gideon. Something reckless—worse now that he was close, his attention focused solely on her.

Curse it all, she was used to being the bold one, the outspoken one. The outrageous one. And yet, with a simple word—or worse, without a word at all; with nothing more than a look—he was stealing everything she did and was. Removing her edge, usurping her position, until suddenly eighteen seemed ridiculously callow.

"I don't smoke," she said, sharply.

"How virtuous of you. Best not to start; it makes it easier to quit." And with a final drag on his cigarette, he grinned and bent to stub it out against the flagstones, tossing the butt into a stand of potted laurels.

"In truth," he continued, "I'm glad to find you here. I hadn't expected such good fortune."

"Meaning?"

He grinned at her arch tone and straightened. "Meaning I was planning to search you out, but I didn't figure Beroe would give you much freedom on your first night here."

"Beroe?"

"The cook. Gracious, didn't anyone take the time to introduce you properly?"

"Not hardly. She was running about too frantically and barking orders too rapidly for anyone to get a word in edgewise."

"Yes, that's our Beroe."

"She seemed kind, though," Jen hazarded, not wanting to malign the staff.

"Oh, she is. Heart of gold. Stamina of iron. Tongue like a razor." Gideon grinned. "Frankly, I'm surprised you're still standing."

"Well, I *was* tired . . ."

"But not anymore?"

Jen shook her head, their eyes meeting with a palpable jolt. Every inch of her skin seemed to tingle.

"Well, then," Gideon said, reaching out and taking one of her hands. His lean, agile fingers—thieves' fingers, Jen acknowledged—played across her skin. "If you're really not too tired, I have a proposition."

"Which is?" She was annoyed to find herself slightly breathless.

"Have you seen the inside of one of the clubs, yet?" Gideon answered, returning question for question.

She shook her head.

"Would you like to?"

"More than anything!"

"Well, then." He released her hand and cocked his head, surveying her. "Why don't you run upstairs and change, and I'll escort you to the best. That is, if your husband won't object?"

"Oh, we're not married."

"Yes, I know." His eyes caressed her. "Who do you think provided the pallet? Run along, now . . . your name's not really Gilyan, is it?"

"No. You can call me Jen."

"And you can call me Gideon. No surprise there, but you do have my permission to use it."

"As opposed to what? The Golden Boy?"

"Yes. Embarrassing, that, if apt. Now, go."

It was the first command all evening that Jen had actually been eager to obey.

*　　*　　*

As Gideon had hinted, the pallet was already in place, but her partner was stretched out on the bed, one of the watery magelights directed at his book.

"Where have you been?" he asked.

"In the garden. Did you unpack already?" And flinging open the closet doors, she added, "Oh, good. Thanks." She flipped though the few racked outfits then, suddenly aware that Thibault was staring, added, "What?"

"I expected you to be in a far worse mood. If you're looking for your nightgown, it's in the drawer."

"I'm not going to bed," she countered, finally deciding upon a pair of harem trousers wildly patterned in green, blue, and gold which she had picked up in Ashkharon, a white shirt, and an emerald vest. "Don't look," she said, shucking her dress.

The pants were soft and recklessly voluminous, the vest a perfect complement to her eyes. A wide green sash bound about her waist completed the image. When she turned, Thibault was eyeing her speculatively. She didn't know when he had violated her injunction not to watch, but for once she didn't care. "Where's my brush?"

"On the dressing table. Where are you going?"

"Out," she answered succinctly, undoing her plait and running the brush through her hair in brisk, firm strokes.

"Out where?"

"Just out. Probably to one of the clubs."

"With whom?"

"Gideon. What's it to you?" She was about to redo the braid when she abruptly decided she liked the fall of her unbound hair. So instead she merely gathered two wings to either side and began to braid them in a small plait down the back.

"I don't trust him, Jen."

"You don't trust anyone," she countered, tying off the tail and leaving the rest of her hair to fall in an unfettered spill, its ends brushing the small of her back. Then she rose and pivoted, her hair swirling about her like a cloak. She liked the effect; she would have to wear it this way more often, and hang the dignity. "How do I look?" she asked, posing.

"Gorgeous. But . . ."

"Don't wait up," she said, and before Thibault could reply she was out the door and halfway down the stairs.

10

Gideon was waiting in the courtyard where she had left him, and his eyes lit up most gratifyingly when he saw her.

"Gracious," he declared. "I had no idea!"

She grinned, and looped her arm through his. "Where are we going?"

"Well, I was debating. But with you looking like that . . . Nowhere but the best, my lady."

"And that is?"

"Why, the Cauldron, of course." And guiding her though the garden, he led her into the narrow funnel of streets that emptied into Sentenniel Street.

"Loyal, aren't you?" she asked as they progressed, using the swelling dome to guide them.

"Oh, always. But it also happens to be true. Most of the older clubs have a set theme. Saul was the first to come up with the idea of rotating decors, and the Cauldron was the first club he implemented it in. He and your Guildmaster both—or so it's been told."

"Told and true, at least according to Owen. I think he's rather proud of his affiliation with the Cauldron. On a strictly confidential level, you understand."

"Of course. Couldn't have a moral man like the Guildmaster publicly affiliated with the illusion clubs."

"I'm so glad you comprehend. Tell me, will your shadow be in residence tonight?"

"Aubrey?" He chuckled, obviously tickled by the description. "Not unless you want him to be. Why? Do you?"

"Most decidedly not!" Then, "Tell me more," she added as Sentenniel Street opened before them, awash in light and color. The more prosaic markets had all shut down, but swaying lanterns of multicolored magelights picked out stall after stall of shops vending brightly colored drinks or gilded trinkets. Merchants hawked their wares above the vibrant, drunken clamor, and men and women with scanty outfits and painted faces worked the crowds.

There was no doubt in Jen's mind as to what they were selling.

"What do you want to know?" her companion answered in amusement.

"Is there a lot of that, then?" she responded, indicating the whores and catamites.

"No more than anywhere else. Why? Are you shocked?"

"Far from it. It's just that . . . It seems more obvious here than anywhere else."

"We Konastans have nothing to hide."

She arched an eyebrow at his brilliant, golden beauty. "You? You're not Konastan. Where are you from? Haar-konis? Scandia?"

"Frieistan, actually. But though I may not be a Konastan by birth, I am nonetheless Konastan. Here we go; the Cauldron."

It was even more impressive at night, with the pulsing white lights that ringed the dome and the deep carmine strobes that backlit the smoke. Ruby lanterns swayed from the porticoed eaves, and the scintillating brilliance of the magelights above the door picked out the name of the club in blinding letters. Blue and green lights, swirling and blending, bathed the external stone, making it ripple and flow like water.

The line for entrance was five people deep and stretched halfway to the topsailed splendor of the Rogue's Gallery.

"How much is admission?"

"For us? Or the hoi polloi?"

"Does it make a difference?"

"Without a doubt," her companion responded, parading her boldly in front of a crowd that murmured and surveyed her with envious eyes. Striding up to the impressively large individual who was guarding the door, Gideon said, "Good evening, Peter."

"Good evening to you, Kyrin Gilvaray." And lifting the red velvet ropes, Peter let them into the porticoed entry where they, too, were bathed in the oceanic light.

"Kyrin?" Jen demanded as they passed.

Gideon shrugged. "A meaningless honorific, seeing as I all but run the place. And"—he leaned closer—"for your future edification, the unwashed masses pay a mere ten bits for entry. But don't worry. Everything else inside is far more expensive."

And, with great ceremony, two smaller guards pushed open the great, iron-bound doors, and they were inside.

Jen's first impression of the Cauldron's interior was one of light and noise. Music was playing—an insidious rhythm, more smoky and seductive than the mannered airs of ballrooms and salons—and above and beyond that was the clamor of voices, intent on drinking, gambling, and blotting out the mundanity of daily existence. Glasses clinked and laughter tinkled. Something, dimly, was rumbling. And bathing it all was an aureate light, emanating from slender golden columns like the bars of some great, gilded cage.

A cage, indeed, Jen realized an instant later as a massive, tawny tiger strolled toward her through the crowd, its golden eyes glinting. For a second she froze, an atavistic terror paralyzing her limbs. She could almost feel the hot, heavily muscled body brushing her leg as the creature slid past, but at the last minute she reached out and made a grab for the tip of its twitching tail.

As expected, her hand closed around light and air.

Gideon chuckled. "Talk about seizing a tiger by the tail! Good, aren't they?"

"Amazing!"

And they were. Everywhere Jen looked, there were creatures—some as mundane as house cats, others denizens of only the most exotic jungles. Still others were products solely of the mages' imagination. Some wore gilded collars as they twined between the golden bars of their equally illusory cages, while others roared or bellowed from behind more tightly massed columns. Tall trees rose at intervals between the bars, their leaves as perfect and glossy as freshly carved jade, and brightly colored birds flitted overhead, their calls blending so melodiously with the din they might well have been scripted. As, no doubt, they were.

If she hadn't known better—if such a display would even

have been possible in the larger world—Jen would almost have believed it, so convincing was the illusion. "I've never seen anything to equal it," she breathed.

"Nor will you," her companion answered, "outside the illusion clubs. Outside the Cauldron, for that matter. Our mages have worked long and hard to perfect their art; no one else gets quite the practice."

As if his words had been a trigger, the light momentarily dimmed. Two great wings unfurled above the crowd, and a gout of flame blasted overhead, momentarily washing bars, animals, and patrons in a fiery glow. Any birds caught in the wash disintegrated, trickling to earth in whimsical bursts of colored feathers. Jen chuckled at the illusion until she caught sight of the vast snaky neck that had funneled the blast, the massive, serpentine jaws that had released it.

Camouflaged behind the gilded bars, a huge dragon lay coiled at the far end of the chamber, its body reposing on a heaped pile of gold and gems. Eyes like agates glowed, and golden scales rippled smooth as silk. Illusion or not, it was the most magnificent creature Jen had ever seen, and she waited with bated breath as the huge head snaked once more over the crowd and then retreated, the light rising again as the membranous wings closed.

She could swear the great beast winked at her as it settled back on its golden hoard.

"Quarter past the hour," Gideon said, laughing at her obvious wonder. "And welcome to the Cauldron of Iniquity. What can I get you to drink?"

"Whatever; you pick," she replied, still too overwhelmed by the spectacle to concentrate on the details.

Gideon chuckled and took her arm, and she wasn't so oblivious that she didn't notice the sudden current that vibrated between them.

"I would get us a private table," her companion continued, "but somehow I sense you'd rather be in the thick of it."

Jen laughed, momentarily tearing her gaze from the projected wonders. "How well you know me. Is that the bar?"

"Indeed it is. Suitable?"

"Infinitely."

"Well, then." And with a flick of fingers, Gideon ges-

tured at one of the patrons, who instantly melted into the
crowd with his companion, leaving two vacant seats.

"Impressive," Jen said, her attention now focused firmly
on Gideon. He helped her up onto one of the bar stools—
a gilded fantasy of intertwined bars.

"One of the advantages of rank," he responded with a
twinkle. "And also of knowing one's employees." He sized
Jen up for an instant, while her face went subtly pinker,
then murmured something incomprehensible to the bartender. Bare instants later, despite a crowd that clogged
and clamored at the bar rail, two tall, frosty concoctions
were pushed into place before them.

Each drink glowed like a sunset, or some nomadic sand-
painting, the colors shifting and swirling. A nimbus of mist
hung above the lip, and gilded straws plumbed the depths.
Wedges of fruit were impaled on tiny, metallic spears.
Mostly illusion, Jen supposed, but the taste was gratifyingly
real: tart and tangy, with the unmistakable fire of some
potent liquor.

It was exactly what she wanted—or would have ordered,
had she been better able to express her wishes—and once
again she marveled at Gideon's perception. *Gideon's perception; Gideon's perfection,* she thought. Scary, how he
seemed to know her desires almost better than she did
herself. Scary, but seductive. And as intoxicating as this
delightful drink.

His gaze was locked on hers and she smiled back at him,
wondering if the subtle golden nimbus that perpetually
seemed to surround him was illusory as well. Or merely
the product of her overwrought imagination.

To keep herself from drowning in those hypnotic orbs—
after all, Jenny, a girl has to maintain a shred of decency—
she deliberately tore her gaze from his, surveying their surroundings with a far more critical eye. The cloverleaf curves
of the bar reigned like an island at the center of the room
so that, over the jewel-like citadel of bottles, the room continued as if mirrored. Terraces and balconies sprouted from
the walls in a riotous yet organic synthesis, like hanging
gardens grown suddenly wild. And everywhere, among the
golden light and gilded bars, the patrons glittered and
sparkled.

Some, Jen suspected, wore their own faces—lines of life and living pulling at their visages, tracing the joys and sorrows of daily existence. Others—their cheeks inhumanly smooth, their eyes preternaturally bright—cloaked their true nature in illusion, be it unworldly beauty or grotesque distortion. Grotesque distortion which somehow managed to be neither grotesque nor distortion, as if it were merely a symmetry of malfunction, a cartoon of disharmony. Wasp-women with floating clouds of ankle-length hair and absurdly pinched waists stood shoulder to shoulder with hunchbacked men whose muscular physiques nonetheless mirrored the perfection of classical sculptures. And all of them laughing, talking, drinking as if their whole world were encapsulated within these walls.

There was something insidious about it, Jen reflected, and suddenly she understood the secret heart of the illusion clubs, the one constant illusion in the midst of all the artifice. Or, perhaps, the largest artifice of all—that everything was beauty. Loveliness and ugliness alike: all, here, transmuted into a surreal, ethereal perfection.

Curious now, she scanned the crowd more sharply, seeing in the ever-flowing ripple of its motions the difference between employees and patrons. It was something like charting the pattern of rocks in a stream—the fixed versus the ever-moving. Only not quite, for the fixtures of the club were far from still. They moved as relentlessly as the patrons. But there was, nonetheless, something solid about them, something grounded, as if they alone could chart the larger patterns, and she suddenly realized who the two people were who had so obligingly vacated their seats.

"What?" Gideon said, seeing her grin.

"Well, it might not be as obvious as it was on the streets," she answered, "but you do have quite your own stable of obliging souls here, don't you?"

One golden eyebrow soared. "What do you mean?"

"Prostitution, my dear. Do I have to spell it out for you?" And she pointed to two of the "patrons" sitting across from them, plus another three lurking in a far-off corner. "To name but a few."

He looked momentarily startled. "But . . . how did you know? We rather prize ourselves on our subtlety."

She smiled. "You know what I do for a living. They don't pay me that much *not* to notice things."

She could almost have imagined his disconcerted expression, it faded so quickly. "Indeed. I am quite impressed by your deductive powers." Those ice-green eyes glinted. "Perhaps I shall have to convince you to stay on in Konasta after your commission is completed. I have a feeling we would make a most formidable team."

"We might, at that." She let her hand stray along the surface of the bar, fiddling almost idly with the edge of his napkin. "Perhaps I shall have to consider it . . ."

He seized on the hint as if born to it, taking her hand and raising it to his lips. "Perhaps you shall." His mouth traced a path of fire across her skin, conjuring images of things to come.

"So," she said, "have you sampled many of the wares?"

"Sampled?" He grinned, startling her in turn. "I should think so, considering I hired most of them myself. After all, we can't have tainted meat in the Cauldron. Another drink?"

She had, she realized, drained her glass in slow degrees. Perhaps that explained the faint haze of disjunction that surrounded her, the almost disproportionate shock his words engendered.

As if sensing her mood, he laughed, the hard edge flowing from him like water until he was the Golden Boy once more. The Golden Boy whose attention and courtesies were for her alone.

"Why not?" she said recklessly, although part of her knew she had already had too much. Besides, she told herself firmly, she was simply getting used to his sense of humor, the inevitable adjustment of any relationship. Nobody ever behaved exactly as you expected. How boring that would be.

Their drinks arrived. Gideon's eyes devoured her. The golden dragon once more stretched his wings above the assembly, blasting out his gout of signature fire.

Jen grinned. "Let me guess," she said, touching her lips to the straw and letting the potent fruitiness fill her mouth. "Half past the hour?"

11

Four more dragon blasts counted out another hour. The crowd grew louder, Jen got drunker, and the music took on a more pounding rhythm, undercut with raw sexuality. To her hazy vision, the gilded bars of the Cauldron morphed and twisted into even more fantastical shapes, and Gideon seemed determined to ape the gentleman, courting her with fraught looks and gestures but each time stopping tantalizingly short of fulfillment.

It was irritating beyond belief.

Yet oddly compelling, to be courted. To be treated as if she were, in truth, the society virgin she sometimes pretended. For Jen, whose specialty was all too often a blunt directness, it was a unique lesson in ambiguity and nuance—and not without its fascination. By the end of the evening, every fiber of her being had been built to a fever pitch.

And Gideon, curse him, seemed to know it. He played her like an instrument, and all the while his eyes told her: *relax, enjoy, follow my lead.* It was a gaze that promised the world while never actually admitting to anything; no wonder she felt compelled to follow it to its conclusion. And so she accepted his drinks and his attentions, his lead on the dance floor, becoming the pliant creature she had always despised—all the while reveling in a game whose rules she couldn't quite understand and for once didn't control.

There was something recklessly exciting about surrendering herself so completely.

He would be a fantastic lover; she could tell that immediately from the rhythm of his body against hers as they danced. He moved with a liquid grace and confidence that mirrored his whole approach to life. And how different from the pristine society dances! Even the waltz, considered so scandalous among polite society, paled in comparison to this primal movement. He dipped and wheeled her, bending her so far back over his arm that her unbound hair puddled on the floor and her fingers grazed the boards, testing the limits. And then just when she was sure he would lose control, dropping her in an ignominious heap, that golden arm would flex, pulling her up with an infinite precision, her body traversing the length of his own. For a few agonizing seconds he would hold her close, not even a cushion of air between them, before whirling her out in an exuberant circle to the length of their joined arms.

Teasing, maddening. It was no surprise her head was spinning when the dragon roared yet again, lapping the dancers in the lurid glow of illusory flame. Blearily, Jen calculated the time, and her eyes widened.

"Gracious, whatever could I have been thinking?" Gideon laughed low in her ear. "Here it is an hour past midnight, and you have been awake since Varia knows when, laboring mightily in Saul's kitchens. And, no doubt, Beroe will want you bright and early for breakfast. We really should get you back."

She opened her mouth to protest, but all that escaped was a prodigious yawn. "Perhaps you should," she admitted reluctantly. The thought of another day in the kitchens made her want to scream. *By all that is precious, please let us finish this job as fast as we can so I can get on to better things!*

Like Gideon.

The Golden Boy grinned as if reading her thoughts—as, no doubt, he could—and offered her his arm. It was, Jen admitted, more than a courtesy; she hadn't realized how drunk she was until she tried to walk. A joined unit, they slipped out through the crowd, and Jen was amazed to see that the throng bunched expectantly outside the Cauldron was as large as ever.

"Great purple piranhas," she exclaimed, around another yawn. "When do they go to bed?"

"Sometime around four," Gideon answered. "That's when the Cauldron closes. And then people like me must supervise the clean-up and count the profits until dawn. For me, I'm afraid, the night is yet young. So don't expect to see me around any time before mid-afternoon."

"Gracious. Must be nice."

"It's a life that does have its advantages. Mind that curb."

Jen straightened from her stumble and tossed back her hair. The night had cooled somewhat, and the breeze that stirred amidst the strands was thin and chill, goading her back to sobriety. Though Sentenniel Street still bustled, the back streets echoed with an odd kind of silence, the muted clamor lying over the paving stones like a blanket.

"Just up here," Gideon said, leading her into an alley which opened into the cultivated spread of the square and House Soleneides. "Are you sure you'll be all right?"

"I should be," she replied, detaching herself from his arm and testing her balance. She took two short steps, then turned back, her eyes drinking in the chiseled lines of his features in the moonlight. "Thank you for a wonderful evening."

"My pleasure." And he took her hand, advancing it to her lips.

For a moment they just stood there, hands touching, and then she said tentatively, "Won't you . . ."

"What?"

"Well, come up?"

He grinned, dropping her fingers and moving closer, one hand curving around the crest of her hip and the other resting intimately at the junction of neck and shoulder. "And what would your partner think of that?"

She cursed dully.

"Besides," he added, his fingers trailing up to the curve of her jaw, tangling in her hair, "you need to sleep. And it's better this way. Better to wait, anticipate. Makes the surrender all the sweeter, don't you think?"

No, she wanted to say, but couldn't formulate the words with his face so close to her own. Bending just slightly—they were almost of a height—he brushed his lips across hers: a feather touch, leaving a searing heat in their wake. "Goodnight, Jen."

And then he was gone, melting back into the shadows of the alley which led to Sentenniel Street.

There was, Gideon reflected, something revoltingly cloying about being on your best behavior. After two hours of decorous flirtation, he felt as if he had been dipped in syrup, and now he needed something to take the honeyed taste from his mouth. Granted he had been good—no, more than good; brilliant—but enough was enough. Jen was his should he want her, and who knew? Someday, he might; at times, his tastes ran that way. But not tonight.

Tonight, flush with triumph from the conquest, from the witting manipulation of another gullible innocent—and an operative of that annoyingly self-righteous Guild, no less— he felt every nerve a-tingle with a characteristic recklessness that always betokened the advent of a truly memorable evening.

In fact, as he reentered the Cauldron through the back door, ignoring for now the more ostentatious front entrance, he could feel himself practically glowing. It was as if a powerful magelight had been ignited somewhere deep within him, streaming out through every pore and fiber, making his hair shine more golden, his eyes gleam like milky jewels. It was an almost tangible power which flowed between him and the throngs of midnight revelers who still clogged the club, rendering him . . . irresistible. He could see the heads swiveling as he passed, male and female eyes alike drinking him in, sending out waves of liquid desire as potent as those of that pitiful assassin. Waves that buoyed and built his own deadly mood.

He had missed this sense of potency and power; he had been wallowing in the mundane for too long. But who to choose to share his exultation?

He looked around the crowded floor, weighing his options. It had to be an innocent; his desire was too sharp tonight to get any pleasure from the seasoned participants who knew what he was capable of and even, in their way, enjoyed it. No, what he needed tonight was submission and terror, the thrill of the unexpected. Almost, he was tempted to go for one of the patrons; he could have had any of them he wanted. But ultimately the repercussions of such a decision would cause far more trouble than it was worth, and Saul did pay his bills; it wouldn't do to antagonize the old man unnecessarily, or draw unwanted attention to the club.

So, one of the employees, then. But not one of the ones he had hired. It had to be someone new, someone who more properly reflected Aubrey's pedestrian tastes. But who had his partner hired in recent weeks?

And then he remembered: Daria. That little mouse of a brunette. The fragile, ethereal type who almost never needed the pap of an illusory disguise. Men liked to dominate that type; it made them feel important. Plus, he supposed she was pretty enough; the more unenlightened seemed to find her beautiful. He preferred a different breed himself.

Still, she would do.

He scanned the crowd, eventually locating her in a corner by the dragon. And once again, it seemed fate was smiling on him, for she was alone. He met her eyes across the crowd and grinned, crooking a finger. She rose, apprehensive and at the same time elated; he could see the warring expressions on her sharp, doe-like features. She had apparently been around long enough to learn of his reputation. Good; all the better. He knew as well as anyone that common club gossip held him as the most revered and feared figure in the Cauldron—primarily because he was so unpredictable. He could send a partner to the heights of ecstasy, or the depths of humiliation, and no one knew quite which way the coin would fall on any given night. Of course, most of his conquests were vain enough to think they would be the one to sway him, to seduce him; others knew better. But, in either case, it would be a memorable experience.

Clearly Daria fell into the former category. As her dewy eyes widened, he could see the calculations stirring in their depths: awe, that she had been chosen; apprehension, for the risk of the gamble. Then denial, like a quick shake of the head: *I will be the one to change him.* They always thought that. And then, finally, hesitant, exultant acceptance.

His smile widened, edgy and brilliant. Silly girl. Countless scores had consistently failed to change him. He held out a hand as she came forward, closing his grip around her translucent, birdlike fingers. She smiled seductively and his heart pounded.

"Daria. Not otherwise engaged, I take it?"

She shook her head, her long flow of silken hair stirring.

"I have a room upstairs," he added. Actually, he had two, and of radically different decor; there was no doubt in his mind as to which one he would be taking her. And it was not the one to which he would have taken Jen. "But then, you know that, don't you?"

She nodded, eyes glowing.

Oh, yes, he would be bringing her to the pinnacle tonight; it was one of his specialties. To make them come even in the midst of humiliation and pain. To make them *enjoy* it.

With another, feral smile, he turned and led her up the stairs.

For an instant, Jen leaned against the walls of House Soleneides—occupying almost the identical position from which she had spotted Gideon several hours earlier—and reflected on the vagaries of fate. It had all seemed so promising; how could he just abandon her now? She considered that for a moment—her faults, and her expectations. Then, pushing herself reluctantly off the stone, she rounded the side of the house and keyed the lock, fumbling the back door open and climbing the rickety flight of stairs to her room.

The upstairs hall was dark, illumined by only a dim bulb of magelight hovering somewhere just above the baseboards, so Jen was able to see clearly when she pushed open the door to her silent chamber.

The pallet was still on the floor. But—obviously far too optimistically—it was empty and Thibault was curled in an amorphous mass beneath the bedclothes, clearly assuming she was not returning. *More fool he,* she thought sourly. She'd be cursed if she was going to spend the night on a pallet—especially not after the indignity of being rejected by Gideon. Not to mention an evening spent slaving in the kitchens. It was simply not the way her life was supposed to be progressing.

Scowling to herself in the darkness, she dropped her clothes into a disordered heap and slithered into her nightdress. Then, probably too energetically, she lifted up a corner of the bedclothes and shoved at her partner.

He woke with a mumbled snort.

"Wha . . . ? Jenny? What are you doing?"

"Getting into bed. I'll be hanged if I'm going to sleep on that blasted pallet!"

"I'm sorry. I thought you were . . . That is . . ."

Thibault was clearly too tired to formulate the polite euphemisms, so she saved him the effort, saying, "Well, that should teach you."

"What, not to think?" By his chuckle, he sounded moderately more awake, but his amusement was the last thing she wanted.

"Something like that. Now, move over; you're hogging the covers."

"I'll get up . . ."

Jen's drunken exhaustion crashed against her in a wave. "No, don't bother. This will be fine for one night. But can't you just . . ."

Obligingly, he shifted, opening a space for her, then curled his body around hers—his only option. His arms enfolded her, her head tucked somewhere beneath his chin.

"Comfortable?" he asked, his breath warm against her ear.

"Mmm," she responded, already feeling the warmth of his presence lap her. She *was* comfortable. There was something reassuringly solid about his oversized body, as if he could protect her from all harm or hurt. No wonder she didn't feel quite so wretched as she thought she would.

"How was the Cauldron?" he asked after a moment. She could hear his voice rumbling deep within his chest.

"Impressive."

"And Gideon?"

"I don't want to talk about it."

The echoes of his laughter followed her into slumber.

It was sometime close to dawn before Gideon reappeared. Aubrey was sitting at one of the upstairs tables, placidly counting the evening's profits and reflecting on how bare the Cauldron appeared when the mages shut down their nightly illusions. There was something achingly sad about that functional grey expanse, as if all of life were no more than a surface gloss over the same dull nothingness. But then, he always got introspective at the end of a particularly successful evening.

Down below, a handful of lackeys were sweeping the scuffed wood floors, and the clink of dishes and glassware from the kitchens spoke of industrious washing and drying. Yawning broadly, several of the Cauldron prostitutes were wandering about aimlessly, comparing notes and collecting coats and bags for the long walk home.

"A good evening?"

Aubrey whirled with a start. Gideon, his golden hair rumpled and his shirt-sleeves rolled up, exhaled gustily and sank into the opposite seat.

"Not bad. And you? I saw you with that Guild assassin . . ."

Gideon chuckled and liberated one of the golden fifties, rotating it idly between his fingers. "Yes, I worked my wiles. Should we need it, I can probably get her to do my bidding."

"How?"

"How do you think?" His partner grinned, flipped the coin, then replaced it in the pile, running a teasing hand along Aubrey's cheek instead.

Scowling, Aubrey seized the fingers—which were playing havoc with his senses—and examined them minutely. "By all that's precious, is that *blood*?"

"Not our assassin's; don't worry." Gideon yawned, running fingers through his hair. "I let her go early, with many promises. But you might want to have the mages see to Daria if you want her in working condition tomorrow."

Aubrey swallowed, trying to ignore the growing ache in the pit of his stomach. The mages' healing spells were costly propositions, both in terms of money and energy, and thus only used in extremity. Or when Gideon was in one of his moods. He had seen the aftermath of some of Gideon's evenings. Poor Daria. Sweet, innocent, beautiful Daria . . . Relentlessly, he pictured her awash in blood, curled miserably at the foot of Gideon's bed like so many others.

He wished the Golden One had given her at least a month before he'd broken her.

"I'll put Reynard on it," he promised.

"Thanks. And you might want to send someone up to clean the chamber as well. I think I may have ruined the floor." His partner yawned again. "Well, if you don't need me for anything else, I'll head home. 'Night, Aubrey."

"Goodnight, Gideon."

Aubrey watched his partner depart, bracing himself for the moment when he would have to face Daria in all her pain and humiliation, and somehow make it all right again.

Blast the man, he thought. *Blast him to perdition.*

Sometimes, Aubrey didn't know why he put up with the Golden Boy. He didn't even like men—not in *that* way. In fact, he had a perfectly satisfactory relationship with a woman he cared for; had for several months now. And yet, it was as if Gideon had tied a string around one of his lower ribs; he couldn't resist its pull.

It was unaccountable. But he supposed he should consider himself lucky, knowing Gideon's proclivities, that the Golden Boy had never let him get any closer than he had. Otherwise, it might be Aubrey in that upstairs room.

Rising reluctantly, he shoveled the money into a bag—he was far too distracted to count it, now—and steeled himself for the climb.

12

As expected, the voyage was a disaster. Although he denied it strenuously, Absalom sulked every time he saw Vera with Captain Black, and each day he seemed to lose months off his age until he appeared almost scandalously young. Scandalously young, yet so heart-stoppingly beautiful that Vera might have been tempted into a dalliance were she not so annoyed with him.

For every time she so much as addressed Kharman Black, there he was, materializing out of the shadows with some outrageous quip or comment. And Varia forbid she should engage in any more intimate contact. It got to the point where she was peering about nervously during love-making, convinced she would see Absalom's ridiculously youthful face peeping through a window.

"He's jealous, your young man," Kharman told her one night, his arms wrapped comfortably around her, after they had just banished Absalom from the rigging.

She shifted in his embrace. "He's not my young man. He's easily as old as either of us. And he is not jealous!"

"Whatever you say," Black answered amiably, but the more she considered it, the more she became convinced it was true. Absalom *was* jealous, and she didn't know why the idea bothered her so much. In part, perhaps, because he was supposed to be her friend and companion—the closest she had ever gotten to a partner—and practical experience had long since taught her that partnerships founded on anything other than friendship inevitably end in disaster.

She and Nick, at the height of their passion, had once considered a partnership. She had almost given up her commission to become his wife. And look where that had landed her. By Varia, she couldn't travel with Absalom if he was going to succumb to such delusions.

And yet, there was more to it than that. What had happened to Nick . . . Well, that was the stuff of tragedy, raw and primal. There had to be a way to partner with a lover without calling down the wrath of the ages.

And yet . . .

Absalom was different; too fundamentally unknown for comfort. She trusted him implicitly, so help her, but who was he? The scruffy mage in the marketplace? Her dapper companion of Arrhyndon? Or this achingly lovely but mercurial youngster? Each time he changed, she was convinced she was finally seeing his true face—even though she knew she wasn't. For instance, this time he was clearly acting out of pique and a certain desire to rattle her—even in the midst of the charade, she could see his eyes twinkle with a teasing good humor—and yet he was too cursed proficient. He didn't just look twenty; he acted twenty, as if he had suddenly removed a mask of maturity.

Was he really just the bastard mage he claimed, or was there something more sinister about him? Was he watching her? Had the Guild caught the eye of the mages?

But that was unfair. She did trust him, and she liked him—even in the midst of her annoyance. She just didn't want to get permanently involved with anyone.

"What's wrong? Can't I even have fun?" she complained to him at one point, several days into the voyage, when he had thrice interrupted her attempts at a private moment with the captain.

"Of course you can. And so can I," he answered, with a wicked grin. "Consider it a challenge."

"Hmph. You're just annoyed I'm getting some action," she countered, hoping for the airy denial he always granted her.

"Am not," he obliged.

"Are too."

He stuck out his tongue, every inch the adolescent, and she had to laugh. But still he dogged her steps, and the unnatural good luck that had accompanied most of his voyages was noticeably lacking. Five days out they encountered a fearsome storm that had Kharman Black in the wheelhouse for hours at a stretch, struggling to keep his ship on course. Following that, they hit a patch of calm that seemed to suck all the wind away as if it had never existed.

"I have sailed these waters all my life," Black complained, "and I have never seen weather like this. Not even in the middle of winter."

"You know," she finally told her companion, after a week of increasingly frayed tempers, "this whole ordeal would be over a lot faster—and Kharman Black out of my life a lot sooner—if you would just get us to Konasta."

"My, my," he answered. "Such assumptions you are making. I assure you, you are more than welcome to your dalliance with Captain Black. And my luck is just as variable as anyone's."

But nonetheless, the wind picked up the next morning and sped the ship tidily to Ephanon without further delay.

They docked on a sunny afternoon a week after Jen's arrival, and the sailors fetched their baggage while Vera bid farewell to Kharman on the wharf.

"A pleasure as always, my dear," he said with a final kiss. "Contact me again when you've tamed your companion."

"Done and done," Absalom answered, debarking in her wake, and Kharman did a sharp double-take, for the mage was back in his familiar guise, all his unnatural youth evaporated.

"Wha . . . ?"

She patted him on the arm. "Don't ask. I certainly try not to."

And leaving the captain of the *Belapharion Traveler* gaping on the docks, she rejoined her companion.

"Where to?" Absalom asked, tilting his face to the sun as if nothing untoward had happened.

Vera considered and discarded several tart rejoinders, eventually saying, "I don't know. A hotel, I suppose, and then wherever the criminal classes happen to congregate. Any ideas?"

"Contrary to popular opinion, I know very little about the criminal mind. And particularly not in Konasta. You realize that, until I met you, I'd never been out of Ashkharon?"

She surveyed him speculatively for a moment, liking him

better now that the grey was back in his hair, then shrugged expansively. "Whatever."

"You don't believe me? Be that as it may. From all I gather, Ephanon is your city; I doubt I could surmount your expertise. Still, I must say it is a relief to be back in a sensible climate."

She grinned and shouldered her pack, taking his arm—all conflict between them forgotten. "How right you are. Just smell the air. That's Konasta all over!"

And Konasta it was: the country of her heart. Every detail called to her, from the heat of the sun to the tang of the air to the quaintly cobbled streets that wound up the hill that was Ephanon. Swarthy navvies, their hair universally dark and curled, grinned familiarly at her as they unloaded crates of freshly caught fish and squid. One young lad, not looking where he was going, upset a bucket of crabs at her feet. Absalom hopped and danced as he avoided the scuttling crustaceans.

"Come," she said. "If I recall correctly, there's a decent inn up on Stabian Street that won't strain our budget too badly."

As Gideon had promised, Jen didn't see him until late the following afternoon, and then only in passing as he breezed through the kitchen on his way to find Saul. He flashed her a luminous smile, full of promise, but by that point she was too busy to pay it much attention. She had been up since dawn, rousted from their warm bed by Thibault, who seemed less than inclined to be sympathetic to her plight.

"I didn't ask you to drink so much last night," he told her as she groaned and tried to bury her head beneath the pillows. "Alcina's expecting us downstairs in half an hour."

And removing her bodily from the bed, he bent her ruthlessly over the basin and upended a pitcher of icy water across her neck.

"Thibault!"

He pressed a bar of soap into her hands. "Wash up. The bathroom's occupied."

Feeling much oppressed, she performed her ablutions, then drifted downstairs to find Beroe waiting.

And so her week progressed as Alcina and Beroe shuttled her from one task to another, seemingly unconcerned by her lack of skill. She would learn, they assured her—and so she did. Reluctantly, and with much grumbling to Thibault after hours, she became adept at wielding a knife for something other than combat, and soon could mop a floor or dust a mantel with the best.

It was thankless, mindless work, but being Jen, she couldn't set her hand to a task without some attempt at mastery. And that, in turn, quickly earned her the praises of her supervisors and a certain degree of enmity from her fellow servants, since her naturally competitive spirit had no other outlet.

And as each evening rolled around, she found herself far too tired to so much as entertain the idea of another night at the Cauldron with Gideon. Although, looking out the windows one night on her way to her chamber, she saw the intermittent glow of his cigarette in the courtyard and knew he was waiting.

It was just as well, she reflected, that the assassin hadn't made a move that week, for she was far too scattered to foil him.

But gradually her mood and energy improved, and by the end of the week she had established an efficient routine that had her scanning all public rooms for anomalies in a daily sequence while keeping her occupied in the kitchens during peak delivery hours. She even found herself with the occasional odd pockets of free time as her skill and efficiency improved. In fact, she was enjoying the luxury of a cold glass of lemonade in the courtyard during one such moment when Saul approached her, emerging from around the back of the house.

She hadn't seen her employer since their initial meeting a week ago—nor any other member of his family for that matter. According to Thibault, Patroch had departed in a dudgeon the day after their arrival for an unspecified stay at a friend's island retreat. And Lydea, likewise, had been engaged in a sudden spate of social engagements, leaving Saul and his son the sole occupants of the house. Granted their freedom from family responsibility, each had closeted himself in his respective office, working furiously. In fact,

Thibault claimed the only time he saw their employer was on the infrequent occasions he was summoned to escort the man from house to Cauldron and back.

But now, grinning broadly, their employer took a seat on the bench at her side, running weary fingers through his hair.

"Should you be out here unescorted?" she asked.

"Why not? You're here, aren't you? Now then, how are you holding up?"

"Better than you, I suspect. According to Thibault, you have barely had a moment to breathe this past week!"

He chuckled. "Yes, isn't that always the case? Calamities never seem to happen one at a time. First one of my most reliable shipping firms goes belly-up, and then a valuable shipment sinks off the Mepharstan coast. And how am I supposed to replace *that* at the last moment? But here I am boring you with my troubles when I should be inquiring about yours. Are you settling in all right?"

"As well as can be expected."

"Yes, I am sorry about that. About the servant thing, I mean. But it honestly seemed like the best way to get you inconspicuously into the household."

"Well," she responded, with only the slightest degree of rancor, "Vera always said I had to learn to play the servant as convincingly as the aristocrat, and this seems as good a place to learn as any."

"Vera?" he inquired, with an arch of eyebrow.

"My aunt. She's also one of Owen's. Have you worked with her? The Hawk?"

"The Hawk?" He seemed shocked. "Your aunt is the Hawk?" Then, pulling himself together with effort, he added, "I had no idea. I've heard of her, of course—who hasn't?—but, no; I've never had the pleasure of working with her. Still, I'm impressed."

She had a sudden feeling he was a little more than impressed—apprehensive, maybe—no doubt at the thought of setting the Hawk's niece to work like a servant. Hastening to reassure him, she added, "It's really not that bad. I'm adjusting."

"I'm glad to hear it. Still, I suppose it's just as well I haven't been much visible for the past few days. No sense tempting fate—or a rogue assassin—until my chosen body-guards are equipped to deal with it, correct?"

"Absolutely!"

"So," he added, settling in more comfortably, "what did you think of the Cauldron? Gideon said he'd shown you around."

"Yes, he did. Most impressive."

He glowed. "I'm glad you think so. Just like Gideon himself, eh? Very resourceful, that boy."

To her mortification, she found herself blushing. "Quite."

"Well, when you're feeling up to it, I'm sure he'd be glad to give you another go. We're always pleased to show off our pride and joy. Now, how are you . . . What is it?"

Jen held up a hand, suddenly alert. She had heard something, she was sure, rustling about in the bushes. A faint movement, just about . . . there! That had to be a flash of emerald fabric, peeking though the leaves. Raising her arm, she hurled her lemonade—glass and all—straight at the laurels.

A faint, muffled, "Umph," confirmed her suspicions.

"Get down. Now!" she cried, pushing Saul from the bench.

He tumbled to the flagstones. The crossbow bolt just missed the descending arc of his body, thudding instead into the mortar between the massive stones of House Soleneides.

In a streak of green, the would-be assassin exploded from the bushes and hurtled down the alley. Even as Jen was debating the wisdom of following him and leaving her charge unattended, there was another muffled grunt and Aubrey emerged into the courtyard, rubbing his elbow in consternation. "Who in tarnation was that?"

With a wordless cry of frustration, Jen exploded to her feet. "Help him," she snapped, jerking her thumb back over her shoulder. Aubrey gaped. Saul's curly head had reappeared from behind the bench. "Now!" she ordered. "And yell if you're in trouble." Then she took off down the alley, her skirts hiked up around her knees and her feet flying.

But it was too late. Whoever the bastard was, he was gone, lost in the warren of streets that surrounded Soleneides Square. She even peered up and down Sentenniel Street in an effort to locate a flash of green, but to no avail. When she returned to the square in defeat, Saul was sitting up on the bench fending off Aubrey's ministrations. They both looked up as she approached.

"Any luck?" the younger man asked. And when she shook her head, he added bitterly, "Curse it all, if I had only known . . ."

Saul started to laugh.

"What is it?" Jen asked. "Are you all right?"

"No more than a few bruises, thanks to you. Oh, do go away, Aubrey, and stop fluttering. I told you; I'm fine." And then he convulsed again, waggling a finger at Jen. "Routed with a lemonade, by Varia! It seems I got my money's worth when I hired you. Oh, you should have seen it, Aubrey; it was a truly magnificent moment!"

"And what about that?" his associate asked sourly, pointing to the crossbow bolt still embedded in the wall.

"Oh, yes; that." Saul sobered. "It seems the Telos vendetta is still in force. Thank you, my dear, for preserving my life."

"My pleasure."

"Gilyan? Blast it all, where's that girl got to now?" Beroe's voice echoed peevishly from the kitchen.

Jen rolled her eyes. Saul, apparently not one for sustained sobriety, dissolved in laughter again. Aubrey looked disdainful. "Here," Jen answered, rounding the side of the house.

"And about time, too," the cook exclaimed. "The bread's ready for kneading, and . . . What happened to your lemonade? Don't tell me you've broken another glass!"

Jen sighed, and suffered herself to be herded back to the kitchen.

13

"So, where to now?"

Night had fallen over Ephanon, a balmy evening breeze stirring among the grape-leaves that wound in a luxurious canopy above the tavern's porch. Vera pushed her plate away with a satisfied sigh and leaned back in her chair. The candle that flickered at their table, and the string of magelights suspended from the eaves, cast an imperfect light over Absalom's features.

"What's your hurry?" she countered. "Why not just enjoy the evening?"

"Because we are out of both food and wine. And who was the one so impatient to contact the criminal underground?"

"I can't even imagine." She yawned. "Who do you think it was?"

The mage raised an eyebrow.

"Besides," she added, "we could always order more food and wine."

"I doubt I could eat another bite, and I think you've had quite enough to drink. At least if you plan on getting anything constructive done, tonight."

"And who was the one who wanted a vacation?" She chuckled, and tipped the dregs of the bottle into her glass. "We sound just like an old married couple, you know."

He regarded her in silence, those bottomless black eyes sparkling, and she caught herself flushing.

"Very well," she agreed, signaling the tavern-keeper for the check. "Sentenniel Street it is."

She threw down the requisite marks with reluctance. It was a beautiful evening, replete with everything she loved most about Konasta. Set against the side of the hill, the tavern's porch afforded a view of the winding streets, picked out with the occasional magelights. And above, through the leafy canopy, shone the vast floodlights that illuminated the palace, soaring high above them on its pinnacle. The wine was tart and fruity, the food succulent and spicy, and she felt at peace with the world.

She was even willing to forgive Absalom his transgressions.

The hotel was exactly where she had remembered it, the rooms as quaintly unchanged as when she had once shared the rickety beds with Nick. She had paid for and received two rooms, her own nestled snugly under the eaves. She wondered why it didn't upset her more, to occupy again the very chamber in which she and Nick had formulated their crazy plans. To eat at the same table at which he had proposed. Maybe because, with time, the hurt had faded, leaving only a faint, nostalgic memory of the happier days.

Yet there was something unchanging about the beauty of the Ephanon nights, and she could almost imagine it was Nick that sat across from her rather than Absalom. The vines had been thinner then, the wood of the porch a little less worn, but otherwise the scene could have been transported from sixteen years in the past. She could almost hear his voice again: "Marry me, Vi."

And her own, twenty-three-year-old response: "Of course, Nikki. How could I not?"

Nikolaos Constantin Navarin; the Lammergeier. Her Nick. How long had it taken her to discover his name? For some reason, he had been inordinately ashamed of his Konastan heritage, and had hidden it for years. When she first met him, he had been plain Nicholas Navarin. As if Nick had ever been just plain anything.

Even from the beginning, there had been a magnetism to him, a dramatic flair that was somehow larger than life. At twenty-one, the Hawk had been the rising star of the Guild; the Lammergeier had almost supplanted her. Not that she had complained; she had been too much under his spell to care. Even now she could conjure his face as if it were yesterday: the soft, dark hair and brilliant black eyes. The thick fringe of dusky lashes. The broad white grin that shone as bright as a hundred magelights. The sculpted arch of cheekbones; the proud, aquiline nose. It was the sort of face that could have graced the ancient coins; she had never seen another like it.

Or known another man like Nick.

Oh, it hadn't always been a honeymoon; they were both too strong-willed for that. In their day, they had fought as intensely as they had loved. That was one thing about Nick; he never did anything by halves. And it was this very country that had prompted some of their hottest debates. She was the one who had reintroduced him to Konasta, who had battled him to acknowledge his parents and his heritage. The noisy three-room cottage in which he had been raised, and which had still been occupied by eight of his relatives the last time she saw it, had left him cringing in shame; she adored it. Much, she assumed, as he would have adored the sprawling, artificial splendor of the Radineaux estates that she so reviled.

They each of them wanted to be what they were not; it had been a bond between them.

"What are you thinking about?" Absalom asked, interrupting her musings.

She smiled, coming back to the present with a bump. "Nothing. Old friends."

"Someone you loved?"

"More than life. Or so I once believed."

"What happened?" His voice was soft.

"I eventually discovered that I loved my life more, when he gave up on his."

"He died?"

"Essentially," she answered. Cryptically, she knew, but she didn't care. She had seen Nick only once since she had left him. That had been ten years ago, and he might as well have been dead. She doubted he was still alive today, sunk in his cycle of recrimination and destruction.

"Well, then," she said briskly, standing. "I think someone's waiting for the table. Come along. Sentenniel Street awaits."

The breeze that stirred among the laurels was soft and balmy, and faintly tinged with Dreamsmoke.

"Gideon?" Jen said, tentatively.

The tip of his cigarette flared and died, and he emerged from the bushes like a ghost, trailing smoke.

"Good evening. I take it you're less tired tonight?"

"Much less tired, thank you."

"Good. I've been waiting for you."

Was she imagining a faint hint of annoyance in his voice? "I know. I've seen you. I'm sorry I've been so busy . . ."

"But here you are at last. Well, then." With a final drag on his cigarette, he flung the butt to the flagstones, grinding it out beneath his boot. The smoke winged from his nostrils like a dragon's breath. "The Cauldron again?"

"If you wish."

"I do. Besides, I owe you a debt. For saving my boss." He moved closer, taking her hand, his voice dropping to an intimate whisper. "My thanks."

Predictably, she flushed. "It was nothing. My job."

"Nonetheless. I think I shall have to conjure a suitably appropriate reward." He cocked his head, regarding her. "Any ideas? Off-hand?"

Under his intent, hypnotic scrutiny, her voice felt thick and unwieldy. "Oh. One or two. That I could think of."

"Ah." He stepped closer, his face bare inches from her own. His hands slid in a languid motion down her sides, eventually coming to rest on the curve of her hips. There was something almost proprietary about the gesture which would have raised her hackles in almost any other circumstances. But somehow, from Gideon, the gesture seemed as natural as breathing.

"About those ideas," he continued, his mouth so close to her own that his lips brushed tantalizingly against hers, their breath commingled. "Might I be on the right approach?"

"I think you could say that," she managed, weakly.

His hand boldly cupped a breast, his thumb circling the nipple.

"Gideon!" she gasped, pulling away.

"What?"

"Well . . . someone might see us!"

He chuckled, low in his throat. "So?"

"I would thank you not to get me fired. At least not before I've had a chance to ferret out the assassin."

"Fair enough; you have a point. I'll put Saul's needs before my own. As usual."

"How very obliging of you."

"Well"—he sounded unaccountably amused—"the man
is a saint. Where else would I find such an accommodating
boss? Now, the Cauldron awaits. Oh, and I hope you're
not acrophobic, O Savior of Saul, because the mages have
put on quite a show this week."

Sentenniel Street was every bit as vibrant as Vera remembered, and more so now, with the newer clubs springing up like toadstools. She didn't recognize half of the
facades, with the exception of the Cauldron—but it seemed
that the more money the clubs brought in, the more elaborate their displays became. The whole district blinked and
twinkled with an energy rivaling even the grandest of
Mages' Quarters.

Absalom was gawking like a yokel, fascinated by the play
of lights and colors; the sights and sound of merriment and
debauchery. Dreamsmoke and alcohol, and grilled lamb on
skewers. Whores and tradesmen, and the grandest of aristocrats. Sex toys and leather, and gemstones beyond compare.
All combined in a decadent frenzy that constituted the average night out in Konasta's largest city.

"It makes Nhuras look like a country cousin," he said,
his head swiveling about like a hawk's.

Vera grinned. "Impressive, isn't it?"

"You're not kidding. I . . . Good gracious, is that
couple . . . ?"

She turned his head. "Don't look; it's rude."

"But . . ."

"You'll quickly find that, in Ephanon, almost anything
goes. Often without the need for closed doors. Honestly,
Absalom, aren't you mages supposed to be world-weary
and jaded?"

"Not the bastard kind. I swear, traveling with you is a
never-ending adventure. Not to mention an education."

"Oh, please. Don't play the innocent with me." She
turned to smile at him and did an abrupt double-take, for
he had once again altered his appearance.

He looked the very image of the young street tough. His

hair was long and stringy, tied back in a tail. There was a scar on his cheek and an earring in his ear. He looked like he hadn't seen a bath for the better part of a fortnight. But there was, nonetheless, a glamour to him—a raw edge of beauty like that knife-thin whip of scar. He grinned at her: a wry, knowing twist of lips above a stubble-shadowed jaw.

It never failed to disconcert her. He could have been anywhere from a jaded twenty to a youthful thirty-five.

She exhaled on a breath. "Well, I'll be hanged."

"Like it?"

"It's certainly different. So tell me, why do your eyes never change?"

"As I see it, we all need something to hang reality on. For you, it's your art. For me, my eyes. I often have an odd feeling that, if I ever let those go, I'd never find my way back to myself again."

She shivered. "You know, I often have the same feeling?"

"What, that I am mutable as air?" He grinned and whirled, waving a hand at the swirling crowd. "So where to, Revered Leader?"

"Oh, hush up." She frowned at the glittering facades, trying to determine where to focus her attention. Then suddenly she gasped and grasped his arm. "Gracious, there's Jen. Hide!" And she towed him behind a column.

The mage was laughing.

"What?"

"No need. I've already done you." And he sauntered out boldly, peering after her niece.

After a moment she joined him, for it was obvious that Jen wasn't paying a jot of attention to anything but her companion. "Great gadding goldfish, but she's caught herself a looker! I wonder who he is?"

"Trouble," Absalom answered seriously.

"What do you mean?"

"He's got an air about him, that one. Dangerous. I can't quite put my finger on it, but . . ."

"Nonsense," she chided. "How can you tell from a look?"

"And you call yourself an assassin? But you still haven't chosen a club."

"Well, not the one Jenny's using; that's for certain. But

then I wasn't planning on visiting the Cauldron. At least not yet." And then her eyes were caught by a billowing expanse of topsail and the soaring riggings of a galleon. And, of course, the name: The Rogue's Gallery. "By Varia, how could any self-respecting rogue pass that up? Do you have the money?" She held out a hand.

Absalom gave a long-suffering sigh. "Why must I always be responsible for the money?"

"Because you don't require pockets."

With another sigh, he plucked a mark from the air and deposited it on her palm. "What would you do without me?"

"Carry a money bag. Come on, then." And she towed him to the club.

14

The mages had indeed put on a grand display. From the doorway of the Cauldron, Jen stepped onto a cloud that had been sheered away in a flat highway, stretching into the heart of the club. The light was white and hard as diamonds, and to each side of the flat cloud-path, puffy billows rose up like decorative hedges. Beyond—and below—stretched an endless vista of sun-dappled fields and shadowy forests, sparkling streams and mirror-bright rivers, lordly manors and tiny bunched hamlets, as if the whole club soared high above the earth.

Nor was there one cloud, but many. Flat-topped and bottom-billowed, their edges rippled in an illusory wind, they seemed to bump at each other like anxious children as the earth scrolled past beneath them. The bar—carved out of the largest cloud, with cotton-puff stools—still reigned at the chamber's center. The hanging balconies of the previous display had morphed into mini-cloudlets, accessible by tenuous, flowing stairways of mist. Hidden fans simulated a breeze, though the air was warm as summer.

It was a flawless illusion—and Jen noticed that most of the patrons stayed resolutely to the designate cloud-paths, prey to the visual trickery. But those who didn't—those who stepped off through absentmindedness or daring—generated, in a fit of whimsy, great arching wings that seemed to hold them suspended.

"I want to sit up there," Jen declared, pointing to one of the mini-cloudlets.

"Your wish is my command," Gideon said, guiding her to the misty stairway.

It must have been still early—or the patrons timid—for most of the upper tables were empty. Perhaps, Jen thought, they simply didn't trust the stairways. The treads felt solid enough under her feet, but when she looked down, it was disconcerting to see her ankles encased in swirling fog.

Miles below her, it seemed, the ground unfurled, dotted with ambulatory flocks of sheep, and herds of cows and horses. Tiny farmers tilled their fields, and miniature chimneys leaked tendrils of steam, fine as cotton threads. Almost, she wished she had brought Absalom's amulet to block the illusion, if only for the pleasure of seeing a multiplicity of patrons leaning out over the borders of the apparent cloud-paths, staring intently at nothing.

She related these sentiments to Gideon, who laughed and admitted, "I've done it a time or two myself. There isn't anything quite like a room of people all intently fixated on the floor boards." There was something fresh-scrubbed about him that evening—pink-cheeked and bright-eyed— that Jen hadn't noticed in the shadowy courtyard. He looked relaxed and eager; expectant.

"So, what now?" she said, with a matching grin.

"We'll wait about an hour, and then proceed upstairs. Providing, of course, that you're still amenable . . ."

She raised an eyebrow. "Of course. But why an hour?"

"You'll see."

And she did. Gradually, as the minutes ticked by, the light became more golden, slanting across the club like the late afternoon sun. It reflected off the clouds, highlighting their humps and valleys, throwing their subtle contours into sharp relief until they seemed to be wrapped in golden foil like the most elegant of confections. Long shadows stretched across the land below as the tiny farmers brought in their herds and burghers disassembled their stalls and markets.

And then the sky began to darken. Pink; salmon; persimmon; red; and finally an improbable twilight blue, picked with the glimmerings of stars. From door to door, blackness crept across the sky, sealing the club under a dome of night. A watery moonlight bathed the clouds so that they glowed pale and insubstantial as ghosts while, above and below, twin firmaments of lights winked slowly into being. Above, an arc of brilliantly cloudless sky, freckled with stars and brushed with wispy galaxies. And below, as the magelights were cued to life in the scattered hamlets, clusters of scintillating illumination like strings and heaps of jewels.

On each of the cloud-supported tables, candles winked joyfully, creating their own scattered constellations.

"We tried hour cycles of light and darkness," Gideon said, "but that only seemed to make the customers edgy. Too much change in too little time, or something of that nature. But these two-hour cycles seem to work just perfectly, don't you think?"

"Indeed." Then, "You planned this," Jen said wonderingly. "Timed it right down to the sunset . . ."

Her companion grinned, admitting nothing, but it was flattering beyond belief that such a man should go so far out of his way to impress her. For something told her that Gideon didn't often make the attempt to impress, letting his natural charms fill that void instead.

"That ain't nothing," he said, with a teasing arc of eyebrow, "to what is yet to come. And now, if you're ready"—he extended a hand—"we go upstairs."

Grinning, she stood, her fingers curling into his, and let herself be led.

The Rogue's Gallery, Vera reflected, was perfect; exactly what she had been searching for. There was a marked piratical theme to the decor, and a more motley assortment of real or imagined rogues she had never seen. Scars and eyepatches abounded, along with missing limbs and outrageous garb.

Of course, she could tell at a glance which were the real rogues and which their illusory cousins. Magerie could mask faces, but not the body: the inherent grace and swagger of the true-born rogue. And there were, she figured, as many rich merchants slumming it as there were honest thieves and scoundrels.

In many ways, that was what amazed her most about her companion. Though Absalom was, she suspected, one of the most moral people she had ever met—forthright and loyal to a fault—he had every ounce of that lowlife swagger; he alone would have fooled her. It seemed his days spent hawking his wares in the Nhuras bazaar had taught him well. That scruffy, bizarrely mangled mage she had first encountered in Ashkharon would have fit into this mix without a hitch, though she infinitely preferred the rough-cut young guise he was currently wearing.

As if sensing her thoughts, he turned and said, "Where to, my dove?"

"The bar, I think. A little loud talk and much flashing of money should achieve the desired results."

She began elbowing her way through the crowd, earning herself some intently startled stares in return. Which was odd, as they weren't the only ones trying to maneuver into an advantageous position. But all the attention seemed to be focused on her—and had been from the moment she entered the club, now that she came to think of it. The hulking guard at the door had given her a frankly admiring once-over, but that wasn't anything unusual. Vera wasn't old enough that she had lost her ability to turn heads. But this . . .

A sluggish suspicion began to stir.

"Absalom!" she hissed after the fifteenth person had done an incredulous double-take. "What have you done to me?"

The mage just grinned. "Look," he said, pointing, "there's a free inch of space at the bar."

She cocked her head and regarded him severely. Then, with a resigned sigh, she shouldered her way into the vacancy, pounding a fist on the polished surface for attention.

The bartender turned, and his eyes went round as saucers.

"Two ales, please," she growled.

"Your finest," Absalom added, materializing a golden fifty from somewhere under the counter and sliding it nonchalantly across the bar.

The bartender blinked twice, then scrambled to do their bidding.

"Absalom," she muttered yet again, when the man was safely out of hearing, "I'm serious! What the bloody tarnation have you done to me?"

"It's working, then," he said mildly. "Good. I wasn't sure if I could compete with a whole consortium of Konastan mages."

"Blast you . . ."

"Shh. He's returning. What's our strategy?" And he draped an arm across her shoulders, drawing her into an impromptu embrace. "Kiss me, my dear."

"What?"

He chuckled at her outrage and covered her mouth with his. It was a showy kiss: lewd; all tongue.

She tromped viciously on his toe.

"Ouch. Just establishing your credentials as a taken woman," he whispered, under pretense of nuzzling her neck. "Protecting you from unwelcome advances."

"Why, do I look as if I need protecting?"

He looked vastly amused. "Well. Perhaps not as such."

"Your drinks, Kyrin. Kyrinne." And the bartender pushed two heavy tumblers towards them, filled generously with a thick, foamy brew. Vera took a tentative sip, then grinned—a genuine one this time.

"Admirable. Most admirable."

The bartender looked relieved.

"Absalom," Vera persisted, when the man had departed yet again. "How do I look?"

"Perfectly delectable, as always."

She suppressed an urge to hit him. "I shudder to think of your idea of delectable," she said instead.

"Well," he replied, hurt. "You did seem to want to be noticed."

"There is that," she admitted. "Very well. Kiss me again, I suppose, then start talking!"

It wasn't a serious kiss—a teasing exaggeration of a kiss—and then he said, loudly, "A perfect evening for mischief, eh, my love?"

"There is that," she answered, equally carrying. "Though I could think of one or two things that might make it better . . ."

He leered, and groped a breast.

"Not that, you silly clunch," she said, laughing and pushing him away. She leaned over to the man next to Absalom: a merchant, for sure. "Cheeky, ain't he?"

The poor man went bright red.

A genuinely disreputable type, lurking over her right shoulder—to whom she'd truly directed the words—leaned over as predicted. "This one giving you trouble?" he growled, closing a ham-handed fist around Absalom's shoulder.

The mage winced.

Vera looked up into the scarred, heavily stubbled face of her savior—front tooth capped with gold and breath redolent of garlic—and managed a flirtatious smile. "Not as such; no. He's got his few good points. I think I'll keep him around for a while, even if he does tend to get above his station." Absalom's eyes twinkled knowingly at her. "Pull up a seat, though," she added, gesturing her new companion closer. "We'll buy you a drink. A girl can never have too many friends."

The rogue's face split in a fearsome grin. The merchant took an ignominious tumble, ending up in a heap on the floor as their new companion snagged the stool out from under him. "I know precisely what you mean," he said, pulling it closer and sitting. "Mighty kind of you, Kyrinne."

"Leta, please," Vera replied. She was beginning to get a sense of how Absalom had disguised her based on the type of men she seemed to be attracting. Beautiful, tough, and deadly, no doubt; the loutish types always seemed to think they deserved that. Whereas the more sanguine—such as the bartender—kept women like her wisely at arm's length. Much as they would a striking cobra.

"Krytos," the lout responded cheerfully, detaching his hand from Absalom's shoulder and thrusting it at her instead.

She gave it a suitably bone-crunching shake. "And this here is . . . Marcos."

"Pleasure to meet you, Marcos."

"Likewise," Absalom said faintly, clearly getting the worst of the handshake.

After liberally dispensing drinks and trading several libelous tales with Krytos, Vera had assembled quite a collection of rogues, all vying for her attention. And for once, she found herself almost glad of Absalom's proprietary arm about her. She was probably a match for any three of them, but half a dozen? It never hurt to have a mage in your corner.

And, admittedly, once Absalom loosened up, he became almost as voluble as she, inventing the most outrageous stories as if determined to outdo every man jack of them for sheer bravado. Though, for all she knew, his stories might be true. Like her own, they seemed to contain far too much detail, and that spoke of a solid grounding in reality.

Would she ever figure the blasted creature out?

After entertaining her impromptu audience with a fictionalized rendition of First Minister Istarbion's death, she yawned and said, "Well, the beer and company are excellent, but can anyone tell me where I might be able to obtain a little Dreamsmoke? Just to make the evening truly memorable?"

There was a moment of silence.

"That's illegal, you know," Krytos said. "Dealing Dreamsmoke."

"I know. What's fun that isn't?"

Absalom arched an eyebrow almost imperceptibly, and she shrugged back minutely in return.

A whispered conference had begun at her words.

"Do you know?"

"Would Natos have a contact?"

"I bet old Constant would know a name."

"Or have some on him."

"If he hasn't smoked it away, already . . ."

Eventually, a consensus was reached: old Constant. Ask old Constant.

"And who's old Constant?" she inquired.

Several fingers poked toward the shadowy corners of the club. Old Constant, it developed, was an almost legendary addict who smoked his days and nights away in the corner of whatever club would admit him. Which was currently the Rogue's Gallery.

After tossing a few more marks around for goodwill, Vera and Absalom extracted themselves from the vociferous group and went in search of the Dreamer. They found him, huddled in the back of the club: a wreck of a man in filthy, overripe clothing, huddled bonelessly over a bottle of pure Ghedrin spirits. His hair was filthy and matted, and reeked of the sickly sweet odor of Dreamsmoke. Vera couldn't tell if it was dirt or age that silvered his hair, but she knew immediately that this was a man on the end of a very long, and very ragged, rope. She doubted that he'd last out the year.

Absalom cleared his throat and the man looked up, dragging bloodshot and dilated eyes in their direction. His mouth moved in a soundless croak. And then, with a hacking cough, he cleared his voice and spoke.

"What?"

It was the voice that cued her. Everything else could have been a disguise. But that voice, beneath the rusty, husky overtones of abuse and disuse . . . That voice was unmistakable.

She swallowed against a sour spike of bile, rising high in her throat. Her voice sounded as corroded as his.

"Hello, Nick," she said.

15

"Do . . . Do I . . . ?"

"Vera, do you know this man?" Absalom seconded, frowning.

She felt the clench of anger like a fist in the pit of her stomach. "Yes, I rather think I do. Take it off, Absalom."

"Take what off?"

"The disguise," she flared. "Take it off. Now!"

He must have complied, for she saw a foggy recognition stir on Nick's face. "Vi?" he said. "Vivi?" He reached out a hand, brushing a finger almost tentatively along her jaw—as if he were a blind man, trying to recall her by feel.

She slapped him, hard, across the cheek.

"Vera!" Absalom exclaimed.

"Curse you, Nick," she growled, ignoring the mage, "how could you? You had a calling! What, by all that is precious, have you let yourself become?"

An obscure kind of confusion registered on his face.

"How much of this have you had?" she demanded, waving the Ghedrin bottle at him.

He looked regretful. "Far too much, I suspect. You . . . You look beautiful, Vi."

It was too much. She threw the bottle against the wall, shattering it—much to the consternation of some of the nearby patrons. "Well, that's bloody enough of that!"

"I'm . . . sorry, Vi," he said, inadequately.

"Right. Of course you are." She ran rough fingers through her hair, pushing the strands away. "You're sorry; I'm sorry. We're all sorry. I need to get out of here. I can't hear myself think."

"It didn't seem to bother you before," Absalom observed.

She had all but forgotten his presence.

"Who's this?" Nick asked, also seeming to notice the mage for the first time.

"I might ask the same of you," Absalom retorted, before Vera had a chance to reply. "Vera, who is this?"

"Nikolaos Constantin Navarin," she said bitterly. "Once known as the Lammergeier. And my former fiancé."

A sudden, awkward silence descended, making the clamor of the club ring all the more stridently in her ears. Absalom looked stunned.

"I like your hair," Nick said at last.

She ran self-conscious fingers along the ends, now just brushing her collarbones. "Occupational hazard," she replied.

For a moment it was the old Nick grinning raffishly at her, sharing what only assassins could share. "You had to cut it off?"

"Afraid so."

"What were you escaping from?"

"A prison cell in Ashkharon."

"A prison cell? Blast it, Vi, are you losing your touch?"

What's it to you? she wanted to cry. Or perhaps: *Look who's talking!* Shouting, accusing. But all she said was, sourly, "Sometimes I wonder."

His lips curved in a world-weary smile. "You do look beautiful, you know."

The old, familiar words just about broke her heart. "I look old," she countered, feeling every minute of it.

"No, *I* look old," he corrected.

"You," she returned, "look dead. Blast it to perdition, Nikki, I never expected you to stay alive this long."

He emitted a rusty chuckle. "Neither did I. But what can I say? Persistence: the one last remnant of my assassin days."

"But that's about it, huh? No desire to go back?"

"Vi, I can't."

"That's a load of crap, and you know it! You were always stronger than that."

"No, that's where you're wrong. I talked big, but . . ."

"You just turned tail and ran at the first sign of trouble?"

"Vera," Absalom chided again.

"Oh, belt up," she flared, whirling. "You know nothing about this!"

He showed an unexpected tenacity in the face of her scowl. "That's not entirely correct. I do know this is a friend whom you haven't seen in a long time. You could at least be civil. Do you think it's any easier for him?"

His quiet tone of reason silenced her. She looked at Nikki; really looked. Saw below the wrinkles and dirt and bloodshot eyes; the reek of Dreamsmoke in his hair and the acrid tang of liquor on his breath. Below the gaze that seemed to struggle for focus; below the features that threatened to slide into drugged incoherence. Saw beneath to the core of the essential Nick, still bleeding after all these years. And here she was, nails extended, ripping the wounds even wider. "It isn't, is it?" she admitted. "I'm sorry, too, Nikki. For everything."

He managed a watery smile, like a ghost of his former nonchalance. "You always had a way of taking on the world, Vi. Owen must have been very proud of you."

"He still is. He's training me to take over the Guild."

Could that be a sparkle of tears welling in Nikki's eyes? But all he said was, "No one better," nodding as if he'd always expected it. "Now, will you please tell me who this is? Your husband?"

"I never married. This is Absalom, my . . ."

He raised an eyebrow.

". . . my partner," she finished.

By Varia, it was almost worse than admitting she had married. She could see the hurt stirring in Nick's eyes, and abruptly regretted the words—true though she realized they were. After all her years of stubborn independence, she had finally acquired a partner—and almost without her conscious volition. And now the one last part of her that had belonged to Nick belonged to someone else.

Absalom looked as stunned by her words as she, but he, too, recognized their truth.

"Funny. He doesn't look like an assassin," Nick hazarded at last.

"That's because he's not. He's a mage."

"A mage." Nick looked almost happy. And then contemplative, adding, "Guildmaster, indeed. How you types always seem to acquire your mages, I'll never know . . ."

"Nikki, you're rambling. Tell me, how long has it been since you've had a bath? Or eaten a decent meal?"

"I can't remember . . ."

"No doubt. Come on, then. A bath and a decent meal is the least an old friend can give you. Can you even walk?"

"I haven't had that much to drink." But his eyes gave lie to the words.

She sighed. "Right. Absalom, help him up. Then both of you, follow me."

And pivoting precisely on her heel, she turned and left the club, no longer caring who saw or recognized her.

Thibault felt someone poke him, and a familiar jolt of alarm surged through him. Over the years he had come to distrust midnight wakings, for little good ever seemed to come of them. First had been a nebulous image of his grandmother, leaning over him and weeping, on the night that his parents had succumbed to a fever. And though many people had told him he shouldn't remember the incident, that he was too young to have any proper recall, he remembered it nonetheless. True, it was more of a feeling than a memory, a reverberating core of emotion tied to a frozen picture—Sylvaine's face, contorted—but still it carried weight.

The second time had been that night when Vera woke him with a touch. She had offered to relieve his endless vigil by Sylvaine's bed so that he might sleep; after thirty-six hours of staving off the inevitable with the last of Sylvaine's potions, his head felt as if it had been stuffed with lead, his eyes filled with sand. Vera had wakened him from a torpid slumber bare minutes before the end, so he could cradle his granny's body as she wheezed out the last of her life.

No, midnight wakings generally meant no good . . . until he recognized the quality of impatience to the shove that was so characteristically Jen's, and recalled where she had been. A spike of happiness impaled him, so keen it was almost painful. He tried to keep the pleasure out of his voice as he asked, "What happened? Rejected again?"

In the warm darkness, he could see the faint pinch of a frown between her eyes. "No. What's it to you?" She sounded vaguely annoyed.

"Oh, nothing," he said, sliding over to make room for her. "Do you want me to . . ."

"No, no point. But you'd better forget sleeping in the bed from now on."

"Why?" He propped himself up on one elbow, peering down at her.

She rolled partway towards him, looking up at him through the darkness. It was an oddly intimate position— her body halfway beneath his, their faces bare inches apart.

"Do you really want to know?" she replied with a grimace.

"Only if you want to tell me."

She appeared to consider. "Well, I don't see what it can hurt. It was wonderful, of course. You have to visit the Cauldron one of these days; it's amazing what those mages can do!"

He shrugged, uninterested. Places like the Cauldron had, at best, a limited appeal for him. It seemed a frivolous pursuit, and he never could understand people's desire to escape from reality. His life hadn't exactly been a picnic, but you faced your troubles with your eyes wide open and resolved your difficulties; problems denied only festered. "Perhaps someday."

"We sat in the clouds and watched the sunset," she said; he wondered if it was some kind of metaphor. "Gideon was . . ." She paused, her face suffused with such a quiet exultation that he felt his heart clench like a fist. "Well, he was wonderful, of course. But he had to work until dawn, and that's about when I get up."

He wondered why he had the sense that she was parroting back excuses that she didn't quite credit.

"That's not exactly love, is it?" he asked.

"I'm not looking for love."

"Well, common courtesy, then."

"He had to work," she repeated, stubbornly.

"So you got what you wanted?"

"I got what I wanted," she agreed, and he knew it for a lie.

He settled back against the pillows, thanking fate for the narrow Konastan mattresses. He extended an arm invitingly. "Tell me about the Cauldron."

She shifted, pillowing her cheek against his shoulder. "It was wonderful." She sighed, relaxing as his arm came around her. "Did I ever tell you about that first night and the menagerie? There were tigers and peacocks, and this great, golden dragon . . ."

He let the narrative lull him, after a while listening less to her words than to the cadence of her voice as it drifted into slumber. And finally, in the midst of an increasingly incoherent mumble about clouds and stars, he succumbed to impulse and ran a gentle finger along her cheek.

"Jenny?"

"What?" A yawn.

"He's an idiot, you know."

A pause. And then, gratefully, "Thanks, Thib."

"You're welcome," he answered, but she was already asleep.

Aubrey had found the body—what was it, the fourth? Fifth? He ought to remember that kind of brutality—about an hour earlier. It was the same modus operandi, filleted like a salmon with a cruel, surgical precision. *Who would do that?* he wondered again, nursing a very stiff drink. *What kind of twisted human being is capable of such*—there was no other word for it—*evil?* It disturbed him, to think of the Cauldron as a receptacle for that kind of depravity. Granted, nothing that transpired within these walls was entirely without corruption—the idea of the Cauldron as a bastion of morality amused him—but still . . .

One had to draw a line somewhere.

He wondered if he should mention it to Saul. His boss had seemed supremely unconcerned by the last few incidents, but Aubrey knew he could make a pretty good case for Saul's involvement. After all, it could be extremely bad publicity should news of this leak out. Besides, even Saul would agree that he was being used, the hospitality of his prized club abused. Couched that way, how could he fail to be moved?

Maybe Aubrey would tell him.

Or maybe he would just wait for Gideon.

Gideon always seemed to know Saul's mind better than Aubrey did. Besides, Aubrey was not about to face the prospect of another clean-up without the presence of his faithful partner.

Where the bloody blazes was the man, anyway?

He had seen him earlier, ensconced at one of the balcony tables with that blasted assassin, performing his duty as only Gideon saw it, blinding and seducing every possible opposition. Not that the girl stood any chance of discovering anything, but that was Gideon. Always alert to the options. They had departed for Gideon's chambers almost three-quarters of an hour ago, which meant they should be down by now.

Aubrey had no illusions as to Gideon's tolerance for the more mundane forms of sexual congress. He should have been utterly bored by now. And indeed, bare moments later, Gideon emerged from the back entrance, stretching and smiling like a cat after a kill. He ran a hand through his tumbled curls and caught Aubrey's eye across the room. He waved and loped over, hooking an ankle around one leg of the opposing chair and pulling it out. Then, flopping into it with his usual boneless grace, he propped his chin on his hand and regarded Aubrey with amused affection.

In an ironic counterpart, dawn was just breaking across the illusory sky.

"Well, what are you doing lurking about in the corners? And taking up valuable table space, I might add?"

Aubrey grimaced and took another slug of his drink, feeling the harsh, potent liquor burning its way down his throat. "It's not that crowded."

"No, it's not, is it? I guess this is not one of our more popular themes. Probably reminds too many people of their mortality. Fleeting time, and all that." He peered over at Aubrey. "What is it?"

"There's been another one," Aubrey answered.

"Another what?"

"Murder."

Gideon laughed, signaling a waiter for a drink. "Honestly, Aubrey, there are murders here almost every night. And government sanctioned, no less."

"You know what I mean. Where's your assassin?"

"I sent her home. And where is yours? Weren't you supposed to be distracting her partner?"

"What's to distract? He never leaves his rooms, except with Saul. And I should know; I've watched him."

"Good man."

Aubrey raised an eyebrow. "So?" he asked, pointedly.

Gideon laughed. "What can I say? Stimulus; response."

"She went home happy?"

"One can only assume. Although presumably she would have been happier if I had let her spend the night. But then, you know I don't do that."

Aubrey knew. Through all the years he had been working with Gideon, his partner had never shared a thing. At least not anything that mattered. Both his sleep and his life went on in a completely separate plane, inviolable. He had known Gideon for nearly seven years—was ostensibly his closest friend—but he had yet to receive an invitation to the man's house. In fact, he didn't even know where Gideon lived. There were, he felt, huge chunks of Gideon's existence that were forever walled off from his perusal.

An endless source of amusement and color, but ultimately untouchable; that was Gideon.

"When did it happen?" Gideon asked, misinterpreting Aubrey's glum expression.

"One hour, maybe two; who knows? I found it a little before the last sunset, while you were having drinks with that assassin."

"And you've been sitting here ever since? My poor sweet."

Aubrey was silent while the waiter fiddled with Gideon's drink, waiting for the man to depart before saying, "No one commissioned me for a revenge, so it must have been you who made the arrangements. Was it?"

"As a matter of fact, it was. Why?"

"What did he look like?"

"Look like?" Gideon seemed vastly amused. "Different from the last time, and—from what you've told me—the time before that. Bloody shades of perdition, Aubrey, this is an illusion club! Do you honestly think these people are going to show us their true faces?"

"This person," Aubrey corrected, stubbornly. "It's one person."

"Whatever. I suppose you want me to help you clean it up?"

"I'd be most grateful."

"My poor squeamish darling! Very well, then, consider me yours. At least for the present." And, reaching out, Gideon playfully tousled his associate's hair before tipping back his head and downing his drink in one fluid movement. "Now," he added, springing erect, "shall we go?"

Aubrey clambered more heavily to his feet. "I suppose so."

"Oh, and Aubrey . . ."

"Yes?"

"I wouldn't bother mentioning this to Saul, if I were you. He's already got enough on his mind."

16

The next few days were supremely uneventful. Thibault accompanied Saul wherever he went, and Jen made the final transition to servant life. She even developed a tentative friendship with two of her fellows, and came to look forward to their company of a morning.

Kore was bold and buxom, with snapping black eyes and a mane of dark, tightly-coiled hair that seemed to fly about with a will of its own. Much, Jen reflected, like Kore herself. Jahnee was milder, the voice of reason, with short mouse-brown hair framing a gamin face, and eyes as big and round as hand-dipped chocolates. They were her unflinching allies against the vagaries of domesticity—even if they still hadn't the slightest idea who she was.

"Brutal evening," Jen said, yawning loudly, three mornings after her first night with Gideon. They had repeated the experience only hours earlier, and she had arrived home exhausted, with barely enough energy to step over Thibault on his pallet and collapse across the bed. That, plus a somewhat overzealous consumption of alcohol, had left her feeling fairly nonfunctional.

She was, she suspected, becoming addicted to the illusion clubs with their aura of decadence and dissolution, their freedom from the trivialities of daily existence. And that wasn't even counting Gideon, who was his own particular brand of addiction. He might not be one of her devoted slaves, but he was, far and away, one of the best lovers she had ever had. The things that man could do with his body . . .

She played through last night's seduction in her mind, then shook herself back to reality, suddenly aware that she had been staring at the wall with a besotted grin. How could she let herself get so distracted? She was on duty, even if her role in Saul's preservation seemed largely redundant. Whoever this rogue assassin might be, he didn't seem to be making any forays into the kitchen. But that didn't excuse her inattention.

"Coffee?" Kore said with a knowing grin, as Jen flopped down at the table.

"The clubs, Ty, or both?" Jahnee added as Jen accepted the cup and took a deep, bracing swallow.

Jen blinked; she had momentarily forgotten that she was supposed to be married to Thibault. How embarrassing. But at least that way she didn't have to hide her foolish, love-struck smiles. Which was a relief; there was nothing worse than having to act nonchalant when you wanted to whoop to the skies.

"A bit of both," she admitted, mentally substituting Gideon's name for Thibault's.

"Honeymoon still on?" Kore teased.

"You could say that," she replied, with a secret smile.

Kore sighed. "You are so lucky. Handsome, kind, and dependable. Does he happen to have any unmarried brothers?"

Dependable? Jen thought. *Gideon?* And then she realized Kore was talking about Thibault, and was amazed at the violent surge of jealousy that seized her. *Handsome? Thibault?* And then, *How dare she?*

It was oddly disconcerting to realize that other people would see her stolid partner as an object of desire. Granted, he was one of the best men of her acquaintance, but she had, she realized, always regarded her affection for him with a certain self-righteousness, loving him despite himself.

How very magnanimous.

She tamped down a spike of anger and fashioned a smile. "No, just the one, I'm afraid. And he's mine."

"Pity. Although . . ."

"What?"

Kore grinned. "Well, Ty is a darling, I admit. But—no offense, Gilly—he can't hold a candle to Gideon. Now *there's* a man!"

Jahnee wrinkled her nose; Jen just laughed.

"No offense taken. Much as I love my husband, I'm far from blind. And Gideon is indeed incomparable!"

"Isn't he, though?" Kore's eyes twinkled. "I wonder . . ."

"Girls, stop chattering!" Beroe scolded. "Kore, there's bread to be kneaded." Kore sighed and ran up her sleeves; her forearms were lean and hard with muscle. "And Jahnee, Gilyan . . . there's meals to prepare. The cold chicken needs to be cut up for lunch, and the rabbits need to be readied for dinner. Now stop gossiping and snap to it!"

Jahnee wrinkled her nose at Beroe's retreating back. "I'll toss you for it," she offered.

Jen laughed. "Don't sweat it; I'll take the bunnies." Skinning and gutting rabbits was one of the few tasks she was actually good at, having learned it at Vera's knee. Moreover, it was one of the duties she didn't feel demeaned her. And since no one else seemed to relish the task as much as she did, it usually ended up falling to her. She fetched a knife, then retrieved the bunnies from the cold-box, lopping off their paws and deftly splitting the skin along their bellies.

"Ugh, I don't know how you do that," Jahnee exclaimed, settling across from her with her bird.

At the end of the table, Kore was industriously kneading. "Because she has more sense than you," she responded, slapping dough to board. "Honestly, Jahnee, what's wrong with Gideon?"

"What, do you want competition?" Jahnee responded, prying off a leg and beginning to slice the meat into neat strips.

"No, but I still don't understand you."

Picking up the first of the rabbits, Jen began peeling back the skin.

"All right, then," Jahnee admitted. "Gideon scares me."

"Scares you? By all that's precious . . ."

"He does," Jahnee said. "There's something . . . too perfect about him. It's creepy." And, at Kore's disgusted look, she added, "You asked me."

"More fool me. Does he scare *you*?"

Jen chuckled, lopping off the rabbit's head with one sure stroke. "Not even remotely."

"See? You're being ridiculous, Jahn. Besides, someone like Gideon could get you out of the kitchens."

"Is that what you're looking for?" Jen asked. "To get out of the kitchens?"

"Of course," Kore declared. "Aren't we all?"

"Absolutely," Jen admitted, immediately resolving to offer the girl a job once she had resumed her proper identity.

"So, who *do* you like?" Kore continued.

Spitted in their regard, Jahnee flushed.

"Patroch?" Jen hazarded.

The women looked at each other, then burst into gales of laughter.

"Girls!" From the cook.

"Very well. If not the Petulant One, then who?" Kore asked, undeterred.

"Why anyone?" Jahnee answered in some agitation. "Why do I have to pick someone when you'll only end up using it against me later?"

"Me?" Kore sounded hurt. "When have I ever done that?"

"Only all the time!"

"What if she promises not to?" Jen said.

"And who will hold her to that promise?"

"I will."

Jahnee regarded her out of too-big eyes. Jen smiled, brandishing her carving knife.

"Very well. How about Aubrey?"

"Aubrey?" Kore shrieked. "Oh, honestly, Jahnee . . ."

Jen cocked her head. "Don't you think he's a bit . . ."

"Pouty? Dull? Lively as a dishrag?" Kore finished in a dudgeon.

"No." Jahnee's voice was surprisingly strong for so slight a girl. "Trust me, Kore, he's got a good heart. In the end, he'll be one of the ones you can count on."

"Aubrey? Great shades of perdition, Gilyan, tell her! Gilyan?"

"Huh? What?" Jen responded, with only marginal attention. A tradesman had come to the door with a carton of lettuces. A perfectly ordinary occurrence, but it set all her Guild hackles to bristling. For one thing, in the week and a half she had been working the kitchens, she had never seen this man before. And while most people tended not to notice their servants, or servants their tradesmen—a useful bit of knowledge under certain circumstances—Jen noticed everything. And there was something not right about this man.

It was not just the trace of a scar, or the hole where an earring might hang. Or the scruffy shadow of a chin that had been too long without a razor. Or the thin lips or rabbity features. Compared to the butcher's boy, this man was a work of art! No, it was the eyes that bothered her, shifty and calculating.

She could have sworn he palmed something when he set down the carton of lettuces.

"Gilyan?" Jahnee prompted. "Are you all right?"

The tradesman was staring at her as if aware of her regard. She looked up at the ceiling, over at a side wall, trying to appear nonchalant; she had long since mastered the art of indirect observation.

"I . . . um . . . forgot the pot," she said, rising.

"What pot?" Kore demanded.

"The one to put the rabbits in."

"But . . ."

Jen scampered for the pot rack, picking the largest, shiniest saucepan she could find. She tilted it as if checking for imperfections until the mirrored bottom caught the man's reflection. And found herself suddenly thankful for all the time Beroe had made her spend scrubbing it as her hunch paid off.

Certain he was unobserved—for Beroe was off fetching the money, Kore and Jahnee were staring incredulously at Jen's turned back, and all the others were either oblivious or otherwise engaged—the man unstoppered a tiny vial, tipping the contents across several of the rising loaves.

"Right, here you are. Ten marks." Beroe returned, pressing the money into his palm. The vial vanished.

Jen paused, weighing her options, then turned and fumbled the saucepan, knocking it into the doctored loaves and sending the lot crashing to the floor. The assassin started and met her gaze; she dropped one eyelid in a wink.

He bolted.

"Gilyan!" the cook exclaimed. "Oh, you clumsy child, look what you've done!"

For an instant Jen considered chasing him, but that would be stretching her cover. Besides, she had to identify the poison. So, with a suitably contrite expression, she bent down as if to rectify the error, picking up one of the loaves and sniffing it surreptitiously. There was a slightly bitter odor, like walnuts, and she raised an incredulous eyebrow. Their assassin must be getting pretty desperate if he was resorting to acarstan; two bites of that, and the whole household would have been dead by midnight!

"What are you thinking?" Beroe scolded. "We can't use those now; they're ruined!"

Too right, Jen thought, and for good measure dumped the lot into the hearthfire.

Beroe was incensed. "What . . . What the blazes are you doing?"

"I thought you said they were no good."

"Yes, but . . ." Beroe's mouth worked; she seemed at a loss for words.

"Look," Kore said. "The fire's burning green!"

As indeed it was, a brief flare of emerald flames licking at the wood. There was a moment of silence.

"Sorry," Jen said at last, contritely, but feeling far from it. She hadn't known that acarstan burned green; it might be a good thing to remember for the future.

There was another silence, then they were ordered back to work by an irate Beroe.

With a little smile, Jen hung up her pot and went back to gutting rabbits, feeling happier than she had in days.

17

"That was a close thing today, wouldn't you say?"

Thibault looked up from his notebook. Jen was sitting cross-legged on the bed, brushing her hair. He watched the bristles fly and crackle through the strands until the unbound mass shimmered like silk, cut through with tawny highlights under the magelights. There was a certain catlike satisfaction to her gaze as she regarded him.

He masked a grimace. There was something disturbingly intimate about being alone with her in their tiny chamber, witnessing such mundane rituals as the nightly brushing of her hair—more intimate, even, than when they shared a bed. Almost as if such an act highlighted the limits of their relationship, taunting him with all he could never have. But, "Two close things, I would say," he responded.

This time the grimace was hers—exaggerated and obvious. She arched her back as she finished, tossing aside the brush and shaking out her locks until they rippled and flowed. He wondered, idly, if Gideon appreciated the effect.

"Don't remind me," she said tartly. "Here I am, stuck in the bloody kitchen all day while you get to explore Ephanon with our employer. Do you realize that, except for my visits to the Cauldron, I haven't set foot in the wider city since we arrived?"

Aware that any placatory remark might inflame her, he wisely remained silent.

After a moment, she continued, "And then, when my true services are finally required, not only does nobody notice, but you have also already outdone me by making your own more public—and more dramatic—rescue."

"No doubt motivated by you."

"Meaning?"

"That if you hadn't so brilliantly foiled his true attempt, our revered assassin wouldn't have been goaded into making such a ridiculously obvious second one. Foiling that was, at best, a joke. Besides, I think your notions of my daily endeavors are a tad romanticized."

"They are?"

"Completely. You talk of exploration? I assure you, my explorations of Ephanon have been strictly limited to hanging about in antechambers. And my views of the city garnered solely through carriage windows. It's bloody boring. At least you're doing something."

"And since when has housework been considered something?" she retorted, but did look cheerier.

He sighed. The things he did for love.

Not that he had lied, precisely. His job with Saul did include a lot of waiting. But the more time he spent with the man, the more his respect for him grew. Up until now, he hadn't realized how much work it took to run an illusion club. Before, he had considered it no more than another exploitation, a step above a street-thief or pimp. But now he saw it for what it really was: a client-related industry, and a deuced lot of good, hard work. There were supplies to lay in, temperamental mages to placate, and a constant awareness of how hard it was to maintain an edge in an increasingly competitive market.

And while Thibault might not exactly approve of the services Saul provided, there was no doubt that the man cared enough to provide the best. Apart from times of crisis, only about a third of each day was spent in the confines of his offices. The rest of the time he was out on the streets or on the docks, meeting with merchants, sampling wares or supervising the unloading of provisions. Twice Thibault's opinion had been sought on the merits of various vintages, and lunches were less a matter of sustenance than a relentless search for the finest chefs in the city. Saul had already, he informed Thibault proudly, wooed at least half a dozen cooks from other employment.

No detail was beyond him. He even wandered the poorer quarters of the city, searching for pretty faces and eager workers to swell his growing staff.

Invariably, the sight of his fine, sculpted visage and bluff charm was hailed with cheers and appreciative grins. The poor revered him; he knew every merchant's name; the rich were all his friends. The only people who seemed to dislike him were the criminal classes. "I may have inherited the business from my parents," he told Thibault, "but I have always tried to rise above the profession."

And as far as Thibault could tell, he had done an admirable job. It was no wonder Owen adored the man. Thibault might even have to revise his own estimation of the illusion clubs—after a judicious examination, of course. Maybe Jen and Gideon would consent to show him around, one night.

If they could be parted for long enough to oblige.

He cast a quick glance at Jenny, now busily plaiting her hair into a tail. Then, stretching out her neck, she rotated her shoulders in an exaggerated motion, peering back at him on occasion. He sighed, closed his notebook, then quit his chair, perching instead on the edge of the bed.

"I take it you want a shoulder rub?"

"Was I that obvious?"

"Varia forfend."

She chuckled and twitched aside her newly completed braid, offering her back.

He curled his hands around her shoulders, fingers brushing her collarbones, and ran his thumbs firmly up the back of her neck. She emitted a tiny, contented moan and gave herself over to his ministrations.

"So, tell me more about today," she said as he worked.

There wasn't really that much to tell, Thibault reflected. It had been an accounting day, and he had trailed Saul about the city like an oversized shadow, toting the thick leather-bound balance book beneath one arm. At intervals in the carriage, as they traveled between some of the more far-flung locations, Saul would check off items on any number of incomprehensible lists, and scribble down columns of figures in his quick, neat hand.

And all the while he would explain to Thibault, as if unaware that anyone could possibly find his doings uninteresting.

"The best spices come from Mepharsta, and the best wines from Magjorca. And we had all the furnishings in the Cauldron built specially in Gavrone. They have to be rather adaptable, you realize, since they are under a different illusion each week. In many ways, it makes my job at single-themed places like the Rogue's Gallery that much easier. There, the furniture can merely be built to the proper thematic specifications, leaving the mages free for better work. Not to mention saving a fortune in their fees. Do you realize that, in the Cauldron, we have a mage whose duty it is to simply maintain the image of the main bar every night? Quite ridiculous, if you think of it."

Thibault could only nod.

"And then, there are the incidentals. You can't enchant everything, you know, and sometimes it reinforces an illusion to seed it with reality. One night, when we did a forest theme, we actually imported a hundred potted trees, because we found that too many patrons wandering indiscriminately through the trunks spoiled the illusion. But once they realized that one in five were real—and that it was impossible to tell which at a glance—they stopped *that* behavior soon enough. By the way, if you have any notions of viable themes for the Cauldron, please tell me. Gideon and Aubrey are always on the lookout for new ideas."

"That's one thing I don't understand," Thibault said, clutching at a strap as the carriage careened around a sharp corner into a narrow alley.

"What? Oh, blast it!" Saul exclaimed, as the jolt blotted a line of figures. He patted at the stain with a napkin.

"Gideon and Aubrey. What exactly are their duties if you are doing all this?"

His employer laughed. "Gracious, my boy, their duties are without number. I merely oversee the issues that affect all my clubs in total. For instance, it's cheaper to acquire certain staples if you buy in bulk. And the more clubs I own, the larger my orders, and thus the cheaper the unit price. It's one of the advantages I have on the single-club owners. I can buy better goods, and thus attract better customers, often for a fraction of the cost. Why, only yesterday, I contracted for twenty barrels of Magjorcan red at a discount equivalent to the purchase of twenty barrels of that Lusanian crap at cost. No offense," he added as Thibault flinched. "I understand you have ties to Lusania.

"But, still," he continued, as the carriage lurched onto a

broader avenue, "each individual club takes its own special management. For instance, after I apportion out the wine barrels to each club, it is up to Gideon and Aubrey to determine how to best maximize quantity and cost so that each portion makes a profit. It's a bit of a tricky thing, convincing patrons they're getting an incomparable deal while in reality you are picking their pockets. And . . . I say," Saul started up from his seat, pressing his face to the pane. "Wasn't that Phytan Street? Remind me to stop there some time. Rumor has it that one of the merchants sells quite fine Ashkharon glassware, and the Cauldron could use some more goblets."

Then, settling back, he returned to the subject at hand. "Don't forget, however, that some of my patrons can leave the gaming tables quite wealthy."

"And doesn't that drain you? I mean, what if chance turns against you one night and more people win than expected?"

"Chance?" Saul chuckled in genuine amusement. "My dear boy, I assure you, chance has nothing to do with it."

Thibault was horrified. "You mean the tables are fixed?"

"Indubitably. I'm running a business, not a charity. Believe me, I give freely to those who deserve it, but the vast majority of the Cauldron's patrons hardly count as the deserving poor."

"But I thought the entry price was kept deliberately low so everyone could enter."

"In theory, yes. But in reality, the only ones that do enter are the desperate or undeserving. In one of life's great ironies, the truly deserving poor seem to regard the illusion clubs as depravities of the worst kind. Or, perhaps, they are simply too weary at the end of their long, hard days to enjoy what luxuries we can offer. No, I'm afraid our patrons are generally a mix of rich men and rogues, and the tables are balanced so the house always pulls in twice what is bet. That's part of Gideon and Aubrey's job, too, you know, figuring out how to best rig the tables. Still," he added, clearly registering Thibault's shock, "a third of the takings is a substantial amount of money paid out each night."

"Paid out randomly?"

"At least in theory." Saul shut the ledger with a decisive snap, passing it over. Thibault settled back against his seat, clutching the book to his chest. It was a lot to think about.

"Here we are," his employer said as the carriage rumbled to a halt. "I'm afraid Kelston doesn't have much of an antechamber. If it weren't for his reputation, I doubt anyone would consent to do business with him. I'll try not to keep you waiting long."

Thibault fiddled with the hilt of the stag's head dagger which he continued to carry around in his pocket. "Thanks. I . . . Just what do you think you're doing?"

"Getting out?" Saul hazarded, his fingers on the handle.

"Not without me in the lead you don't. Why do you think I'm here, otherwise?"

"Right. I keep forgetting. I must say, it's distressing to be hated; I'm used to quite the opposite reaction. But you're right; it won't do to get careless. Even if our assassin hasn't made a move since that day in the garden."

"Nevertheless. You know Owen would never forgive me if I got you killed."

"Yes. Dear Owen."

"Actually," Thibault added, "I'm surprised you walked all the way down to the docks by yourself to meet us the day we arrived."

"By myself?" Saul laughed. "Hardly. I may be a bit forgetful in the short term, but I assure you I'm not suicidal. Avram and Lucinda were around until your ship docked. After that, I figured I'd let you two earn your keep." And gesturing for Thibault to proceed him, Saul scooted back, exchanging places with his defacto bodyguard.

Thibault poked his head out, checking for suspicious activity before unfolding himself from the conveyance. Then, standing aside in proper suhdabhar form, he extended a hand to help his employer down.

"You're getting quite deft at that, my boy," Saul declared in some amusement as he descended. Thibault grimaced and handed him the ledger. Then, two paces behind his employer, he entered the spice merchant's place of business.

As promised, the antechamber was no more than an outer office, cluttered with books and papers. A surly-looking assistant occupied a desk in one corner, and the lone window was streaked with soot. There were a number of yellowing sea charts tacked to the walls, and the only unoccupied chair was piled high with ledgers. So Thibault propped his back against the wall and waited while an effusive and seemingly anxious Kelston ushered Saul into his inner sanctum.

Thibault expected the usual long and boring interval while Saul conducted his business, and at first he was not disappointed. After several minutes of idle toe tapping and staring out at the street through the filthy windowpane, he began to prowl the outer chamber, studying the old sea charts with their spice routes marked out in faded ink. At intervals, the sour-faced assistant would shoot him disapproving glances, then return to his papers.

But after a while, the unmistakable sound of raised voices began to resonate from behind the closed portal. Casually, Thibault drifted closer, not wanting to appear too interested, but nonetheless curious. After a moment, he noticed that the industrious scratching of the assistant's pen had likewise ceased. He turned and met the man's eyes deliberately. The assistant shrugged.

Thibault grinned, and installed himself flagrantly beside the inner door.

The walls were thick and it was hard to make out the individual words, but apparently the expected shipment had gone astray. And neither party seemed to want to shoulder the financial burden.

". . . hardly my fault it was taken by pirates," Saul bellowed at one point. ". . . paid for that shipment in good faith . . ." And, ". . . don't see why I should be responsible . . ."

"But if I return . . ." The answer came in fitful snatches. ". . . not enough to purchase the next . . ."

"Hmph." From Saul. ". . . risks of the business, I would say . . ."

There was some incomprehensible muttering, followed by, ". . . anything I can do to make it up . . . ?"

Thibault drifted closer.

"Other than returning my money, you mean?" Saul's

amusement registered clearly. Another mutter, and then, ". . . one thing . . ."

"Yes?" Eagerly.

"Occasionally . . . certain special shipments . . . cancel the debt . . ." Saul's voice phased in and out of audibility, then dropped out of range entirely.

There was some more muttering, and then ". . . illegal?"—rising in a panicked squawk—followed by Saul's rumbling chuckle. A sound which Thibault knew was meant to sound reassuring, but suddenly seemed anything but.

Saul emerged from the room several minutes later, looking supremely self-satisfied despite a plastered-on scowl. "Blasted pirates," he announced. "Scourge of the sea. Someone really ought to do something about them." Thibault could sense it was a performance put on solely for the assistant's benefit, for the man's eyes were flicking rapidly between the two of them.

"Indeed," Thibault responded blandly, cocking his head to let Saul know he was aware of the deception.

His employer grinned. "Well, then, shall we go? It appears Lydea and that appalling son of hers are due home tonight, and I daresay I shall be expected to be in attendance."

Thibault opened the door and proceeded Saul into the street. Then, when the door had closed behind them, he remarked, "So, what was that all about?"

Saul winked. His face, despite his age, shone like a schoolboy's. "Turning a situation to your advantage. I needed those spices, blast it"—and his frown, for an instant, turned genuine—"but it never hurts to have people in your debt." He handed the account book to Thibault.

"Thanks, but . . ."

There was nothing remotely subtle about the attack. The rat-faced assassin, complete with identifying scar, popped up from behind the carriage and cocked his arm. The resultant flash of movement was too swift to be anything other than a hastily thrown dagger. Automatically Thibault pivoted and flung up the ledger. The point of the weapon sank into the thickly tooled leather and stuck.

"I . . . Blast it, that was a perfectly good book!" Saul exclaimed reflexively.

It was too much. Thibault started to laugh.

The assassin started, then fled, spewing epithets. And by the time Thibault had gotten Saul safely into the carriage, he was long gone.

"And that's it?" Jen demanded, when he finished the tale.

"That's it."

She muttered something incomprehensible.

"What?" Thibault asked.

"You're right; that is nothing," she clarified, around a yawn.

"Are you sleepy?"

"No, just very relaxed." She stretched, catlike, and he stopped massaging her shoulders. "Thanks, Thibault; that was lovely."

"My pleasure." He paused for a moment, then asked, "Did you know that the gaming tables in the Cauldron are rigged?"

"It stands to reason. Saul's running a business, after all. And there's only so much you can leave to chance. Why, are you shocked?"

He grimaced and muttered something noncommittal. Sometimes her callousness surprised him.

"So, do you really think I rattled him? The assassin, I mean?"

Thibault sighed. "Yes, Jen. I do."

"Excellent." She rose and began searching the floor, peering intently under the bed. "Have you seen my nightgown?"

"It's where it always is. In the drawer," he elaborated, in response to her stare.

"That's not where it always is; that's merely where it ought to be. Honestly, Thibault, you should be the house-maid, not me!"

"Mmm. I doubt I'd look as good in a dress."

She laughed.

There was a moment of silence.

"Well, then." She retrieved the requisite item, clutching it momentarily to her chest. "At least things are finally starting to happen!"

"Perhaps. Or perhaps they've already happened. That

second attack smacked of desperation to me. Perhaps our boy has run out of funds at last."

She frowned, then stamped her foot. "Curse it, Thibault, don't get all pessimistic on me. That was *not* desperation. Just stupidity. The assassin will strike again."

He smiled at her tone, but all he said was, "We'll see."

18

She couldn't, Vera discovered, take Nick back to that same inn in which they had once lived, that same attic room in which they had once made love. Instead, she ordered Absalom to escort Nick to one of the more disreputable of the seaside bathhouses—the only one likely to take him in his drunken, filthy condition—and bathe him while she moved them to a different lodging. Partly because of the unassailable discrepancy between past and present, but mostly because of the solid steel shield that had sprung up around her heart at the sight of Nick.

Somehow she couldn't let him know that the wounds still bled, though slowed to a sluggish trickle over the years. Couldn't let him believe that she still sought out the old places, whether through nostalgia or some more enduring feeling. That left her too vulnerable. Besides, one of them had to be strong. And after all these years, Vera had grown accustomed to feigning strength.

So she packed her own and Absalom's belongings, and moved them to a quaint boarding house on the respectable border of the docklands. It had once been a private house, owned by a shipping magnate and his wife. But in the years since the man's death, the family's fortunes had gradually dwindled and the slums had encroached until his widow was forced to rent out rooms to support her declining years. Now, the house had settled into a quiet decay, its lines still handsome but its paint fading, its wallpaper yellowed with age.

There was a back garden, its statuary and benches fighting a losing battle with the weeds, and through its overgrown hedges, a faint sliver of the bay and the harbor lights could be seen. The back parlor, which opened onto the

gardens, doubled as the residents' sitting room. The piano
was slightly out of tune, but usable. For a small fee, a
breakfast could be provided.

All this her hostess explained to Vera as she bustled
about opening the rooms and settling the accounts. She was
a charming old lady—slightly faded, like her house, but
nonetheless with a solid air of competence and caring. Her
residents, Vera suspected, were less tenants than guests,
and granted all the courtesy as such. In fact, Vera found
herself unbending enough to relate the bare bones of Nick's
tale, receiving in return the woman's sympathy and
compassion.

"Why, of course he can stay here until you get him on
his feet, my dear. I've always felt there were far too many
Dreamsmoke casualties in the city. And it's so tragic,
though there's only so much one woman can do. Still, it's
nice to know that somebody cares. I'm sure they all wish
they had friends as fine as you."

Vera had managed a watery smile at that, and returned
to the bathhouse to find Absalom supporting a much
cleaner, but only marginally more sober, Nick. Together,
they had managed to force a quantity of food—and, more
importantly, coffee—down him, until he could actually
manage a half-stumble, half-shamble of a walk that got him
back to the boarding house with only a minor incident.

Absalom, bless him, had made no comment about the
move, and proceeded to settle in with a placid equanimity
that had their hostess charmed within minutes. Nick, tucked
into one of the downstairs bedrooms, passed out cold and
slept for thirty-two hours without waking.

It was, Vera reflected later, her last moment of peace.
From the moment Nick returned to consciousness, she
spent every waking hour at his bedside. For the space of
three days, her life revolved around the painful symptoms
of his withdrawal. He whined and pleaded, dissolving at
intervals into sloppy tears. She was iron and adamant. She
cajoled and bullied and sometimes even screamed, fueled
by a constant dull throb of anger.

"You must really love me, Vi," he said at one point,
when he was in a particularly maudlin mood. His voice was
soft with wonder.

"No, I despise you," she flared. "I despise what you've become. Look at yourself, Nikki."

That had prompted another spattering of tears, and a whimpering plea for "Just one smoke. To help me forget."

But the last thing Nikki needed was forgetting. What she wanted to do was remind him, of all the failed promises and broken vows. Of everything he could have been and yet so clearly wasn't. There had been a time when she had believed Nick could do anything; now she would be happy to get a coherent sentence out of him.

And worse, the more she tried to remind him, the more she herself remembered. Details, so help her, that she had thought buried beyond recall. Nikki singing, his rich resonant voice rising on a clear moonlit night, just for the joy of it. (She had forgotten how lovely his voice could be until she heard it, rasping and broken, crying out for Ghedrin.) Nikki sparring, his every movement a dance of economy and beauty. The incandescent flash of his smile when he bested her; his laugh of delight when she triumphed. He had always loved pitting himself against the best, had lived to test his limits. And now, it seemed, the best he could do was shake in her arms and puke in her lap as the dreadful cravings tore through him.

And yet . . .

She was older and wiser now, suddenly able to see new truths in the old behaviors. And in the posturing she had once thought so strong she now saw only weakness. That lust to challenge, to succeed—to shine brighter than any star—now seemed to stem out of a fundamental insecurity that had always left him proving himself. And not to the world, but to that toughest of all possible judges: himself. So that what she had once seen as belief she now understood was doubt, a constant battle to find value in the face of apparent valuelessness. A crazy, undying quest to convince himself he was *worth* something.

No wonder he had caved in under the pressure of that one fatal mistake. It must have seemed then as if all of his worst suspicions about himself were true, spilled out irredeemably along with his family's blood. And so he had run, straight into the arms of oblivion. Oblivion that came in small brown packets of crumbled weed and shattered dreams.

Funny that she had never noticed that until now. Not that it made the pain any less.

Fortunately, throughout it all, Absalom was the soul of support, fetching her meals and relieving her when she needed a rest or a bath. And the jealous trickery that had flared in Kharman Black's presence was nowhere in evidence. She had chosen well that day in the Nhuras bazaar, perhaps unconsciously seeing in that lone black eye the depths of wisdom and compassion that seemed to lie at the core of Absalom the mage—no matter how annoying he might be on occasion.

And after a few days, the core of the Nick Navarin she remembered began to emerge through the brutal haze of withdrawal. There was something about his eyes that remained bruised, as if some essential structure within him had collapsed, but his smiles were readier and his acerbic wit partially restored, even if he himself was often its most brutal victim. And, relieved and exhausted, Vera retired to her bed to sleep away the last few days of anger and betrayal.

She awoke around dusk to find Absalom and Nick occupying the back parlor. Absalom, with a garish silk dressing gown wrapped atop his clothes, was lounging on the sofa like some sort of eastern potentate, reading. Nick was seated at the piano bench, idly tuning the instrument. She had forgotten that about him. Nick had once played the piano like a virtuoso, for all that he had taught himself on the University's rickety instruments. And within three months of first touching a keyboard, he could already play better than Vera with all her years of childhood training.

It might have irritated her more if she hadn't been so in love with him.

"Well, well." They both looked up at her approach. "It seems that some of your old skills are still intact, Nikki."

He had the grace to flush. "One or two, I suppose."

"Can I get you anything to eat?" Absalom inquired, forestalling her tart rejoinder.

"That would be lovely. But I thought our accommodations didn't run to dinner."

"Oh, Hannah's given me kitchen privileges. She loves me, you know."

"I don't doubt you've thoroughly charmed her, you rogue. But don't put yourself out on my behalf."

"Nonsense. It's no trouble, I assure you." And Absalom unfolded himself from the couch, revealing the lurid expanse of the dressing gown in all its glory.

"Great blowfish of oblivion," she choked, "where did you get that ghastly creation? You look like a parrot!"

The mage waggled his eyebrows comically at her and departed, leaving her alone with Nick.

There was a long moment of silence.

"Hannah offered me one as well," Nick said at last, his fingers temporarily stilled on the keys. "Even more hideous than Absalom's. I turned it down."

"Well, at least one of you has sense." Vera drifted over to the window, peering out over the moonlit swathe of the garden. She could feel the tension in her back, engendered by the intensity of his gaze.

"Vi . . ."

"What?"

Another silence, and then, "I like him."

"Yes. I do, too." They were stark words—hard and unforgiving, affirming the presence of the other man in her life. But she wasn't quite ready to grant Nick his absolution.

"Vi . . ."

"What?"

"Nothing." He sighed and went back to the piano, picking out the notes. They echoed behind her like a patter of liquid raindrops, each plinking tone edged subtly from discord to harmony as he occasionally rose from the bench and fiddled in the depths of the instrument.

"Hannah should be grateful," she said, unable to mask the bitterness in her voice. "It's so hard to find a good piano tuner these days."

"Vi . . ."

"Tell Absalom I'll be out in the garden if he wants me." And throwing open the doors, she escaped into the night, settling alone on one of the worn stone benches.

Behind her, Nick's fingers faltered, stilled, and then resumed their rhythm. The marble was cold beneath her thighs, and she rubbed her fingers idly across the lip of the seat, feeling the imperfections that stemmed from years of use and weather. Between the gaps in the hedges, the harbor lights winked back at her. A thin breeze penetrated the fabric of her shirt and she shivered, wrapping her arms about her.

By Varia, she felt old. There were aches in her muscles, stiffnesses in her joints, that she had never imagined at the age of twenty-three. She seemed preternaturally aware of every failing system in her almost forty-year-old body and this, more than anything, reminded her of how many years had passed. How long would it be before she was forced to retire? Before her own physical essence betrayed her?

Behind her, Nikki had apparently finished tuning the piano, for his fingers picked out a descending series of scales, releasing a shimmering glissando of notes. The harbor lights blurred and sparkled like diamonds.

"Want to tell me about it?" Absalom said softly, slipping onto the seat beside her.

She scrubbed an impatient hand across her face. "Where's my dinner?"

"Heating."

She turned, then, shooting him an accusing glance. "You mean Hannah's cooking it."

He grinned, and she suddenly realized what she had always found so disturbing about his appearance. In his current guise, he looked much as Nick would have done had Nick matured rather than just decaying. "Guilty as charged." He peered more closely at her face. "Are you all right?"

"I am *not* crying!"

"Of course not. Are you cold?"

"A little."

He scooted closer, raising an arm and draping it about her shoulders. A palpable warmth seemed to radiate from him, probably something to do with magerie. After a moment, she relaxed, resting her head against the heavy, gold-stitched silk of that hideous dressing gown. It felt smooth and comforting beneath her cheek. His hand stirred lightly among the shortened tendrils of her hair, but otherwise he made no move to disturb her.

Back in the parlor, Nick's fingers began to pick out the familiar strains of a Deykharchie sonata—one of her favorites. Slowly at first, and then more confidently, the notes spilled from the piano in ripples of sound. Passionate and poignant, the old melodies tore at her heart, and she shut her eyes against the sudden, betraying spill of tears.

Absalom's voice echoed against the notes. "Tell me, Vi."

"Don't call me that." Her voice sounded tight, congested.

"I'm sorry. Vera. Tell me. It might help."

"Who? You or me?" she answered bitterly.

He didn't answer.

"I'm sorry," she said eventually. "That wasn't fair."

"Life isn't fair."

She managed a strangled laugh. "Cursed right."

Nick fumbled a phrase, lost the rhythm, and stumbled to a halt. After a moment, he picked up the melody again, seeming to make up in passion what he no longer possessed in skill. The piano whispered and wept with the changing flux of the music—at once soft and poignant, then charged with thundering intensity despite the occasional flubbed notes. She could almost envision him, eyes half-lidded, hunched over the keyboard as if he would devour it, his face rippling with the music's changing emotions. He had always played as he lived, with an all-embracing intensity. Nick never went half-measures at anything.

Another stumble of sour notes interrupted her reverie. "Can you imagine he actually used to be good at this?"

"If you ask me," her companion answered, "he's still very good. Just a little out of practice."

"Yes, practice. Do you realize there was a time when I thought Nick could do anything?"

"What happened?"

"He couldn't, apparently." And since Absalom didn't press her for details, she felt compelled to add, "They always warn you never to take personal jobs, you know."

"And do you ever listen?"

"Rarely. You're always the one to think you will prove the exception. That you can beat the odds. Of course, that's never the case. Ashkharon nearly destroyed me."

"But you got out of it."

"Only because I was older and wiser. Nick was twenty-four when fate got the better of him. He thought he could handle himself. Alas, so did I. He was young and cocky, then; it was the greatest part of his charm. Though I doubt he would have taken the job if he didn't feel he had something to prove."

"Prove? To whom?"

"His family. Himself. For some reason, Nick has always been ashamed of his Konastan heritage. I was the one who made him come back here, face his roots. For a while, I even felt responsible."

"Why? What happened?"

She shifted slightly against Absalom's shoulder, but didn't raise her face from the silk. "If I hadn't made him reconcile with his family, he would never have accepted the job that got them killed."

"You can't think like that," he said, almost sharply.

"I know that. Now." She was silent for a moment, then added softly, "I wonder if that's the reason he's still here."

"What?"

"Penance. Repentance. Like he owes it to his family to destroy his life in Ephanon because this is where he destroyed theirs. Funny, I never thought of it that way before."

The sweet strains of the sonata poured over her, then abruptly merged into a medley of music hall numbers in Nick's old, mercurial style. There was something oddly bracing about that sudden, raunchy spray of notes. She hummed a snatch of song.

"Remember this one, Vivi?" Nick called, his voice rustier than its fluid, youthful tones.

" 'The Sailor and the Goat'?" she answered. "Isn't that the one we sang under the Dean's window?"

"With one two many flagons of ale under our belts?"

"We nearly got ourselves expelled that night."

"Only I talked them out of it." His fingers danced over the melody.

"You?" she scoffed. "I was the one who went begging to Owen the next day."

"Yes. He always did like you best." And with barely a

pause, Nick thundered into the final strains of Benadene's Third Concerto. The angry, pounding chords hammered over the garden.

"What happened?" Absalom asked softly, under the sudden outpouring of musical fury.

Vera raised her head. "Are you sure you want to hear this?"

"Why?"

"It's not exactly a pretty story. It doesn't reflect well on any of us, I'm afraid."

He met her eyes unflinchingly in the moonlight. "And you believe I'll think any less of you for it?"

She bit her lip, listening to Nick's musical rage. They had, neither of them, made it out of those days unscathed.

"Very well," she agreed at last. "Fetch me my dinner and I'll tell you."

19

"Constantin? They named you *Constantin*?"

"Now do you see why I didn't want to return?" Nick growled.

Vera just laughed and pulled him down the dock. "What's the matter? I think Konasta is lovely."

"You didn't grow up here. Try spending time in one of the poorer fishing villages like this."

"Try spending time on the Radineaux estates."

"Like that's any punishment."

She had never been able to convince him that it was just as possible—and just as painful—not to belong on a grand estate as it was in an impoverished fishing village. "Still," she added, "I think it's sweet of you, moving your family to Ephanon."

"If they'll go," he said sourly.

She laughed. Nick wasn't usually so grouchy, but he hated being coerced. And the battle that had brought them here had been the ultimate test of wills. Having been cut off from her own family, Vera was determined that her lover should not make the same mistake. And since few people ever won a fight with Nick Navarin, she was feeling absurdly proud of herself for getting him this far.

It was, everyone agreed, what made them such a perfect pair. Nick Navarin could have had any woman he wanted, but Viera Radineaux was the only one who could match him, equal to equal.

She looked around her with curious eyes, eager to see where her insistence had brought them. Granted, the village of Evadre was everything Nick had said it would be, and more: dingy, filthy, and crawling with vermin, exactly the opposite of the tailored Radineaux estates. It was no wonder Nick had wanted to escape. But family was family, no matter how lowly born.

Nick had assured her that no one would be there to meet them but, as usual when it came to his family, he was wrong. His mother, Irini, was at the docks: a small, thin wraith of a creature who shared none of her son's flamboyant elegance. A life of hardship had boiled away all excess until what was left seemed no more than a shadow of a woman. She had iron-grey hair and black Konastan eyes, and there was a tracing of bruise on her cheek. When she spoke, Vera noticed that several of her side teeth were missing. But despite the outward appearance of a woman much abused by life, she nonetheless seemed to possess a core of iron.

Though perhaps that was simply an erroneous impression, given by a frame that had been whittled down to nothing more than bone and a few wisps of hard muscle, covered by skin cured to the consistency of fine leather.

Her son certainly appeared to think no differently, for the first words out of his mouth were, disgustedly, "Has Father been beating you again?"

Irini merely shrugged and exchanged a look with Vera, who knew instantly that she accepted the blows not because she had to, but rather to protect the rest of her family from their frequency. "Well, you know your father's temper," she said. "It is good to see you home again, Nikolaos."

She made no move to embrace her son, which Vera thought odd until she saw the prickly defensiveness of Nick's stance. His eyes were shuttered, his arms crossed guardedly across his chest, as if he sought to shield himself from these unpleasant reminders of his past.

Finding it oddly sad, Vera sought to bridge the gap. "Kyrinne Navarin," she said courteously, extending a hand. "It is a pleasure to meet you."

For the first time, Irini seemed flustered. "Who is this, Nikki?"

Nikki? Vera mouthed, in some amusement.

Her lover shrugged imperceptibly, as if to say: *I told you this wouldn't be a good idea.* "This is my lover, Mother. Vera. Viera Radineaux, from the Radineaux estates in Hestia."

"An aristocrat?" the woman breathed.

Vera shrugged, embarrassed. "Disinherited," she said.

His mother appeared not to notice the disclaimer. "Oh, Nikki, I always knew you were bound for greatness. An aristocrat! But," she added, suddenly flustered, "we have no lodging fine enough for the likes of you, Domina. I . . . Oh, dear. It is a pleasure to meet you, of course, but . . . Perhaps you shouldn't have brought her, Nikki."

"Perhaps neither of us should have come," Nick responded.

Irini's face crunched with hurt. "When your letter came—Taryn read it to us—I was so happy. I thought, my son is coming back at last. That is good; it is time. But . . ."

"Family is family," Vera inserted, before anyone could say anything they would regret. "Nikki wanted to come"— this with a stern look at her lover—"and I begged him to let me accompany him. Believe me, you needn't worry about the accommodations for either of our sakes. I have not been part of the aristocracy for a good many years, and Nick and I have both slept in far worse places during the course of our work. Remember that night we put up in that leaky barn, love?"

Nick snorted.

Irini's face relaxed into a grateful smile that made her ravaged features look almost pretty. "I thank you for that, Domina. It is good to have my son back at last. But— pardon me for asking—what is it you do for a living that brings in so much money yet has you sleeping in leaky barns?"

"We kill people," her son responded dryly.

Irini blinked and looked appealingly at Vera, who shrugged. "I have to admit that's a part of it."

Irini looked sharply from one to the other. "I will not deny the money you sent us has been helpful, Nikki. Your sisters are now in school, and your brother has been able to start his own business, but I have to ask. What you do . . . it's not illegal, is it?"

Vera and Nick exchanged an amused glance—hers not entirely free of question. She had not been aware he was sending money to Konasta.

"Not entirely," Nick answered with a grin.

Another quick glance—it never ceased to amaze Vera

how much information they could exchange with their eyes—and she added, in accord with their new agreement, "You've heard of the Guild, I take it?"

"You mean . . . The Guild?" Irini's whisper gave it suspicious capitals.

"Precisely so," her son responded. "Meet the Hawk and the Lammergeier. Apprentice stage only, of course. But not for long."

"Well," Irini said almost briskly. "That settles that."

Half a day later, Vera almost began to understand why Nick had tried to sever the ties with his family so completely. His father, Kostas, who arrived home shortly before the evening meal—a thick, oily fish stew, imperfectly prepared by the eldest daughter, Melantha—was a crass, belligerent bear of a man who seemed to sow discord the way other men sow smiles.

"Well, the reprobate has returned at last," he commented with a sneer as he thumped into his place at the head of the long, worn table. "Still full of your foppish airs, boy? Still think you're too good for the likes of us?"

"Kostas . . ." his wife began.

"Hush up, woman, and let the boy answer. Still think you're too good for us, Kyrin High and Mighty?"

"I am too good for you," Nick retorted. "Most of the people at this table are too good for you. *Father.*" His voice twisted the latter with a vicious scorn.

Irini cringed, and the eldest son, Stefan—a younger copy of his father with an even meeker wife—scowled. But Kostas merely slapped the table and roared with laughter. "So, the pup's developed a backbone after all these years! Will wonders never cease. Your mother says you kill people for a living, boy. Is that true?"

Nick nodded tersely.

"Bet you're thinking, even now, how good it would be to kill me. Ain't that right?"

"Don't tempt me," Nick responded, with a feral smile. If Vera hadn't known better, she would almost have thought he was enjoying himself.

Kostas took a bite of his stew, which Melantha had slapped down before him, then choked, spitting the mouthful across the room. "Faugh! This is revolting, girl." Vera couldn't help but agree. She had been pushing the unappetizing mess around her plate since it had been set before her. "No wonder your brother gets an aristocrat while we can't even get you married off to the village idiot!"

"Has it ever occurred to you that perhaps I don't care to get married?" Melantha flared. "And if you don't like the food, you can bloody well starve for all I care!"

"Tell him, Melly," Nick cheered.

"And what business is it of yours, Nikki? When have you ever done anything other than run away?" And tossing back a mane of thick, black hair, his sister scowled at him fiercely. There was such an iron resolution to her stance that Vera immediately itched to recruit her to the Guild.

"Run away?" Nick countered. "Like I haven't done what each of you secretly wishes you had the courage to do! I made something of myself."

Nick was glowing with that particular passion that he always reserved for his fiercest battles, and Vera suddenly understood where he had developed that larger-than-life magnetism that had always drawn her. A lifetime of fighting the chaos in this house couldn't help but solidify one's sense of self. Either that, or annihilate it completely.

She felt a sudden surge of pride that Nick had survived. His two youngest sisters, sitting wide-eyed and pale at the foot of the table, seemed unlikely to mirror his fate.

"So," his younger brother, Taryn, snapped, "having made such a success of yourself, why bother coming back? To rub our noses in it? You think you're the only one who can make good? Or bring in money?"

Nick merely laughed. "Yes, Mother said you had a job. So what games are the big boys playing?"

"No games." Taryn puffed himself up proudly. "I deal Dreamsmoke."

"Dreamsmoke?" Nick grinned. "That's illegal."

"Taryn," his mother began worriedly. "You never said . . ."

"Tell it to my buyers," the boy responded cockily. "Free smokes, Nikki?"

"I never say no."

"Zenia and Thea are in school," Irini said placatingly.

"Good for you," Nick said, and the twins smiled shyly. "Tell Vera what you've learned."

Immediately, Vera was surrounded by the press of two twelve-year-old bodies as the soft-voiced twins began to repeat their lessons.

"Yesterday we learned about the . . ."

". . . war for Konastan independence. Teacher said that the . . ."

". . . forces were divided between . . ."

It was uncanny how they completed each other's sentences, but there was something charming about it as well. Nodding and smiling at appropriate intervals, Vera kept one ear tuned to the conversation that flowed around them.

"So why did you come back," Taryn added, "if not to gloat?"

Because Vera insisted, she thought. *More fool me.* But Nick merely grinned and said, "To take you all away from this, if you want."

"Away from what?" Kostas sneered.

Nick gestured around the squalid hut. "This."

". . . five regiments, two hundred horsemen and three elephants," Zenia was saying. Or maybe Thea.

"Evadre's always been good enough for us," Kostas responded.

"And Ephanon wouldn't be any better?"

A sudden silence fell. Even the twins' soft confidences stuttered to a halt.

"Ephanon?" Irini breathed, with something like reverence in her face.

"That's what I said. Ephanon. I bought you a house."

"Ephanon has a university," Thea breathed. Or maybe it was Zenia.

"A whole new market," Taryn said.

"No more bloody fish," Melantha added.

"Ephanon," Irini said again, softly.

"Belt up, all of you," Kostas flared. "We are not going to Ephanon. Particularly not on that boy's tainted money!"

"A three-story house on Ione Square, two blocks from Sentenniel Street," Nick added.

Another silence.

"Why?" Irini asked at last.

Nick didn't answer, but Vera noticed that his cheeks were slightly pink.

"We are not going," Kostas roared, "and that is final!"

If Vera had any further thoughts on the matter, they were drowned out by the immediate outcry that met Kostas's words—support, not unexpectedly, from Stefan, and protest from the rest of the children.

But from the look in Irini's eyes, Vera had a feeling that the discussion was far from over.

20

"See, I told you they wouldn't go for it," Nick said later in the privacy of their room. They had, from the scowl on Stefan's face, displaced him and his wife, Rhea, but Vera didn't care. After the tensions of the day, she gloried in the comfort of Nick by her side. He was stretched, naked, atop the covers, and she couldn't keep her eyes from his body, as smooth and sculpted as a masterwork.

The Dreamsmoke cigarette he had begged from Taryn hung languidly between his lips, its tip glowing red as he drew the thick, sweet-smelling smoke into his lungs. His black eyes held that limpid look that Dreamsmoke lent him, his toughness mixed with a vulnerable sensuality.

He extended the smoke to Vera, exhaling in a sleepy cloud. She took her own drag, feeling the odd, cotton-wool swaddling of Dreamsmoke comfort enfold her. It was still a relatively new sensation to her, and at first she had been hesitant; tales of Dreamsmoke addiction had haunted her childhood. But according to Nick, every Konastan had been raised with the stuff, and the stories of its addictive powers were greatly exaggerated. A little willpower and common sense, and it was no worse than alcohol. Better, even, in that its effects wore off without any enduring misery.

And, in truth, since she had become involved with Nick, she had partaken on occasion and suffered no ill effects. So she no longer protested when he procured a fag—for unlike alcohol, which often made him giggly and impotent, Dreamsmoke relaxed the last bastions of his reserve and did wonders for his sex drive.

Besides, when you were twenty-two and in love, the consequences no longer seemed quite so dire.

So as she exhaled her own lungful of Dreamsmoke and

passed back the fag in the cozy warmth of his brother's chamber, she ran a lazy hand up the muscular smoothness of his chest and rested her cheek on his shoulder.

"I think you might be surprised," she answered.

"What about?"

"Ephanon. What else were we talking about?"

He grinned then, that mischievous twinkle that liquefied her joints. "You know, at this point, it doesn't matter whether they do or not. Still . . . Thank you, Vivi."

"For what?"

"For making me do this. It's not about the house, in the long term. It's about me making my peace."

"Or having your revenge."

"Whatever." He ran sensual fingers along the curve of her spine, and as usual she was infinitely well aware that those long, deft digits were killer's fingers; that they could as easily destroy as comfort. It made her feel oddly loved and protected, that she alone saw the soft side of Nick. That he trusted her enough to cradle her own assassin's body against his naked and defenseless side.

"All my life, I have been fighting against this house and everything it represented. The poverty, the cruelty, the end-less abuse. I always imagined it still had the power to harm me. But it doesn't any longer. By Varia, I almost enjoyed fighting with the old bastard tonight! And I owe it all to you, my love. For making me come back and face my fears. He's a disgusting old sot, isn't he?"

"He's not the finest of fathers, I'll admit," Vera said judiciously.

"Ah, diplomacy," he teased. "A noblewoman until the end."

"Hmph." She snorted. "You only love me for my breeding."

"And for the fact that it impresses the blazes out of my family. Little Nikki, sleeping with the aristos."

"Disinherited aristos."

"Whatever."

She snatched the cigarette from him in mock anger and took another puff.

"Ah, my lovely Vivi," he purred, coiling himself around her. He often became maudlin in his smokes. "Beautiful, intelligent, and deadly as a striking snake. I would love you even if you had risen from the gutter like me. We're a matched set, are we not?"

"Perfectly matched, my noble Lammergeier. Now, show me how high you can fly."

But apparently not all his insecurities were excised by one night of fighting with his father. For a month later, her face proudly bearing the last of Kostas's resistance, Irini brought her family to Ephanon. Thea and Zenia thrived, but the rest of the family did not. Kostas, once the king of his small fishing pond, was suddenly a tiny fry in a very large sea. Bitter and disillusioned, feeling the last of his authority slipping away, he soon spent his days drinking and smoking himself into an early grave in the worst of the illusion clubs. Stefan became fat and indolent, and took to beating his wife. Melantha, with no concrete target for her rebelliousness, joined a gang of street toughs, and spent as much time in jail as out. And as for Taryn, with the arrogance of youth, he assumed he could carry out his chosen trade in Ephanon as easily as in Evadre.

He was wrong. A brush with the master supplier later, and, Nick got a frantic summons from Irini. He and Vera had been in Konasta a time or two since the move, but somehow had never managed to visit the house in Ione Square. But now his family wanted to hire him, to teach the master supplier a lesson in tangling with the relations of a Guild assassin.

Owen had advised Nick strenuously against taking the job, even going so far as to offer the services of one of his current top operatives in Nick's place, but the Lammergeier had scorned the suggestion. He was mature enough to handle it and, to her shame, Vera had backed him.

"Honestly, Owen, how hard could it be? They intimidate him, he intimidates them. Nick's a big boy; he can take care of himself."

"How many times have I told you never to take jobs in which you have a personal stake? It's far too dangerous."

"Owen, you're overreacting. Vi's right. Besides, how much control can one man legitimately have over an entire industry?"

More than they had counted on, apparently—though at first that trip had seemed so perfect. True, Vera had initially been shocked at the change that had come over Nick's family, but she was never one to give up on anything without a fight. She got Stefan a job on one of the big shipping boats. She talked Melantha into applying to the Guild, and even gave her a few rudimentary lessons. Nick proposed to her, and she accepted. She even began to envision a life for herself in Konasta, settling into domestic routine and cutting back on Guild assignments until she got her family-in-law straightened.

But Taryn refused to be intimidated. Threats and counter-threats had been traded, and still the boy persisted in dealing. It wasn't as if his small trade in any way infringed upon the wider domain of the master supplier. But the boy refused to pay his cuts, and Nick still thought it was a battle he could win. The night the family house went up in flames, Vera began to suspect that they might be up against larger forces than she had suspected, but Nick and Taryn refused to back down, moving the family to an inn instead and going on with their business.

Over the weeks, the two had grown closer, discovering a new fraternal feeling in their determination not to be intimidated. And Vera, so help her, had seen this as a good sign, thinking that Nick had finally buried the last of his ghosts. Even on the day they had received their "last warning," they had both laughed.

Nick and Taryn had been a little drunk, and Nick had waved his glass of ale about in sodden determination, one arm around his brother's shoulders. "It's a question of morals," he declared. "No blasted trader is going to get the better of a Navarin."

"Or the Lammergeier," Taryn added. "Don't know what the blazes they're dealing with, eh, brother?"

"Not by a long shot."

"But don't you think they might be serious?" Vera cautioned. "After all, the last time they burned the house . . ."

"Vivi, my own, my love, are you honestly telling me you're going to let yourself be intimidated by manipulative scum such as these? They're only bluffing."

But they hadn't been, and as Vera and Nick lay entwined

in their attic bed across the city for what was to be the last time, the Navarin family had, one by one, been slaughtered in their inn.

Kostas had taken a knife to the gut. The twins had their eyes gouged out and their throats slit. Stefan was drowned, and Rhea and her baby were smothered. Irini and Melantha were raped and then bludgeoned to death. And as for Taryn, she didn't even want to think about what tortures he had undergone before he had finally died. One night, and everything that Nick had fought against—everything that he had loved and despised—was gone.

"What happened then?" Absalom asked softly, and Vera came back to the present with a bump. She had been so caught up in her memories that she had forgotten the mage at her side, the soft air that swept over a Konasta sixteen years in the future. She was thirty-nine now, a mature woman with a life of her own and an eternal grudge against the Dreamsmoke trade that had so wrecked the man who now sat in the next room, his fingers wandering brokenly over the piano.

It was a tender air this time, a lullaby or childhood lament, that set her heart to aching, so sad and innocent was its tune. It reminded her, intimately, of everything she had lost.

"As you see," she answered bitterly. "To this day, I don't know why Nick was spared—but perhaps that was the ultimate punishment. Because it ate him alive, the very trade he had tried to defy. Within a week, between the drink and the Dreamsmoke, I had lost him, though it took me longer to realize it. What could I say? I was young, and I still thought love could heal the world."

"And?"

"Vi?" Nikki's voice drifted plaintively over the garden. She hadn't even been aware he'd stopped playing. "I'm hungry."

"I'm not surprised," she called back, tartly. "You threw up everything for three days."

"There's food in the kitchen," Absalom added.

A shadow fell across them, and Vera turned to see Nick's hurt face contemplating them. She supposed it looked suspicious to see her curled in the mage's embrace, the streaks of tears still on her cheeks. But, blast it all, what right did Nikki have to feel betrayed? He had given up on her years ago, had repudiated the fact that her love could save him. He had no bloody right to look like a child whose favorite toy had just been snatched away.

As if aware of her thoughts, Nick turned meekly and disappeared toward the kitchen.

"And?" Absalom repeated.

Vera scrubbed angrily at her tear-streaked cheeks. "Obviously his guilt was too much. Or my love was not enough. Or maybe both. But after a month, I realized that there was nothing more I could do. Nick was dragging me down. I could either get on with my own life and leave him, or I could follow him into doom." She paused, then added, "It was the toughest decision I have ever made. I resolved never again to let someone have that much power over me."

"Is that why you never married or took a partner?"

"What do you think?" she answered bitterly.

Absalom was silent for a moment, then said, "I think you're an incredible woman. And I'm very glad you made an exception for me."

"So am I," she said, meaning it. "You're a blessing in disguise, Absalom."

"And what particular disguise might that be?" he answered, leering. And then he surprised her by leaning down to kiss her, lightly. It was the first time he had touched her in affection, and that feather-light brush of his lips disturbed her out of all proportion to its intensity. "So, it's not just the Dreamsmoke trade you're after," he said. "You want the master supplier."

"I want the master supplier. After all, it's the least I can do. I owe Nikki that much, for setting the whole thing in motion."

"It's not your fault."

The mage's voice was bracing in its assurance. "I know. But still, if I had left well enough alone, Nick would never have come back here, would never have attempted that reconciliation. And his family would still be alive."

"And you would never have been the top-rate operative you are now, being groomed for Guildmastership. And Jen wouldn't have met Thibault and become an assassin. And you and I would never have met in Ashkharon, and so would not be sitting here enjoying this fine Konastan evening."

"Oh, Absalom." She gave a shaky laugh. "You do have a way of putting everything in perspective. And as usual, you are right. But you do understand why I have to try, at least one more time, to save him?"

The mage's face, for an instant, looked infinitely sad. "Of course I understand. You will always follow your heart, and for that I value you. But I only hope . . ."

"What?"

"Do you want a piece of cake, Vi? Hannah baked it, and it really is quite delicious."

They both turned to see Nick framed once more in the doorway, holding out the confectionery like an offering. He was wearing an oddly hang-dog expression.

Vera sighed gustily, and pushed herself out of Absalom's embrace.

"Fine, Nikki, if you'll do one more thing for me."

"What's that?"

"Get me a plate and a fork. And play that Deykharchie piece I like so well again."

He grinned, almost like the Nick of old, and her heart inverted.

Blast him to perdition. She was getting too cursed old for all this emotion.

21

As usual, the attacks seemed to come in waves, and so for several days after the rogue's dual attack, life in House Soleneides settled down into a boring and uneventful routine. Thibault was closeted with Saul, and Jen measured her hours by dusting and chopping, gossiping with Kore and Jahnee, and occasionally clubbing with Gideon. Though admittedly that latter was coupled with a growing frustration, for she had begun to sense a core of reticence to the Golden Boy, or perhaps just a sense of potential reined in. There was a dangerous edge to him—which was more than half of what had attracted her—yet she had begun to feel there was a wall between them that she could not breach, behind which he kept his truer self concealed. And Jen was not used to being kept out of anything.

So as she straightened cushions and tidied mantels and counted knickknacks, she began to devise ways of breaking that barrier. And, in truth, the mindless routine of housework proved the ideal balm to keep her fingers occupied while her assassin's mind turned over the possibilities.

The only distraction was that Patroch, newly returned from the islands, seemed to be constantly underfoot, and his unique brand of awkward obnoxiousness was one she found particularly galling. She tried to vary her routine to avoid him, but every time she entered a room he would appear as if by magerie, scant minutes later, looking chagrined to find her there. Which was a travesty, for he somehow managed to turn every guilty flinch into a prurient leer, followed immediately by some tastelessly lewd comment until she became convinced he was stalking her.

It was, according to Kore and Jahnee, a common pattern with him, and she found herself forced, on more than one occasion, to explain that she was married—and to remind him, rather pointedly, of the size of her husband. Which was even more of a travesty, for she could have taken him in seconds had she not a disguise to maintain.

Blast Saul, and blast the Guild, she thought on more than one occasion. *This is the Dagger he's insulting! Two minutes after I'm off this job, I'm going to pound that soft, ineffectual face into pulp!*

But overall, there were compensations to the job. Being in Konasta was better than idling the winter away in frigid Ceylonde or provincial Bergaetta. And her Golden Boy was amazing, even if he never did let her spend the night. So what if she had to tidy houses for the privilege? There were worse fates—and even she had to admit that, after a month in Bergaetta with nothing to do but shop, she would truly have drowned Thibault under a tide of useless possessions.

And so it was that she found herself humming tunes as she dusted, not even regretting the lack of attacks. Which was how Thibault found her, several days after the failed assassination attempts, wielding her duster in the parlor.

"You seem to be adjusting well," he said, coming up behind her and wrapping his arms about her waist.

She broke off in mid-hum and swatted him with the duster.

"Ouch," he complained, mildly.

"Aren't you supposed to be working? Where's Saul?"

"In his study with Gideon and Aubrey. After all, even suhdabhars need an occasional break to check on their beloved wives." He turned her towards him.

"Thibault . . . what are you doing?" she demanded in a furious whisper.

He inclined his head toward the door in a barely perceptible gesture. Jahnee was sweeping the hall, her big eyes fixed on them. Jen stifled a sigh and tilted her face for Thibault's kiss.

He had the good sense to keep it short, but she still couldn't help noticing that his lips were softer than Gideon's, and that it really wasn't that far of a reach for all he seemed so tall. . . .

She jammed the butt of the feather duster into his ribs

to make him release her and moved away, her gaze fastened to the mantel while she willed the flush to recede from her cheeks, glad that Jahnee had disappeared down the hall.

And then she started, gazing intently at the narrow shelf above the fireplace, her interest no longer feigned. "That's funny," she said.

"What?" Thibault retorted, retreating to the couch and flopping down, his legs stretched out before him—promptly flattening all the cushions she had just plumped. But for once she was too distracted to chide him.

"When did this get here?" she asked, lifting a silvery sphere off the mantel and holding it out to him.

He sat up marginally straighter, the slightly knowing smile wiped off his face. Bless Thibault; he did seem to know when she needed him.

"What is it?" he asked.

"Cursed if I know. I was hoping you might have some idea."

"And why should I?" He accepted the sphere and turned it over in his big, deft hands. "I'm hardly the expert on aristocratic knickknacks, having never really possessed a mantel—let alone a house—on which to showcase them." He made as if to toss it back to her, but she quickly took a seat at his side, plucking the object from his fingers.

"Stop it, Thibault; I'm serious. Our employer asked me to look for anomalies, and that's what I've been doing. This wasn't here yesterday."

His eyes sharpened. "So what do you think it is?"

"Well, I'm wondering if it might not be some sort of weapon."

"In the house? How did it get here?"

"I don't know . . ." But before she could turn her attention to the question, he had the object out of her hands and halfway across the room.

"Bright blue blazes, Thib," she exclaimed, torn between annoyance and laughter, "this is no time for chivalry. What good will it do me if you get yourself killed?"

And indeed, her partner was now standing uncertainly on the rug with the object cradled gingerly in one hand, looking about in some confusion.

"Give me that," she added, and snatched it back. Then, tilting the sphere into the band of sunlight that poured in through the wide windows, she examined it more closely. It was about the size of her fist, and there were fines lines in the silver that she suspected were joins, creating a pattern rather like a furled flower. An elaborate tracery of etched swirls and spirals covered the whole.

"Well, it's a pretty thing, I'll grant you. And it looks as if it's meant to open. I wonder what's inside?" She ran her fingers over the surface in search of some sort of button or hinge, but the globe was smooth as a marble. "Blast it." She levered a fingernail under one of the petals and tried to pry it up.

"Jen!" Thibault exclaimed in horror, wresting the globe from her and tossing it into the fireplace. It pinged off the bricks and fell noisily into the grate, nestling between two unburned logs. Almost as an afterthought, he threw open the flue.

"What did you do that for?" she demanded.

"And who has the suicidal impulses now? What if it *is* a weapon? And you had activated it?"

She felt immediately chastened—and not a little shaky— but couldn't help saying, "Then you'd only have one more of my messes to clean up after. Though admittedly a pretty spectacular one."

"This is not a laughing matter, Jen."

"No?" She offered a tentative grin. "You know, we're both going to feel pretty foolish when this turns out to be a music box or something."

"Well, better foolish than scraping your intestines off the carpet. What in blazes were you thinking?"

"Apparently not much—or so you'd have me believe," she flared in response. "I was simply trying to figure out what we were up against."

"At the cost of your life?"

"Oh, do hush, Thibault; nagging me is not going to solve anything. And don't talk to me about acting impulsive. You could have set it off just by hurling it." And picking up a poker, she began prodding at the globe, trying to dislodge it from the logs. "As it is, you probably broke the blasted thing. Whatever it is. And what we are going to tell Saul now is anyone's—"

There was a faint pop, and the next thing she knew she was halfway across the room with Thibault's big body crushing her to the floor. He was stretched atop her like a felled tree, his arms crossed protectively over her head. Her cheek was ground into the carpet, the poker buried uncomfortably in her ribs.

"Thibault, you great big oaf. Get off!"

He levered himself tentatively onto one elbow, which only served to mash her lower body more firmly into the floor, and stared incredulously at the fireplace.

With a grunt of pain, she shoved at him, and he shifted fractionally.

"Look," he said, pointing.

She turned her head in time to see a thick cloud of yellow smoke disappearing up the chimney. The blackened remains of the globe, its petals unfolded, nestled between the logs like a charred lotus. A faint curl of ocher rose from the ruins.

Jen drew a shaky breath, then rolled over to look up at her partner. Their eyes met and locked for a long tense moment.

"Is everything all right in there?" Jahnee's voice filtered in from the hall. "I thought I heard shouting, and something fell . . ."

Jen and Thibault turned to stare guiltily at the door.

Jahnee's face poked tentatively around the jamb, and when she saw Thibault sprawled atop Jen, her eyes went wider than ever.

"Oh, you two . . ." she said, clearly torn between amusement and embarrassment. Her face whisked from view, and Jen could hear her footsteps receding down the corridor.

Slowly, Jen let out the breath she had been holding.

Thibault's body still covered her like a blanket, rooting her to the earth, but for once she didn't have any desire to move.

"Well?" he said eventually, seeming to drag the words up from a deep well.

All manner of responses flickered through her head,

ranging from accusation to apology. But all she said was, "It just goes to show you . . ."

"What?" He seemed to be grinding his teeth.

"That I was right. It seems our rogue is not finished with his work yet."

And with Thibault's incoherent bellow echoing in her wake, she wiggled out from under him and beat a hasty retreat.

Nonetheless, it was a much chastened Jen who bearded Saul in his den an hour later and confessed the whole thing. She didn't know quite what reaction she had expected, but she needn't have worried. Saul was his usual charming self, accepting her explanations with equanimity from her first, tentative: "Um, I believe there's been another attempt . . ."

In fact, all he said to that was, "Indeed? Tell me everything."

And so she had, with Gideon nodding and smiling encouragingly, and Aubrey hunched in his armchair, frowning querulously.

"I'm amazed Sauron Telos still has funds left for his vendetta," the latter commented sourly, when Jen had finished. "For a two-bit dealer, he certainly seems to have amassed a fortune."

"Which he is squandering on me," Saul said. "I'm flattered."

"Is that how you measure your success?" Gideon quipped. "By gauging how much people are willing to expend in order to eliminate you?"

"Well, it's certainly one method," Saul returned cheerfully. Then, turning to Jen, he added, "I'm just amazed you noticed it when you did."

"As I said, that's my job. And don't let my junior status in the Guild fool you. I may be one of their newest recruits, but I spent my life training under a master. Observation has always been one of my stronger points."

"But not considered action?" Aubrey asked tartly. "You should have brought the device straight to Saul; we might have been able to learn something from it."

"What, and risk setting it off in the vicinity of its intended victim?" Gideon countered, winking surreptitiously at Jen. "The threat was neutralized. What more do you want?"

"To know how it got there, for one."

"Yes, Thi . . . I mean . . . Ty and I were discussing that."

"Perhaps it was spirited in by magerie," Gideon suggested.

"Perhaps, but that implies a prior knowledge of the house to place it. As near as I can figure, the rogue has never penetrated past the kitchens."

"Who else has access to the house?" Aubrey demanded.

They all considered this in silence for a moment. Then, "It's a mystery to reflect on," Saul concluded, "but for now, one that has been averted by the Dagger's quick thinking."

Jen flushed. "Well, more due to the Cloak, actually. I may have set it off, but it was my partner who prevented it from killing us both. Or killing us all. If he hadn't thought to set it in the fireplace and open the flue before I started poking at it . . ." Her words trailed off with a shudder.

"Well, regardless of who claims responsibility," Saul decreed, "the disaster has been averted. The mystery will save."

Gideon grinned at her—a gesture Jen knew was intended to be reassuring, but which still left her feeling oddly hollow. There remained a feeling of cotton batting around her brain, a sense of sawdust packed under her skin. Worse, the ghost-pressure of Thibault's body still lingered on her own, and she found herself clutching at the sensation like a comforting blanket.

There were disadvantages to always being right, she reflected, as Saul dismissed her after a few more questions.

Gideon trailed her to the door, somehow managing to turn the gesture—which in Thibault would have seemed abject—into one of dignity and poise. Which, perversely, annoyed her more than ever. "The Cauldron tonight?" he whispered under the guise of opening the portal.

She paused for a moment, startled to realize that the last place in Varia she wanted to be tonight was in Gideon's bed. Or perhaps it was the inevitable act of getting thrown out of Gideon's bed after that rankled. She whispered back, "Thanks, but no. Not tonight, I think."

A brief flash of anger hardened his eyes, subsumed almost instantly beneath his usual urbane charm. But for a moment her heart soared in triumph for having penetrated that wall, if only for a second. Perhaps the problem was that she had been too easy; too willing. Sophisticates like Gideon required a little more mystery and challenge.

In the future, she would endeavor to play harder to get.

22

Thibault had grown used to the nightly routine, and by now could face most of it with equanimity. Although there were times—such as turning his back while Jen changed, brutally attuned to the whisper of fabric puddling around her feet, catching tantalizing glimpses of her in the filthy glass of the window—that the pain of the impossible lanced through him. But mostly he was learning to ignore it, and was bitterly proud of himself for the victory.

There had been times, during the earliest stages of their partnership, when he couldn't imagine a life without her. When he couldn't conceive of a time that his proximity and devotion wouldn't wear down the walls between them. For how could such loyalty go unrewarded? But, as usual, fate had proved fickle. And after three-quarters of a year continuously in her presence, he was beginning to understand that Jen's essential nature would never change. To her, men were nothing but diversions, something to be taken and accepted as her due.

Unlike him, whose very identity was caught up in what Jenny thought and what Jenny did. He had built a future around a hope as transient as the shifting decor of the illusion clubs.

He sighed.

"What is it?" Jen said brightly, obviously recovered from whatever reflectiveness came in the wake of her brush with death. Clad in only a nightgown, she undid the tie that held her plait and shook out her hair, sighing in pleasure as the last of the strands unfurled. She turned and tossed him the hairbrush, and he tried not to notice the way her breasts shifted under the fabric. He remembered all too clearly the feel of her body under his as he crushed her into the rug.

Clamping down on his unruly thoughts, he gestured her onto the bed and began running the brush through her hair. He supposed he should feel thankful that she wasn't out celebrating with Gideon. Still, he couldn't help saying, "I thought facing your mortality was supposed to be a sobering experience."

"What mortality? Nothing dire happened."

"No thanks to you." His voice was sour.

"Ouch." She pulled away from his ministrations. "Mind not ripping my hair out in your zeal?"

"Sorry," he said—not at all contritely, he supposed. His hands stilled for a moment, then resumed their labors.

"Besides," she added, "much as you might disapprove of my methods, at least I proved my point."

"Which is?"

"That our rogue assassin is far from finished."

He snorted.

"What?" she demanded, irately.

Despite himself he laughed, shaking his head. "Only you, Jenny, could turn an occasion for potential gratitude into a first class 'I told you so.'"

She turned and grinned, momentarily startling him by locking her arms around his neck. He stiffened and she released him, dropping a teasing kiss on the point of his nose instead. "Thank you for saving my life, Thibault," she said. "But I'm still right."

He stared at her incredulously. "What's it like?" he demanded.

"Always being right?" She grinned, vastly misinterpreting his question. "Trying, of course, but one must endeavor to bear up under adversity." Then she presented her back to him and gave a little shimmy, making her hair ripple and dance.

He picked up the brush again, reflecting that his real question was: *What is it like being you?* Or: *What is it like to never know a moment of doubt—even when you are so blatantly wrong?* For he couldn't help feeling that she *was* wrong, despite all evidence to the contrary. Despite the fact that trusting his own instincts wasn't something he excelled at.

"What now?" she exclaimed, sounding almost offended.

She was becoming too attuned to him. For a minute, he was tempted to let it go—to leave her safe in her delusions—but he was still angry at her for risking her life so foolishly. He didn't know what had set the device off, but he couldn't help feeling that her meddling hadn't helped. And, coupled with the fact that he knew there was something to this whole affair he was missing—some vital clue that would cast it into a more comprehensible light—he was rather less than charitable.

"I still think you're wrong about the assassin. I can't shake a feeling that this is not part of the same picture; that we're looking at something else entirely."

"Such as?"

"For one, how the device got into the room in the first place."

"Thibault, we've been over and over this. The house isn't alarmed during the day. Anyone could have gotten in."

"Past you and all the servants?"

"I can't be everywhere. And perhaps the rogue was under an invisibility spell when he planted it." She paused, then added, "By Varia, what if he starts using invisible *devices* next?"

A long silence reigned. Then, "Maybe you should get an anti-illusion amulet," Thibault said.

She grinned. "I already have one of Absalom's. I liberated it from Vera's box. I'm going to start wearing it tomorrow. Happy?"

"No. Because something about this still doesn't feel right. Not like the other attacks."

"And the other attacks *did* feel right?"

"You know what I mean."

"Actually, I don't, so why not enlighten me?" There was a hint of condescension in her tone that made him bristle. Why did she always assume that his instincts were inferior to her own? Unless it was the fact that, up until now, he had always deferred to her?

He cast his mind back over the afternoon's events. His sudden flash of fear as Jenny had juggled a potentially lethal weapon and tried to pry it open. An unavoidable surge of smugness when his pleas for caution had been justified, followed by a sudden, sharp stab of guilt. And the shameful

knowledge that, even in the midst of danger, he had enjoyed the feeling of her body beneath his own.

It was no wonder he'd been on edge for the rest of the
day.

Nor was he alone in those sentiments. Word of the potential attack must have filtered out faster than he imagined, for all of family Soleneides had seemed jumpy when
they gathered in that chamber for their pre-dinner drinks.

Well, perhaps not all of them, Thibault amended upon
further reflection. Saul seemed unaccountably amused, and
Stavros' dour demeanor would have given a rock a good run
for its money. Lydea was querulous and demanding, but
then Lydea was always querulous and demanding. But Patroch—younger or less gifted with the fine art of dissem-
bling—kept glancing involuntarily at the mantel and
flinching visibly every time his grandfather's name was
mentioned.

Nor would the servants go near the place, and Lydea was
further discomfited by having to pour her own drink. Which
was perhaps why she snipped more than ever at Saul for
his nightly consumption of brandy. Still, such behavior was
nothing he could point out to Jen as overtly suspicious.
Or even out of the ordinary. So, "I don't know," he said
again, helplessly.

"Well, you'll have to be more specific if you're going to
convince me."

"I can't be. I don't have anything more specific."

She arched an eyebrow. "And you lecture me about my
crazy instincts?"

"Except that, unlike you, I don't persist in hanging my
life on those instincts."

"That's not fair," she said sharply, pulling away from him
and springing from the bed. Almost absently, she gathered
up her half-brushed hair and began to plait it into its
nightly tail.

The old, familiar platitudes rose to his lips but died unut-
tered. Instead, he found himself saying, "Why not? It's
about time you opened your eyes to the truth. You've spent
your whole life getting everything you wanted—mostly delivered on a silver platter—and now you take it for granted
that the world revolves around you. That everything that

happens does so by your contrivance. And for your benefit." *Where were these words coming from?* a part of him wondered. He heard them pouring from his lips in stunned disbelief, yet he seemed unable to stop them. Forth they came—bitter as bile, and as caustic. "Some of us haven't been so lucky."

"Oh," she retorted, "like you can talk? Don't pull your righteous peasant act on me, Thibault! You benefited from Vera's bounty as much as I did. Look at you! A house, an independent income, and five hundred a job as an up-and-coming assassin. If you're so bloody unhappy, why don't you go back and sulk in Sylvaine's cottage like the poor, oppressed peasant you are rather than wintering in Ephanon with me?"

"Because who else is going to keep you out of trouble?"

"Please." Her voice dripped scorn. "I don't need your dog-like devotion. Do you know how wearying it can be, constantly having someone running herd over you like you're incapable of looking after yourself? Like you're some sort of simpleton child who can't even make a proper decision?"

"I hardly think that's justified, Jenny . . ."

"Justified? *Justified?* Now who's the arbiter of truth? If you can't take it, Thibault, don't dish it out!"

"After all the scrapes I pulled you out of . . ."

"Scrapes that were more than half your fault because I was trying to bloody *impress* you—Varia only knows why I bothered!" The words, quite literally, stunned him, but she was not done yet. "And as for everything going my way, do you really think I wanted Vera to risk her life in Ashkharon just so I could get a job? That I wanted to chase every wrong lead in Arrhyndon so that what should have been a three-day job turned into a three-month disaster? That I want to be thrown out of Gideon's bed every night like I'm nothing more than some cheap whore?"

Her deliberate crudity struck him like a blow. And while he would have preferred not to have been reminded of that particular complaint, he was horrified to see the betraying glitter of tears in her eyes. She always seemed so tough and competent, he sometimes forgot she was only eighteen. Part of him longed to gather her up and murmur the soothing platitudes he knew she wanted to hear, but the angry accusations were still too brittle between them. She would not have tolerated his touch—and, besides, a deeper part of him refused to utter the words. He had spent too many years smoothing her ruffled feathers; he was tired of being the one who always made the peace. Tired of being—*face it, Thibault*—her devoted cur.

So, "There, you see, Jenny?" he said instead. "It always comes back to you in the end."

A long, fraught silence stretched between them.

Eventually, she scrubbed her fists roughly over her eyes. "I thought I knew you, Thibault. I thought you were something better. But I guess you've proved for once and for all that while you can take the peasant out of the gutter, you can't take the gutter out of the peasant. Turn off the lights whenever you like; I'm going to sleep."

They retreated to their separate beds in silence, and Thibault cued off the lights.

The tiny room was unaccountably cold that night.

"What's the matter?" Aubrey demanded. He had never seen the Golden Boy looking so distracted, and especially not on a night like this.

This week the club was swallowed beneath the sea. A diffuse green light, rippled with currents, mimicked the waves, and a whale lolled ponderously in the shallows where once a dragon had roared and blasted out the hour. Anemones bloomed like exotic flowers, and heaped corals mounded into weird, attenuated figures. Seaweed waved. A pod of dolphins arrowed past, their sleek bodies punching through a school of fish, sending silver bodies darting.

The balcony table where Gideon and Aubrey sat was dripping with weed like an old man's beard, cupped in a prodigious shelf of rock and coral. When Gideon spoke, bubbles rose from his mouth, so flawless was the illusion. A fish, brightly colored as a parrot, wriggled past his left ear. "The bitch turned me down," he said. *"Me."*

"So? You never liked her much anyway, right? Unless . . ." A thought occurred. "You're not . . . by Varia, you're not *falling* for her, are you?"

"That insipid bit of fluff? Of course not! But she was supposed to be better behaved than that."

"Incapable of turning you down, you mean?"

Gideon's grin flashed out: the one that could make you lie down and die. "Precisely."

Foolish girl, indeed, Aubrey thought. But aloud he said, nonchalantly, "Shit happens." Predictably, Gideon laughed. "She's not worth wasting your anger on. So, tell me, what do you think of our mages' offering?"

"Flawless as always. Except . . . Don't you think that whale is a tad too phallic?" Gideon pitched his voice louder for the benefit of one of the lurking mages, who, in a fit of pique, tossed an illusory octopus at his head.

Aubrey grinned.

"So, any other business?" Gideon asked eventually, as the silence stretched out. "Or are we free for the night?" He was making lewd gestures at the octopus, which had settled down beside his drink. The octopus was returning as good as it got. Better, really, with the extra arms.

Aubrey swallowed. "No. I mean . . . yes. That is, we're done."

"You're lying," Gideon said. He poked at the octopus with his fork, and it vanished in a cloud of noxious, black ink. He waved a hand through the muddied water and the mage, reluctantly, cleared it. "Don't you have customers to entertain?" Gideon added, pointedly. The parti-colored fish circled back and took an illusory nip out of his ear, then darted away, mouth gaping in a piscine grin.

Aubrey sensed more than saw the mage move off.

"Now, Aubrey," Gideon continued, returning his attention to his associate. "What is it you're not telling me?"

Aubrey grimaced. "We got a disturbing request today. I'm thinking of turning it down."

"Why? How much is it paying?"

"He's willing to go as high as two thousand."

Gideon whistled. "And you want to turn it down? What for?"

"The subject matter."

"You don't think he's our secret killer, do you? Honestly, Aubrey, I'm beginning to sense an obsession . . ."

"No, it's not our favorite lunatic."

Gideon's mouth tightened. "What is it, then?"

"He wants a six-year-old."

"Oh." A long moment of silence stretched out. And just when Aubrey was convinced he had finally uncovered Gideon's moral threshold, the latter said, calmly, "That's not going to be easy. Not many six-year-olds in the public jails."

"Gideon, you're not . . ."

"Considering it? Of course I am! For that kind of money . . . Check around; see what you can find. We may get lucky."

"And if not?"

"We'll embrace that problem when we get to it. But tell the client we're on the case."

Swallowing against a sudden bout of nausea, Aubrey prepared to do his bidding.

A feather-light touch on his wrist wakened Thibault—not that he had really been asleep. He had tossed restlessly throughout the night, trying to figure out how to retract his words without seeming weak. After all, a man had to maintain his dignity. Still, the hours of doubt and recrimination had stretched interminably, and so he was almost surprised to find the room still swallowed in darkness as his eyes popped open. It was a heavy darkness, unrelieved by the moon and compressed by the narrow alley. Jen was no more than an indefinable blot against the blackness.

"Thibault, I . . ."

"I'm sorry," they blurted together, and Jen snuffled a laugh.

He reached out blindly and enfolded her, drawing her down onto the pallet. Her arms locked convulsively around his neck, and her head settled into the hollow of his shoulder. It was all right; everything was all right. And he hadn't had to come to her . . .

"I am selfish, I know," she said. "And I think of myself far too often." Her voice was oddly thick, and he reached out a wondering finger to find her cheek wet with tears. Not because of him; not because of what he said . . .

He tried to inject some levity into his voice. "And I'm a stubborn bloody peasant, one step up from the gutter . . ."

"No, you're not. You're the greatest. Sometimes I wonder why you put up with me. But the fact that you do . . . well, sometimes it's the only thing that gives me any hope I am redeemable."

It was the nicest thing anyone had ever said to him, and it stunned him speechless. He fumbled for words.

"Your opinion matters more than anything, Thibault," she went on, unaware of his struggle. "It always has."

He managed to unstick his throat long enough to croak, "I shouldn't have said those things . . ."

"No. You were right. About everything. But that's why we make such a good team. Who else would have the gumption to tell a trained assassin, to her face, exactly what is wrong with her?"

He laughed at that, as she had intended, and she relaxed against him, her stranglehold loosened from his neck. Her voice was oddly tentative as she said, "I still don't believe our assassin is finished, or that the device we found today was in any way different from all those other attempts—mainly because my own instincts, which we both agree are somewhat overdeveloped, tell me the opposite—but I do trust you. If you can prove to me that this is different, I'll believe you."

"And if you can find me proof that our assassin is still operative, I'll believe that as well.

"Good," she said softly, "because that's exactly what I intend to do tomorrow." And her tone was so humble and yet so determined all at once that he stifled a grin. That was Jen; a creature of contrasts to the end.

It was as inevitable as breathing, their lips meeting briefly in the dark. He tasted the salt tears on her mouth, and then she was laughing—a sudden, spontaneous explosion of schoolgirl giggles.

"What?" he said.

"Jahnee's face," she gasped. "When she came in and thought we were doing it on the rug . . ."

He paused for a moment and then roared, their mirth rising into the darkness like a song. And he knew then that everything was going to be all right.

23

"Good morning."

Vera looked up from her toast and tea. Nick was looking more like himself—although, admittedly, a little more ragged around the edges. The ravages of addiction still showed in his pouchy, yellowed eyes and the haggard lines that drew his face into unfamiliar angles. But at least his hair was washed and trimmed, and he had made a passable attempt to shave. He was clad in clean pants and a shirt that she had last seen in Absalom's luggage. His feet, as lean and graceful as she remembered, were bare.

He flashed her a grin that bore shades of his old insouciance, and she found herself smiling back.

"Mind if I sit?"

She waved him to the seat in silence. It was a lovely morning, one of those ineffably fine days when potential seemed to ride the breeze. The sun was rising in a cloudless sky, sparking glints off the harbor waters, and there was a crisp saltiness to the air that seemed to sweep all cobwebs away. Absalom had transported one of the tables to the patio, and even the overgrown tangle of Hannah's garden couldn't detract from the mood.

Narrowing her eyes against the sun, Vera watched Nick sit and pull the teapot across the table, pouring himself a cup. With an ancient familiarity that should have irritated her yet oddly didn't, he reached over and helped himself to her toast.

Sometimes, she reflected, it *was* too blasted easy to go home. Seeing him sitting across the table like this, she had the sudden feeling they had never been apart. Yet, hand in hand with that sensation, was another, newer acceptance. Or perhaps recognition. In his presence, her heart no longer clenched so painfully, reminding her of all that could have been and never was. And while a corner of her did still belong to Nick—and always would—she was pleased to discover that it was a very small corner, indeed.

From the distant kitchens, Vera could hear the echo of laughter and the lilt of Absalom's exaggerated drawl as he worked his charms upon their hostess. She smiled—although it took her a moment to identify the feeling that twined so palpably in the wind. It was peace. For the first time in a long time, she felt at peace.

Thus she was able to say, without any rancor, "How long has it been since you've seen the daylight?"

"Eons, I think," Nick answered, biting into a corner of the toast. He ate with the same catlike neatness, a minimum of fuss and crumbs. "You're getting grey."

She resisted the urge to touch her hair. "So are you. We're neither of us getting any younger, you know."

"Mmm. How long has it been?"

"Sixteen years. I'm thirty-nine, now," she added, after a pause.

"Which makes me . . ."

"Forty."

"Oh," he said, softly. Then, "I had kind of lost count."

She was silent.

"Have I thanked you yet, Vi? For saving me? Because it means a lot . . ."

"Then try to make it stick this time," she answered, with a trace of bitterness.

"I'll try," he responded, but his voice lacked conviction. "You always were better than me, Vi."

"Why? Because I was the aristocrat and you were the fisherboy?"

"No, because you were Viera Radineaux, and I was Nick Navarin. You were always the strong one, much as I tried to deny it. And now look at us. You are being trained to take over the Guild, and I am . . ."

"Keeping the Guild in business by supporting the Dreamsmoke trade. Which is illegal, in case you hadn't recalled."

He managed a sickly smile.

"Is this a party for two, or can anyone join?" Absalom's

cheerful voice interrupted them. He was carrying a steaming platter, and was still wrapped in that hideous dressing gown—which, amazingly, looked even worse in the daylight.

Vera grinned, and pushed a chair towards him with her foot. "Pet mages are always welcome."

He grimaced comically, and placed the tray down on the table. It was laden with fresh-whipped eggs and muffins, olives, and cheese. She groaned.

"I think we're bringing out Hannah's maternal instincts," the mage said. "I suggest you eat something. She'll be offended if you don't."

"I don't think we need worry," Vera said dryly. "Nick looks capable of taking care of it all by himself."

And, indeed, Nick was tucking avidly into the repast, piling his plate with Hannah's bounty. He looked up almost sheepishly at her words. "In addition to everything else, do you know how long it's been since I've eaten a decent meal?"

"Last night?" she retorted.

"Apart from that, I mean."

"Let the poor boy eat in peace," Absalom drawled, leaning back in his chair and nudging her feet with his own. "And be thankful that one of us has an appetite."

"Well, I don't know how he could," Vera retorted, nudging him back, "when you're sitting here still wrapped in that dreadful creation. It's enough to put anyone off their food."

The mage blinked at her in feigned hurt. "I'm quite attached to the thing."

"If you even try to take it back with you . . ." Vera threatened.

Absalom just grinned. "So, what were you two arguing about when I arrived?"

"The Dreamsmoke trade."

"And your desire to shut it down, one presumes?"

"Well," she conceded, "I hadn't advanced quite that far in my argument, yet."

Nick choked on a bite of egg and stared incredulously from one to the other. "You're *serious*?"

Vera could feel her lips curve in a smile. "Absolutely."

"And, unless I miss my guess," Absalom added, "you are going to help."

"Me?" Nikki spluttered, for once inelegant. "What can I possibly do? I'm not an assassin anymore, remember?"

"Clearly. But you are an addict. And you know the dealers."

"Only the minor ones, I assure you."

"Every trail leads somewhere, if you follow it far enough back."

Nikki flinched. "You want the master supplier."

"Indubitably."

"But . . . You remember what happened the last time we went up against him."

"All too well. That's why I want him."

"I can't go through that again, Vivi. I can't."

She regarded him for a long, silent moment. He flushed.

"Absalom, feel free to jump in here any time you want," Vera added levelly.

"Why? I think you're sufficiently persuasive all by yourself."

"One way or another, Nikki, I am going to do this. It would be easier with you, but I'm perfectly prepared to do it without you."

He glanced between her and Absalom, his jaw slack, an uneaten bite of egg depending from his fork. She could almost see the thoughts stirring sluggishly behind his eyes. And then he sagged slightly, and she knew she had him.

To the uninitiated, the assassin's life was one of mystery, intrigue, and endless adventure; Vera knew better. More than half of it was drudgery and interminable boredom. And waiting. Lots and lots of waiting.

Which was what she was doing now, shadowed under the umbrella of Absalom's invisibility spell. Waiting for the Dreamsmoke trader Nick had fingered to make a move. They had sent Nick in earlier to make a buy, hoping to exhaust the dealer's supply. Figuring that it was best to lie with the truth—or as close to it as possible—they had not altered Nick's essential story much. Besides, enough of the regulars of the Rogue's Gallery had seen him leaving in company. So he had claimed that an old friend had located

him and was trying to rehabilitate him. That he had taken
the money he was meant to spend on food and clothing
and was using it to maintain his habit. All the while under
Vera's vigilant—and invisible—gaze.

They had trailed him into the Rogue's Gallery under
Absalom's spell, and Nick had seemed more disconcerted
that he could not see his companions than that he was
shortly to be placed in the path of temptation.

"Are you still there?" he would whisper on occasion,
rotating his head in a frantic, pointless search. And would
invariably flinch when Vera's invisible hand rose to clamp
his elbow.

"We're right here. Now, relax, and stop making a spectacle of yourself." Though Vera had to admit that his nervous
peering over shoulders only added credence to his story.
To the uninformed, he seemed a man apprehensive about
being caught. As well he should be, she thought grimly.

Absalom's spells were working with their usual efficiency,
fooling even the standard body count spells which prevented the masses from sneaking into the clubs as they
were doing, in invisible guise. Handy to have a bastard
mage on your side, Vera reflected for the umpteenth time.
The door guard didn't so much as blink—not even when
Nick stumbled from a slightly overzealous push.

"Why did you do that?" he demanded in a hurt whisper,
once they were inside.

"You were hesitating," Vera informed him. "Now, which
one is it?"

"That man over there. See? In the ragged cap . . ."

"Well, then. What are you waiting for?"

Nick sighed audibly. "Where will you be?"

"Right over there, by that post," Vera said. "Watching
you."

"Don't you trust me?"

"Not by half. Besides, it's my money. Now, move."

Nick sauntered off with obvious reluctance, and she felt
the mage exhale, his breath warm against her cheek.

"What?" she demanded, turning to regard him. They
were under a shared spell, so she alone could see him,
lurking balefully over her right shoulder. His dark eyes
were reproachful.

"Must you be so hard on him?"

"Sorry. Force of habit."

"That's all very well and good. But it's not me you should be apologizing to."

"Oh, stop being such a sanctimonious prig."

The mage chuckled.

"I swear," she added, "you do it deliberately. Just to annoy me."

"That, of course, is my primary pleasure in life," Absalom declared, and she hit him. "Ouch. Now, shall we take up our appointed position? And maybe try to be a bit quieter? The place may be noisy, but we're not exactly inaudible."

Vera nodded and followed Absalom across the club, propping her shoulder against the post.

"Do you want a drink?" Absalom asked.

"Why? How long can this possibly take?"

"You might be surprised," the mage answered.

"Very well, then, but be . . ." Her voice trickled off as Absalom winked from view.

"Be what?" he prompted, from a foot to her left.

She stifled an involuntary yelp and frowned. No wonder Nick had been disconcerted. ". . . careful," she finished. "What the blazes did you do?"

"Uncoupled the spell. Otherwise we'd suck everyone between us into an invisible well. Back in a flash."

She grumbled something unintelligible, and watched as Nick approached the dealer and negotiations commenced. He seemed unduly nervous—though she wasn't sure how much of that was genuine and how much was an act.

"Should we have had him buy more, do you think?" Absalom asked, winking back into view.

She jumped, and scowled at him anew. He was bearing two brimming mugs of ale. He grinned, and offered her one. "I can't vouch for the quality, alas."

"Where did you get this?"

His dark eyes twinkled in answer.

"Oh, no. You didn't . . ."

"Steal them?" Absalom answered cheerfully. "Of course not. After all, it's not my fault the bartender wasn't watching what he was doing . . ."

She gave a heartfelt groan, then stepped hastily aside as a drunken patron swayed against their post, almost colliding with her invisible body.

"Here. Perhaps we'd be safer under this plant-thing," Absalom advised, steering her into a more advantageous position against the wall.

"Right," she said, when they were settled. She took a pull of her ale. It was of indifferent quality; not the worst she'd tasted, but certainly nothing spectacular. She turned her attention to Nick instead, who was surreptitiously exchanging her marks for a small, flat package.

"Here we go," she said, handing her drink back to Absalom.

The former Lammergeier strode away from the dealer, glanced nervously about, then whispered, "There, I'm done. Are you happy?" at the now-vacant post.

Vera grinned and intercepted him, slipping the package deftly from his hand. "Very," she said. "And thanks. Now, stop talking to the walls."

He started. "What are you doing over *there*?"

"Enjoying a drink, courtesy of Absalom. Now, scamper. We'll take it from here."

"Are you sure? I . . ."

"Positive. We'll meet you later, at the appointed rendezvous." She paused for a moment, then added, "Will you be all right?"

"I'll be fine," he answered, with a trace of bitterness in his voice, and exited the club.

That had been over two hours ago, and still the dealer had not moved, his supply apparently unexhausted. In that time, Absalom had liberated two more indifferent ales and one fairly fine brandy, and Vera was getting bored.

"How much extra money do you have?" she asked. "We had Nick do a fairly large buy; the man can't have much more on him. Should we put on another disguise and throw some extra money at him . . . ?" And then another customer approached, sidling up to the dealer, confident he was alone and unobserved.

"See?" Absalom said. "A little patience is its own reward."

Vera forbore hitting him in favor of knocking back the rest of the brandy. And, when the dealer stood and stretched, slipping from the club, she and Absalom were right behind him.

24

Jen woke before Thibault the next morning, still uncertain of how to face him. Despite their nighttime reconciliation, which she still wasn't certain had not been a dream, recalling their angry words in the light of day was quite a daunting proposition. And, truth to tell, she was still smarting from his accusations. Cold and selfish, was she? Uncaring of others? Well, the last thing she recalled was that she had thrown a challenge at him—one that she fully intended to keep.

She *would* prove the rogue was still up to his tricks. She would follow him back to his den and make him confess.

Thus resolved, she rose and dressed in silence, then tiptoed from the room before the sun had fully crested the sky. She was intending to beard Saul in his den and request a day off . . . after breakfast. But as luck would have it, Alcina was in the kitchen when she entered, in search of sustenance, and greeted her with a start.

"Good morning, Gilyan, lass. You're up early on your day off."

"Day off?" Jen squeaked, pausing with her hand halfway to a muffin. Was Saul now adding clairvoyance to his considerable list of talents?

But the housekeeper merely said, "Didn't Beroe tell you? I swear, sometimes I wonder where that woman keeps her brains. Well, you've more than proved your worth, and now it's time for your reward. We cleared it with the master yesterday."

Jen felt an absurd surge of pleasure in the words, and almost laughed. How sad her life had become if she measured her worth by a housekeeper's praise! But still, at least someone appreciated her talents.

"Cleared what?" Kore asked, entering the kitchen with a yawn.

"Gilyan's day off. How late were you out last night, young lady?"

Kore laughed. "You don't want to know." She swallowed another yawn, and swiped the muffin Jen had abandoned. "How are you going to celebrate, Gil?"

"She's going to spend some time with her poor, abandoned husband," a quiet voice said from behind them. Jen turned slowly, not sure what to expect from her partner this morning. But Thibault's face was calmly neutral: neither openly welcoming nor coldly censorious. "That is, if she'll have me," he added, with a sudden look that set her stomach to fluttering.

"Of course," she agreed, with as much aplomb as she could manage, and felt faintly outraged by Kore's envious sigh. Then, "You didn't say you had the day off," she accused.

His lips curved in a lazy grin. "Surprise."

"Oh." Kore clapped her hands together. "You must go to the Hanging Gardens; they're ever so romantic!"

"We'll take it under advisement," Thibault returned, swiping muffins for himself and Jen. He draped a light arm about her, squeezing her shoulders in a way that let her know all was forgiven, if not forgotten.

"But what about Saul?" she asked him, when they were alone. "Someone planted that device, meaning he's now vulnerable in his own dwelling. Will he be safe without you?"

"I thought of that, and I've already extracted a promise that he won't budge from either office without Gideon or Aubrey. Or both. For today, we're free to follow our assassin and see if we can't stop this in its tracks."

A sudden surge of happiness seized Jen—and not only because he was endorsing her theory. Why, it was almost as if it were meant to be. A day off, dropped like a gift into her lap, and Thibault's presence at her side. She would prove her case, and then they would see who was laughing!

Unfortunately, tracing a rogue assassin back to his source was not as easy as it sounded. Jen began at the grocers,

relieved that Thibault seemed content to merely trail along
and let her do the talking. Still clad in her servant's garb,
she dimpled at the grocer, feigning a shy confusion.

"A week or so ago you hired a new delivery boy? Sort
of scruffy, with a scar just here?" And she trailed a finger
down her cheek. "Well . . . oh, how shall I put this? One
of the girls, Varia knows why, evinced a certain interest in
him, but didn't dare to approach him directly, so she asked
me if I wouldn't mind . . ." And Jen let her voice trail off
suggestively, batting her lashes.

Thibault rolled his eyes.

The grocer raised a grizzled eyebrow and propped an
elbow against the cabbages, regarding her. "That one?" he
said, with liberal contempt. "I remember him, but only because he was one of the worst workers I ever laid eyes on.
Only showed up for one day, and I was happy never to see
the fellow again."

"I sympathize." Jen feigned a shiver. "But there's no
accounting for taste. And I did promise Mary. Do you happen to know where he works?"

"No. He just showed up on a day when my regular lad
was sick, and I was too desperate to turn him away. Don't
even know how how found me, or how he knew Henry
was ill."

"I see. Well, thank you. Do you think . . . Do you think
I might talk to Henry?"

"No skin off my nose, lass. But I'd tell your friend to
beware. That one ran out on three deliveries, and pocketed
over fifteen marks of my profits." And the man disappeared
into the depths of his shop, calling, "Henry? Young lady
to see you."

Jen turned to her partner, who was lounging indolently
against a crate of tomatoes. "What?"

He grinned. " 'Evinced an interest'? At least try to sound
like a servant, why don't you?"

"Look who's talking!"

"Who, me?" He feigned horror. "I was brought up a
peasant, remember?"

She flushed, but any rejoinder she might have made was
preempted by Henry's arrival. He was a gawky adolescent
with far too many pimples—a situation which was not aided

by the hectic flush that suffused his cheeks at the news of his visitor.

"You wanted me?" he asked, his voice cracking abruptly at the end of the sentence. His cheeks flamed even brighter as he realized belatedly what he had said.

Jen softened her voice. "When you were sick, a week or so back, did you ask anyone to take your place?"

"No. Why? Was there a problem?" the boy asked in increasing agitation.

"Not at all. I was just curious how the man who replaced you knew there was work. Did you happen talk to anyone before you fell ill?"

"No, but . . ."

"Yes?" Jen prompted.

The lad wiggled in an ecstasy of indecision. "I . . . wasn't really sick," he admitted in a rush. "More sort of . . ."

"Hung over?" Thibault supplied.

The boy shot him a grateful look. "Yes. I mean, I honestly don't drink that much, normally. Just one, to sort of . . . loosen me up. And I didn't think I had more that night either, but . . ." He frowned in memory, then shrugged. "I guess I did. You won't tell, will you?"

"Of course not," Jen assured him, exchanging a triumphant glance with Thibault. "Only . . . would you mind telling me which tavern?"

"The Fish. On Drakos Street."

"Thank you. You've been most helpful. I'll make sure Beroe gives you a big tip next time."

The boy flushed again and hurried off, as if pursued by a flock of harpies.

"There," Jen said triumphantly, as they left the grocer's. "How much do you want to bet the boy was drugged?"

"Nothing. You'd win. And I don't exactly have the money to spare."

"Oh, stop it. And may I add . . . No one said this would be exciting, but need you fidget quite so blatantly? It's distracting."

"Excuse me?"

"Come on; you know exactly what I mean. The whole time I was talking with Henry and the grocer, you were fiddling with something in your pocket."

"I was not."

"Were, too."

And suddenly they grinned at each other, reminded of their frequent childhood battles.

But, "I was not fidgeting," Thibault persisted.

"Oh? And what else would you call it? So, tell me, what's so fascinating?" And Jen made a grab for his pocket, which he deftly evaded, stepping nimbly out of her reach and stuffing his hand more firmly into its depths.

"Back off, Jenny."

"Why? What is it you don't want me to see?"

"Nothing," he countered, with considerable aplomb. "I just don't want you fishing around in my pockets is all." But she knew him too well; the faint, residual flush on his cheeks let her know he was lying.

"So, do you know where Drakos Street is?" he added.

Magnanimous, she let him change the subject. She'd figure out his secret soon enough; she always did. "No. But we can ask."

They set out again, and though it was still early, with a faint nip of chill to the air, it was shaping up to be a beautiful day. Sunny, as always, and clear, the sky arcing like a jewel overhead. Once again, she thanked fate—or Vera— for introducing her to the Guild and getting her out of Ceylonde for the winter. Even now, she imagined, the wide, gracious streets of Hestia's largest city would be choked with snow, turning slowly to frigid, grey slush beneath the wheels of the hansoms.

No, better far to be here—despite the fact that she now cleaned houses for a living. No wonder Vera loved this city so much. And the Cauldron . . . Tonight, Jen resolved, she would finish the day by rejoining Gideon at the Cauldron.

Feeling abruptly companionable, she slipped an arm through Thibault's. His hand still remained firmly in his pocket—further proof that he was trying to hide something—but after a time he began to relax.

It wasn't even a conscious decision on her part; she really hadn't intended it as a ruse. All she knew was that, the minute his hand began to slip out of his pocket, hers was there, triumphantly dragging out what she found.

He gave a startled yelp and tried to snatch it back.

"Jenny . . ."

"What?"

He scowled at her. "That was low."

"So is trying to hide something from your partner," she answered, and turned her attention to her prize. It was an oversized dagger, simple in execution, its hilt engraved to both sides with an antlered stag's head in a lozenge, its blade a shimmer of rippled steel. It was one of the loveliest things she had ever seen.

She stared at him in consternation.

A long silence stretched out.

"Thibault," she said at last, almost reverently. "This is beautiful. Where did you get it?"

He ducked his head; she could barely hear his answer.

"What?"

"Vera," he repeated, flushing.

"Why is Vera giving you daggers?" She didn't want to sound petty, but she couldn't help the hurt in her voice. She was Vera's niece, after all; he was merely her neighbor. So what had he done to deserve it? Or, more importantly, what had she done *not* to? Did Vera, too, see her as shallow and selfish?

"Um . . . my birthday," he answered sheepishly.

"Your *what*?"

"My birthday," he repeated. "My twenty-first birthday, actually. My majority."

"When?"

"Halfway through exams."

"And you didn't tell me? Why not?"

"I thought you knew," he said. "Vera did."

Selfish, again, she thought bitterly. And, *Blast it to perdition!* Unsure of what to do, she handed back the dagger. He started to return it to his pocket, but she said, curtly, "No point in hiding it anymore, is there?"

"I suppose not." He seemed almost self-conscious as he fastened the lovely thing to his belt. "You'll get one, too," he added placatingly. "On your twenty-first. Vera promised."

"Well, at least that's something." Then realizing that sounded ungracious—or, at least, selfish—Jen essayed a smile. "It really is lovely, Thibault. And well-deserved."

"Thank you."

"But I still can't believe you didn't tell me!"

He flushed slightly, and shrugged again. "You were busy. In the middle of exams. I didn't want you to have one more thing to remember."

"And were you that convinced I would forget?"

He didn't answer, and somehow that omission hurt her more than anything. He *did* see her as self-involved, and yet he still cared for her, despite it. Which made her feel as low as a crawling worm.

She would do better, she promised herself. She would deserve his friendship and caring. And if a small part of her suspected that his feelings ran deeper, she assiduously ignored it. For that would only make her all the less deserving.

They walked on in silence, and found the Fish with only minimal directions: a run-down tavern fronting an indifferent street and backing an alley. The interior was seedy and locked into a perpetual twilight, as if the proprietors couldn't afford to fully charge their magelights. But then, Jen decided, it was probably a good thing that the watery light did not penetrate some of the deepest corners; there were undoubtedly things there that no one wanted to see.

The bar was pitted, and sticky with spilled beer; Jen planted her elbows on it with reluctance.

The bartender sauntered over in no particular hurry, pulling a filthy rag from behind the counter and swiping halfheartedly at the stains. "What can I get you?"

"Information," Jen countered, reaching into a pocket for a bit of silver. It flashed between her fingers.

The barman continued to stare at her, stony-faced.

"And two of your best ales," Thibault added with a smile.

The man's demeanor softened noticeably, and he pulled two tall mugs, extorting from them a sizable sum.

"What kind of information?" he asked after a moment, when Thibault and Jen had both taken pulls of their ale.

She wiped a hand across the back of her mouth. "Do you know Henry, the grocer's boy?"

The man stiffened again. "And what is that to you?"

"Sweet kid, isn't he?" said Thibault. "Vulnerable. We're worried about him."

"We think someone drugged him a few days ago," Jen added, taking up the narrative.

"In my establishment?" That seemed to incense the bartender more than anything.

"Not that it was your fault," Jen hastily supplied. "We just want to make sure it doesn't happen again. Do you recall a man who was in here with Henry? Must have been, oh, ten days or so ago? Disreputable looking; shifty eyes? Scar about here?" And she released the coin to the bar.

It vanished. "Yes, I might have seen someone like that. Hung around here for several days, as I recall. Didn't like him much. Stingy tipper."

"Have you seen him before or since?"

The man shook his head.

"Not one of the regulars, then?" Thibault added.

Their host snorted. "This might not be the greatest of establishments, but even we have our standards."

"So you have no idea where we might find him?"

"What do I look like, a mage?" And then, "Anything else?"

Jen shook her head disconsolately. The man moved away.

"What now?" she said to Thibault, when they were alone.

"I don't know. This is your show." His face was neutral, so why did she have the feeling he was absurdly pleased?

And the worst of it was, she had no idea what to do next.

25

"Well?"

Vera exhaled gustily and flopped into the chair Absalom indicated, resting her elbows on the table. The café she had chosen for their meeting was surprisingly unpopulated despite its fashionable location a few streets off Abelard Square. Ropes of magelights were strung over the tables, and wrought-iron chairs and tables with green marble tops completed the decor. A spill of honey on one of the neighboring tabletops was attracting a small gathering of wasps.

Vera pushed her hair off her face, and grinned ruefully at her companions. She was an hour late for their scheduled rendezvous, and counted herself fortunate she had gotten off so lightly. For a man who made his livelihood in the Dreamsmoke trade, their target had been surprisingly leisurely about restocking. Upon leaving the Rogue's Gallery, she and Absalom had trailed the man for what felt like an eternity, reluctant participants in the sordid daily minutia of the career criminal. They visited two bars and a bathhouse, and were even forced to witness one unimaginative and sweaty grope with a hired prostitute behind the bathhouse wall.

"Who would have thought the common dealer led such a boring existence?" she had whispered disgustedly, at that point.

"Oh, I don't know," the mage temporized with a grin. "He seems to be rather enjoying himself."

"Although one cannot say the same for his companion. Have you ever seen such a face of indifference?"

"Not in such a similar situation, I must admit."

"Meaning?"

He leered at her. "Meaning that when I make love to a

woman, she has no cause for complaint. Rather the opposite, in fact."

Despite the teasing corners of his grin, there was an un-
deniable intensity to his gaze that brought a flush to her
cheeks—and a scowl to her face. Why did he always manage to unhinge her? "We weren't talking about you," she
informed him tartly. He smirked. A moment passed, and
then, unable to resist, she demanded, "Even in your scab-
rous guise?"

"Well," he drawled. "For some, scars are a turn-on."

That's when she had hit him, but fortunately the dealer
was too engrossed in his noisy climax to register the faint
yelp of pain from one apparently empty corner of the alley.

When the dealer moved on, they were behind him, Absalom rubbing his arm in pointed silence and shooting Vera
the occasional wounded-puppy look, which she blatantly
ignored. "Now maybe we'll get somewhere," she whispered, but was doomed to disappointment. Instead, their
quarry decided to renew his apparently failing vitality with
a large, greasy, and stunningly inedible meal at one of the
dockside taverns.

"Ah, the glamorous life of the professional Smoke-
trader," Absalom declared, leaning up against a nearby
wall while the man consumed his repast.

Vera frowned. The rancid smells of old cooking oil and
even older fish were beginning to turn her stomach, and
from the look of the sun, they were already going to be
late for their rendezvous with Nick. Who, to be honest, she
didn't trust leaving alone for any longer than was strictly
necessary. So eventually she had surrendered to necessity
and sent Absalom after Nick, counseling him to keep her
ex-lover at the café until she could rejoin them.

Which, as it happened, was earlier than she expected—
and later than she deserved.

"So?" Absalom prompted again, as she signaled for the
waiter and settled back more comfortably in her chair, wondering how the sun could still possibly be so high after such
a seemingly interminable afternoon. "Any success?"

"A modicum. Eventually," she conceded, ordering a coffee and casting an avaricious eye at the uneaten remains
of Nick's pastry. He pushed the plate across to her. She

seized his fork and began to eat, feeling the heady rush of sugar dissolving her incipient headache. "I never would have believed one man could dawdle so, but he must have had a set rendezvous, because precisely on the hour he met a man behind one of the dockside warehouses, and exchanged a packet."

"And?"

"I followed the other one home, of course," Vera responded, attacking her coffee when that was delivered. "He went to a rather seedy address on the far side of Penhalion Square. When he didn't come out after half an hour, I figured he was at home and left."

"Was that wise?" Absalom asked.

To Vera's surprise, it was Nick who defended her. "She's been doing this longer than either of us. She knows what she's about."

Absalom arched an eyebrow. "I bow to your superior judgment, of course."

Nick scowled.

"Now, you two," Vera counseled, sensing in their bristling postures the imminence of a first-class pissing contest. "Nick, thank you. And Absalom, you're going to have to start trusting me sooner or later. If there is one thing I do know, it's the criminal mind. The disreputable ones always come out at night. After I get some decent food in me— something other than that greasy fish-fry our friend seemed so enamored of—we'll shadow the new target's residence and see what transpires."

"Tonight?"

She looked hard at Nick. There was an eagerness in his eyes—and an apprehension. The stirrings of the Lammergeier, ready at last to resume his former profession? Then she looked more closely, seeing the tell-tale dilation of his pupils, and his faint guilty flinch as he acknowledged her notice.

"Blast it to perdition, Nick!" she exclaimed, slamming her fist down on the tabletop. Cups jumped in their saucers, slopping a puddle of coffee across the table.

"What is it?" Absalom demanded.

"He's . . . I . . ." She threw her fork at Nick's head as words failed her. "How did you manage it, Nikki?"

He flushed. "I held back some of the money you lent me."

"For what?" Absalom asked, still puzzled.

"Dreamsmoke," Vera spat. "Didn't you notice his eyes?"

"No, I didn't," Absalom confessed, peering at their companion more closely.

"Well, no surprise there," Vera countered bitterly. "You haven't spent years learning to recognize the signs. Blast it, Nick, how could you?"

"It was only one smoke . . ." he protested.

"You betrayed my trust."

A spark of anger stirred in his eyes. "I didn't ask for your trust. Or your supervision. So stop treating me like a child."

"Then stop acting like one, and take some bloody responsibility for your life!"

"I have; I did. Just because they're not your choices . . ."

"You call addiction a 'choice'? How could you be so stupid?"

"And how could you," he fired back, "to trust an addict?" He paused, then in a duller voice, added, "And it is a choice, no matter what you think. It's a choice to take the easy path, the path of least resistance."

There was a depth of self-loathing to his voice that she hadn't heard since the days after he had lost his family, and something within her broke. "Nick . . ."

"What? Don't tell me what I could have been. I am what I am. A poor, pitiful addict who long ago chose death over life, loneliness over love. It's too late for me to change, Vera—and I'm not even sure I want to anymore. So just leave me alone."

"To die?" She was so furious that her voice cracked.

"If that's what I want, yes."

"And do you?"

There was a long moment of silence. Then, "Maybe. Sometimes. Yes," he admitted. "And if that offends you, I'll leave." He rose, the iron chair scraping across the paving stones.

"Nick . . ."

It was still there, that bond between them. Another might not have even heard the words, but her whisper halted him mid-flight. At least she still had that much power over him

He turned to look at her, the tell-tale traces of the drug still visible. She took a deep breath and added, "There's no point in missing dinner. And anyone can watch a house. I was going to suggest adjourning to the Five Crowns, in Griffon Square. If I recall correctly, they make a wicked lamb stew . . ."

He paused for a moment, then shot her a shaky grin. "I was always partial to lamb stew."

"I remember." But it wasn't until she tried to rise that she realized she was clutching Absalom's hand like a life-line under the table.

Jen stared morosely at the pitted bartop, and swirled the dregs of beer in her mug. The bartender's words echoed accusingly in her head: *What do I look like, a mage?* Blast him; blast them all. And most especially blast her cursed partner who hadn't even trusted her with his birthday, and who now sat radiating a false solicitousness. When he tried to pat her hand consolingly, she kicked him.

"Ouch. Jenny. I was only trying to . . ."

"Gloat," she finished.

He shot her a sour look, and moved away. Wonderful. Now she'd alienated him as well. So she had no rogue, no lead; nothing. The bartender had long since vanished.

She drained the dregs of her beer and set the tankard down with a bump. "We might as well leave," she said.

Thibault regarded her, his gaze deliberately blank. "Giving up already?"

"No, curse you, I'm not giving up. I just need to regroup until I can find a new bloody strategy."

His lips twitched slightly, but he wisely refrained from laughing. He tipped the last of his beer down his throat. "Very well. Let's go, then."

The Ephanon sunlight was blindingly bright after the murkiness of the bar, making Jen's eyes water suspiciously. She blinked back the moisture furiously—*I am* not *crying; it's only the sun*—and so for a moment didn't notice the tugging at her sleeve.

"What?" she said crossly. "Thibault . . ."

"Excuse me, Malina, but did I hear you inquiring about a man with a scar?"

Jen turned to regard the speaker in surprise. He was as scrufulous a specimen as she had ever seen, but at least he had the decency to address her as a young lady of the middle class and not as the servant she so clearly appeared. Her voice was almost warm as she said, "You did. How astute of you."

He smirked. "In certain circles, I'm known for my hearing. And my eyesight."

"And what things have you seen with this remarkable eyesight of yours?"

"Alas," he replied, "I am also known as a man of very little means. And a very light purse. Sometimes excess of hunger makes me lightheaded, and I don't see quite as clearly."

"Well, we must remedy that, mustn't we?" Jen countered, beginning to enjoy herself again. She exchanged a glance with Thibault. "Hunger can be a tragic thing. If we can supply you with the means for your sustenance, can you tell us where we might be able to get a decent bite of our own?"

"But of course. I know just the place."

Heart pounding with a giddy excitement, Jen fished in her pockets and counted out the coins into the man's outstretched hand, her eagerness for a lead—any lead—almost outweighing her distaste at touching her informant's filthy fingers. There was a wound on the back of his hand that looked barely healed and, come to think of it, he didn't smell that appealing, either.

"And where, pray tell, might that be?" she asked, when a look in his eyes indicated she had bestowed sufficient bounty.

"Don't rightly know the name of the place," he said, and she stifled a surge of panic. "Don't even know if it's got a name, to be honest. But I think it's got just the dish that might whet your appetite."

"Will you take us there?"

"And reveal that I was the one who recommended the establishment? Not on your life! I'm far too modest a man

for that. But I will"—he leered—"tell you how to get there.
Do you know Griffon Square?"

Thibault nodded. Jen would have to defer to him in this;
thanks to Saul, he had spent more time exploring Ephanon
than she. "Rather a posh area, though, isn't it?" her partner added.

"Right posh—but where you're going's not in Griffon
Square. That's just the nearest convenient landmark. Now,
here's what you do. Take the first street south of of Griffon,
leading toward the harbor, and when you reach Thalassa
Road . . ."

As the complex directions unfurled, Jen couldn't quite
mask a smile. This time, they were on to something. This
was the genuine article. She could feel it.

And then she'd show Thibault who was right.

26

"You're in a good mood," Thibault said, as Jen's voice, raised briefly in song, echoed along Romana Street.

"And why shouldn't I be?" she countered, breaking off mid-warble.

"Because we've been to seven bars, two bathhouses and one whorehouse in the past three hours, we're almost out of bribe money, and we still haven't seen hide nor hair of our quarry."

"Yes, but at least we're in the right area. Here people actually know who we're talking about."

"Yes, and fortunately there's no honor among thieves. Still, if we don't flush out our quarry today, the scope of our inquires will scare him out of the neighborhood forever."

"Don't worry. We'll find him."

"What makes you so certain?"

"Just a feeling, Thibault," she said, hooking an arm through his.

He sighed inaudibly and studied the top of her head, noting idly the way the sun picked out red fire from among the dark strands. He much preferred Jen cheerful to Jen moody, but he preferred her realistic most of all. And it was beginning to seem that, in that, he was destined for disappointment. She had a remarkable talent for self-deception.

"Jen . . ."

"What?"

He permitted himself a gusty breath. "Nothing."

"Come now, Thib," she said, squeezing his arm. "Don't be such a stick in the mud. Of course we'll find . . ." She felt him stiffen, and froze. "What is it?"

Barely breathing, as if their quarry were a bird or a wild deer that the slightest breeze could startle, he whispered, "Look—slowly—to your right. That's him, isn't it?"

Jen's lips curved upwards in a grin. "By all that's precious, Thibault, we've got him! You wait here; I'll drive him to you."

She was good; he had to give her that. She blended so seamlessly into the crowd that he actually lost sight of her until she popped up behind the rogue assassin. "You, there," she said, pointing. "I know you . . ."

The assassin flinched, then bolted. Jen took off in pursuit, herding him straight into her partner's grasp. The man squeaked in alarm as Thibault tightened a hand around each arm and hauled him off his feet. As Jen trotted up, he was kicking and flailing, spewing an impressive array of imprecations.

"Nice job, Ty," she greeted her partner.

"Thank you." He tightened his grip around his quarry's biceps, and was delighted to hear the man's yip of surprise. "Is that any way to talk in front of a lady?" he chided, emphasizing his position with a shake.

The man trailed into silence.

"Better. Thanks again." Jen acknowledged her partner's efforts with a nod, and the two exchanged a grin over the rogue's head. "It's all right, Ty; you can put him down, now. You won't attempt to run away, will you?" she added to the rogue.

He shook his head sullenly, and Thibault set him down with a chuckle. The man shot him a wounded look and rubbed his biceps pointedly.

"You'd better be thankful a sore arm is all he gave you," Jen said, drawing the rogue's attention. It never ceased to amaze him; just when Thibault was convinced she was nothing more than a flighty girl with an inflated ego, the mask fell away, revealing an implacable killer. Or maybe this was the mask and the other the reality, but either way the transformation shocked him. Her mossy eyes went cold as agates, and her face was impassive and deadly. She stood poised, every line of her body expressing a violence barely held in check.

This was no well-bred society flirt but a true-born member of the Assassin's Guild. This was the Dagger, honed and whetted, and it took his breath away.

The assassin's, too, it seemed.

"You . . ." he stammered. "I know you."

"I should hope so, seeing as I foiled your plan."

"You're . . ."

"The genuine article, yes. To which you only can aspire."

"Then what are you doing . . ."

"Playing servant to the Soleneides? I should think that would be obvious."

The little man flushed. "So?" he persisted. "What can you possibly want that you attempt to abduct me in broad daylight?"

"Abduct you?" Jen grinned. "My dear fellow, if we had really wanted to abduct you, you would have been missing by now."

"So what, then?" he demanded sullenly.

"A little talk, nothing more. A friendly warning. No more attempts. Whatever you left on Saul's mantel yesterday—and whatever other tricks you have up your sleeve—they won't work. We're wise to you."

"Tricks? Mantel? Wise to me? What the bloody blazes are you talking about?"

Jen looked momentarily startled. Then, "The silver sphere?" she elaborated. "On the mantel? With the yellow smoke inside?"

"Yesterday, you said?" The rogue laughed harshly. "You've got the wrong man, Malina. And if you were really so all-fired good, you would have known the money for *that* job ran out a long time ago! Saul Soleneides has been safe from me since you foiled my little poisoning plot. And, come to think of it"—he turned and regarded Thibault speculatively—"since you blocked my knife throw with that ledger. That was it. The end. Understand?"

Jen deflated. "Then you weren't responsible for yesterday's attack?"

The assassin crossed his arms. "No offense, but little silver balls aren't exactly my style."

"Any idea whose style they are?" Thibault prompted, as Jen's initiative evaporated.

"I haven't the foggiest, but if the Telos clan is fronting

the cash, then they're seriously scraping the bottom of the barrel. I was the best they could afford, and they ran out of the wherewithal to pay me a while back. The rest of the rogues in this city?" He shrugged. "Not even worth their commissions. Shouldn't be hard even for a pair like you to foil them."

"Tell me," Thibault said. "Do any of those rogues use invisibility spells?"

"Invisibility spells?" The assassin scoffed. "I don't bloody think so! Do you know how much those cost?" Then, "Why?" he added. "*Is* someone using invisibility spells?"

"We're not sure," Thibault admitted. "Perhaps."

The rogue hooted. "Then you're up against something far more serious than anything I was involved in. Maybe this one will actually prove a challenge for assassins of your caliber!"

"So you're not mad we foiled you?" Jen asked, with a sudden childlike naïveté.

The rogue looked amused. "Mad? Why should I be mad? I got paid, didn't I?" He looked around. "Can I go now?"

Jen shrugged, and Thibault stepped back, clearing a path.

The man took two steps, then paused. "Can I ask a question?"

Thibault nodded.

"Who are you? In the Guild?"

"The Cloak and the Dagger," Thibault answered; there seemed little harm in that.

The man snorted: a derisive spurt of laughter. "A little hackneyed, isn't it?"

"It was a deliberate choice," Jen said tightly.

"No doubt; no doubt. I just would have thought two geniuses such as yourselves could have come up with something slightly more original."

Jen frowned. "Will that be all?"

"Yes." Their quarry started to walk away, then turned again, adding almost wistfully, "Is it hard? To get into the Guild?"

"That depends on the applicant," Jen said coldly.

"Of course. And how did *you* get in?"

"Family connections," Thibault said, with a disarming grin.

"Hmph. Figures." And turning for good this time, the rogue assassin vanished into the crowd.

The words *I told you so* had never been further from Thibault's mind, but they echoed between them nonetheless as he and Jen trudged disconsolately out of the maze of streets that comprised Ephanon's poorer quarter. Or rather, as Jen trudged disconsolately and Thibault tried to match his pace to hers without seeming as if he were humoring her, or catering to her mood.

"Someone *is* still out to get Saul," he informed her. "As that device we found proves."

"But you were right that it wasn't our rogue."

"So?" And when she paused to look up at him indignantly, he shrugged. "This is a job, Jenny, not a competition. We're partners, and we've been hired to protect Saul—no matter who is behind the attacks."

"True." She continued to walk along in silence, oblivious to the squalor of the neighborhood. But to Thibault, it stood in unpleasant counterpoint to the decadent opulence of the illusion clubs. Ephanon might be some people's idea of paradise, but no paradise Thibault was aware of contained such stinking back streets, smelling of dead fish and offal and too many people in too tight a space. The buildings were crumbling and, from the stench of it, the sewers had ceased to function some time ago. Worse, every corner seemed to contain a Dreamsmoke addict, locked into his or her own private and sordid oblivion.

"So who do you think *is* responsible?" Jen said after a time, still dwelling on their assassin. "If the Telos clan really is out of money?"

"I don't know. But it does bring up one disturbing possibility. If none of our rogues can afford illusion spells, then we are either dealing with a freelancer, or . . ."

"Someone in the house," Jenny breathed.

Thibault nodded glumly. "But which one? Patroch? Stavros? Lydea?"

"Or Gideon or Aubrey?" Jen added. "Maybe they want the illusion clubs."

"Stavros certainly doesn't. What if he were planning on getting rid of them?"

"The illusion clubs? Would he do something that stupid?"

"If he decided he didn't want to be tainted with their profits. What if something illegal is going on in the clubs and Stavros learned about it, too?"

"Illegal? Like what?"

"How should I know?"

"Then why not just eliminate Stavros?"

Thibault was silent for a moment, then said, "Maybe that's the next step."

Jen shivered. "We're speculating, Thib. Maybe we should try to gather some evidence first."

"Such as?"

"How should I know?" She wasn't angry any longer, just frustrated. He could feel it pouring off her in waves. "Where are we anyway?"

"Two streets north and three west should put us back in Griffon Square."

"Fortunate that someone's paying attention." She sighed. "If Ephanon has so much money to spend on the illusion clubs, then why do slums like this still exist?"

He started at her in surprised respect.

"What? Oh, for Varia's sake, Thibault," she said crossly, "of course I noticed! I'm not *that* self-centered."

He smiled at her. "I was wondering the same thing myself. About the streets, I mean."

She was silent for a moment, and then surprised him by reaching out and taking his hand. "Thibault . . ."

He curled his fingers around hers. "Yes?"

"I'm sorry I missed your birthday. I . . . It won't happen again, I promise."

He nodded and squeezed her fingers. "I know."

She stopped, jerking him to a halt, and stamped her foot. "You don't believe me!"

"What?" He stared down at her incredulously.

"You're just humoring me. Admit it."

"I am not!"

"Prove it, then."

He looked down at her, at that familiar, beautiful face

now furrowed in lines of indignation. Mossy eyes sparkled beneath pinched brows; the delicate arch of cheekbones was stained with a faint, hectic flush. And beneath it all, invisible save to those who knew her best, the tremulous insecurity that quivered on her lip and crouched like a frightened animal in the depths of her eyes. He could almost read her thoughts: *What if it were true? What if he couldn't prove it?*

A sudden wave of tenderness assailed him. She was such a funny mix of self-doubt and supreme, overweening confidence: ironically assured when she was mistaken, and forever questioning things about which she should never have had a doubt. His lips curved in a fond smile—which only seemed to irritate her more.

"Now you're laughing at me," she accused.

Slowly, deliberately, he met her eyes and shook his head. And something of his true feelings must have shown, for a wave of painful color slammed across her cheeks, and she dropped his hand as if burned.

"Well, that settles that," she said brusquely, her eyes darting from cobblestones to buildings—anywhere but to his face. "We should get back; it's getting late. And Saul will wonder where we've got to."

They entered Griffon Square in silence. A tantalizing whiff of roast lamb from the magnificent sprawl of the Five Crowns tavern made Thibault's stomach rumble loudly, and Jenny laughed.

"We are overdue for dinner, aren't we?"

"Yes, and if we had a little more of our bribe money left, I'd treat you to some of that magnificent food. But, alas, we are poor." He cast his eyes longingly over the spread of outdoor tables and the throngs of contented diners.

"A pity, indeed . . ." Jen's regretful tone mirrored his own, then she broke off as he stiffened. "What is it?"

For the briefest of instants, as the crowd shifted, Thibault thought he caught a glimpse of Vera's profile, imperious and framed in that too-short hair, flanked by two dark-haired men like enough to have been twins—either of whom could have been the irrepressible mage. But what, in Varia's name, was the Hawk doing in Ephanon when they had left her safely in Bergaetta?

He paused, craning his neck and peering intently across the tables, barely aware of Jen tugging urgently on his arm.

"What is it?" she echoed.

"I thought I saw . . ." There; the crowd shifted again, revealing the table in question, and Thibault sank back with a disgusted snort. Three women, and none of them even remotely like the Hawk. His eyes must have been playing tricks.

"Saw what?" Jen persisted.

"Nothing," he admitted, offering her his arm. "Just silly Thib, seeing things again. Shall we go and see what Beroe can provide us in compensation for missing this delicious meal?"

27

The sky was fading into twilight as Jen and Thibault arrived back at House Soleneides. Jen was feeling surprisingly sanguine for someone whose hunches had all been proved wrong, but while her quarry hadn't exactly said what she wanted to hear, at least she had found him. She had proved she could follow a trail to its end, and Thibault had witnessed it.

So what if the presence of that magnificent dagger at his side reminded her how little he had trusted her? She would prove him wrong in that one, too. She would do something wonderful for him—something he would never, in a million years, expect.

She suppressed a little smirk as she formulated her plans. She couldn't wait to see his face!

And tonight . . .

Tonight she would renew her acquaintance with Gideon and the Cauldron; it had been far too long.

As they entered Soleneides Square, the Golden Boy himself was crossing the courtyard with Saul and Aubrey. Saul, just back from the Cauldron, was talking and gesticulating with his usual animation; Aubrey was sullen and withdrawn. But Gideon shone like the sun. Even in the fading daylight, his hair flared around him like a nimbus.

He met Jen's gaze, dropping one eyelid in a wink. A rush of pleasure went through her, and she laughed, her smile igniting like a magelight. Between them, she had the feeling they could illuminate the garden, and she masked a surge of awe. There was no way such a man could be responsible for the attacks.

Sullen Aubrey, on the other hand . . .

Gideon advanced to meet her, and she would have

walked straight into his arms had Saul's cheerful voice not jolted her back to a belated sense of propriety.

"There you are, you two! How was your day off?"

"It was . . . enlightening," Thibault said dryly.

"Did you enjoy the sights of Ephanon?"

"Some better than others," Jen said, glancing sidelong at Gideon.

The Golden One grinned.

Aubrey's mouth pinched, as if he had tasted something rotten. "If you'll excuse me, I have to get back to the Cauldron. Someone has to supervise the unloading of that new wine shipment."

"Oh, don't be such a stick in the mud, Aubrey," Gideon retorted. "The wine can wait a few minutes. I'll go back with you. Even though it is their day off, I'm sure Gilyan and Ty can see Saul safely through the front door."

"Of course they can," Saul declared. "Ty, my lad, walk with me a minute. We need to discuss the logistics for tomorrow. I need to travel out of Ephanon for the afternoon, and since you're not letting me out of your sight . . ."

Jen tuned out the discussion, turning her attention to Gideon instead. He lingered in the square although Aubrey was clearly intent on departing. *Tonight?* he mouthed.

Jen nodded, her lips curving in a grin.

"Here? An hour to midnight?" he added aloud.

"What?" Aubrey asked.

His associate grinned. "Nothing."

"Yes," Jen replied.

Gideon winked and was turning away when a percussive crash split the air. Jen whirled. Time froze, suspended in a single moment of protracted horror.

One of the huge cornice stones must have come loose, for the wreckage of the block lay strewn about the courtyard, shattering the paving stones for a good eight feet in every direction. Pieces ranging from the size of a fist to that of a human head bounced and settled. One of the latter lay at Saul's feet, while the master of House Soleneides, his face drained of blood, looked down in disbelief at the crumpled form of his latest bodyguard.

The edges of Jen's world crimped and greyed. Thibault had never looked so small and disjointed as he did lying there on the shattered flagstones like an unstrung puppet, his limbs all askew. His back was to her, but a crimson puddle was leaking inexorably from beneath his right cheek. She couldn't see him move or breathe, and in that instant it seemed that all vitality and purpose had drained from the world. Her breath locked around a panicked howl, but before she could utter it, her narrowing vista snapped shut, spiraling her into blackness.

Thibault didn't know what had alerted him—maybe a subtle shift in the patterns of light and shadows, maybe a noise or an unexpected breeze—but when he had looked up to see the massive cornice stone falling, he had nearly frozen. Only years of training and an innate instinct to place the lives of others before his own had galvanized him into action. Leaping into a run, he had shoved Saul out of the way—for it had been he who stood directly in line with the massive block—then continued on through the block's path until he judged himself a safe distance away.

But he must have been more rattled than he'd realized, for he misjudged either the time or the distance. One corner of the stone glanced painfully off his shoulder, flinging him to the ground. Unable to break his descent with an arm suddenly gone numb, he crashed headlong to the paving stones, tearing a painful gash across his cheek. The side of his head bounced forcefully off the ground, setting both ears to ringing.

It was a prodigious height from which to fall and he lay there for a moment, stunned and winded, still in shock and cursing himself silently for every kind of a fool. And then the pain came flooding back, and he groaned.

The frozen moment shattered. Saul stumbled over the broken stones to kneel beside him, helping him to sit. Simultaneously, a dull thud from his other side indicated a second body going down. With an agonizing slowness, he turned his head to see Jenny, crumpled on the flagstones.

Patroch, who had materialized seemingly from out of nowhere, had been running full tilt toward the scene of the crime when Jen collapsed; he took a purler over her prostrate body.

"Grandpa . . . oof!" Patroch exclaimed, going down in turn.

Thibault winced. "Jen!" he cried, forgetting momentarily the ruse of their names. He lunged for her, but a spike of pain from his shoulder halted him, forcing a scream from his lips. Instead, it was Gideon who disentangled Jen from Patroch and scooped her up.

Her eyes fluttered open. "What happened?"

"You fainted." The Golden Boy sounded amused. "And then Patroch fell on you."

Her eyes alighted on Saul's grandson, who flinched. "I did not faint," she declared indignantly. And then, "Thibault!" Her eyes sought him out, half supported in Saul's embrace. "You're alive!"

He smiled ruefully, stretching the scraped skin of his cheek uncomfortably. "No thanks to my reflexes." He became aware of a trickle of moisture tracking down his face, and he rubbed at it absently. His fingers came back red.

Disentangling herself from Gideon's embrace, Jen flew at him, jarring his arm and making him yelp.

"What's the matter?"

"I think I dislocated my shoulder," he gasped, after the dizzying waves of pain had receded.

She was abruptly gentle, probing the joint. Above them, he was vaguely aware of Patroch chittering something anxiously at Saul—and Saul's curt rejoinder. "No, just bruised," she informed him. She wiped the flow of blood from his temple with her sleeve. "But you're bleeding like a stuck pig."

"Head wounds. They're always supposed to be the worst. Blast it, I could have sworn I was clear!"

Her brow furrowed. "If you ever try a stunt like that again . . ."

He managed a shaky grin. "What?"

"I'll . . . I'll kill you myself!" she finished in a rush.

He laughed—although it made his head ache abominably.

"Are you all right, my boy?" Saul asked anxiously. "What I owe you . . ."

Thibault waved this away with his good hand. "Nothing," he managed. "My job."

"Can you stand?" Jen asked him.

He took a deep breath, then gasped. "Debatable."

"Not to worry," Saul said briskly. "Gideon and Aubrey can carry you. And Patroch, if he'll condescend to sully his hands."

"Of course, Grandpa," the boy said, suddenly meek.

"Right, then." Saul glanced at the roof, where a hole in the cornice taunted them like a gap-toothed smile. "Though, on further reflection, perhaps it might be better if we used the back door, this time."

When Thibault was finally settled in their bed—his head wrapped in bandages and his cheek resembling raw meat, his shoulder swelling and turning five shades of purple— Jen curled up beside him, resting her hand on his arm.

"You *are* all right, aren't you?" she asked, for what must have been the fiftieth time.

"Apart from the obvious, yes. And you?"

"Me?"

"You fainted," he reminded her.

"I did not!"

"I suppose I should be flattered. The unassailable Jen, prostrated by the sight of my lifeless body . . ."

"I did not faint!"

He smiled. "If that's the way you want to play it . . ."

If he hadn't looked so well-tenderized, she would have hit him.

Then, abruptly, his face became serious. "Jen?"

"What?"

"Do me a favor, huh? Go up to the roof and check for evidence."

"Evidence? Why? What are you thinking?"

"That it's looking more and more like an inside job. And I am beginning to suspect I know who is responsible."

"Who?" she demanded.

Annoyingly, he shook his head. He could be bloody close-mouthed when he chose to be. "I don't want to prejudice your observations with my theories. Just go up and see if you can find anything that points to a household member. Then we'll talk."

She surveyed him for another moment, raising a faint

flush on his cheeks. "Very well," she conceded. "Where did you put the portable magelights?"

"In the back of the top drawer."

She uncurled herself from the bed and retrieved one of the small portable globes. "Hullabaloo," she said. The globe flared to life in her hands, spilling a cool green light from her fingers. "Well, at least that's one thing that still works. I'll be right back."

He nodded his acknowledgment and she eased out the door, making her way to the upper reaches of the house. In the drama, she had forgotten to fetch dinner, and now her stomach rumbled imperiously. When she was finished on the roof, she would drop by the kitchens and beg a plate of something from Beroe. By now, the story should have made the rounds, and doubtless the staff would be falling over themselves to coddle Thibault.

She snorted, and eased open a small door at the far end of one of the upper corridors. Behind lay a small, spiral staircase that led to the roof. As usual, it was swallowed in darkness, making her grateful for the magelight that banished the shadows in a sweep of verdant illumination. It was better than the flickering candles that had lit her way when she'd snuck up here on occasion with Kore and Jahnee to gossip over a bottle of pilfered wine.

In the twilight, the roof was a magical place, caught beneath the purpling sky with the lights of Ephanon and Sentenniel Street winking in the distance. In one corner, a handful of empty wine bottles lurked like conspirators. Jarred loose by her tread, a lone bottle toppled and rolled unerringly toward her. She kicked it out of the way, sending it rolling to the far side of the roof.

The gap in the cornice loomed, creating a low, wide door to the sky. It would have been a dizzying prospect to anyone afraid of heights, but Jen didn't count herself among that number, so she merely walked to the gap and poked her toes out over the edge, peering down at the stones below. The fragments of the block still lay scattered across the court, radiating out from the star-shaped crater that marked the center of the impact. Spider-web cracks in the flagstones, stretching tendrils halfway across the square, were further testament to the force of the blow.

It was amazing her partner hadn't been crushed flat.

She suppressed a shudder, then frowned, leaning further out into the void. By Varia, Thibault hadn't misjudged the distance—at least not if he assumed the block was intended to strike the doorstep. Because the crater was decidedly off-center, displaced to the left by a good few feet, which Thibault could never have predicted.

But why? No one standing in the doorway was likely to be injured by a block that fell that far off center, and certainly not killed by it. Unless—a horrible thought occurred—unless Thibault was right and it was an inside job. And the culprit knew Saul was guarded and expected Jen or Thibault to push him out of the apparent path and into the intended one. And of the people in the household who knew Jen and Thibault's true identity, that left only two real suspects: Aubrey and Gideon.

That is, providing the block's trajectory was intended and not a mechanical failure.

Jen knelt in the gap, examining the stones more carefully, the handheld magelight winking in her fingers. If Thibault had expected her to find any apparatus remaining, this long after the fact, he was doomed to disappointment. A few dark skidmarks angled out from the neighboring block, but otherwise the roof was clean. Still, unwilling to leave until she had solved the puzzle, she brushed her fingers across the stones and against the skids, determined to wrest some kind of order from the chaos.

On her third pass, running her hands along the neighboring stones on a whim, she found a tiny crystal glued to the outside of the right-hand block. She pried it out of its moorings, nearly snapping a fingernail in the process, and examined it. Like the shards she had used to spy on Iaon Pehndon, this appeared to have been split from a larger mass, making it likely that it was some sort of viewing and signaling device. She slipped it into her pocket and leaned precariously out over the cornice, pressing her cheek to the area on which the crystal had rested.

As near as she could figure, it commanded a perfect view of the doorway.

She considered this for a moment, still hanging half off the roof, then pulled herself back onto solid ground, wrap-

ping her arms around her knees as she waited for the pieces
to fit. A tenuous picture was beginning to form, composed
of swirling fragments. She was just missing the link . . .
And then her eyes fell once more on the angled skidmarks,
and the whole thing coalesced. Instantly, she was down on
her knees, her fingers questing across the gap.

The scratches where the stone had rested—artifacts of
shoving the heavy block from its moorings—ran not per-
pendicular to the edge of the roof but rather angled off to
the side, in the same direction as the skids. She could see
it now. It had to have been a tripartite system. The spy-
eye had peered down into the courtyard, linked to some
sort of viewing crystal, awaiting Saul. And then, when he
had appeared, a code had been uttered which fed into yet
a third crystal, that one activating some sort of pushing
device which had skidded across the roof in the opposite
direction to the line of force.

Leaving only one conclusion: that the block had been
deliberately set to strike off-target. And by someone near
enough to activate the crystal array.

With her fingers wrapped tightly around the crystal shard
in her pocket, she hastened downstairs to tell her partner.

28

Aubrey didn't know what it was about this job that was bothering him so badly. Certainly he had done worse things in the course of his duties—or, at least, equally reprehensible things. But paired with the grisly murders that were haunting the club, he was feeling more on edge than usual. They had found the sixth body late last night, and the brutality had only gotten worse, the wounds rendered with an increasingly chilling precision. This particular killer, it seemed, was refining his craft in leaps and bounds. And there was nothing Aubrey could do to prevent it.

Nor was Gideon helping. The fact that the Guild girl was not jumping though his hoops had put him in an intolerable temper, and that made it impossible for Aubrey to broach the topic of his current assignment, which he had been putting off for too long. Yet when Gideon had asked him this morning how he was progressing, he hadn't had the nerve to protest. Or lie. Which was why he was here now, at the prisons, attempting to find a six-year-old girl so another depraved maniac could rape and then kill her—and all in the name of filthy lucre.

Was it any wonder he was starting to become disillusioned with his job?

There was an absurd kind of double-speak he had to go through with the prison officials as they attempted to negotiate a territory that was technically illegal and utterly reprehensible.

"What are you looking for?" they asked him.

"Someone small."

There was a dwarf, too wizened to pass as a six-year-old even under magerie, and male to boot. The next smallest was a five-foot harridan who would as soon kill as look at you. Aubrey was almost tempted to take her, if only for the damage she would inflict upon the client. But who had ever seen a five-foot six-year-old?

He tried a new tack. "How about younger?"

There was a twelve-year-old thief, slated to lose his hand for breaking into a magistrate's house, and a seventeen-year-old whore condemned for stabbing a rapist. Seeing Ephanon's sins laid out like this made him feel vaguely sick. What sort of society would maim a young boy for trying to survive, or castigate a young woman for self-defense? But it didn't come any nearer to solving his dilemma. As he had suspected, there were no six-year-old criminals in the Ephanon prisons. So what was he going to tell Gideon?

The truth, he decided. Not that it would make his associate even remotely happy. But the Golden Boy took the news with more equanimity than Aubrey had expected, shrugging off the latter's explanations.

"It was a remote chance, anyway. A six-year-old criminal? And female? You did your best."

"Well, there was always that five-footer," Aubrey said, still not willing to give up his dream; it would create a most satisfying confrontation. But Gideon just snorted.

"And when was the last time you saw a five-foot child? No, we'll just have to find an alternative. Any suggestions?"

"Cancel the contract?"

"Honestly, Aubrey, you have a very strange sense of humor sometimes."

I wasn't joking, Aubrey wanted to say, but knew well enough when to keep his mouth shut. In the face of his continuing silence, Gideon just shrugged and added, "Don't worry. I'll take it from here."

Which, Aubrey reflected as he departed, was precisely what he was afraid of.

Jen awoke early the next morning, rising from the pallet and dressing in careful silence to avoid waking Thibault. Thanks to an extra-strong infusion of poppy late the previous evening, her partner was finally asleep. Until then, the blasted man had attempted to be noble, muffling his groans in the pillow—which had only served to keep Jen awake, startling her from a light doze every time he so much as twitched.

But when he finally slept, so had she, and she felt surprisingly refreshed for how little rest she'd gotten. Which was just as well, because the next few days proved distressingly harried. For a time she was performing double duty, doing Thibault's job as well as her own: escorting Saul about the city in the guise of his temporary suhdabhar, squiring him from house to Cauldron and back as he required it, while still managing to execute her kitchen duties during prime delivery hours. And while she was temporarily excused from house cleaning—Alcina was not without compassion—she did still survey all the public rooms each morning, afternoon, and evening.

In some ways, it was a nightmare; in others, a revelation. For the first time in her life, she felt committed. There was a weight of responsibility on her shoulders that was hers alone to carry. That she could—that she *did*—was a neverending source of satisfaction to her. But yet . . . For all she had complained about being confined to the house while Thibault explored the city with Saul, she had to admit that her partner was right. Her time with Saul was mostly spent in carriages and waiting rooms, and she began to wonder more than once about her aunt's decision never to take a partner.

It was bloody hard work, doing everything yourself. Not to mention unaccountably dull—at least during the waiting periods, of which there were far too many. She almost longed to clean house again, if only for something to do. Moreover, her new-found suspicion of Gideon and Aubrey had made those periods of lurking about the un-magicked Cauldron, gathering what employee gossip she could, more than a little tense. On the first day, she had visibly flinched when Gideon crept up behind her on noiseless feet and slipped his arms about her waist, whispering, "Where were you last night?" She had managed to pass off her jumpiness as exhaustion—and her defection as worry over Thibault—but she hadn't missed the flare of anger in his eyes.

And throughout it all, she still hadn't managed to put her secret plans for Thibault into action. His days of captive bedrest were rapidly drawing to a close as he regained mobility in his shoulder and recovered from a minor concussion, so one morning, rising revoltingly early, she set about it before it was too late. A hasty pass through the washroom roused her, and then she braved the kitchens. It was so early only Beroe was up, but the cook had endorsed her plan. Within a few minutes, Jen was ensconced at a table in the back of the kitchen, surrounded by bags of flour, bowls of eggs, and mixing bowls, a book of recipes open before her.

After all, she was a trained member of the Hestian Guild. She could kill men—at least in theory—and had tracked an assassin to his lair. How hard could it be to bake a cake?

Her recipe of choice was for two cakes, but she would just remember to divide everything in half. And for a few minutes, her concentration reigned supreme as she pored over the book and divided, following the instructions meticulously. And then her attention was caught by Jahnee's arrival, coughing pitiably, and she accidentally added a double portion of the flour. And perhaps of the milk; she couldn't remember.

"What are you doing here so early?" Jahnee asked, wandering over.

"Baking a get-well cake for Ty. What about you?"

Jahnee coughed again. "Can't you tell? I've come for some of Beroe's disgusting syrup. It tastes like rancid fish, but it actually seems to work. Beroe?" Her voice rose plaintively, interrupted by another cough. "Can I have . . ."

The cook reached for a bottle on one of the tallest shelves and passed it to Jahnee. "A spoonful an hour," she counseled, "and no making faces!"

Jahnee dutifully swallowed the requisite dose and winced at Jen, masking the grimace behind one raised shoulder. Jen grinned back.

"Good luck with your cake," Jahnee added. "I hope Ty *is* feeling better." And with another series of grimaces and a shudder of revulsion, she departed, valiantly trying to clear her mouth of the medicine.

Jen turned back to her recipe. There was no extracting the excess flour, so she just decided to double the rest of the ingredients. And as to whether or not she had added the milk, well, if the cake didn't show any signs of setting, she could just add a bit more flour.

When she had finished mixing, she dipped a surreptitious finger in the batter to taste it, then decanted the mixture into the two prepared pans and popped them into the oven. She dutifully cleaned up her mess and bundled all the ingredients back into the cupboard. Then, with a small amount of time on her hands, she performed her morning survey.

But an hour later, the cake still hadn't set. Determined a mere pastry was not going to best her, she cast her mind back through the recipe, analyzing its components like the trained logician she was. More flour, certainly. She fetched that out, and mixed it into the pans while still in the oven. And to ensure it set, perhaps another egg or two. She stirred those in. And to compensate for the extra volume . . . perhaps more baker's powder was warranted, to ensure it rose. She shook that in as well, feeling unaccountably pleased with her analysis.

Really, there was nothing to this baking at all.

Then, as a last minute impulse of which she was particularly proud, she sprinkled a few more drops of vanilla into each pan for flavor. How many other untrained young chefs would have thought of that?

Grinning, she stirred the contents of each pan one more time for luck, and shut the oven. And, indeed, not long later, the mixture was fluffing and firming quite nicely. Well, perhaps not quite nicely, for it was bubbling over the sides of the pans and falling to char on the oven's floor. But then again, she had filled the pans rather full, so she supposed that was natural. Whatever was left over should be edible.

When the mixture had set, she lifted the pans out of the oven and scraped the charred edges off the sides of the containers. What was left did look properly cakelike, so she turned her attention to the icing. As the recipe instructed, she whipped the butter and sugar together with a mage-powered mixer and—on an inspiration that a little taste never hurt anyone—dribbled in some more vanilla.

It certainly had the consistency of icing when she was

done, but she had to admit that the rancid tan color was a bit startling.

"What is that?" Jahnee asked, wandering back in.

"Icing, I thought."

"Funny color."

"Yes, it is, isn't it? I wonder if Beroe has any food dye . . ." And retreating to one of the nearby cabinets, she began rummaging through the shelves. "What are you back for?"

Jahnee masked another cough. "My medicine. I think this thing's getting worse. Have you seen . . . ? Oh, there it is. Thanks. Good luck with the icing."

Her footsteps retreated. Jen's search revealed nothing but a jar of lurid red dye, which she was hesitant to use as it reminded her too much of Thibault's wounds. The cut in his temple had required five stitches to close.

Abandoning the dye, she returned to her bowl and peered at it critically. Really, the color wasn't all that bad. As long as it tasted all right . . . She swiped a bit off on a finger and stuck it in her mouth.

No, something was definitely off. Too much vanilla, or not enough? She looked around for the bottle, but the compulsively neat Jahnee must have already put it away. She rooted around through the cupboard, and found the bottle lurking behind the flour. She uncapped it and dipped a finger in, putting it to her lips, but when it hit her tongue she recoiled. Revolting stuff! No wonder the icing tasted off; she must have added too much by mistake.

Then her eyes lighted on a jar of cocoa powder, and she grinned. Of course! She shook some into the icing, feeling wonderfully inspired, and ended up with a rich, dark mix that disguised both color and—marginally—taste.

How could Thibault fail to be touched? And impressed?

The cooling cakes had collapsed more than she had expected. One of them had actually sunk in the middle, forming a sizable depression. She decanted them anyway, putting the sunken one on the bottom and suppressing an uneasy twinge at the audible thud they made as they fell out of the pans. But then, she *had* doubled the recipe . . .

Seized by a sudden inspiration, she iced the bottom layer and filled in the sinkhole with some of the least-burned pieces she had scraped off the outside of the pans. Then, adding the top layer, she iced the remainder and surveyed it with pride.

It was most decidedly a cake. And she had baked it herself.

Well, Vera, she informed her absent aunt, *you were right. There is a certain satisfaction in learning the skills of the lower classes!*

It really was a lovely cake. It just needed . . .

She cast her eyes about the kitchen. The rest of the staff had arrived by now, and Kore was slicing strawberries for Saul's oatmeal. Jen begged a few, slicing them thin and laying them in a scalloped pattern around the edges. Then darting out into the garden, she seized one of the late-blooming roses, snipping it off the bush along with a hand-span of stem. Then, stripping off the thorns, she impaled it in the center of the cake, where it reigned, blush-pink and lovely.

"What do you think?" she said to Kore, displaying her handiwork.

Her friend grinned. "Gorgeous. Ty will be impressed."

"That's the point," Jen returned, feeling excessively smug. "I'll leave it in the cold-box until right after lunch, then, shall I?"

"You might as well," Alcina responded, bustling in at the tail end of the conversation, "because Saul is awake and asking for you. Take him his oatmeal while you're about it, won't you?"

Masking a sigh, Jen stowed the cake and located her employer. He was in the breakfast room, with the morning paper spread out before him. "It's the Cauldron this morning," he told her cheerfully. "Then to Phytan Street to pick up my glassware."

"Yes, Saul."

"Bored of the suhdabhar's life already?" he teased, successfully divining her expression. But after more interminable waiting in the Cauldron—and a jouncing session in the carriage, listening nervously to the rattle of glassware—she was finally able to return to the house and her partner for lunchtime, carrying him up a tray.

Thanks to the concussion, Thibault had been sleeping a

lot, so she was glad to find him awake and less groggy than she expected. He was sitting up in bed when she entered, bared to the waist and poking experimentally at his shoulder, which had gone almost black with bruise.

"You look knackered, love," he said, glancing up as she entered. "Is Saul running you off your feet?"

"You could say that. How does your shoulder feel?"

"Not as bad as it looks. I'm sorry for abandoning you."

"It's not your fault." She sat beside him on the bed and pushed back his hair, checking to see how badly the bandage was stained. "I should change this."

"Later," he said, reaching for the tray. He tucked a piece of bread into his mouth, then added, "There'll be a scar, you know."

"Lucky you. A souvenir of Ephanon." She helped herself to a slice of the cheese.

"So, any new evidence to report?" he asked. "Any new suspects?"

"No, but . . ." She paused. "I did hear some of the employees talking this morning in the Cauldron. A few of them mentioned something about a series of murders, but only when Saul wasn't listening."

Thibault paused, a spoonful of soup halfway to his lips. "Yes, I had heard something about that, too, though I actually hadn't given it much credence at the time. Do you think there *are* murders going on at the Cauldron?"

"I don't know what to believe anymore. But if there were, it would certainly be cause for Stavros to shut down the clubs, if he were indeed the one to inherit. Now, are you almost done with lunch? Because I have a surprise for after."

"A surprise?" Thibault's eyes glowed. "What?"

"If I told you, it wouldn't be much of a surprise, would it?"

But it was a surprise, and a wonderfully successful one judging from the look on his face as she presented it. It was even more impressive than she had remembered.

"What is this for?" he asked, wiping the icing off the rose's stem and tucking it jauntily behind his ear.

"Happy birthday," she answered. "Belatedly. I baked it myself."

"*You* baked it? Great leaping polliwogs, Jen, I'm impressed!"

"Aren't you just?" She grinned. "Want some?"

"After a hug," he said, enfolding her with his one good arm. She hugged him back, careful not to jog his bruises. Then, proudly wielding her knife, she cut him a generous slice of cake—which admittedly did seem a little dense—and handed him a fork. He waited until she had cut a more conservative slice for herself, and then saluted her with his utensil.

"To majority," he said.

"To majority," she echoed, clinking her fork against his own. Then she watched him anxiously as he speared off a corner and put it in his mouth.

A spectrum of expressions flitted across his face, eventually settling on one of pointed interest. "Jen, this is . . . indescribable," he said.

With a sinking heart, Jen pushed her own fork through the leaden layers and took a taste. She took a breath, chewed twice . . . and then spat the disgusting mass back onto her plate.

All right, so it wasn't perfect. She just hadn't expected it to taste so strongly of rancid fish.

Thibault was valiantly masticating his way through a third mouthful. She slapped the plate out of his hands and confiscated his fork. "Don't you dare eat another bite!" she commanded, caught between laughter and tears.

His face was almost comic in its distress. "Well, I appreciate the gesture," he began, "but . . ." A grin threatened. "How . . ."

"Did I manage to make it so epically revolting?" she supplied, scrubbing at her eyes. "I have no idea." But of course she did; the taste gave it away. And suddenly the whole situation struck her as so absurd, she had to laugh. "Well," she managed, shaking a finger at Thibault, "at least this is one birthday you'll never forget!"

"Yes, the year Jen tried to poison me with rancid fishcake," he responded. "What the bloody blazes did you put in there?"

She could barely talk for laughing. "Cough syrup."

"What?"

"Cough syrup," she confirmed. All those valiant additions of vanilla of which she had been so proud had only managed to liberally dose the cake with Jahnee's medicine.

"It's a fortunate thing I'm a good assassin," she added, "because I've just managed to prove myself irrevocably hopeless at everything else!"

29

The following day, Thibault was back on his feet, although feeling a little worse for the wear. Headaches still plagued him, and his cheek still looked like raw meat. Moreover, if he hadn't been so assiduous about exercising it, his shoulder would have long since seized into a lump of immovable muscle. As it was, it still screamed at him when he moved it too enthusiastically—by which he meant anything that required over an inch of flexibility.

His bodyguarding skills were distinctly shaky, and his suhdabharing wasn't much better. He could hold a tray mostly one-handed, but when it came to serving, he quickly reached his limits—as evidenced by the ladle of soup he accidentally spilled into Saul's lap during his first evening back at the table. Saul was excessively gracious about it, and Stavros and Patroch, albeit reluctantly, did consent to serve themselves from the various dishes Thibault presented. But Lydea fussed nonstop at what she perceived as his deplorable lack of courtesy and talent.

Just another dysfunctional evening in the Soleneides household.

Patroch was whining about money and the club he wanted to open, and Saul was ignoring him. Stavros was trying to convince his son to take up a more reputable career than illusion club owner, which even Thibault could see was unsuited to Patroch's personality—such as it was. And Lydea was talking over all of them, complaining endlessly about her day.

From what Thibault could tell, listening with half an ear, it apparently had been quite trying, having something to do with miscut gowns and rude salesclerks, and so-called friends who hadn't been home when they'd promised. *Try standing under falling masonry,* he thought dryly as her litany unfolded, flexing his shoulder experimentally. It hadn't gotten noticeably better since the last time he'd checked.

Once again, he wondered about Jen's suspicions. That the block had fallen off-center was undisputed; he had been up on the roof earlier that afternoon, confirming her findings. And the cold foresight of that act had chilled him as much as it did her. Worse, even, since the one he had been suspecting seemed so incredibly feckless.

And yet . . .

He kept a weather eye open and watched events unfold. Which they did with a suddenness that startled him. And, for once, he was glad of his injury, which gave him an excuse for clumsiness.

It all began with Lydea, who said curtly, as Thibault unstoppered the brandy decanter, "You might as well bring an extra glass tonight."

It was such an uncharacteristic statement that the whole table went silent. Stavros gaped at her, and Patroch started violently. Saul's eyes began to gleam.

"Oh?" he taunted. "And who might that be for?"

"Me, of course. I've had a wretched day."

"Oh, ho! So it's all right to ridicule it until it becomes a necessity, is that it? I always suspected you were an opportunist at heart, Lydea."

"Mind your manners," she snapped in return. "I admit it's a filthy habit, but for once it might help, seeing how badly my poor nerves have been shaken. Not the least of which is the responsibility of your wretched suhdabhar, who can't seem to master the basics of serving!"

"Mother . . ." Patroch began, looking flustered.

"My suhdabhar," Saul interrupted, exchanging an amused glance with Thibault, "is clumsy only because he was wounded trying to save my life."

"Well, I hardly see how the one connects to the other. If he's that badly incapacitated, he shouldn't be at the table."

"Mother . . ."

"And who else would you have?" Saul countered. "Neither Jahnee nor Kore seemed to suit yesterday, and we're rapidly running out of servants."

"And whose fault is that?" she snapped. "What about Avram? He was always marginally competent."

"Avram's been on Phykoros for the past three weeks, in case you hadn't noticed."

"Well, anyway . . ." Lydea thrust out the glass Thibault had placed before her. "What is that wretched man waiting for?"

"Mother, I . . ."

"And you're sure you want to do this?" Saul asked, in obvious amusement.

"Yes, Mother," Patroch piped up. "I don't think you want to . . ."

She whirled on her son. "Don't you try to pretend *you* have morals!"

"But, I . . ."

Thibault shot the boy a hard look. His face was flushed, his protests too vigorous. Usually he cared not a whit what his mother did, so why the sudden solicitousness? Unless he had slipped something into the brandy . . .

The boy had been acting decidedly odd of late, and all too jumpy—especially in Saul's presence. So as Thibault uncorked the decanter, ostensibly to fill Lydea's glass, he passed it surreptitiously under his nose. He didn't smell anything odd, but then the brandy had a strong odor. And most poisons didn't have a distinctive scent, anyway.

He began to pour, watching Patroch's face go white, then deliberately fumbled the decanter, sending brandy cascading over Lydea's dress. He hoped it didn't act topically, for while he wasn't excessively fond of Lydea, he didn't wish her overt harm. But then, he supposed—if he had really wanted to—he could have missed her dress entirely. He masked a grin at his petty revenge, and recovered the spill while there was still a little brandy remaining in the decanter.

Lydea gave an irate shriek and dropped her glass, saving him from the necessity of knocking that over as well. "Why, you great, clumsy oaf . . . !"

"Are you all right, my boy?" Saul asked in concern, as Thibault straightened.

Patroch had visibly deflated, caught between relief and annoyance.

"Yes, yes; I'm fine," Thibault answered, wincing as he rotated his shoulder. At least he didn't have to feign that one. The sudden movement had pulled something, he was sure. "I am sorry. Let me uncork you another bottle."

And, carrying out the decanter, he stashed it and its remaining contents behind one of the hallway curtains for later collection.

"What, by all that is precious, were you thinking?" Jen demanded, as Thibault snuck into their room later that evening, pulling a crystal decanter from beneath his jacket. She had been reading a book as he entered, but now laid it down and uncurled herself from the bed. "I admit, I've stolen the occasional bottle of wine from the cellars, but this is ridiculous! What are we celebrating?"

She reached for the decanter, but he jerked it away. "Don't! Poisoned," he said. "At least, I'm assuming it is. You didn't happen to notice where the Mages' Quarter was, did you? I need to have this analyzed." He placed the decanter in their basin, checked the seal, then began pouring water over the outside.

"What are you doing?"

"Removing the residue. I had to fake a spill . . . No, don't touch it!"

"Don't be silly," she countered, taking the ewer from his hands. "You can barely move." And indeed, he was wincing exaggeratedly as the ablutions pulled at his bad shoulder. "Besides, it's not like I'm unfamiliar with poison." She continued to douse the decanter, scrubbing a washrag over it, then removed it from the basin. "Mind opening the window?"

Thibault released the catch and she swirled the water once through the basin, then tossed the lot—washrag and all—into the alley.

"There," she added. "Now, come with me." She dragged them both to the wash room down the hall, and scrubbed both their hands and the basin with the harsh lye soap.

"There, that should do it," she said at last. "Now, perhaps you'd better explain yourself. Who was responsible for this?"

"I'm not exactly sure, but . . ." He looked around surreptitiously. "Um, perhaps we should go back to our room, first?"

"Very well." She escorted him back, then curled up against the pillows, regarding him expectantly. He folded his bulk onto the foot of the bed, cradling his bad arm against him. She extracted one of the pillows from behind her head and tossed it to him. "Now," she said. "Talk."

He settled himself with obvious reluctance. "My theory?" he said at last, looking slightly embarrassed. "Patroch."

"Patroch?" she yelped. "That insignificant little piece of . . ."

"Shh!" he interrupted. "Not so loud."

"Why do you think *Patroch* is responsible?"

He flushed. "A hunch?"

"Oh, honestly, Thibault . . ."

"No, wait. Listen to this." And he related the evening's events.

She frowned. "It's intriguing, I'll admit. But . . ."

"I think it's more than intriguing. I mean, didn't it strike you as odd that Patroch showed up so conveniently as that stone fell?"

"No," she responded with a certain humor. "I actually found it moderately painful. You're not the only one with bruises." And lifting up the corner of her shirt, she revealed a smear of purple across her ribs, courtesy of Patroch's elbow.

Predictably, Thibault blushed. "But what if he were trying to push his grandfather into the path of the stone in an attempt to look like he was saving him?" he persisted.

Jen went very still. "That does pretty much eliminate Gideon and Aubrey, since it doesn't presuppose knowing Saul was guarded. But why in Varia's name would *Patroch* want to kill Saul?"

"Maybe Stavros isn't the one set to inherit."

"Or maybe he'd be the next victim. We should try to find a will."

"And check that murder angle. If there is something illegal in the clubs, Stavros might refuse the inheritance. And deny it to Patroch. Maybe we should ask Saul who inherits."

"And what if he asks the reason for our interest? Are we supposed to tell him we suspect his grandson is out to destroy him? We've mucked up enough assignments leaping to conclusions. Maybe we should research this one, first."

"How?"

Jen shrugged uncomfortably. "By searching Saul's office?"

"Jenny! Saul is our employer. And one of Owen's oldest friends. We can't just . . ." Thibault's voice trailed off, and he sighed. "I'll have the brandy analyzed. But maybe we should wait until we get the results back. We might be chasing a false lead . . ."

"Do *you* think we're chasing a false lead?"

He shook his head ruefully.

"And do you think Patroch suspects you are wise to him?"

"I think he might."

"Well, then. We shouldn't waste any more time. If it turns out we were wrong, we apologize—and no harm done. But if not . . . By the time the results of ycur tests are back, we'll have all the proof we need. If your hunch is correct, that is."

Thibault was silent for a long time. Then, "You're probably right," he admitted. "Much as I dislike it. I've become fond of the old man."

"I'm fond of him, too. But it's not Saul we're gathering evidence against; it's Patroch."

"I know. So how do we go about this?"

Jen sighed. "Well, we know the codes to his home office. I can search that tonight."

"And if you don't find anything?"

"I'll search the Cauldron."

"And that means . . ."

"Gideon; yes."

He looked uncomfortable. "Jen, I don't want you . . ."

"What? Using Gideon? I'm already sleeping with him," she said, rather more harshly than she intended.

There was another moment of silence. Then, "Jen, you shouldn't be doing this alone," Thibault continued.

"Why not?"

"Because I have a bad feeling about it. I should be there."

"Doing what? You can barely even move! You'd just be a liability."

He began cursing then—fluently, passionately. Her eyes flew open in alarm, and she clapped a hand over his mouth.

"Stop it! You're scaring me. I'll be fine. I've burgled plenty of offices before. Remember Iaon Pehndon? And who found Dougal's secret workroom?"

"Vera," he said dryly, but he accorded her the point. "So, how will you get into Saul's Cauldron office if it's shielded?"

She shrugged. "Saul doesn't seem overly imaginative with his codes. It'll probably be the same."

"And if it's not?"

She grinned crookedly. "Then I'll wing it, as I always do."

30

"So?" said Saul, resting his elbows on his desktop. "Report."

Gideon leaned back in his chair. "Very good residuals for the week. And the underwater theme is, once again, proving extremely popular. We'll undoubtedly bring back another variation on the same in a month or two. Perhaps something a little more tropical to herald the coming spring."

"Good; excellent. And?"

"There's been another murder," Aubrey inserted darkly, from his corner.

Saul stared at him. "Honestly, Aubrey, you're becoming positively obsessive. Forget the murders."

Gideon chuckled. He loved it when his boss proved him right. "That's what I've been telling him. You might want to watch this one, Saul; I fear he may be losing his edge."

Aubrey, ever humorless, flushed an unbecoming magenta at the words. "What do you know about edges?" he fired back. "You've never had one."

"On the contrary." Gideon smiled. "I'm all edge."

"Truer words were never spoken." Saul arched an eyebrow. "Now, you two, will you stop snipping at each other and tell me about my club? First off, Gideon, has that assassin girl been tractable?"

Gideon frowned; it was not a topic he cared to engage in. The bloody chit was proving distressingly unpredictable. Just when he thought he had her figured—had her wrapped around his finger, no less—she evinced startling moments of independence. She had refused his invitations twice— and once committed the unforgivable sin of actually *forgetting* about him—and Gideon was not used to being ignored.

Worse, a hidden link into Saul's home office that not even his employer knew about had revealed her searching that office late last evening—the very thing he was supposed to have prevented her from doing. Not that she would find anything of value there. Still, despite his anger, he was curious to see what she would do next, so he hadn't told Saul. Nor would he until the other shoe had dropped.

Which he was certain it would, at any minute now.

"Frankly," he said, "I have my doubts. I'm beginning to believe she's a lot cannier than she lets on—which in turn makes me wonder if your precious Guildmaster didn't know precisely what he was about, sending those two."

"Owen? Spying on me?" Saul sounded horrified.

Gideon shrugged. "I'm not saying he is. I'm just saying you shouldn't blind yourself to the possibility. My instincts never lie, and my instincts are telling me now the girl is trouble."

And more than just my instincts, he thought sourly. *Blast her.*

"Why, just because she's proved herself capable of resisting your charms?" Aubrey asked.

If it was meant as an insult, the comment went wide of its mark. Poor Aubrey; he was so transparent. "But, of course," Gideon answered, with a devastating simplicity. "People can't. Take yourself, for example."

His associate scowled, but Gideon knew the barb had struck its mark. Aubrey was as much under his spell as all the rest—Gideon had made certain of that—much as the man tried to deny it, even to himself. It was in his eyes as he gazed at Gideon, a look of sullen fascination and resentful devotion that let Gideon know he could have Aubrey when, where, and how he wanted. That he hadn't acted on the knowledge was less due to predilection than power—seducing Aubrey would gain him nothing.

"Very well, then," Saul conceded. "Keep an eye on the girl if you feel you need to. But I remain unconvinced that Owen is behind this. Now, is there anything else?"

Gideon glanced at Aubrey, almost a challenge. *Tell him,* he dared his associate silently. *Let him see how loyal you are. And who really holds his interests at heart.*

As usual, Aubrey seemed to misinterpret everything Gideon did and was, for the poor naif took this as tacit permission to speak of something which, until now, had been only a private matter between them.

Gideon masked his smile, relishing what would follow. He almost regretted setting his associate up like this, but Aubrey brought it on himself.

"What is it?" Saul demanded, sensing the unspoken dialogue that passed between them.

Aubrey glanced once more at Gideon, who just raised an eyebrow as if to say: *On your head be it.*

"We had a new client come by the club," Aubrey began.

"Wanting?" Saul inquired. And when Aubrey was silent, he prompted, "Revenge fantasy?"

Aubrey's face twisted in disgust. "With a six-year-old."

Gideon held his breath, absurdly pleased when Saul justified his faith by laughing. "By Varia, he starts young! That's going to be a tough one. How much did he offer?"

"Two thousand," Aubrey responded. "But . . ."

"Quite right," Saul agreed. "This one isn't going to be easy to fulfill. I take it you've already tried the prisons?"

"Aubrey did," Gideon answered with a grin. "No luck. Unless we can do anything with fifty-year-old male midgets . . ."

Saul chuckled. "My mages may be the best, but I think that's beyond even their powers! Well, it was nothing less than I expected." He stroked his chin. "Still . . . good instincts, Aubrey. If the man wants it badly enough, he'll be willing to pay substantially more than two thousand. Tell him the assignment is a difficult one, and that the price is three. I'm willing to negotiate down to two-fifty, but that's the absolute lowest. Understand?"

"Yes. But . . ."

"Come now, Aubrey. Don't get greedy."

Gideon didn't know what amused him more—Aubrey's self-righteous horror, or his employer's complete lack of comprehension. "Oh, Aubrey's not greedy," he informed the man. "I believe he's having a momentary attack of morals."

"Morals? Aubrey?" Saul exclaimed.

Aubrey crossed his arms and scowled at them.

"Alas, it's true," Gideon confirmed.

"Well I dare say he'll get over it soon enough; he always seems to. Meanwhile, you'll handle this matter, won't you, Gideon? I know I can trust you to accommodate the client without immersing the club in any adverse publicity or scandal."

"Of course. It would be my pleasure." Gideon exchanged a triumphant look with Aubrey. If possible, his associate looked more sullen than ever. "I'll report to you when I have matters tied up satisfactorily."

"Not literally, I hope?"

Gideon chuckled. "Good gracious. Now you've given me an idea."

"Varia forfend! Very well, then, is that it? Then you may go."

Gideon saluted and strode jauntily from the office, Aubrey trailing him in offended silence. They were halfway to House Soleneides before his associate said, "What did you have to do that for?"

"To prove a point. Aubrey, you know I love you. And I find your intermittent morality charming, honestly I do. But this is a business we're running. And occasionally even the best of us needs a little reminding." He followed up the words with his most ingratiating grin, and watched Aubrey melt enough to give him a grudging smile. By all that was precious, he hadn't lost his touch!

"But not for you, eh?" his associate countered. "You never need a little reminding, do you?"

"Of course not. That's why I'm so good at my job." They rounded the corner into Soleneides Square, and Gideon saw a furtive movement at one of the downstairs windows. "And, hark," he added, "here comes my delightful conquest, right on target! Get lost like a good man, will you, Aubrey? I dare say she has certain intimacies to impart. And"—his expression hardened—"apologies to tender."

Aubrey rolled his eyes but dutifully vanished, nodding curtly to Jen as he passed her on his way into the house. She, in turn, skipped eagerly across the paving stones—but then, Gideon reflected, who wouldn't be anxious to see him?

He almost forgot, for a moment, that he was annoyed with her.

She hastened up and took his arm. "Walk with me," she said, towing back along the path he had just trod, until they were screened from view by the laurels. There he paused, mustering the appropriate degree of coolness, and stared down at her.

"I'm sorry again about the other night," she began, sounding frighteningly uncontrite. And a little apprehensive? "But I've been trying to find you for the past three days to make it up to you . . ."

Knowing it never was good to forgive too quickly, he drew a silver case out from his pocket and extracted a smoke, lighting it in measured silence. He took a deep drag, then exhaled in a languid cloud, regarding her through the haze. The mild narcotic massaged gentle fingers into his brain. He put the appropriate level of hurt pride into his voice.

"Do you love him?" he asked.

"Not in the slightest! But then, I don't love you, either. Although admittedly I do appreciate your . . . finer points." And she stepped closer, trailing a finger down his chest. An expression she undoubtedly believed to be seductive adorned her face.

He grinned at her delusion, and brought the cigarette back to his lips. "I was wondering," he drawled, then inhaled. "Well, then," he added, the smoke trailing lazily from his nose and mouth. "How do you intend to make it up to me?"

Was it his imagination, or did she flinch imperceptibly as the mix of tobacco and Dreamsmoke flowed over her? She was oddly prudish in the midst of what she clearly thought was outrageous rebellion, and her aversion to the drug was clear. He didn't even know why he had lit the smoke, except maybe to rattle her.

"Well," she countered, attempting to mimic his drawl, "I can think of a thing or two. If you're willing."

Gideon had highly developed instincts; it came with the job. And his instincts were telling him now that she was lying. But about what? And, more intriguingly, why? And then it hit him: she was planning to burgle the Cauldron offices as well. And she was trying to use him to get close.

The other shoe, indeed.

He stepped closer until there was barely a handspan of air between them and inhaled deeply, ostensibly smelling her hair, her scent. But in reality, he was after a deeper truth, and his efforts were rewarded with a faint acrid tang. Barely even perceptible—invisible to the untrained—it was the elusive stink of fear he was after. And found. She was afraid of him. Afraid of his reaction to her desertion?

Maybe she knew that he had spied on her, last night. Or maybe she had finally realized what it meant to keep the Golden Boy waiting.

The thought cheered him immeasurably, and—abruptly magnanimous—he entered the game. "Tonight, then," he said. "You won't"—he let a trace of vulnerability show on his face—"abandon me?"

Her relief was palpable. "I'd rather die."

And you might, at that, he thought. *If you keep trying to use me.*

Really, he felt almost cheerful.

He took another drag on his cigarette, then lowered his mouth to hers, confounding her by exhaling the smoke down her throat. To her credit, she didn't cough or choke. And he had to admit she was a decent kisser.

Leaving Jen in the courtyard with Gideon, Thibault slipped quietly out the back door, the doctored brandy in a vial in his pocket. He didn't much like abandoning her to Gideon's mercy, but Jen was a big girl; she could take care of herself. And he supposed it was time he started acknowledging that fact. She had proved quite competent in her office raid the other night, locating Saul's will among his papers. And Stavros did inherit. Which meant he was either the next victim, or those murder rumors Jen had overheard at the Cauldron had to be investigated.

No, his partner was frighteningly competent, when she set her mind to it; she could handle Gideon Gilvaray. And he had a mage to locate and a poison to analyze. They would each be fine.

Thibault had begged leave from Saul earlier, saying only that he was following a lead; he had refused to give details when pressed. He still felt guilty for the lie, but Saul was safely ensconced in his office and not likely to leave for another few hours. By then, Thibault would be back to resume his duties.

And tonight . . .

Jen really would be on her own. Thibault wondered if she was nervous. With her bravado, it was hard to tell. But if it were him, he would be terrified.

Once again, he cursed the fate that had temporarily crippled his shoulder. He should be with her. Experimentally, he flexed the joint again, and was rewarded with the usual flaring of pain. He didn't know why he kept expecting it to get better.

The Mages' Quarter in Ephanon was less vainglorious than any other Mages' Quarter he had ever seen—almost humble, really—but he supposed that was due more to the illusion clubs than anything. Why advertise your powers when a whole culture was based on your prowess? The clubs of Sentenniel Street were grander than any three Mages' Quarters combined, so why waste the energy?

He found what he was looking for down a narrow alley and under a surprisingly tatty sign. He opened the door. A scruffy man looked up at his approach and scowled.

"What do you want?"

"Are you Mal Abelard?"

"Just Abelard will be fine," the man snapped. "And I repeat: what do you want?"

"I need to have something analyzed, and I've been told you can help me," Thibault answered, feeling oddly comforted by the man's brusque demeanor. He never trusted the more unctuous mages.

"I probably can; I have a knack for those sorts of things. But I'm not a mind reader. Well, I suppose I could be if I wanted—I am a mage, after all—but why waste the energy? Or time? Most people's thoughts aren't worth the perusal, anyway. Well, if you aren't going to tell me what you want," he continued as Thibault grinned, "get out. I'm a busy man."

"No doubt." Thibault pulled the vial from his pocket. "I want you to tell me what's in this."

The man uncapped the vial and sniffed it. "What kind of nonsense are you wasting my time with? That's brandy, boy. And a rather fine vintage, too, if I don't miss my guess.

Northern Lusania, I'd say; probably the Argossy vineyards. About . . . oh, twenty years old. I'm not surprised you don't recognize it."

Thibault chuckled. "Twenty-two, actually, but otherwise correct. Congratulations. However, it's not the brandy I'm interested in, but rather what's in it."

The mage's gaze sharpened. "Meaning?"

"Which poison?"

"Poison?" The mage's eyes gleamed. "Now that's more like it! Why didn't you say so before?"

Because I thought I was dealing with a scrupulous man, Thibault thought, but didn't say it. "Can you help me?"

"If I can't, nobody can. How's a week?"

"How's two days?" Thibault countered.

The mage stared at him for a long moment, and Thibault suddenly wondered how many of his thoughts *were* being probed. But apparently convinced of his earnestness, the man's only response was, curtly, "It'll cost you."

"How much?"

"A hundred for the analysis. Twenty-five for the rush."

"I'll give you one-ten for the lot."

Another long glance, and then, "I'll take it. But only because your problem intrigues me. Such a fine brandy obviously comes from one of the noble houses, but who's trying to kill a lordling?" The man chuckled: a rusty wheeze. "I can see you're not going to tell me. Never mind. I'll signal you when the information's ready."

"How?"

The mage chucked him a crystal shard. "When this goes black, come see me. I'll need half the money up front."

With a rueful grin, Thibault counted out fifty-five marks, and reckoned it a job well done. He was on his way out the door when another thought occurred to him.

"Do you work the clubs?" he asked.

The mage scowled. "What's it to you?"

"Information; I'm trying to find something out. I can pay."

"How much?"

"Fifteen."

The mage considered him. "What's the information?"

"Umm . . . does anything illegal ever happen in the illusion clubs? Anything concerning murder?"

The mage stuck out his hand and Thibault placed his remaining coins into it. Then the man began to laugh, magicking the coins away before Thibault could reclaim them. "Fifteen marks for telling you something half the lowlifes in this city could reveal? I'd consider that coin well earned."

"Then what's my answer?

The mage arched an eyebrow. "Ever heard of revenge fantasies?"

31

"I did it," Thibault said, entering their room when his night of service was over. "We'll know what's in the brandy in two days."

Jen was curled on the bed in her evening's finery. "How did you manage that?"

"A healthy infusion of cash. How else?"

"Of course; mages. So do you trust him?" she added as he took what was becoming his traditional place at the foot of the bed.

"Who, the mage?" And when Jen nodded, Thibault laughed. "Implicitly."

"Why?"

"Because he was rude. Curt and rude."

"Oh. Now *there's* a recommendation."

"Actually, it is. Besides, I piqued his curiosity. He wanted to know who was poisoning the aristocracy."

She showed the first signs of animation he had seen all evening. "What did you tell him?"

"Nothing." Thibault smiled ruefully. "Unfortunately—or perhaps fortunately, as the case may be—I located a mage with taste. He recognized the vintage of the brandy."

His partner actually looked impressed. "Perhaps a worthy mage, after all. Two days, you said?"

He nodded. Then, "There's something else," he said. And he relayed all the mage had told him about the revenge fantasies.

She went silent, looking down at her hands, folded demurely in her lap. "So do you think Saul sanctions this?" she asked at last.

"I guess that's what we need to find out."

She shivered. "Well, that certainly would revolt Stavros." She extended her arms. "How do I look?"

He surveyed her critically. She was wearing an ostensibly boned bodice—whose struts, he knew, contained her lockpicks—belted into a pair of voluminous pants with a wide belt he had seen her employ as a garrote during training. Her hair was braided down her back. She looked both competent and alluring, and he felt a sudden wash of apprehension at the thought. She would be seducing Gideon again—and this time with motive.

Dangerous motive, as it now seemed.

He forced a smile. "You look beautiful. As always."

"I tried on five different outfits, trying to find the right balance between seductive and functional. I'm still not sure I got it right."

"Trust me. You did."

She was silent.

"What is it, Jenny?"

"Nothing."

"Are you sure? Will you be . . ."

"Don't be silly; I'll be fine," she said, preempting him. "After all, it's only Gideon. Nothing I haven't done before."

He wondered why he felt a shudder of dread at the thought. But he surprised himself by forcing the issue. "I'm serious, Jenny. Do you want me there?"

Something in her seemed to snap. "More than anything," she said, then looked at him imploringly. "But you can't, Thibault; you know that as well as me."

He nodded ruefully, and opened his arms. To his vast surprise, she came to him, nestling her head against his shoulder. He closed his arms around her, feeling only a mild twinge of protest from his wounded shoulder. Her face was buried in the curve of his neck, her breath warm against his collarbone.

"Are you nervous?" he asked.

"Terrified," she admitted. "But I don't think Gideon noticed anything, earlier. I'm not that bad of an actress."

"I know." He brushed a hand across her hair. "And I'm sure he is just as besotted as the rest."

She gave a short bark of laughter. "Not Gideon. He's

the only one I haven't been able to figure out. Which is probably one of the reasons I find him so cursed fascinating."

He forced himself to equanimity. "So?"

"So?" She grimaced. "I'm going to find out if Saul is guilty of murder, if Patroch is really out to benefit from it, and at what expense to Stavros."

She looked up at him, and he had the sudden, over-whelming urge to kiss her. Her face was so near his own, her lips so uncharacteristically tremulous. But something of his intent must have communicated itself for she abruptly stiffened, pulling out of his arms and pushing back his hair.

"How's your head? I should change that bandage . . ."

He captured her hands. "My bandages are fine."

"Oh. Well, then. What time is it?"

"Close to midnight, I'd imagine."

"I should go . . ."

"I never thought you'd show so much reluctance to meet the Golden Boy," he said, unable to help himself.

She seemed to rally at that. "Yes, of course. What could I be thinking?" She grinned at him sardonically, and surprised him by dropping a kiss on his forehead. "Wish me luck."

"Luck," he said reflexively. Then, as she was halfway out the door, he added, "Wake me up when you get back, no matter what time."

She waggled her eyebrows comically at him and departed.

Jen hadn't lied when she said she was terrified, or that Gideon was one of the few men she couldn't predict. She had played this scene out in her mind infinitely many times, and each time she had received a different answer. He would go down like a felled tree beneath her spell; he would see right through her. She wouldn't find Saul's office; she would locate all the answers like magic among his papers.

It was as she had said to Thibault: she was a good actress, but betrayal on top of betrayal was weakening her. By all that was precious, she didn't even want to sleep with Gideon tonight, much as he excited her. She had once sus-

pected him of engineering these crimes; maybe she still
suspected him, despite her attraction. Instead, she had
nearly thrown herself at Thibault. Sweet, gentle Thibault
who was her best friend and strong right arm. Thibault,
whose touch seemed to cure all her doubts. Thibault, whose
big, ungainly body masked a wealth of sensitivity and compassion. Thibault, who deserved better than to be the sop
to her insecurities. She had almost kissed him tonight, and
that wasn't fair. If she ever slept with Thibault, it would be
because she couldn't stop herself any longer, and not because she needed someone to bolster her flagging ego.

And where, in Varia's name, had *that* thought come
from? Thibault was her partner; almost her brother. So why
was she wondering what those lips would *really* feel like on
her own?

Nerves, of course. That was all. Bloody nerves.

Gideon was waiting for her in the courtyard as promised,
smoking. If he offered her the cigarette this time, she would
take it; she felt the need for a little artificial courage tonight. But instead he stubbed it out on her approach and
straightened.

She walked up to him and took his hand. Her palm was
damp, but it was easy enough to blame that on the heat.
It was an unseasonably warm evening, even for Ephanon,
with a tropic fragrance on the breeze.

"I was beginning to wonder," he said, his voice rich with
amusement, "if you were planning to show."

She forced a smile. "And how could you doubt me? My
partner has not been injured; Saul does not need me.
Where else would I be?"

And suddenly, it was true. It was better, being near him.
A nervousness still churned in her belly, but this was Gideon, her Golden Boy. She had made love to this body; she
knew all its secrets. And despite everything, that reckless
chemistry was still between them, sizzling through her veins
and weakening her knees. He was not stolid Thibault; he
was heady and exciting. And there was no way he would
betray Saul. She brushed his lips with hers, tasting
Dreamsmoke and brandy.

The lights from Sentenniel Street flared across the sky
like an aurora.

"Are the mages still doing their underwater theme?" she asked. "I would hate to miss that one."

"For you, my lady . . ." He grinned. "It's the last night, actually, so you're just in time."

"Well, thank Varia for small favors. Are we going?"

He hesitated for a fraction of a second, measuring her, then offered his arm.

She looped her elbow through his and then, surprising them both, said, "Aren't you going to offer me a smoke?"

"I wasn't aware you wanted one. But far be it for me to deny you all the pleasures of Konasta . . . Shall I light it for you?"

"Please," she said, feeling suddenly worldly, as if having gorgeous and vaguely dangerous men light Dreamsmoke-laced cigarettes for her was the most common of occurrences. And how much damage could one smoke do? All she wanted was enough to relax her, to take off her betraying edge.

He paused and, without dropping her arm, extracted his silver case. He shook out a cigarette and placed it between his lips. With a graceful economy of motion—and an obvious familiarity—he lit it and took a deep drag before handing it over to her.

Recklessly, she seized it, imitating his motions. The smoke sank into her lungs, thick and pungent. She coughed slightly, but pulled it deeper, embracing its effects. She could feel the traces of the narcotic beneath the tobacco, filtering throughout her body. Warm, languid; erotic. Heady. Like Gideon.

She laughed and took another drag.

"Nice?" Gideon asked.

"Very." Her nervousness *was* vanishing, praise Varia.

"Ah," he sighed, and grinned. "Another innocent corrupted."

"I am not," she replied, "an innocent."

"Of that, my lady," he said, his eyes smoldering, "I am infinitely aware." He began to walk, extending his fingers for the smoke, and she passed it back to him. He drew on it contemplatively, the smoke trailing languidly from his nostrils as they strolled.

She giggled.

"What?" he asked.

"You look like a dragon."

He turned and growled at her, and she giggled again.

"I don't think I'm going to let you have any more of this," he said mildly. "It's making you silly." But he passed the fag back to her anyway.

She discovered she liked the feel of it in her fingers; liked the dramatic way she could blow out the smoke. It made her feel old. Almost thirty, really.

She had smoked the thing to a nub by the time they reached the Cauldron. Gideon plucked it from her fingers and dropped it to the cobblestones, grinding it out under his boot. Then, bypassing the crowds of jealous gawkers, they entered the club.

The decor was stunning. Swathed in a shimmering, aqueous light, fish darted and kelp forests swayed. Whales swam by with a ponderous grace. But for once, Jen was not able to concentrate on the illusion. All she kept wondering was which sculpted coral bed, which waving tendril, masked the door to Saul's office. Was it downstairs with the bars and the gaming tables, or upstairs amidst the trysting rooms? If she were the one who had designed this club, where would she keep it?

"You seem preoccupied," Gideon said. "Doesn't the illusion please you?"

"Infinitely. But . . ." Suddenly all the posturing struck her as ridiculous. Why should they spend an hour engaged in inane chatter and mindless flirtation when they both knew they were going to sleep together? She wanted this evening over with—all of it: the lies, the seduction, the burgling. And the sooner the better.

She stepped fractionally closer. "Gideon . . ."

"What?"

"Take me upstairs."

"Now?" He sounded vaguely scandalized. "Don't you even want a drink?"

"No. I want you." *And then I want to burgle Saul's office. And then I want to be home, before dawn, with all of this behind me. All right?* she added somewhat petulantly to herself.

"Well. This is a change. But as I said before, who am I

to deny you all the pleasures of Konasta?" And he grinned, holding out his arm. She tucked herself beneath it, belatedly realizing that her consumption of the Dreamsmoke was the perfect excuse for her unprecedented behavior.

Clever of her, in retrospect, to have thought of that.

"What are you smiling about?"

"Oh, nothing. You. Us. Have you ever noticed that those whales look particularly phallic?"

She was definitely lying, Gideon thought, as he led her upstairs. Lying, lying, lying, lying.

She *was* planning to burgle Saul's office.

He would have to make certain the experience was one she would never forget.

32

It was wonderful; it was wretched. Their bodies meshed, their chemistry sizzled. And then fell hopelessly, horribly flat. He wouldn't quit. She wouldn't come, although she strove in vain for release. *Nerves,* she told herself. *Nerves.* But it was more than that. There they were in his private haven, ensorcelled to look like a potentate's chamber—all rainbow silks and glinting gold hangings, as plush and romantic a setting as she could desire—and all she wanted was to be somewhere else. Saul's office; the servants' quarters she shared with Thibault. Bergaetta; Ceylonde; Nova Castria. Even Arrhyndon, the scene of her disgrace.

Worse, Gideon was with her, his golden body a marvel, and all she could think about was Thibault. Her partner's big, ungainly form kept inserting itself onto her vision, replete with blackened shoulder and scabbed cheek, the white swathe of bandage cocked jauntily over one eye. He was saying, "Are you sure you'll be all right? I should be with you . . ."

Not here, Thibault, she thought. *Definitely not here!* But it was no use. Real or imagined, his implicit disapproval tore at her.

Blast it, Thibault, will you never let me be? Must you always be my de facto conscience—even when I don't want one?

Briefly, she considered faking her release, just to be done with this travesty. But in the end, she was just too tired.

"Not working, is it?" Gideon said at last.

"No." She rolled away from him, pulling herself into a tight, self-contained ball. "I'm sorry."

He reached out to caress her back, and suddenly she

couldn't bear even that intimacy. She flinched away from his touch.

"It happens sometimes," he said.

Not to me, she wanted to rail, but wisely held her peace.

"I suppose it wasn't meant to be," he added eventually.

"I suppose not." Her voice was curt. She sprang from the bed and began to gather her fallen clothing.

"Do you want . . . ?"

"No." She didn't even rightly know what he had been asking, but suddenly it didn't matter. There was nothing she wanted from him. Nothing at all. Except for him to abandon her as completely as he always did after the act so that she could get on with her burglary. And her life.

But, ironically, it seemed the one time she actually wanted him gone, he was determined to play the solicitous suitor.

"It could be the Dreamsmoke," he said. "I've never seen it take anyone quite this way before, but there's always a first . . ."

She drew on the voluminous pants and began lacing up her bodice, surreptitiously checking the seat of her lockpicks in the struts. "It's not the Dreamsmoke, it's just me. Haven't you ever had an off-night?"

He shook his head with a certain amusement, and she masked a scowl. *I'll just bet, you bastard!* "Well, I have," she lied, and almost laughed that the statement galled her more than all the other lies she had been spouting. It was the one thing about herself she had always relied on. That, and her assassin's guile.

Guile, don't fail me now.

"But if you would rather I stayed . . ." she said, her hand going back to her bodice lacings.

That did it. "Alas, no," he replied. "I mean, as much as I would love you to stay, you know I have to work to do. The club doesn't shut down just because I desire it to."

It was his standard litany, and she had never been more glad to hear it. She pasted on an expression of mock-contrition and bound the sash about her waist. "I know," she said. "Next time?"

He rose and began dressing himself, his movements a

study in grace and economy. "Absolutely. I wouldn't miss it for the world."

"Good." She scooped her hair up into a tail and began plaiting it down her back. "And I'm sorry again."

"Think nothing of it. Will you be all right?"

The words were such an inadvertent echo of Thibault's that she couldn't help laughing. "I'll be fine."

"Really?"

"Positively."

"Well, then."

And as there seemed to be nothing more either of them could say, he kissed her quickly and departed—as he had so many times in the past—leaving her to find her way out alone.

Jen hoped that Gideon hadn't noticed, in the process of undressing her, that her pants were a different color inside from out. It was not much of a disguise, but it might fool the most superficial of scans. If Gideon were looking for a young woman in a white bodice and scarlet trousers, he might pass over, at least once, a vision in dull white and tan.

Hastily stripping off her leg-wear, she reversed it, completing the most basic of transformations. Then, easing out of the room, she descended to the lower reaches of the club. She had already determined that Saul's office would most likely be on the ground floor—solely for convenience—and so decided to commence her search there. And the one advantage to the illusion the mages had picked for this week was that the undersea lighting was hazy and indistinct, and the throngs of people hid her furtive movements.

Burgling a club at the height of its activity—how stupid was that? Except that, with all the people, it was the time she was least likely to be noticed. Besides, she did have one advantage: Absalom's amulet, which she had been wearing since they found the silver ball. The tricky part had been where to hide it on her person tonight.

She had at first considered wearing it around her neck or bound against her wrist, but any new piece of jewelry was bound to look suspicious—and especially such a thing as Vera's amulet. Granted it was carved into a pretty design, but it was still a dull lump of greyish stone, hardly worthy of special attention. She had considered weaving it into her braid, but that, too, would look odd. Not to mention that the Golden Boy had a penchant for unbinding her hair and spreading it out around her on the pillows. She couldn't hide it among her clothing, as he would be undressing her. And it might fall out of her shoes. Which, in the end, had left her with only one alternative.

So she had swallowed it, hoping that wouldn't affect the magic. Or that, at about the length of her top thumb bone, it wouldn't hurt too badly coming out again.

It was yet another of the things she hadn't told Thibault.

Taking a deep, preparatory breath, she invoked it. There was a long, anxious moment which seemed to stretch out for an eternity, and then the veil of illusion shuddered and tore, the optical trickery melting from the room.

It was a startling sight.

The light was still a dull green, but it no longer shimmered. Instead, it seemed to impart a depressing tawdriness to the room—which, admittedly, was tawdry enough without the added help. Worse than in the daylight hours, the dull illumination only emphasized walls that hadn't seen a decent coat of paint in years; floorboards that were scuffed and pitted from thousands of passing feet; tables and chairs that were rickety affairs, teetering on the verge of collapse. The long sweep of the bar was scarred with old cigarette burns.

And throughout it all, awed patrons gaped at nothing.

As for the patrons themselves . . . For one thing, they were far less beautiful or exotic than they had appeared before—though Jen supposed that was to be expected when your own image could be changed as easily as those that adorned the walls. There were also a surprising number of famous faces mixed in among the common. Jen thought she recognized the Minister of Finance, huddled in a corner with a hooker who must have been well over fifty. Moreover . . . was it just her imagination, or did there seem to be somewhat fewer of those patrons than there were before?

Did the illusory scam extend to fake guests as well?

Well, whatever the case, she would have to be careful. It

would be all too easy to blow her cover by walking through some carefully crafted illusion she could no longer see. So she paid close attention to her fellow revelers, gaping when they gaped, and avoiding the spots they seemed to avoid.

Appropriately enough, she felt like a fish in some rather mindless school, following the pack. But at least she could see some things they missed, like the hidden doors.

She dismissed the two in the main part of the club immediately; they were too obvious, and probably led to storerooms. The long hall that led down to the gaming tables was featureless, but in the gaming hall itself there were any number of interesting possibilities.

She hadn't been in this part of the club before. Gideon hadn't seen fit to show her, and she wasn't a gambler. But judging from the throngs that flocked the tables, this was one of the more popular rooms. Money changed hands with a frightening rapidity as bets were laid and wagers taken. Some of the club's hookers prowled the room like circling sharks, searching for the big spenders. And the big winners—of which there were not many.

As Saul had told Thibault, it was all engineered for effect.

Nonetheless, she had a feeling about this chamber, a gut impression that it would appeal to Saul's sense of humor to locate his private sanctum in the midst of such controlled chaos. There were five doors in the room, one on the far wall across from the entrance, and two each on the side walls. Curious, she reversed the amulet's effects and caught her breath.

Sprays of lights in the form of phosphorescent plankton fountained into the air above the tables, winking and twinkling. Sinuous eels writhed, their sides luminous rainbows that morphed and shifted. Everything was a dance of color and lights and stimulation—guaranteed, no doubt, to keep the patrons off-balance and less than perfectly focused on their bets or the club's abominable manipulations. And over it all—illusion or reality—lay a steady thump of music, hypnotic and driving, which only enhanced the effect.

Two of the doors Jen had located without illusion were still present, only illuminated with sprays of colored lights, instantly ruling them out. But the other three were invisible behind gargantuan sprays of coral towers, and she invoked the amulet again to reveal them. Her gut, again, told her it would be the center one, which held the position of most prominence, but how to proceed? Would it be locked? And if so, how could she get her lock-picks out without anyone noticing? And then, providing she could pick the lock, would opening the door interrupt the illusion, creating a gaping hole in the oceanic wall?

She didn't have answers to any of these questions, but she wasn't a trained Guildmember for nothing.

Sidling closer to the door, she jiggled the handle—locked—and then examined the keyhole. It seemed a simple enough mechanism; obviously Saul trusted more to illusion than hardware to protect it. Or his shield spell, which Jen could only hope she had the codes to.

Revoking the amulet again, she let the illusory splendor descend, and strolled from the room, in search of the public lavatories. There, locked into a stall, she extracted her lock-picks and tucked them into the sash at her waist. There was an anxious moment as she left the lavatory, almost colliding with Aubrey on the Cauldron's main floor, but fortunately Gideon's associate seemed too preoccupied to notice her.

With a sigh of relief, she slipped past him, heading back for the door at the end of the gaming room. Once there, she banished the illusion, and set to work, her hands crossed behind her back, ostensibly leaning up against the coral castle that hid the club's far wall.

It was harder to work that way, but Jen was eventually rewarded by the twin clicks of the tumblers falling. The lockpicks returned to their temporary resting place at the small of her back, and she reached for the knob.

It turned freely under her hands.

Revoking the amulet's power one final time, she turned sideways, seeing her hand resting on one protuberant knot of coral. Cautiously, she whispered, "Open," then held her breath and eased the door wider, a fraction at a time, all the while watching the illusion. No alarms sounded, no magical barriers met her questing hand.

She heaved a sigh of relief.

She didn't have much clearance before the coral bed began to ripple and distort with the door's movement, but fortunately Jen was slim, and the crack was just wide enough for her to slip through. Almost, she thought, as if it were meant to be. She cast an anxious glance around, making sure none of the patrons were looking, then eased closer to the door and nipped inside.

It would, she supposed, look mightily odd to see a girl just disappearing into a bed of coral, but if her actions raised a hue and cry, she didn't hear it, for the door was thick and muffled all but the barest hum of voices and faintest thump of music from beyond it. The room was windowless, swallowed in darkness, and she fervently hoped that, were she right, Saul did not share his friend Owen's penchant for cuing his magelights to all sorts of ridiculous phrases.

"Lights up," she whispered. Nothing.

"Illuminate?" she hazarded. Still nothing.

"On?"

That did it. The globes of magelight slipped sweetly into life, banishing the shadows. She grinned in triumph at what was clearly Saul's office. Bookshelves lined one wall, stacked with ledgers, and filing cabinets covered the other two. The desk was large, with wide, deep drawers. It would take a while to search it all—even cursorily—but she had time. It was barely midnight, and the club didn't close until dawn. She had escaped Gideon's notice, and no one would be looking for her. She would start at one end of the room and work her way around it methodically. And she would find what she was looking for, something, anything, that would give Patroch a motive.

She felt like singing. For all her worries, it had been so easy. All her hunches had paid off; all her fears had proved unfounded. She was here. She would find out why Patroch wanted to kill his grandfather, she would bring that information back to Thibault, and how they would laugh at his groundless fears!

So easy.

Too easy, a sardonic voice whispered in her head, but she ignored it. She was the Dagger, after all. Making it look easy was just part of the job.

She locked the door behind her, then opened the first of the cabinets and started searching.

33

Gideon knew the moment Jen entered the office; after all, he had already cued off the shields. She couldn't fool him with her talk of off-nights and Dreamsmoke. He was willing to bet she hadn't had an off-night in her life. She was like him, a hedonist; like always recognized like.

No, what was wrong with Jen tonight was fear, plain and simple. Fear, clotting her gut, crippling her nerves; he could smell it in her sweat as she writhed atop him. And it wasn't fear of him—although, had she a brain, it should have been—but more fear of some act, some betrayal, that was eating away at her.

Betrayal, indeed. He had watched her sneak downstairs in her reversed trousers, pitiful disguise that it was. Did she honestly think such a puerile ruse could fool him? The only thing that confounded him was where she had stowed that blasted amulet she had been wearing around lately—the one that invalidated his mages' illusions—for by her behavior she quite clearly had it. He had searched her quite carefully as he undressed her and hadn't found a thing.

It almost made him re-evaluate his estimate of her intelligence. But did she honestly think that his boss—the smartest, most manipulative man he had ever known—would trust to nothing more than a flimsy lock and some random illusion to protect him? Or to the same codes that guarded his home office? Not that there was anything worth protecting in either place—like all smart men, Saul conducted his more nefarious dealings elsewhere entirely—but it was the principle of the thing that mattered. Offices were protected; private papers were guarded. For if you got careless with one, then all of them would suffer.

Gideon had learned that lesson at a very young age, indeed.

Besides, there were one or two items in that office that, while not particularly incriminating, might raise questions that no one wanted answered. And Saul had commanded his Golden Boy to keep her out of any areas he didn't feel she belonged in.

Saul's Cauldron office quite definitely qualified.

He didn't go down right away, though. He'd give her some time to become complacent; it would make his revenge all the sweeter. So he sipped his drink on one of the upstairs balconies and trimmed his nails meticulously with his dagger, and when he was convinced sufficient time had elapsed, he stood up and stretched, meandering his way down the stairs to Saul's office.

It was later, now, and the crowds around the gaming tables had thinned. Those that were left had the lean and hungry look of professional gamblers; they were not likely to notice his actions. But the surge of light from the office would attract some attention, so he approached one of the lingering mages keeping watch over the scene.

"A surge of water," he said. "Two feet off the back wall, in twenty seconds."

The mage nodded his comprehension, and Gideon sauntered to the door. He didn't need an amulet to locate the doorknob; years of practice guided his hand instinctively. He wiggled the knob. It was locked. As the backside of the wave surged past him, he inserted his key into the lock and turned.

Yellow light spilled from the portal, hidden from view by the mage's illusion. Gideon grinned and slipped inside, pulling the door shut behind him as the last of the wave trailed past. Then he rested his shoulders against the thick wood and waited.

Jen was about two-thirds of the way through her search; he hadn't expected her to be that efficient. Some of the filing drawers still gaped open, spilling papers across the room. Ledgers had been returned haphazardly to the shelves. Three files of notes in Saul's bold, black hand were strewn across the top of his desk. That, above all, seemed the crudest violation.

He remained silent, waiting for Jen to notice him. It took her a moment. Then slowly, inevitably, she looked up, as if sensing the weight of his stare, the force of his presence. She started guiltily as his curls caught the light.

"Gideon!" she gasped, her hand going to her throat. "What are you doing here?"

She tried to keep her voice neutral, but he could hear the betraying tremor.

"I might ask the same of you," he said, in what he had always considered one of his most reasonable tones.

Her embryonic smile died a-borning. "I was just . . . that is . . ."

"Betraying my master?" he finished, his voice going flat and deadly. It was a tone he had practiced often, and which, he had been told, was frighteningly effective.

In response, the sheaf of papers dropped from her nerveless fingers, spilling about her feet like so much dry snow.

He grinned again, and advanced.

This was going to be fun.

Wrapped up in her thievery, Jen hadn't heard him enter the office. But how could she have missed it? And how could she have missed what Gideon truly was? How could she have envisioned true feeling in the Golden Boy apart from her own thwarted imaginings? There was certainly none, now. His eyes had gone flat and dead as a shark's: ice-cool as always, but without a glimmer of emotion. And yet, incredibly, he was smiling—*smiling*—as he advanced on her.

An atavistic horror rooted her to the spot, and she froze like a rabbit caught in a falcon's regard.

"What, no glib words now?" he taunted. "No pretty platitudes or explanations?"

Sick. He was sick. A wave of nausea swept her. She had slept with *this*? She had let these hands, now raised in menace, touch her body? Had let these lips, so cruelly twisted, linger on her own?

She had flirted with a madman, smug in the depths of her own ignorance and infallibility. And now she was about to pay the price.

All her assassin's training flitted through her head, goading her to move, to fight—*anything*—but by then it was already too late.

"Is that *blood*?" Aubrey's voice was horrified.

Gideon examined the spot on his shirt front meticulously. "Blast. The wretched stuff never comes out properly in the wash."

"What have you been up to now?" Aubrey demanded. "Or don't I want to know?"

Gideon grinned. "Most likely the latter." He turned his scrutiny to his knuckles. Not too badly bruised. Excellent. The girl *had* been weaker than he expected. Gideon always liked it when the world conformed to his assumptions.

"I'm serious, Gideon," Aubrey continued, unusually persistent in the face of his companion's silence. "What have you been doing?"

Gideon surveyed his associate critically. "You *are* losing your nerve, aren't you?"

There was a moment of silence. They were sitting in the Cauldron's main room as dawn streaked the sky, counting out the evening's take. All the club's other employees had long since gone home and to bed.

Aubrey's face contorted, masking a yawn. "It is you, isn't it?"

"What is me?"

"The psychopath. Murdering the clients."

Aubrey's expression was a study in contrasts: righteous and fearful; sullen and triumphant. It was too much. Gideon threw back his head and laughed.

"Oh, Aubrey," he declared, wiping the tears of mirth from his eyes. "You are an endless delight!" And, reaching out, he tousled his companion's hair.

Aubrey scowled, but more from reflex than annoyance; Gideon could feel his hard edges melting.

"So it's not you?" Aubrey persisted.

"Of course it's not me! Go check the upstairs rooms if you don't believe me."

Aubrey sighed heavily. "No; that's not necessary. Sorry, Gideon."

"For what? Confusing me with . . ." And Gideon again convulsed with laughter. "Wait until I tell Saul!"

"I wish you wouldn't."

"I know."

"Which is precisely why you are going to," Aubrey finished, with yet another sigh. "I don't even know why I bother."

"Because we are partners, Aubrey, united to the end. One for all . . ."

"And all for you," Aubrey finished dryly.

Gideon chuckled.

"So what *were* you up to tonight?"

"Nothing dire, I assure you. Just a little business for Saul. Strictly according to his orders, of course. Now, shall we shut up the Cauldron?"

Thibault was frantic. He had been up half the night waiting for his partner, drifting in and out of an uneasy doze, startling awake at every whisper of movement or creak of floorboard in the hall outside their room. Midnight passed, and then the dark of the night when even Sentenniel Street seemed quiet, and still no Jen. By the time the sun was reaching tentative fingers across the sky, Thibault was in a frenzy. Where the blazes was she? A thousand times over, he berated himself. Injury or no injury, he should have been with her. His shoulder was almost . . .

He winced and bit back a cry at the injudicious movement. His shoulder still hurt like the dickens. But that shouldn't have prevented him from being at Jen's side.

He waited as long as possible before necessity forced him from their chamber. Saul would be looking for him, and Alcina for Jen. And despite the fact that he wanted to raise the household with his cries and send them all searching, he did the only thing he could under the circumstances.

He reigned in his anxiety and lied for her.

No, Gilyan wouldn't be making it downstairs this morning, he told them. She had contracted a flu and was up half the night vomiting. No, he didn't think she wanted anything to eat. It was probably best to just let her rest and recuperate.

He hated lying, but how else could he avoid annihilating her cover? After all, maybe she had been locked into the club, trapped in Saul's office and unable to leave. Or maybe she had gone haring off, following another lead. That would be typical. But it had to be something that simple, that innocuous, because the alternatives were unthinkable.

Thibault didn't know how he made it through the day. But his acting abilities must have been better than he thought, for though he possessed not one ounce of concentration, Saul appeared not to notice any change in his behavior, and kept him running. He managed to slip away briefly at lunchtime, ostensibly to check on his wife, but Jen had still not returned. He left a frantic note on the pillow—*Where are you? Find me! I told everyone you were sick.*—then returned to duty and to a prolonged trip out of the city that Saul had been planning for days but had put off until Thibault had recovered enough to drive the trap one-handed.

The day passed in a muddled haze, and they didn't return to Ephanon until close to dark. Frantic, Thibault almost flew up the steps to their room. He flung back the door, expecting to see Jen—not sure whether to hug or berate her—but the room was still deserted, washed only in the low, slanting beams of the late afternoon sun. It cast a golden glow across the empty bed, throwing his note into stark relief.

He didn't think it had even been moved.

He flung open the casement and peered futilely into the alley below, not even sure what he was expecting to see. Then he shut the windows again and began to pace, his long strides measuring the tiny chamber.

"Jen," he groaned. "Jenny, where are you?"

A sound, faint and almost inaudible, stopped him in his tracks.

"Jenny?" he called again, a note of hope in his voice.

The noise was clearer this time, caught between a sob and a moan. It sounded almost involuntary, as if emitted against the utterer's will. It also sounded suspiciously like it was coming from the closet.

He flung open the door. "Jen?" He almost didn't see her, huddled in the darkest corner. "Jenny? Is that you."

She seemed to shrink from view, burrowing deeper into the shadows. "No . . ."

Her voice was so thick he could barely make it out.

A sudden anxiety assailed him, but he kept his voice as gentle as he could. "Jenny? What's the matter? What's happened?"

If he hadn't known better, he would have thought she was crying. But Jen never cried.

"Nothing. Everything . . ."

She *was* crying. Bloody blazes!

The closet was tiny and Thibault was not, but somehow he managed to wiggle inside, wrapping his arms around her as best he could in the narrow confines. She gave a muffled sob and burrowed against him. She smelled, now that he noticed it, of blood and stale urine.

His heart inverted.

"What's everything?" he whispered, stroking her hair. It was tangled, and stiff with what he feared was clotted blood.

"This," she said, and hiccoughed.

A sudden anger seized him. But he kept his voice gentle as he asked, "Can you come out of the closet now?"

She shook her head frantically.

"No? Why not?"

"Because you'll hate me."

"For what?"

"For . . . for . . ." Another muffled sob escaped her, her tears hot against his chest.

"You know I could never hate you, Jenny," he said. "Not now; not ever."

"Even if I failed? Even if you could say: 'I told you so'?"

"Have I ever said 'I told you so'?"

"No." She almost laughed.

"And if I promise never to say 'I told you so' in future, will you come out?"

She hesitated for a moment, then sniffed and nodded her agreement.

"Right, then." He gently disentangled her from his arms and took her hand, carefully backing out of the closet with her in tow. When the late afternoon light poured over her, he began to curse—viciously, fluently.

She cringed and pulled away. "You promised . . ."

Cold fury seized him. "Not you, love," he assured her. "Him. Whoever did this to you. Was it Gideon?"

"Yes . . ."

"The rat bastard!"

She gave another snort of what might have been laughter, but Thibault was ready to kill. Her eyes were swollen half-shut, her mouth clotted with dried blood. A deep gash on her right cheek had bled freely down her face. Her clothes were torn and filthy, and what little he could see of her skin was already purple with bruises.

It *was* dried blood in her hair.

"Blast him!" he exclaimed, though the oath seemed stale and puerile, no match for the brutality Gideon had inflicted on his partner. "What happened?"

"He caught me. In Saul's office. He . . ."

"Never mind; I can guess the rest. Did he . . . did he rape you?"

Jen shook her head miserably. "No need. He already had done. Time enough, and more." Her voice was thick with self-loathing.

Thibault sighed and touched her torn cheek lightly. "You need a bath," he said. "And some dinner. When you didn't come home this morning, I told the staff you were sick. So no one will question me if I request a tub and a tray."

Again, another snort of that almost-laughter. "It's not that far off a lie. I've certainly felt better. I think he broke some ribs."

"Let me see." Thibault ran his hands lightly along her sides, searching for breaks. "No, merely bruised, I think. Not that it's going to make you any more comfortable. Oh, Jenny, I'm so sorry . . ."

Another involuntary spill of tears cascaded down her cheeks, ceasing almost before it had begun. But, "Not your fault," she said. "Mine."

"No! Not yours," he insisted. "Gideon's."

"But I couldn't handle him . . ."

"Hush, now. No one expected you to take on a monster." He peered down at her anxiously. "Will you be all right for a few minutes? I'm going to go fetch you a bath. And some food. Don't go anywhere."

"Don't worry." She rewarded him with a shaky smile.

"If I were going to fling myself from the window, I'd have done so already."

He managed to smile back, though his heart was breaking. "Good girl. Now, hold tight. I'll be right back."

34

Thibault pounded down the stairs at a run, his thoughts a muddled confusion. What had happened? What had she discovered? And what could have prompted Gideon to take such dire action? But such answers, he knew, would have to wait. What he needed now was to help her, and for that he required a reasonable calm—and a demeanor that wouldn't alarm the servants. So he slowed his steps and marshaled himself to composure.

He found Kore in the front hall, and asked her to bring up some hot water and a tub, and to leave it in front of their room because his wife didn't want to be seen. He asked the same of Jahnee in the kitchens for food. Then, returning upstairs, he found Jen staring blankly at the wall, her position unchanged from where he had left her.

He gathered her up, rocking her like a child as she wept onto his shoulder.

When the tray and bath finally arrived, she had gone limp and complacent in his arms. She didn't even fight him as he stripped off her soiled clothing and kicked it into a corner, helping her into the tub.

It wasn't how he had envisioned it, seeing her naked for the first time. But even battered, the sight of her awed him, and he tamped down an embarrassed surge of desire. She needed his love and caring, not his intrusive passion. So he tried to remain impersonal as he ran a cloth over her body, washing away the blood and urine, but he was still achingly aware of all those curves he had longed to touch. It was a subtle torture. He ran the cloth over her breasts and between her legs, across the perfect curves of her collarbones, now mottled with scrapes and bruises. He rinsed her face, and washed the clotted blood from her hair.

The water was pink with blood when he had finished, and the cut on her cheek had begun oozing sluggishly again. He wrapped her in a warm blanket, then dressed the wound with some of the extra bandages she had saved for his head. Then, with the tray on his lap, he fed her until she pushed him away, irritably.

It was fully dark outside when he finished, a faint trace of moonlight leaking into the alley. Saul would need him soon. He stroked her damp hair. "Do you think you can sleep now?" he inquired.

She gazed at him blankly.

"Are you tired?" he persisted. "Were you in the closet all morning?"

She managed to rally. "No. I . . . I think I must have passed out in Saul's office. I woke up some time in the afternoon and managed to sneak out of the club. But I couldn't bear for anyone to see me, so I hid in the . . ." Her voice cracked.

"Yes; of course. But I think you should try to sleep now. I have to go serve dinner, but . . . Great bloody blazes, I hate to leave you like this!"

"I'll be fine," she assured him. And she squeezed his hand lightly, the first time she had initiated contact all evening. "I'll try to sleep, I promise."

"Good girl." He hefted her into his arms and carried her to the bed, tucking her—blanket and all—beneath the covers.

"I'm not a girl," she protested.

"I know. You're a beautiful woman who has had a very bad day. And it's time for you to rest."

She snuggled into the pillows and—greatly daring—he kissed her once, lightly, before he departed.

For almost two days straight she slept, whether in pain or denial. And when Thibault entered the room to check on her in the spare moments between his duties, or when he stretched out on his pallet at night, she was invariably curled away from him, her eyes tight shut, her head buried into the pillow and one fist clutching the blankets like a lifeline. Her face, pale against the sheets, was marred by the ugly spread of bruises and the dark crusting of the gash on her cheek.

At times he almost wondered if she weren't faking it—if sleep could really be that taut and contained—but her breathing never hitched or varied, not even when he leaned over the bed. And respecting her need for either privacy or rest, he did not disturb her further.

Then one night, nearly two days after the attack, he found her awake, the two half-slits of her eyes staring blankly at the ceiling.

"Welcome back," he said softly.

Her lifeless gaze shifted toward him, and a little shudder seemed to run through her. "Thibault," she said. "How long was I out?"

"Long enough. How do you feel?"

She shook her head; shrugged. Attempted to frame a reassuring smile and failed. "How are things in the house?"

"Surreal." He didn't elaborate further, but it *was* surreal, to see everyone acting so naturally, so normally, while Jen lay battered and all but lifeless in their bed. Surreal in that this one act, which he instinctively knew would change their lives forever, caused so few ripples in the wider world.

Save for themselves and Gideon, no one even seemed aware it had transpired.

And what did that say about their place in the universe?

"Does anyone know?" she persisted.

"No." He didn't bother with the lights. The moon was nearly full and high over the alley now; it provided enough light to see as he washed up. Besides, the silvery glow was kinder to his partner's battered features.

Jen was silent as he worked over basin and ewer, but he could tell there was something on her mind. Eventually she said, "Thibault . . ."

"Yes?"

"You can turn on the lights if you want. Or can't you stand to look at me?" Her voice was unaccountably thick and he started, almost spilling the washwater down his shirt. *"What?"*

"I won't ever be beautiful again, will I?"

He abandoned his ablutions. "Out of all that's happened, *that's* what you're worried about?"

"Well . . ." Her hand strayed unconsciously to her bandaged cheek. "I did wonder. It's always been a part of who I am. Who I was," she corrected. "But . . . I'm never going to be the same again, am I?"

He was abruptly sober. "No, Jen, you're never going to be the same again—but not because of your physical appearance." He dried his face and went to sit beside her on the bed. "What happened to you . . . that would change anyone. Emotionally. And, yes, there will probably be one bloody great scar. But if you think that's going to make you any less beautiful, then you are downright insane!"

She clutched at him. "So you wouldn't turn me away? Looking like this?"

He tried to keep his voice light around a suddenly constricted throat. "Of course I wouldn't."

"Oh." She was silent for another long moment and he worked free of her grasp, rising from the bed to change into his nightclothes. He was infinitely aware of her gaze on his body, and he felt himself flush hot and bright as he tried to imagine what she was thinking. He wanted to turn away, to retreat into the closet himself, but it didn't seem fair to hide, not after he had seen and exposed her in all her shame.

So he finished undressing and reached for his nightclothes, willing the hectic flush to recede from his cheeks and chest as he pulled them on. Then, kneeling beside the bed, he reached underneath to draw out the pallet.

Her hand on his head halted him, the touch searing like lightning.

"Thibault . . ."

"What?" he managed; he didn't quite know how.

"Hold me."

Her voice was so small and tentative that he abandoned the pallet and climbed onto the bed without hesitation, lying atop the covers and wrapping his arms around her, careful not to jar her bruises.

She was silent for a time, her head cradled against his shoulder, content merely to be held. But then her hands began to move, trailing across his back and shoulders. At first he thought it was simply her response to his gentle stroking of her hair, but after a while—when her hands crept under his pajama top, questing shiveringly across bare skin—even he couldn't deny that she had something else in mind.

He was beginning to respond, and his heart was pounding like a drum.

"Jen . . ."

She pushed herself away and stared back at him, eyes glitter-bright in the moonlight.

"I don't think . . ." He didn't know how he got the words out. "I don't think this is a good idea."

She seemed to stiffen; her voice sounded as thick and muffled as his felt. "Why not?" He couldn't even think where to begin, but she spared him the battle, adding, "So you were lying, then. About not turning me away. About me being beautiful."

"No!"

"Oh." A long silence reigned. Then, "Aren't you cold?" she asked.

"Maybe a little." And, indeed, a thin, cool slip of a breeze had insinuated itself through the warped window frame and was gusting across the small of his back. But how much of his cold was due to the breeze and how much to sheer panic he simply couldn't tell.

He was very far out of his depth, and it terrified him.

Jen tugged the blankets out from under him and flung them over his body as best she could. Then she scooted closer, wrapping her arms around him, and he gasped.

He had forgotten he had put her to bed naked, over two days ago.

"Great bloody blazes! Jen . . ."

"What?" She pressed distractingly close. His nostrils were full of her scent, and he couldn't think clearly. Especially not with her hips so hot and tight against him. "Don't tell me you don't want me," she added.

He flinched. "That's not the point. We're . . . we're partners, Jen. We can't complicate things with . . ."

"With what?"

"With . . ." Words failed him.

"Please, Thibault," she said, in a voice pregnant with tears. "Don't make me beg."

"Jenny . . ."

"For two days I've been lying here, thinking about my life, about the attack. About what I could have done to stop it. Wondering if anything would ever be the same for me again." So he was right; she *had* been faking that studied slumber. "I'm not asking for love or commitment. I'm not asking for an eternity. I just want one night. To feel some kind of tenderness. To know that I'm still beautiful to someone. Please."

By Varia, she was hurting and vulnerable, seeking comfort in the only way she knew. And to answer her needs would fulfill every one of his most deeply held desires.

How could he deny her?

How could he deny himself?

Only . . .

"What is it now?" she demanded. He could hear the hurt in her voice, her fear of rejection. And that alone pushed the words past the impossible barrier in his throat.

"Jen, I don't know how. That is . . . I'm still . . ."

"A virgin?" she finished incredulously.

He didn't know how, but he managed to confirm it.

"At twenty-one?"

"To my eternal shame."

"But what about Kati?" He shook his head. "Carolie?" Another shake. "But surely there were willing girls in Gavrone? Or in Nova Castria?"

What could he say, that he had been saving himself for her? "The opportunity just never came up," he stammered, then gave a nervous laugh at his choice of words. "Um. So to speak."

"Do you think," she whispered, her breath warm against his mouth, "that you could manage it? Just this once?"

"I think," he responded, equally tremulous, "that I could try."

And he did. Successfully, as it happened—for the most part. It was both wonderful and awkward, at once anticlimactic and the answer to all his dreams. And the only thing he held back were the words that continually threatened to spill from his lips: *I love you, Jen.*

That much he would spare her. She had made it clear from the start that this was a thing of comfort, a thing of the body only. So that was what he would give her. And in the morning, he would gift her with the words she most needed to hear: *It meant nothing, Jen. It meant nothing.* Even though that was the biggest lie in the world.

It was the least he could do for her.

35

Jen awoke to a languid feeling of contentment—which quickly transmuted into agony as she stretched and the events of the past few days came flooding back. Thibault was lying naked beside her, still asleep, one arm curled lightly yet protectively across her belly. Her cheeks flooded with sudden color. By Varia, she had done it! She had slept with her partner.

Great shades of oblivion, what would Vera say?

But it had been . . . Wonderful.

More than wonderful.

Marvelous.

She couldn't mask a grin. Everything would be different now. Men like Gideon were abominable cads, thoroughly untrustworthy, but Thibault . . . Thibault was the salt of the earth. Thibault would keep her safe, shielding her with that big, ungainly body of his. That body she had never thought she would find attractive but which suddenly she could not get enough of. For while he might look awkward, the assassin's grace with which he could move—and which had always fascinated her—was equally apparent in his lovemaking. He was big—*all* of him was big—but he was gentle. Gentle to a fault, and yet . . . There was also a passion to him, and an intensity that took her breath away just recalling it.

Of course there had been some awkward moments. How could there not be? He had come to her—and what a revelation *that* had been!—a virgin. He had been almost afraid to touch her at first, and not just because of the bruises. He had stroked her as if she were fragile porcelain, ready to break. And even though those subtle caresses had aroused her, it had still taken her a while to convince him that she welcomed a firmer touch. But eventually his hands had become more assured—though careful, always, of her hurts.

He had not lasted all that long, at first. But he had later proved that he had staying power when it counted, which she always suspected.

Thibault, Thibault, Thibault. Who would have thought it? Certainly not she, when she had led him on their merry adventures in the woods so many years ago. Her peasant playmate. Her lover.

She couldn't wait for him to wake.

She looked over at his tousled, mouse-brown hair, his scabbed cheek, the stitched cut on his brow, the fading purple bruise of his shoulder. Matched pair, she thought, and then shuddered as the memory of Gideon's beating came flooding back. Praise Thibault for that, too; for making her forget. Maybe if she thought about him some more, the other memories would be pushed from her head forever. So she focused on the firm curves of his chest, the subtle swell of muscle on his upper arms. Tried to drown the echoes of the endless, concussive blows against her flesh with remembrances of those large, gentle hands moving across her skin, as if the one could erase the other.

How could she have trusted Gideon, despite his pretty face? How could she not have seen? In retrospect, the clues were all there. The way he had never let her linger in his bed. The way his passion never seemed more than a thing of the moment. The way his dangerous swagger had excited her.

How could she have been so bloody stupid?

She shivered again and choked back a sob, wondering how she could go from being so happy to so frightened and miserable in so short a time. But then, her life had been one of extremes in the past few days. Almost, she began to understand the attraction of a placid life. Lacking, perhaps, the exorbitant highs, but also without the crushing lows. Just . . . normal.

As if her life could ever be normal again.

Gideon had broken her. Despite her assassin's training—despite all her knowledge and confidence—she had been unable to fight him. He had been too strong, too fast. Too powerful. First he had broken her will, and then he had broken her body. And that one fact would forever color the rest of her days.

Jen Radineaux, the Dagger, could be broken.

Granted, she had found what she needed. But how could she ever trust her judgment again?

A spate of self-pitying tears flooded her eyes and tracked down her cheeks, and she scrubbed at them angrily, hating this weakness.

As luck would have it, her movement awoke Thibault, who grunted slightly and rolled towards her . . . then abruptly stiffened. His eyes—as nondescript a brown as his hair—popped open, and they regarded each other for a long, frozen moment. She could see the remembrance of the previous evening replacing the momentary confusion in his gaze, and she froze, suddenly terrified to see his reaction.

What if he, too, rejected her? How could she bear it?

The blasted tears came washing back and she blinked furiously, but at the sight of them Thibault melted. He reached out a finger and lightly stroked her injured cheek.

"Are you all right, Jenny?" he asked, his voice soft and concerned.

She longed to throw herself into his arms and bury herself against that impressive breadth of chest, but she was seized with a sudden, uncontrollable bout of shyness. She, Jen Radineaux. Shy.

A little spurt of laughter escaped her lips at her predicament. Jen, the hoyden, suddenly unable to look at a man she had known over half her life. How positively ridiculous.

"I'm fine," she said. And, in response to his questioning look, added, "Really." But she still couldn't help the faint, bashful flush that crept across her cheeks.

By all that was precious, you would think *she* was the bloody virgin!

"Jen . . ." he began.

He looked so beautiful lying there, so plain and nondescript, so utterly transcendent, that she burst out, awkwardly, "Thibault, I just have to explain . . ." What? That she was sorry she had taken him for granted for so long? That she had never realized how much he mattered? That no matter what she might have said, last night meant so much more than another of her flings?

That, so help her, she was beginning to realize she was falling in love with him? And maybe had been, for a considerable number of months?

The thoughts flew at her so thick and fast that the words clotted on her tongue, choking her with all she longed to say. All she needed to say to make it right between them.

But before she could untangle her thoughts, Thibault reached out and took her hand. A moment of pure happiness seized her. "It's all right, Jen," he said gently. "You don't have to explain anything."

Of course, she thought. *Our rapport is that perfect. There has never been much need for words between us, has there, Thibault?* Even in the earliest days of their friendship, he had always seemed to know just what she was thinking.

She smiled at him.

"It meant nothing," he added.

She felt like she had been doused with icy water; her breath came in ragged gasps. He couldn't mean it. She had to have misheard him. "Thibault . . ."

"No, I mean it," he insisted, squeezing her hand gently. "You needed comfort last night, and I gave it—gladly. But . . ." He shook his head slightly. "That's all it was, really. It meant nothing more than that."

His eyes were sad—melancholy, almost—as if he knew the hopes she had harbored and hated disappointing her. As he probably did, she realized; Thibault had always known her mind better than she. And he was doing it in the only way he could: gently and honestly.

So why did it hurt so much?

By Varia, she had thought . . .

But, no. That way lay madness.

And then a spurt of panicked laughter escaped her. By all that was precious, she hadn't gone so far that she was spouting bad clichés?

For an instant she was tempted to fight him on it. But, thanks to Gideon, she had already lost enough dignity for one lifetime. She forced a smile.

"Of course," she said. "It meant nothing."

Thibault reached out to touch her again, his thigh accidentally brushing her leg, and she felt the shock of that contact throughout her body. And he must have felt it, too, for he abruptly pulled back, rolling from the bed. He reached unerringly for his abandoned pajamas, drawing on the bottoms.

A crushing depression swamped her.

"Are you sure you're all right?" he asked, returning to sit beside her. His chest was still bare. He laid a hand lightly on her shoulder.

She nodded, blinking back the tears.

"Bloody Gideon!" he muttered.

"Yes. Gideon," she managed.

"He won't get away with this, I promise."

Don't be noble, she wanted to snap. *Don't protect me. I'll be fine. Despite him. Despite you. Despite everything.* But all she said was: "Mmm."

"I think you should rest some more. Remember, the staff still think you have the flu. So you have a few more days reprieve, if you want it."

"Yes." Suddenly the thought of facing everyone in all her humiliation was too much for her. The minute she emerged from her room, it would be obvious that the last thing she suffered from was the flu. Questions would be asked, and she didn't have the answers. What could she say, that the Golden Boy had her beaten for searching Saul's office without permission, searching for evidence to explain why Saul's grandson may or may not be trying to murder him?

"Yes; yes. That's good. Thank you, Thibault." She tried to sound grateful and probably succeeded, for he smiled at her briefly.

"For what?" he said. "We're partners, Jen."

"Yes," she parroted dully. "Partners." Then, "You never asked me what I found."

Thibault looked almost startled. "In Saul's office? You found evidence?"

She managed a bitter smile. "Saw it, anyway. Gideon . . ." Her voice cracked. "I looked for it the next morning, but it was gone. So you only have my word for it. But, yes; part of the Cauldron's profits derive from revenge fantasies."

"So, we were right."

She nodded tersely.

"Bloody blazes." He placed his palm on her forehead. "Well, we can figure out what it means later. For now, sleep. You'll feel better tomorrow."

"Of course I will." *Because I will become as hard as iron,* she vowed. *Because I will never allow myself to be hurt again.*

But she would fucking kill Gideon if she ever got her hands on him.

It was almost impossible to leave Jen in their room when all Thibault wanted was to take her in his arms and never let her go. Being with her last night was everything he had dreamed of—and more. He had never been more certain in his life that he loved her. And she hadn't laughed. Not once, for all he had been so bloody awkward.

He wanted her so badly, and yet he could barely make himself touch her at first, for fear of doing something wrong, something stupid. Something any twelve-year-old would know and which felt, at twenty-one, like an appalling lack. If she had ridiculed him . . .

But she hadn't. She was patient and caring—and cursed funny, now that he thought of it. The way she had allayed his fears by telling him of her own wretched first experience . . . He had almost laughed himself sick. And after, she had merely said, "Now how could this possibly be as bad as that? For one thing, we don't have to worry about the apples . . ."

In retrospect, he hadn't expected her to be so sensitive to his needs. But it was one of the things he always valued about Jenny. As flighty, self-centered, and superficial as she sometimes appeared, she had surprising depths of character. And the minute you thought you had her figured, she would surprise you all over again.

She had surprised him endlessly last night. Which, in turn, made sticking to his resolution even harder.

But because he was Thibault, he had done it. And every one of her reactions had proved his instincts were correct. She had stiffened as he awoke, and when he had touched her, she had laughed nervously—obviously uncomfortable with their sudden intimacy. And when he had tried to talk to her, she had instantly set about justifying the act.

What other choice did he have?

She had even laughed with relief when he had finished.

Poor Jenny. Her life was uncertain enough as it was. No need to confuse her by altering the only relationship that held any real stability.

But still, on occasion, he sometimes wished he were just a little less noble and self-sacrificing.

36

That final day of forced inactivity, confined to her chambers and bed, had left Jen restless and twitching. So the following morning—despite virulent bruises and still raw-looking wounds—she rose and dressed. Thibault watched her anxiously as she climbed from the bed and reached for her clothes, biting back another round of useless protests. All his previous attempts had fallen on deaf ears; Jen remained as stubborn as ever.

She moved with such a studied deliberation, though, he could tell her body still pained her. But when he attempted to make a comment, she cut him off, her lips pressed into a thin, unyielding line. He masked a sigh. Jen's stubbornness might not have changed, but she had. There was a hardness to her now, as if she had erected a wall around her heart. But it wasn't the bruising of her body that bothered him most; it was the bruising in her eyes. He hadn't realized how much a part of her that spark of life had been—that indefinable joy in her existence and all its absurdities that had once shined like a beacon from her gaze—until Gideon had killed it.

He wanted to wrap his hands around Gideon's throat and choke the life out of *him,* but in lieu of that he simply said, "Are you sure this is a good idea?"

"And why wouldn't it be?" Indifferent to his gaze, she stripped off her nightgown and tossed it to the floor.

A hot surge of embarrassment swept him. "Do you want me to . . ." He pantomimed turning.

"Why?" she said harshly, reaching for her clothes. "It's not like it's something you haven't seen."

He didn't know what to say to that, so he said nothing. She pulled her shirt stiffly over her head.

"Besides," she continued, as if the interruption hadn't occurred, "I can't keep up this fictitious flu forever. The truth is bound to come out."

"But one more day . . ."

"Is hardly going to make any difference in the way I look." Her words came in sharp, staccato bursts, like angry footfalls. "And I'll be cursed if I'm going to sit here and cower in this room until every last trace of Gideon's beating is gone."

He thought her voice cracked slightly on those last words, but he couldn't be certain. Nothing about her voice seemed natural anymore. Nothing about *her* seemed natural. He wanted to cry. Or howl. Or maybe just shake her firmly by the shoulders and say: *This isn't courage, Jen. It's just a different sort of denial.*

But then again, what did he know? Maybe for her it was courage. Maybe for her, crossing that threshold with her shame writ boldly on her face, was the hardest thing she had ever done.

He let another soundless sigh trickle past his lips. "So what are you going to do?"

"Do?" She shot him a scathing look. "My duties."

"I meant, how will you explain?"

For a moment he saw a fracture in her armor, and then the wall slammed shut again. "As for the staff, I'll figure something out. But Saul deserves the truth. He needs to know what sort of maniac he hired."

He reached out a hand to her almost without thinking, but she turned from him, cinching her skirt around her waist instead. She gathered her hair into a tail, looking around for the hairbrush.

He handed it to her. "Why do you think he . . ."

"Because he's a madman, that's why! No one with those eyes could possibly be human. That's why I have to warn Saul. Who knows what he could do to that sweet old man in a fit of passion? Or perversity?" She dragged the brush roughly through her hair, wincing as it pulled against her wounds.

"Here, do you want me to do that?" Thibault offered, holding out his hand for the brush.

She scowled at him, and jerked from range. "I'm not a baby, you know. I can take care of myself."

A few more rough strokes sufficed, and then she clubbed her hair at the back of her neck, not even bothering to braid it.

"There, how do I look?" she said at last. "No, silly question; forget it. I look a fright. But that, too, will pass." And without another word, she pulled open the door and stalked down the hall.

Thibault stared after her for a moment, then closed the door and sank down on the bed. It simply wasn't fair. Granted, Jen had been getting cocky of late, but no one deserved a lesson of this magnitude. He wondered how she would come out on the other side—if she came out at all. Her current brittleness worried him, making him think she could as easily snap as soften.

But moody reflections would gain him nothing, so he rose after a moment and started his day—as he always did— by straightening their chambers. He smoothed the rumpled sheets and plumped the pillows, then slid his pallet beneath the bed. The water in the basin, still slightly bloodied from Jen's morning ablutions, got tipped out the window and into the alley. He picked her discarded bedclothes off the floor and folded them neatly, stowing them in the dresser drawer. He was turning away when a shard of crystal atop the dresser caught his eye. It had turned a dusky black, almost disappearing against the dark and pitted wood.

For an instant, he thought it was the crystal shard Jen had discovered atop the roof, but then he remembered the poisoned brandy, and his bargain with the mage. Blast it all to perdition; Jen's beating had driven it straight out of his mind! And judging from the mage's previous surly temper, he wouldn't be remotely happy about the delay.

Thibault grimaced and pocketed the crystal. He would check with Saul and see if he couldn't get an hour to himself to conclude this business. And then, he and Jen could leave this cursed household forever.

Walking out of her chamber was akin to a nightmare. Jen was acutely aware of every cut and bruise, throbbing with a subtle accusation. Each one was a mark of shame, a blatant reminder of her weakness and failure. No matter that her face was still puffy, that it hurt just to stand erect; those were only physical worries, hardly worth contemplating. The real wounds ran deeper, and would take more than mere bed rest and time to conquer.

It was one of the deepest of those that had driven her out of her bed today: terror. A certain knowledge that if she didn't face the world now, she might never leave the safety of that chamber again. As it was, it took every ounce of courage she had just to keep from shaking, and an adamantine shield between herself and the world to keep back the tide of tears that every second threatened to overwhelm her.

Her spirit felt as frail and bruised as her body. How the blazes could she face the rest of the household when the sight of Thibault alone was almost enough to unhinge her?

Again, she remembered the feeling of his hands on her body the night they had made love, and that alone seemed the ultimate betrayal. He had barely touched her since. Maddeningly, his words echoed through her head: *It meant nothing.* Maybe it would be easier to see Jahnee and Kore, Alcina and Beroe.

And if she saw Gideon, she would kill him. She would. No matter what Saul said.

Saul . . . Owen trusted him, and yet he was countenancing murder. Or was he? Did he even know what Gideon and Aubrey were up to in the depths of his club?

How could he not?

But then again, how could he?

"Gilyan, lass, it's good to see you up and about," Alcina's cheerful voice declared from behind her as she came down the last of the steps from the servants' floor. "I trust you're feeling better this— Sweet shades of oblivion!"

The housekeeper's hands flew to her mouth as Jen slowly turned, revealing her battered face in all its glory. They stared at each other for a long, tense moment, Jen frantically blinking against the flood of tears that threatened again to spill.

"Oh, my dear, sweet child, what happened to you? That is certainly no flu . . ."

The deep and genuine caring in Alcina's voice almost

undid her; a single tear slid down Jen's torn cheek, stinging in the wound.

"I was . . ." she began, trying to muster the lie despite a voice which wavered and threatened to crack with every word.

To her surprise, the usually brisk housekeeper strode over and took her into arms which were almost motherly in their uncaring acceptance. It had been so long since Jen had been held—certainly not since her childhood nannies. Her long-dead mother had never been much for affection, and Vera was . . . well, Vera. The last of her control faltered, and she found herself weeping bitterly against Alcina's breast, wondering why she had ever believed such a release was shameful. There was something so soothing about letting go; she wondered if Alcina might not hold her this way forever.

But eventually her frantic sobs quieted, and she found herself with enough presence of mind to choke out some remotely plausible story about a late night out clubbing, a back alley, and a robbery. And when she had finished, Alcina patted her comfortingly and said, "Now, don't you fret about the rest of the staff, my dear. You just sit here for a moment and compose yourself, and I'll tell the rest of them your story so you won't have to repeat it."

Astounded at the depths of Alcina's perception and caring, Jen blinked up at her in gratitude. "I . . ."

"No, don't thank me, lovey; it's the least I can do. You've been a good worker, and a cheerful presence in this house; I wish there was some way we could keep you when Avram and Lucinda return. All I can say is I hope you don't judge our city too harshly for this one bad incident. It's a lovely place despite that, and you are welcome here any time you want." And reaching out briefly to touch Jen's undamaged cheek, she bustled off towards the kitchens.

Jen sank down on the nearest riser, feeling oddly humbled. Vera was right; it never did to judge the serving classes for their lack of education and advantages. Nine out of ten aristocrats would have dismissed her pain with no more than an offhand word and perhaps a cup of tea. But this woman, whose highest ambition in life was to keep a well-run house and whose voice was ripe with her gutter upbringing, had understood more of Jen's needs than her partner.

Brushing the residual water from her eyes, she drew her knees up to her chin and sat on the bare wood riser until she judged a sufficient interval had elapsed. And then she followed Alcina into the kitchen.

The brusque Beroe actually smiled at her, and Jahnee's soft brown eyes were wide with horror. Kore crossed her arms irately over her breast and scowled at the world as if she wanted to take a saucepan to its head. "That beast!" she whispered to Jen as she passed. "Did you get a good look at his face?"

Jen experienced a moment of disorientation, forgetting for a minute that she had supposedly been robbed at knifepoint in some nameless back alley. But she managed to shake her head with reasonable aplomb, all the while choking down a surge of hatred for the golden-haired vision that rose in her head. "No. No, I didn't."

"Curse it! Still, I don't blame you for fighting. I hope you gave as good as you got!"

Jen managed a watery smile. "I certainly tried to," she said, and this lie, more than any other, tasted like ashes in her mouth.

Jahnee sidled up, still regarding her out of eyes as large and round as dinner plates. "Will you be all right?"

"I'll be fine," Jen responded with a certain curt bitterness. Then, forcing a leaden humor into her voice, she added, "Fine case of flu, is it not?"

"Certainly not one I want to contract," Kore said.

"Kore!" Jahnee exclaimed, but Jen almost laughed. Kore's bluntness was exactly what she needed, the perfect antidote to her creeping depression.

"Do you have anything to chop?" she asked Beroe. "I have the sudden urge to inflict violence on something, and it's probably best if you give me something inanimate to work on."

The tense atmosphere of the kitchen—with all eyes fixed nervously on her as if waiting for her collapse—instantly lightened at her words. A few chuckles winged about the room, and she could sense the collective release of breath as the servants broke their frozen ranks to continue their tasks, smiling encouragingly at her as they passed. They had obviously decided that she would be fine.

She only wished she could believe it herself.

When Thibault finally left their chambers, he had been in time to see Jen standing at the base of the front stairs, dissolved in tears in Alcina's arms. A momentary surge of jealousy had gone through him, followed by an inchoate relief. It should have been him holding her, his words comforting her. He was her partner, after all. And the release she was pouring out, which he had tried to elicit for days, was now being gifted to a relative stranger whereas all he had received for his efforts had been her bitter and chilly silence. But then, he supposed, whatever precarious equilibrium had reigned in their relationship had been upset, and Varia only knew how the cards would come down when a new balance was achieved.

Yet for all that it wasn't him, he was abruptly grateful that someone had broken through her brittle wariness, and he was suddenly less worried that she would break under the strain.

So, reluctant to disturb her, he had crept down the back stairs instead, and made his roundabout way to Saul's chambers.

"Saul?" he said, peering through the open portal and knocking briefly on the door jamb in emphasis. "Do you have a minute?"

His employer looked up from his papers, his face brightening in a grin. "Thibault, my lad! Come in, come in. What can I do you for?"

Thibault pulled up a chair, unable to integrate Saul's cheerful mood with the events of the past few days. He was relieved that they had, at least temporarily, been able to keep the truth a secret, but it still seemed incongruous.

Was this man really a murderer?

"Will you be needing me any time in the next hour?" he asked.

Saul cocked his head. "Why?"

"I have . . . an errand to run."

"What sort of errand? Pardon my curiosity, but you seem nervous. Is it anything I can help you with?"

"Not precisely, though it may well have some bearing on your case."

"Some bearing on my case?" Saul repeated. "Whatever do you mean by that?"

Thibault thinned his lips. "I'd rather not say just now, not until I'm certain. But trust me when I say it might be important."

"Of course I trust you. And if you believe it's important, then it's important. I think I can manage to spare you for an hour. But you will tell me what it is should your suspicions be confirmed?"

"Of course."

"Good lad. Well, then." Saul shuffled a few papers on his desk, then waved Thibault away with a smile. "Go. Enjoy yourself, if it's that kind of mission. And I'll see you when you return."

Thibault sketched a bow and departed, wishing that he felt happier about the whole endeavor. If he was right, Jen's life wouldn't be the only one forever altered. But he wasn't a man who shirked his duty, no matter how unpleasant it might be, so with his fingers wrapped convulsively around the crystal in his pocket, he ventured off to see the mage and confirm that Saul's grandson was indeed trying to poison him.

37

"Ah, Gideon. Just the person I wanted to see. Come in, come in. And Aubrey, too. Sit, both of you."

Gideon plunked himself into a chair as if he had no cares in the world; Aubrey followed more cautiously. He wondered what was on their employer's mind that he had summoned them so early. He usually didn't bother with their reports until much later. But maybe, Aubrey thought with a sudden hope, it was about the six-year-old. Maybe Saul had finally come to his senses.

"So?" Saul asked pointedly. "Anything to report?"

Gideon grinned and said, "Aubrey thinks I'm the one behind the murders in the club." Which is precisely what Aubrey had been afraid he'd say.

But—for once—instead of ridiculing Aubrey, Saul merely replied, "Are you?"

Gideon looked offended. "Of course not! But the point is . . ."

"The point is," Saul finished, "there are apparently things you are not telling me. What did you do to Jen?"

Aubrey flinched, looking between his associate and his employer. Gideon almost never got dressed down by Saul. Besides, Aubrey hadn't been aware there was anything wrong with the girl.

Gideon, too, looked almost startled. "How did you know about that?"

Saul's brows drew together ominously. "I didn't found an empire by being stupid. Or unobservant. Give me some credit, Gideon! What the bloody blazes did you do to her?"

"Nothing that you didn't sanction."

"Meaning?"

"Meaning that I had express orders from you to stop her

if she went too far, poking around in places she didn't belong. 'Use any means necessary,' I believe were your words. Or at least your implication.''

"And was she? Going too far?"

"You tell me," Gideon said in disgust. "I found her riffling through your Cauldron office five nights ago. And that was after I saw her poking around this office. So I beat her."

"You did *what*?" Aubrey exclaimed.

"She was doing *what*?" Saul echoed simultaneously.

"Going through your offices," Gideon replied, ignoring Aubrey.

"And you didn't see fit to tell me?"

Gideon shrugged. "It's not like she would have found anything."

"I hardly think that's the point. If she suspects . . ."

"If she suspects," Gideon interrupted, "she has no proof. But all she found was information about the revenge fantasies, and I confiscated even that. I'm sure about this, Saul; she has nothing. Nor is she likely to find anything. I'm afraid I was rather . . . resolute in my persuasions."

"Gideon! How badly did you beat her?" Aubrey exclaimed.

"What makes you sure?" Saul demanded, again in concert. "Wasn't it you who said she was unpredictable?"

"Have you seen her?" Gideon countered. "You tell me how persuasive I was! Look, I saw a problem, I fixed it—as per your orders. She hasn't said anything to you, has she?"

"No. But then again, she only just emerged from her room. The story is that she was robbed in a back alley."

"Well," Gideon said proudly. "I am nothing if not good at my work."

Aubrey felt sick. "You really beat her?"

"To within an inch of her life," his associate responded. "Well, honestly, Aubrey, she was breaking into Saul's offices. What else was I supposed to do?"

"Tell me, for a start!" Saul flared. "Blast it, if Owen suspects . . ."

"He has no proof. Neither does she. I told you. Besides, there's no way to connect you to Veridien Street—at least not through the Cauldron office. Trust me, all she found

were the revenge papers, and no city authority is going to
jail you for that. Especially not if it's your word against
hers."

"But . . ."

"Saul, would I jeopardize your empire for a few cheap
thrills? I'm as much a part of it as you are. And you've
always trusted me to care for it properly before."

"You've never assaulted a Guild operative in my private
office before. But if I can't trust you, then who can I trust?"

"My point exactly."

Aubrey felt his stomach roil.

"Very well," Saul concluded. "Anything else?"

"One thing," Gideon responded. "The matter of the six-
year-old. It's been concluded."

"What?" Aubrey yelped.

"Successfully?" Saul inquired.

"You tell me. The man seemed too embarrassed to hag-
gle. I got the full three thousand."

"Excellent! But dare I ask . . ."

"Where I got the six-year-old? Ah . . . Aubrey's all ears."

Aubrey was indeed all ears—though he wasn't so sure
he wanted to hear the answer.

"Medina Street."

"You kidnapped her?"

Gideon nodded smugly. "What's one less gutter rat?"

Saul chuckled. "My boy, your resourcefulness never fails
to amaze me! Did you . . . Aubrey, where the blazes are
you going?"

"To stop this!" Aubrey exclaimed, already out of his
chair and halfway out the door. Assaulting Jen was bad
enough. But kidnapping an innocent six-year-old just to fulfill some monster's fantasy? It had gone too far; everything
had gone too far.

It was time someone drew a line in the sand.

"Aren't you going to stop him?" Saul demanded
incredulously.

Gideon just shrugged, sitting back and crossing his legs.
"Why bother? He's too late."

"It's finished, then?"

"Last night. I was going to dump the body by the docks

this evening. No one will be able to trace it back to the club."

"Well, that's that, then. As usual, you've succeeded beyond my highest expectations." Then Saul chuckled and added, "Three thousand! For that, I almost forgive you assaulting Jen."

Gideon grinned.

"But you might want to watch that partner of hers," Saul added. "He may look slow, but he's deceptively strong. And fast. Plus, I suspect he harbors grudges."

"Thanks for the warning, but I've been taking care of myself for more years than I care to mention. I'll be all right."

"Yes, somehow I suspect you will."

"Is that it?" Gideon added. "Can I get back to the club now?"

"By all means. And see what you can do about Aubrey while you're at it. I hate to lose such a promising employee after all these years, but you always seem to know how to handle him. Work your magic."

"If I can. But there's only so far unrequited love will go."

"True. Still . . ." Saul frowned, suddenly serious. "If he doesn't come around, you'll have to take care of him. He knows too much, and I can't have that sort of knowledge running about uncontrolled. You understand, don't you?"

"Of course."

"Yes, I thought you would. And, needless to say, the same applies for that assassin. If she suspects—really suspects—then . . ."

"Do whatever is necessary," Gideon finished. "We've been through this before, Saul, remember?"

"And you haven't disappointed yet. Point taken."

"You're too kind." And with a jaunty grin, Gideon saluted his employer and strode for the door. But no sooner had he put his hand on the knob than a knock sounded from the other side of the portal. Jen's tremulous voice followed.

"Saul? Are you there? Can I talk to you for a moment?"

Gideon exchanged a look with his employer, his eyebrows winging upward in amusement. "Well, the prodigal arrives." He pitched his voice low so Jen couldn't hear him. "This should be intriguing."

"Indeed," Saul replied, regarding him speculatively. He unlinked the shield spell, then called, "Of course, my dear. Come in."

The door swung open with unexpected force. Gideon stepped back hastily to avoid getting a panel in the face. From his position behind the now-open portal, he couldn't see Jen at the threshold, nor could she see him, but he had a clear view of Saul and felt obscurely satisfied when his employer gasped and half-rose in his chair, his jaw falling open in shock.

Not that Saul was surprised by the fact of Jen's beating—though, to his credit, he gave a credible performance. It was more the nature of that beating that awed him. Gideon could see the glimmer of respect hiding deep in his employer's eyes.

That would teach Saul to discount the strength of his deterrents.

Gideon hadn't seen the girl since he had left her on Saul's office floor, but he had a reasonable confidence as to her appearance. He had administered enough beatings to know their subsequent effects. And she must look a treat.

"Bloody blazes!" Saul exclaimed on a breath. "What happened to you?"

"Long story," she said tersely. "May I sit down?"

Saul waved her forward, shooting a quelling look at Gideon as she advanced. Unable to help himself, Gideon was dissolved in silent laughter behind the door. He was supposed to slip out quietly in her wake, he knew, with the girl none the wiser, but he just had to see the results of his handiwork. So he nudged the door with his foot, and she whirled, startled, as it swung shut behind her.

They regarded each other for a long, silent moment—she with a murderous gleam in her eyes, he with a faintly superior smile lurking about his lips. She did look horrendous, and was moving stiffly, as if every movement was an agony—which no doubt it was.

He had done his work well.

Best yet, though palpable hatred sparked from her eyes, it was overshadowed by fear. A blissful, paralyzing fear that kept her feet frozen to the carpet and her fists clenched impotently at her sides. He had suspected he had broken her, but he hadn't realized how completely until now. He started to laugh.

Her whole face rippled and clenched.

"Beast!" she hissed through clamped jaws—the greatest act of defiance she could manage.

"Jen? Gideon? What's the meaning of this?" Saul demanded, feigning ignorance. But his eyes, boring into Gideon's, spoke clearer than words: *Get out. Now.*

Gideon grinned and complied, shutting the door behind him, leaving Saul to the delights of his interview.

Jen was shaking—badly—as she took a seat across from Saul, though she tried to hide it behind an irate scowl. Of all the reactions she had expected, this was not one of them. She blinked back furious tears, hating herself for her impotence. She had wanted to scratch out Gideon's eyes, to claw his perfect face to ribbons—to pay him back blow for blow and wound for wound. But she couldn't.

She *couldn't*!

Just the sight of his face, the tone of his laugh, catapulted her back into Saul's office, the helpless victim of his abuse. She was literally paralyzed beneath a flood of memories so potent it left her shaking. So that she, the assassin—master of a hundred different forms of death—had let him walk out of the room.

Just walk out.

Unscathed.

And laughing.

And in that instant, she knew that everything she had once trusted about herself—everything she had once thought of as fixed and immobile—was now mutable as air. For if you could not depend on yourself, then who could you depend on?

"What is this all about?" Saul persisted, and cued his shield back on.

She looked up, startled. She had almost forgotten his presence.

"Jen, talk to me. What is going on?"

She drew a deep breath. "Well, I don't think you're going to like this, but . . . Perhaps I had better start at the beginning."

38

The mage had installed a bell. It clanged discordantly as Thibault opened the portal, but the shop seemed deserted as he entered and shut the door behind him, prompting another jangling chorus. There were cobwebs in the corners he could have sworn hadn't been there before.

"Is anyone here?" he called after a moment.

"I'm not deaf, you know," came a sour voice from one of the back rooms.

Thibault leaned a hip against the counter and tried to quell his growing impatience, occupying himself by watching a fat fly that had bumbled into the shop by accident and was now hurtling itself mindlessly against one grimy windowpane.

Eventually Abelard shuffled out of the back, muttering to himself. His eyes flicked over Thibault, then settled on the fly, which had temporarily alighted on the scarred wood of the counter. With a contemptuous glance, he reached beneath the counter and extracted a swatter, which he proceeded to employ with a brisk efficiency, reducing the intruder to a fat yellow smear.

Thibault stared at him in consternation.

"What, haven't you seen a flyswatter before?" the mage asked sardonically, tucking it away.

"Yes. But . . . you're a mage!" Thibault managed.

"There's no fooling you, is there? And here I was convinced I was a lightshade."

"No, I mean . . ." Thibault collected himself with an effort. "Aren't you supposed to just smite it or something? With magerie?"

"Why? Would you rather I wasted my time and energy reinventing the wheel? Or, in this case, the flyswatter? No, the simplest solutions are often the best. Not to mention the least draining."

"Hence the doorbell?"

"Precisely. Never could remember to look at the bloody visual. Bells serve perfectly well." He peered down at the remains of the fly, as if recalling its presence, then wiped up the mess with the edge of one stained sleeve. "Now," he added, transferring his attention to Thibault, "what can I do for you?"

Thibault drew the blackened shard of crystal out of his pocket and laid it on the counter. The mage frowned.

"Now I remember you. You were the one with the brandy who was in such a blasted hurry. You're three days late, you know."

"I know. And I'm sorry. There was a . . ."

The mage waved a hand. "Don't bother. I'm not interested in your excuses. You paid for the rush. As long as I get my money, you can come back in fifty years for all I care."

"Oh. I . . ."

"Want the results?"

"Well . . .of course. I mean . . . Yes."

Abelard held out a hand. "Fifty-five."

Thibault arched an eyebrow. "So you don't remember my face, but you remember my debt?"

The man laughed. "Of course. I'm a mage."

"Of course," Thibault agreed, reaching for his purse and counting out the coins. "So?"

Abelard was looking extremely smug as he pocketed the marks, and Thibault had the sudden feeling he had just been badly cheated. But in what way he had no idea.

"What was in it?" he asked instead.

"Emetic."

"*What?*"

"Emetic. Common, garden-variety emetic. Might have led to a nasty bout of flux, but nothing more. Poison, indeed!" He chuckled. "Overreacting a bit, weren't you?"

"I . . ."

"You know, at first I was annoyed at you for wasting my time, but then I figured: What the blazes? He's paying."

Thibault barely heeded the words. "Emetic?" was all he could say. Mindlessly. Like a parrot.

"Emetic," Abelard confirmed.

Thibault frowned. What the bloody blazes was going on here? This changed everything. What if Patroch *hadn't* been trying to kill his grandfather? Where did that leave them?

Blast it all to perdition, he thought savagely. *If only we had waited two more days, then Jen wouldn't have had to face Gideon.* After all, what were two mere days in the scope of things?

The mage cleared his throat pointedly. "Is there anything more I can do for you? More secrets about the illusion clubs I can reveal, or are you just waiting to get your brandy back?"

Thibault shook his head distractedly and thanked the mage, then left the shop, caught in a cycle of recrimination and confusion. What had seemed a neat puzzle had suddenly shattered into odd mosaic fragments which resolutely refused to fit.

What was Patroch doing if he *wasn't* trying to kill his grandfather?

Absently, Thibault rubbed his shoulder, recalling the block of masonry which had been set to fall off-center. And now the brandy. What the blazes was the point of setting trap after trap that were deliberately designed to fail? Was Patroch setting up a series of assassination attempts designed solely to keep his grandfather *alive*? What was the point of that? And, moreover—the thought brought a whimsical smile—what did that make it? A series of *anti*-assassinations?

Thibault defied anyone in the Guild to find an odder assignment.

Still, it was no use trying to figure it out now. His thoughts were chasing each other around in ever-tightening circles, so he banished the entire mess from his mind, watching instead the bustle of people going about their business on the streets of Ephanon. Merchants haggled; beggars extended their bowls. Ladies of fashion tripped between dressmakers and milliners. A young boy, no more than six, darted into the street, straight into the path of a hansom.

Before Thibault could react, the boy's mother shrieked and dragged him back; the cab thundered by with inches to spare. She began lecturing him furiously, her voice high and tight with panic, while the boy—rattled from his narrow escape—burst into noisy tears.

Thibault stared at the spectacle for a moment, then abruptly smacked a hand to his forehead.

"By Varia!" he exclaimed. "Of course." And took off down the street at a run.

"I think you should know," Jen blurted. "He's a madman!"

"Who's a madman?"

"Gideon. Your so-called Golden Boy. He did this to me."

"*Gideon?*" Saul repeated incredulously.

"A fine bit of work, no?" Jen said bitterly.

She glimpsed a flicker of repressed emotion, glittering deep within Saul's eyes. Anger, probably. And outrage. He needn't have bothered. She was outraged enough for both of them.

"But . . . why?" he demanded.

"Who knows? Just because I was in your office four nights ago doesn't mean . . ."

He fixed her with a stare. "You were in my office? Which office?"

"The Cauldron office." She abruptly flushed. "Perhaps I *had* better start at the beginning."

"Yes. Perhaps you should."

She took a deep breath, aware that she owed him an explanation, no matter how misguided her actions now looked. "As it happened, I *was* sneaking around in your office after hours, and quite without authorization, but Thibault and I had an idea who was behind these latest assassination attempts and we didn't want to present you with our suspicions without some sort of evidence to back them up."

"Evidence of what?"

"Duplicity."

"Whose duplicity?"

"Someone close to you, which makes it so hard to relate."

"You mean it wasn't the Telos clan?"

"Yes, it was. Initially. But they ran out of funds weeks ago."

"And you're certain of that?"

"Absolutely. I tracked their assassin down and asked him directly." She spread her hands, palms up, as if offering him a present. "No more Telos funds. Therefore, no more attacks. At least not from that quarter."

"But subsequently?"

"Yes, subsequently." She scrubbed both hands over her face, temporarily forgetting her many wounds and bruises. Blast Gideon!

"I have often found," Saul added, "that bad news is best delivered quickly." He attempted a smile, then demanded, "Who has been trying to kill me?"

"Well, you understand that we're not certain about any of this, that it's all just hunches and speculation . . ."

"Jen," he said sternly.

She took a deep breath and blurted, "Patroch."

Maybe he was right about the advantages of a sudden delivery, because for a moment he just sat in stunned silence. And then, like a breaking tide, he began to laugh.

"Patroch?" he said incredulously.

It wasn't the reaction she had expected; she nodded tentatively.

"Patroch?" he repeated. "That soft, useless fop of a grandson of mine? He doesn't have the guts!" He startled her still more by adding, "By Varia, perhaps there's hope for the old boy yet!"

"Excuse me?"

His mirth vanished, and he seemed to come abruptly to his senses. "Are you certain about this?"

"As certain as I can be," Jen said quietly. "All the evidence points to him. But like I said: no proof. That's what I was looking for in your office. Some sort of motive that would tie him into this, that would explain his behavior or show how he would profit by your death."

"He profits nothing by my death. Somewhat deplorably,

that honor goes to Stavros. Who has the imagination and personal magnetism of a cheese.''

"I know," Jen admitted. "I found the will. But if Stavros refused to inherit, and tried to deny Patroch as well . . .''

"Because of something I was doing?"

Jen flushed.

"You've found out about the revenge fantasies, haven't you?" Saul said. "But I assure you—nasty as it sounds— it's unofficially government-sanctioned. And the victims are only those already slated for death under public law. But it would disgust Stavros if he knew. Sometimes," he added speculatively, "I wonder if that boy is even my son. But no matter. Do you think it would disgust him enough to make him repudiate my money and my clubs?"

"What do you think?" Jen countered.

Her employer chuckled. "I think it's very likely. So, he refuses the inheritance. But what if he doesn't let Patroch inherit, either?"

"Then maybe he ends up as Patroch's next victim."

"Well, then." Saul's face hardened, a frigid expression sheeting over it like ice. "Perhaps we should ask him." He reached for the bellpull.

"Now?" Jen squeaked, suddenly conscious of her appearance.

Saul's expression softened. "Yes, I had forgotten. You haven't quite finished your story." He tugged at the bellpull sharply. "Please, continue."

"What more is there to say? Gideon found me, and . . . Well, he overreacted. As you can see. Saul, you really shouldn't have him around, knowing what he's capable of. I'm worried he might hurt you. He really is a monster!"

Saul looked troubled. "I admit, Gideon can be a bit . . . unstable at times, but it's complicated. I owe him, and he owes me. We've been through too much together for me to abandon him now."

"But . . ."

"I know, and I regret it. Honestly, I do. But . . ."

A soft tap on the door interrupted him. "Yes?" he called sharply, cuing off the shield.

Alcina's voice echoed from beyond the portal. "You rang?"

"Indeed I did; come in. Excuse me for a moment," he added to Jen.

Alcina opened the door, waiting expectantly on the threshold. "Sir?" she queried, and then, catching sight of Jen, added irately, "So you heard what happened to our Gilyan, then?"

Saul cast Jen a probing look, but she shook her head minutely in return. He relaxed visibly.

"Those low-life street thugs," Alcina rattled on, oblivious. "Something should be done about them. They're nothing but petty criminals—every last one of them!"

Her indignation was so real—and so palpable—that Jen felt like hugging her. But instead, Saul just said, "Yes, we were discussing that. Alcina, is Patroch at home?"

"I believe so, sir. I just saw him leaving the breakfast room."

Saul consulted his watch. "Almost noon, the lazy sod. Hmph. Fetch him for me, will you? I wish to speak with him directly."

"Yes, sir." She departed, pulling the door shut behind her.

There was a long silence, then Saul added, "Gideon will pay for this, I promise. But don't judge him too harshly. He's had a hard life. He . . ."

Jen didn't want to hear it. The man was a beast. She opened her mouth to protest when another knock came at the door.

Patroch's whining tones sounded through the portal. "Grandfather? You wanted to see me?"

He tried to keep his tone light, but his voice sounded constricted; nervous. Saul exchanged a weighty glance with Jen, then replied, "Yes, my boy, I did. Come in."

Patroch opened the door, his too-pretty face pulled into sullen lines. "Always glad to oblige, Grandfather, but can we keep this short? I have some people to meet in a little under . . . By Varia!"

He was so startled by Jen's presence—and even more so by her appearance, which even she had to admit bordered on the grotesque—that he failed to hide the object he cradled surreptitiously in one hand.

Jen lunged for it, wresting it from his fingers with a triumphant cry.

It was, as she expected, another of the silver globes, like the one she had found on the drawing room mantel.

She clutched it firmly—careful not to drop it—and waved it irately under Patroch's nose. "Ready to plant this, were you?"

Her angry accusations, combined with her ghoulish appearance, must have been too much for him, for Patroch paled noticeably and began to stammer. "No . . . That is . . . I . . . Grandfather!" He appealed desperately to Saul.

"Yes?" his grandfather answered repressively. "I believe you have some explaining to do. What is this?"

Patroch opened and closed his mouth several times soundlessly, like a fish.

"Sit," Saul commanded.

"No," Jen said abruptly. "I've seen one of these things go off before and, trust me, none of us wants to be anywhere in the vicinity when it does. Let me get rid of it before we continue."

And before anyone could say another word, she was out the door and down the hallway, heading for the courtyard at a run.

39

As Jen pounded down the hall, thoughts tumbled freneti-
cally through her head, spinning and colliding like children
at play. She was infinitely aware of Saul at her heels, pro-
pelling Patroch forcibly before him, and with every step she
took her battered body screeched at her, protesting the
abuse as vehemently as Patroch.

How to get outside before the blasted thing exploded?
What was the cue? If Patroch had carried it—and stored
it—presumably it was safe to transport. Which meant that
something highly specific had to trigger it. Something highly
specific and quite simple, since it had to be cued outside
of his presence. But what?

Frantically, Jen cast her mind back to her previous encounter with one of these globes, trying to determine how
Thibault had inadvertently set it off. What had happened?
He had flung it into the fireplace, there was a delay while
she chastised him, and then . . .

She loosed a spate of curses, prompting Saul to exclaim
from behind her, "Gilyan? What ails?"

She ignored him, her mind spinning over the revelation.
It was so bloody obvious; why hadn't she seen it before?
Voice-activated, cued to the name of its intended victim.
And the last time, she had nearly killed them both.

Well, not this time! She skidded into the courtyard, raising her arm to fling the deadly thing far from her—although
something about the whole situation still troubled her,
something about the cue. . . . But before she could complete the thought—or the toss—Thibault came tearing into
the courtyard from the opposite direction, halting precisely
where she had intended to deposit the globe.

She uttered a wordless cry of frustration and rage.

Her partner, caught up in some mindless concern of his own, seemed oblivious to her distress. "Jen," he said, blinking. "What are you doing out here? Have you seen . . ."

"Don't say it!" she shrieked.

But it was too late.

". . . Saul?" he finished, cocking his head in inquiry.

She heard a faint, fatal snick from the object in her hands. The silver petals fell open, and a yellow cloud of gas hissed forth, billowing from her fingers.

Blast it all to perdition, she thought. *What a bloody stupid way to die!*

And then oblivion claimed her.

Aubrey raced through the Cauldron, tearing open storeroom door after storeroom door in an attempt to find the child. And it wasn't until he was in a hurry—in a race against Gideon and time—that he realized how extensive the place truly was. You could have hidden an army in the warrens of basements and subbasements that stretched beneath the Cauldron. The girl could be anywhere.

Even more distressing was the condition of the hallways: brightly lit and immaculately clean, their stone walls painted pristinely white. The very ordinariness of it only made his search all the more surreal. Such a quest should have been conducted in dusty dungeons with twisting corridors covered in dust and cobwebs, smelling of misery and dimly lit by flickering torches or scattered globes of magelight. But instead the brisk, businesslike progression of storeroom doors only served to heighten the horror. These were corridors he had trod almost every day for the past ten years, fetching up wines and brandies, and food for the kitchens.

Not kidnapped six-year-olds.

He had first checked the modified cells where they kept the prisoners purchased from the city jails, but they were all empty. Though, in retrospect, he wasn't surprised. That would have been too easy. So from there, Aubrey turned to the maze of storerooms, searching wine cellars and root cellars, and rooms piled high with bags of rice and flour, dried sausages and herbs.

Still nothing.

Worse, the longer he searched, the more chance there was that Gideon would find him. At every turned corner he expected to see Gideon's face, his pale green eyes glittering like ice and his mouth twisted into a mocking sneer. "Aubrey," he would say. "What are you doing? You truly have gone soft . . ."

Gone soft, Aubrey thought. *Gone sane would be more like it!*

But still he searched, and still no Gideon. And still no girl. Maybe she was in one of the upstairs rooms, like Gideon's chamber. Or maybe—the thought horrified—she wasn't in the Cauldron at all. Maybe Gideon, in his infinite deviousness, had hidden her in the one place Aubrey couldn't find her: his own apartments, wherever the blazes those were. Again, Aubrey found himself cursing Gideon's unnatural privacy. Once (and he acknowledged this with a shudder), he might have welcomed Gideon's touch and the chance to be a part of his life. Now he had other options, and the thought made him want to retch.

Gideon truly *was* a monster, and this time he had gone too far. Not only in his beating of that assassin, but also in the way he had appropriated an innocent off the streets, as if his needs supplanted her own.

Granted, Gideon had seized her from among the indigent, and the fate of such a girl was dubious. At best, she would have been a servant in some minor house; at worst, dead or addicted to drugs, selling her body on the streets before she'd hit eleven. But still, she deserved the chance. The *choice*. And Gideon would take that away forever unless Aubrey stopped him.

And then, between a wine cellar and a room dedicated exclusively to liquors, he found her. She was in a chamber meant for meats, the walls kept cold by a mage's spell, and he knew then why Gideon hadn't tried to stop him. She was dead. And not only dead—viciously dead. She was naked, and at least one of her arms had been broken so that she lay like a disjointed puppet. Both her mouth and groin were a smear of blood, and there were bite marks on her jaw and about her prepubescent nipples. Aubrey wasn't sure if it was the cold of the room or some other cause that had turned her skin so subtly blue.

Bile rose in his throat, and he swallowed it down. It wasn't the worst death he had encountered; the serial killings that had recently been plaguing the club were infinitely worse. But she was so young. She would be one of the ones that would haunt his nights, he knew, waking him from troubled sleep.

If so, she would be in good company.

He sank down to the floor, ignoring the cold, and took her tiny hand in his. Her bones were so fragile, like birds' bones. She had deserved protecting, this daughter of the streets. And who had been there for her? Not Gideon, certainly. And not Saul, "philanthropist" extraordinaire. For all he was worshiped as the savior of the common man, only a select few knew the true motives for his generosity or the secrets it was hiding. Or even that whatever he did distribute was such a vanishingly small fraction of the whole that it made not a dent in the accounting books.

Here was one of the citizens Saul was supposed to be protecting, and he had sold her out for three thousand marks, as if she hadn't even mattered. As Aubrey supposed she hadn't. Not to Gideon, and not to Saul. But as for Aubrey, he was beginning to recognize some bitter truths. And one was that, while money was nice, it could not substitute for a conscience. And, trite as it sounded, there were some things that money could not buy, like caring. Or compassion.

But worse was a growing comprehension of his own community, and the price it extracted. He had an obligation to humanity—at least so long as he desired to count himself among its number. So he squeezed the frail, dead hand, and promised, "It will end. I swear it."

He felt a sudden rush of pleasure at the words, as if it were the first worthwhile thing he had done in his life. As perhaps it was. But—a grin, disused and rusty, curved his features—who better? He had knowledge. And, as Saul had often told him, knowledge was power.

How foolish they had been to trust him. With one word, he could bring Saul's empire crumbling to its knees.

He dropped the dead girl's hand and rose—filled with a sudden heady resolution—and not a moment too soon. Gideon appeared in the doorway, his face identical to Aubrey's imaginings, down to the cynical sneer that twisted his lips.

"So. You found her, I see."

Aubrey cultivated an air of indifference. "It seems I did."

"And?"

"And what?"

Gideon arched an eyebrow. "You went tearing out of Saul's office fairly precipitously. It seemed your conscience was pricking you." He grinned, then gestured to the body. "Are you still thinking of rescuing her?"

"Hardly much point in that now, is there?" Aubrey was amazed at how cool he sounded, lying to Gideon like this. There wasn't even a tremor in his voice.

Who would have thought?

"So how's your conscience feeling now?"

"Fine." It was no less than the truth. If Aubrey had ever realized that doing the right thing felt this good, he might have done it years ago. But to allay Gideon's suspicions, he added, "Providing, of course, that I get my commission . . ."

"Well." Gideon measured him. "I don't know why you should, since you did just about everything possible to sabotage the deal. But then, you were the one that took the request in the first place, so . . . why not?" He grinned, and clapped Aubrey on the shoulder. "We'll split the three hundred."

Aubrey managed to quell his shudder of revulsion. "Thank you."

"Think nothing of it. Saul will be so pleased to hear that you've come around."

That's what you think, Aubrey reflected. *But I guarantee that, whatever Saul feels, it won't be pleasure!*

He followed Gideon from the chamber.

Consciousness sifted back in slow stages, as if Jen were battling through the yellow fog that had claimed her. She almost expected to see a citrine haze when she opened her eyes, but instead all she saw was Thibault's face, his mouth split in a grin. She was, she realized belatedly, cradled in his arms as he knelt beside her, her head against his chest. But his expression was so far removed from the frantic worry she had expected that she instantly assumed the worst.

"Are we dead?" she asked, her voice a croak.

"Not even close. Can you sit?"

"I think so." She struggled upright, the world tilting and then reorienting to reveal Saul staring at her with frozen horror—now *that* was more like it!—and Patroch, his face pulled into resentful lines.

She turned back to Thibault. He looked almost . . . triumphant. Was he so relieved to be rid of her after their ill-advised night of passion?

And then she realized what it was about the globe that had been bothering her. If it had indeed been cued to Saul's name—as now seemed to be the case—then at least one other person had to be in the room to trigger it, for Saul wasn't about to go saying his own name in private. And Patroch—despite his spoiled demeanor—didn't seem the type to kill *two* people simultaneously. Especially if one was an innocent. Which left only one option.

"It wasn't poison?" she croaked.

"No," Thibault agreed. "It wasn't."

"But . . ." Whatever that blasted gas was, it had ruined her voice. She cleared her throat noisily and then said, in a more normal tone, "Why are you smiling?"

"Because I was right."

"But . . . You were the one who suspected Patroch!"

"And I still do. But we were wrong about one thing, you and I. It was never Patroch's intention to murder his grandfather. Quite the opposite, in fact."

"I'm confused."

"You're not the only one," Saul grumbled, interrupting their conversation. "Into my office, the lot of you. It's time to resolve this for once and all."

40

It was an interesting group that gathered in Saul's office several minutes later. Jen, whose bruises made her seem both tough and vulnerable, nonetheless looked like a woman who had just had several large rugs pulled out from under her. Patroch looked scared and sullen all at once. Saul was scowling. And as for Thibault . . . Well, he knew his face reflected a certain smugness for Figuring It All Out.

At last.

It had been a long and tortuous road, but it had finally ended. All the pieces fit. And now they could leave this crazy house forever.

"Well?" Jen said at last, looking pointedly at Thibault. "Isn't someone going to explain this?"

"Yes," Saul agreed, training his scowl on Patroch. "Why were you trying to kill me?"

"I . . . I wasn't!" Patroch stammered, with convincing horror.

"He wasn't," Thibault confirmed, then abruptly regretted it as every pair of eyes swiveled toward him.

There was a moment of silence. Then, "Why are the servants here?" Patroch demanded.

"Because they are not the servants," Saul responded.

"No? Who are they, then?"

"The Guild."

Jen smiled pleasantly at him, and Patroch went pale, obviously trying to calculate when and how badly he had last offended her.

Saul chuckled, turning his attention back to Thibault. "You were saying?"

"He wasn't trying to kill you," Thibault continued. "But, blast it all, he very nearly killed me!" And he rotated his shoulder absently, glaring at Patroch. The boy went paler still.

"The falling masonry?" Saul guessed.

"Quite. And the first globe, and the doctored brandy . . ."

"Doctored brandy? Curse it, boy, not the Argossy?" And when Patroch nodded, Saul added, "Do you know how much that costs?" And then, "Doctored with what?"

"An emetic," Thibault supplied. "I'm not sure which one; the mage wasn't that specific."

"Still," Saul opined, steepling his fingers, "it doesn't seem all that dire."

"It's not. As I said, the object was never to kill." Thibault glanced over at Jen, who was still looking puzzled. "I didn't figure it out until this afternoon, when I saw a mother drag her boy away from a speeding hansom."

A light came on behind Jen's eyes. "He was trying to save him," she breathed. "He was deliberately engineering harmless attacks that looked deadly, so that he could 'save' his grandfather without any risk to himself!"

"Precisely." Thibault's eyes applauded her; he would have hated Saul to have figured it out first. "Attacks which we, alas, ended up consistently foiling."

"Yes," Patroch flared. "And blast you for that, anyway!"

Saul arched an eyebrow. "But why was Patroch engineering attacks just to save me from them?"

Thibault looked at Patroch. "Do you want to tell him, or shall I?"

Patroch scowled.

"Very well," Thibault said. "Money."

Saul looked more stunned by this than anything. "But . . . why? I've been more than generous."

"I wanted to open my own club, Grandfather," Patroch whined. "And you never listened to my plans . . ."

The timing couldn't have been more perfect. A shrieking cry preceded Lydea into the room, brandishing an armload of brightly colored silk.

"And what do you think I found in my son's room this time?" she railed.

"Mother!" Patroch exclaimed. "I've told you that you have no right to be in my room!"

"I have every right, as long as you are living under my roof," she fired back.

"My roof," corrected Saul mildly.

Lydea whirled on him, her face purple with rage. "Look at this!" she choked, thrusting the bundle at Saul. "And tell me what the depravity in this house has done to my son!"

With an expression bordering on contempt, Saul unfurled the wad of silk, revealing a bright scarlet dress.

"So?" he said. "A trophy of conquest. What's the harm in that? Proves he's a man who appreciates his women."

"Look closer," Lydea said tightly.

Patroch went as red as the dress, and shrank down in his chair. Saul unfolded the fabric further, revealing frilly underclothes and a wad of long, dark hair.

He killed someone else? was Thibault's first thought—until Saul dangled the wig before his grandson. The dress, now that Thibault noticed it, was several sizes larger than expected.

"What is this?" Saul demanded.

Thibault didn't think it was possible for Patroch to get any redder, but he did.

"It seems he doesn't like women, he likes to *be* women," Lydea informed them.

Jen began to giggle—half from nerves, and half from genuine amusement. Thibault didn't entirely blame her; the absurdity was beginning to get to him as well.

Saul turned to Patroch. "Is this true?"

"I blame this all on you," Lydea interrupted, scowling at Saul. "You and this amoral household. It's a wonder something like this didn't happen years ago!"

"That's enough, Lydea." Saul's voice was sharp. "If you will kindly leave us, I would like to settle this matter with my grandson in private."

For a moment, Thibault thought Lydea was going to protest. But she merely flung up her hands, shot each of them a disgusted glance in turn, then departed in a huff.

"Well, Patroch?" Saul repeated, when she had gone. "Is this true?"

His grandson shrugged sullenly, but said, with more spirit than Thibault had given him credit for, "Yes. And what of it?"

"You mean *this* was the type of club you wanted to open?"

"Yes," Patroch repeated, with that same defiance. "And it will make money, I assure you."

Saul actually looked thoughtful. "I don't doubt it. Well." There was a long moment of silence.

"Well, what?" Patroch asked at last. He was clearly starting to panic, a trickle of sweat tracking down his brow for all his resolve.

Saul broke into laughter. "Well, it seems your plan worked after all. I may not be grateful to you for saving my life, but I am most certainly listening."

"Then you're not mad at me?"

"On the contrary." Saul grinned at him, leaning back in his chair like a fond old uncle. "You've shown more initiative and persistence than I would have thought possible. I'm actually quite proud of you."

"You are?"

"Indeed." Saul surveyed his grandson for a moment, and then added, with a decisive nod, "Yes, I think you'll do. How much capital will you need to start your venture?"

"Well, that was anticlimactic," Thibault said later.

Jen looked up from her contemplation of the bedspread. Night had fallen, and the two were alone in their chamber. She frowned at him distractedly. "You think?"

"Don't you? We unmask the villain, he turns out to be the hero, and makes off with a fortune."

She gave a spurt of laughter. "When you put it that way, it does seem a bit absurd." Then her eyes sharpened, and he knew he had her full attention. "It also feels . . ."

"What?"

"A little too unfinished. Like we don't have the whole story, yet."

"But what is left? The first assassin stopped when the Telos clan ran out of money, and Patroch confessed to the second round and was forgiven."

"I know. But I still think something is missing."

"Like what?"

She exhaled gustily, and returned to her contemplation of the bedspread. "That's the annoying part; I have no idea." She ran a finger absently along the cloth, tracing patterns in the fabric.

He knew better than to say she was overreacting, so instead he said nothing, going over to the open window and gazing out into the alley. A cool breeze caressed his face. Besides, for all he knew she was right. There *was* something unfinished about the job—but maybe that was only his sense of anticlimax speaking. Because for all that had happened, the solution seemed ridiculously trivial.

But Avram and Lucinda would be back from Phykoros in four days, and Saul figured he could survive that long now that all the would-be assassins were uncovered. He had released them from service, and their classes at the university would not start for another month. Which, discounting transit, left them almost two full weeks of leisure. Two weeks to wander around the Konastan islands while their wounds healed and their bruises faded. Two weeks to figure out what new balance their relationship would settle into.

"Well, finished or not," he said, "we are free to go, and we have two weeks to wander the islands. So unless you'd just prefer to go back to Bergaetta . . ."

"No, I would like to see the islands, particularly Phykoros. And since I never did get you into the Cauldron . . . maybe we can spend a night at the Kettle?"

He shot her a wry smile. "You know, after all this fuss, I admit to being kind of curious as to what the illusion clubs are all about. The Kettle it is. We'll book passage tomorrow morning, and then you, me, and our bruises will travel to Phykoros and finally reap a few of the rewards this job has denied us. Silly, isn't it, that all we have to show for our time here is a motley collection of wounds and scars . . ."

Her face froze, and he instantly cursed himself for eighteen kinds of a fool. He knew how sensitive she was about her appearance.

"Jenny, I'm sorry. I didn't mean . . ."

She waved him to silence with one imperious hand.

"Jen, what . . ."

"No. Don't say anything," she snapped. "I've almost got it, what's been bothering me about this job." She steepled

her fingers to either side of her nose and closed her eyes,
her brow furrowed with concentration.

"Jen . . ."

"Shh! What was it? Something you said. Something
about . . ." Her eyes popped open, and she stared at him
incredulously.

"What?" he demanded.

"Answer me one question. Why, if all this consisted of
was Patroch's petty attempt to extort money from Saul, did
Gideon react so strongly when he found me in Saul's
office?"

"Because he's a maniac?"

"No. I tried that," she admitted, "and, in part, I believe
it. But it still doesn't explain the facts. There was something
else at stake, almost as if Gideon were protecting Saul in
some way. But what did he have to protect him from?"

"The revenge fantasies?"

"No, Saul explained that, too. It's unpleasant, but marginally legal. They only offer alternate executions for condemned criminals. It has to be something more."

Thibault frowned. To him, it sounded like another way
of rationalizing her experience, to add motive and meaning
to a random act of violence. Still, he owed her some answer
that wasn't quite so stark—if only he could think of one.

In the face of his continued silence, she finally grimaced
and said, "You're right; I'm being silly. And we should
start to pack if we're to leave for Phykoros tomorrow."

"So we should."

"And remind me that, before we leave, I also want to
speak to Kore and Jahnee."

"What for?"

"To offer them jobs."

He chuckled. "Is that how you repay Saul? By stealing
his servants?"

She began to grin. "I'm making quite a habit of that,
aren't I? But, like Elia, they deserve a chance. Besides, I'm
going to need someone I trust to work the Radineaux estates once I inherit them. Which reminds me . . . How
much did Saul end up paying you for your servant's work?"

"Eighty-five. And you?"

"The same. So counting our commission from Owen, we haven't done all that badly."

He laughed. "I thought money was no object."

"It's not. But a little extra never hurts."

He couldn't fault her logic. He saluted her and was about to open his trunk to start packing when a sharp, furtive knock sounded on the door.

They exchanged a look.

"Who do you think *that* could be?" Jen whispered.

"I have no idea," he returned, in a similar tone.

The knock came again—louder, and more insistent.

"Well, whoever it is, they're determined," Thibault said. "Shall I?"

Jen motioned him forward. He opened the portal and Aubrey pushed past him, hastily swinging the door shut behind him.

Jen instantly stiffened at the sight of Gideon's associate and Thibault stepped between them, but not before Aubrey had caught a glimpse of Jen's face and arms.

His mouth twisted, and he loosed a spate of curses.

"Why are you here?" Jen asked sharply. "Come to gloat?"

In the teeth of her murderous expression, Aubrey paled visibly and took a step backward, holding up his hands. "No! I'm here because . . ." Then his face clenched, and he said, "I'm sorry. I heard he had beaten you, but I had no idea how badly. Blast him! Blast them both!"

"Both?" Thibault queried.

Aubrey's expression darkened. "Saul, of course. Who else do you think gave the order?"

The air in the room seemed suddenly brittle, as if a word or movement could shatter it.

"Saul?" Jen said eventually, in a voice so tight you could have constructed castles on it.

"So he's got you fooled, too?" Aubrey said bitterly. "Listen, I can't stay; I'm taking enough of a risk just coming here. But if you want to know what is really going on, pay a visit to Number 17 Veridien Street. You won't be disappointed, I promise."

Another silence, and then, "Why are you telling us this?" Thibault demanded.

Aubrey's face was tight. "Let's just say I have my reasons." He put his hand to the doorknob, then abruptly turned back. "And if you tell anyone this came from me, I will kill you myself. I swear it."

And with those words, he pulled open the door and slipped through it as swiftly as he had entered, disappearing down the hall before the portal had even closed behind him.

41

Vera was rapidly growing bored—or frustrated; she couldn't decide which was worse. It had all seemed so easy, at first. Too easy, in retrospect, which perhaps should have alerted her to the truth. But then she had figured that perhaps the world had owed her a favor.

She ought to have known better. The world owed her nothing; it was merely having a little fun at her expense. But while it lasted, the luck was heady. Absalom was the perfect partner, and his own unique methods of magerie had opened doors that were previously impenetrable.

Not that Vera was any stranger to the drug trade, or to following a trail to its conclusion. But while she had made several runs against the master supplier in the past dozen years, each one had been doomed to failure. The drug trail was, of necessity, a tortuous one, involving several dozen intermediaries and not an inconsiderable number of false leads. And the higher placed the master supplier's henchmen were, the less they seemed inclined to trust. Each was bristling with anti-magerie amulets, and not even Vera's most carefully designed disguises or most expensive invisibility spells could outfox them.

Until she had met Absalom, whose spells could circumvent even the most rigorous battery of amulets by sneaking in the back door. Protected beneath the cloak of his invisibility spell, they had penetrated to the very highest levels of the organization, locating the suppliers of the suppliers of the suppliers. And then, without warning, the trail had dead-ended at a nondescript warehouse on Veridien Street. And no matter what Vera did, she could not crack its secrets.

At first, to determine this was in fact the storehouse of

all Ephanon's Dreamsmoke, she had gone back to the start of the trail on no less than three occasions, sending Nick to a new supplier each time. And no matter how vastly different Nick's contacts were, or what area of the city they originated from, all paths eventually led to Number 17 Veridien Street.

Which confirmed that she had found the right place— but who was behind it?

The cantankerous caretaker had been unable to tell her anything, not even under threat of death. And while Vera was not enamored of torture, even she sometimes saw advantages to a system that sacrificed one for many. Dreamsmoke had destroyed more lives than she cared to contemplate, and Absalom was expert at crafting them bodies that seemed reasonably likely to carry out their threats. But even at the height of the interrogation—while the man had shivered and gibbered and fouled his pants—he had revealed little of value. He had never seen his employer, or the owner of the warehouse; all his contact came through typeset notes, deposited randomly on his desk through magerie. Which made them impossible to trace.

And as for the contents of these notes, they revealed no more than which vessels were bringing shipments and when. And to what dealer the resultant stash would be delivered.

"And should you need to get back in touch with your master?" Vera prodded. "If shipment is late, or a dealer doesn't pay and you need to inform him . . . How do you go about that?"

"No different. Leave a note. It gets picked up. Somehow."

In the end, she hadn't had the heart to kill him—but she needn't have worried. Two days later, the man had mysteriously vanished and another faceless caretaker had taken his place. Two days after that, the first man's body had floated to the harbor's surface, bloated and nibbled by fishes.

Vera hadn't the heart to risk another innocent by asking the same questions all over again. She had enough blood on her hands already.

So she had turned to other methods of detection, strain-

ing the limits of her creative powers. Her next targets were
the housing offices and government buildings as she tried
to trace the deeds of the warehouse back to their owner.
But in that, too, she was thwarted. The warehouse was held
in the name of a fictitious corporation, which in turn led
to other fictitious corporations, and around and around in
a great circle, like a snake eating its tail.

Someone owned the warehouse, but she'd be cursed if
she could figure out who.

So, in despair, she had turned to the shipping manifests
in the harbormaster's office. Not that she expected the illegal shipments to be listed, but perhaps she could find some
thread of commonality between the ships whose captains
eventually made a drop at the warehouse. Some customer
common to all of them, whose name might be the connec-
tion she needed. But that, too, led nowhere. The only name
common to every manifest was Saul Soleneides, and simply
because he commanded a portion of every cargo hold of
every ship that ever docked in Ephanon—regardless of
whether they visited the Veridien Street warehouse or not.
Only last week, Kharman Black had carried a shipment of
preserved pears from Grometiere to Ephanon, bound for
the Cauldron. And Kharman, she knew, was as honest as
day.

Until that moment, she hadn't appreciated how vast
Saul's empire was. If Saul Soleneides went down, all of
Ephanon might follow—not that such a fate seemed likely.
Vera hadn't entirely forgotten her niece or her partner, and
at intervals she would ghost past House Soléneides in her
shroud of invisibility, just to make sure all was proceeding
smoothly. And, indeed, from what little she could gather,
all seemed fine. Jen was cheerfully involved with that glori-
ous blond Absalom found so threatening, and she and Thibault seemed to be happily following leads. Vera had taken
to frequenting the Five Crowns with Absalom and Nick,
and one evening about three days after she had begun her
campaign, she had seen her niece and Thibault proceeding
past the square, eyeing the restaurant longingly. She had
willed them to pass, and it seemed to have worked—although she could have sworn that Thibault had spotted her.
Fortunately, Absalom had also noticed Thibault, and the

mage hastily slapped an illusion over them which seemed to have distracted the boy.

However, this still didn't solve the problem of the warehouse.

So, fresh out of ideas, Vera was sitting morosely at the table in Hannah's back parlor one night, staring at the congealing remains of her dinner and wondering if it wasn't time to give up the quest.

"You have to eat *something,* you know," Absalom counseled mildly.

Vera grimaced, and poked at Hannah's stew absently with her fork. "I'm not hungry," she said.

He arched an eyebrow.

"Don't push it, Absalom. You don't do the maternal thing well."

He just smiled, and for a moment someone suspiciously like her mother—had the aristocratic Lady Marguerite ever stooped to wearing a mob-cap and servants' garb—smiled back at her.

Nick seemed oblivious. "So what do we do now?" he asked.

"We?" she answered, pointedly.

He had the grace to flush. She had smelled Dreamsmoke on him three times since his first infraction, and once he had tried to mask the scent of Ghedrin on his breath by chewing a handful of mint leaves. He was never changing; they both knew that now. Yet instead of depressing her, she felt no more than an odd nostalgia at the thought. Perhaps it was just acceptance of what she could no longer change, an acknowledgment that there were certain things beyond her control. Nick had chosen his road; it was no longer her battle to fight. If indeed it ever had been.

Or perhaps it was the depths of compassion and caring in Absalom's dark eyes that eased her.

"So are you going back to the warehouse again tonight?" that worthy now asked, abandoning his attempts to get her to eat.

"Of course." No matter what she discovered—or didn't—during the days, she haunted the warehouse each night like a vengeful spirit, with Absalom at her side. Waiting for the one missing piece that would resolve the whole blasted puzzle.

The one piece that never seemed to materialize.

But she didn't want to return to Owen in defeat. Not this time.

"Can I come?" Nick asked, as always.

Her anger at Nick was more a reflexive thing. Still, without his assassin's edge, she'd be cursed if she let him ruin her schemes. Or place him voluntarily in the path of such great temptation. So, "No," she answered, also as always.

He sighed deeply, but what more could she do? He was no longer an assassin. No longer her partner. Absalom was all she needed.

She met the mage's eyes again; they were infinitely deep and compelling. Comforting, somehow, in their unrelieved blackness. Perhaps reminding her that there were still absolutes in this muddy, grey world.

"Midnight?" he said.

"Midnight," she confirmed.

"Well, then." He rose from the table and stretched luxuriously. She tried not to notice the play of muscles beneath his loose shirt; they were probably more than half illusion, anyway. "Time for forty winks. My beauty sleep, as it were. You'll be the death of me yet, Vera, keeping such hours."

"She does tend to have that effect on people," Nick observed dryly.

"Well, it keeps me on my toes," Absalom replied. Then he added, leering at both in turn—only because he knew it annoyed them—"Anyone who wants to join me is welcome."

And he quit the back parlor as he always did, trailing quiet laughter like clouds of Dreamsmoke, leaving two flushed and scowling faces behind him. Nick because he still didn't like being mocked, however subtlely. And Vera because she was more than half-tempted by the teasing offer, and hated herself for the weakness that implied.

"So, do you think it's a trap?" Jen asked, in the wake of Aubrey's departure.

Thibault frowned. "I don't know. He seemed sincere enough . . . but it could be."

"Yes, it could. So?"

"I think we go anyway."

Jen nodded. Her jaw was set in a hard, tight line he was coming to know far too well of late. "I agree. There is more going on here than meets the eye; I know there is. And this only confirms my suspicions. It's close to midnight, now. We'll go out the window."

"Yes. But perhaps we should pack, first. Just in case we need to make a hasty departure later."

She considered this in silence for a moment, then nodded. "Right. But quickly. I don't want to delay this any longer than necessary."

As expected, however, Thibault ended up doing most of the packing while she changed her clothes—once again coolly ignoring his presence and regard—tucking her various weapons and assassin's implements about her person. Her movements had a false formality, as if she were engaged in some important ritual, a talisman of protection against the dark. He didn't like it. It felt brittle to him, and needy. And for all the times he used to revile her casual, off-the-cuff confidence, he now found himself mourning its loss.

This taut, considered creature—shadowed with the violet afterimage of violence—wasn't his partner, and he wanted her back. Annoying habits and all.

He muffled a snort of laughter at the thought, making her glance up sharply.

"What is it?"

He forced a nonchalant expression. "Nothing. Just thinking what Vera would say if she could see us now."

She almost smiled. "Not so incompetent, are we? Still, I'm glad Saul freed us from our duties. I'm not keen to linger in Ephanon any longer than we have to, especially not if we discover something significant tonight. I'm getting tired of pretending."

And what do you think a lifetime of being a Guild Assassin entails, he wanted to say, but he didn't. For where would he be if she decided to leave the Guild the minute he was getting used to it? A Cloak without a Dagger was a sad thing, indeed.

So he remained silent, shutting and locking the last of

the trunks. Then, undergoing no more preparations than settling his dagger at his waist, he opened the window wider and set the grapple, cueing off the room lights and gesturing for her to precede him.

She swung a leg over the window ledge, then turned back to regard him. She was framed in the casement and frozen in mid-motion, backlit by a thin sliver of moonlight. With her tilted head and her chestnut braid hanging loose over one shoulder, one hand raised and resting lightly on the jamb, her body was caught in a graceful curve of attenuated motion, rather like the curl of a wave in the instant before it smashed itself into oblivion against the shore. He hoped it wasn't an omen, but nonetheless found himself drinking in the sight, as if he could file it away for posterity.

It struck him as suddenly poignant: the ending of one life and the beginning of another. He hoped. But all she said was, prosaically, "Do you know the way to Veridien Street?"

He sighed and nodded, the moment fading, and she threw her other leg over the window frame and was gone, swallowed into the darkness of the alley below.

42

Thibault may have claimed he knew the way to Veridien Street, but his knowledge was obviously more sketchy than he implied. He had led them into the heart of the warehouse district with reasonable confidence then faltered, peering up at darkened street signs and muttering, "I know it was around here, somewhere."

Jen remained silent; she was hardly in a position to criticize. The dark, hulking warehouses loomed, their blackened windows winking like accusing eyes. Shadows pooled thick in every alley and corner. And the cobblestoned streets and high, narrow walls conspired to bounce the echoes of their footsteps around until it sounded like an army of ghosts was pursuing them.

Jen hated herself for jumping at every footfall and seeing ominous ripples of motion in the stillest of shadows, but she rationalized it by telling herself that anyone would be nervous on these silent streets so late at night. Anything could be hiding in those darkened buildings, and the beady pinpricks of rodent eyes might not be all that was watching. But that was only an excuse. Her partner wasn't nervous. He strode along as if navigating the busiest promenade, his hands thrust deeply into his pockets, disconcerted only by his inability to find the way.

He muttered and cursed at the street signs, shooting her the occasional placatory grin. She would have hated him if she could. But how could she hate that peasant face, now more familiar to her than her own? The more she looked at it, the more she found in it to admire. How could she have thought it nondescript when the moonlight etched its firm, clean lines so clearly? His cheekbones and chin held an unexpected strength, balanced by an infinite gentleness in those soft, brown eyes. The thick, straight fall of his hair with its forelock that always threatened to fall into his eyes—which she had once thought so foolish—now seemed to impart a boyishness to a face which otherwise had become frighteningly hard and competent. Even his slow-footed peasant grace was reassuring in its solidity. She wanted to throw herself into those comforting arms and never emerge again.

Two weeks ago, she would have trod these streets as fearlessly as he, confident in her ability to handle anything she might encounter. Foolish boy; didn't he know that life was rarely dependable? Didn't she know?

Since when had she become afraid of the dark?

But that hardly required more than a moment's thought. Ever since each shadow seemed to contain a golden-haired monster. A golden-haired monster with ice-green eyes and a deadly beauty whose very presence could undermine every last ounce of her courage. She was a walking arsenal tonight, yet all it would take to neutralize her was Gideon's smile.

Fortunately, her partner seemed oblivious to her distress, merely uttering a soft cry of triumph as he finally located the sign for Veridien Street. He touched her arm, guiding her down the proper path, and she hoped he couldn't feel her shaking.

Veridien Street seemed no different than any of the other streets: dark, narrow, and frosted by moonlight. Warehouses loomed. Sharp points of starlight burned high overhead. Certainly, there was nothing to imply that a secret lurked behind these shadowed facades.

A secret . . . or a trap.

Number 17 was three blocks down, a nondescript warehouse like every other nondescript warehouse, its dark paint flaking. Its front loading door was chained and padlocked, but the side door was caught with a shiny lock.

"You or me?" Thibault whispered, cocking an eyebrow.

"Me," Jen responded, with more confidence than she felt. She extracted her lockpicks from the roll at her waist and set about finessing the lock. It was trickier than she expected, and several times she fumbled and nearly dropped the lockpicks. She wasn't sure how much of that was due to her sweaty palms and how much that the lock was a deuced tricky one.

"Do you want me to try?" Thibault whispered, after her fourth fumble.

She shook her head angrily. "It's just a stubborn lock; way too many tumblers. I'll have it in a minute." And wiping her hands resolutely on the seat of her pants, she attacked the lock anew, and this time felt the tumblers falling under her picks.

She masked a surge of triumph as the final cylinder fell. At least she hadn't lost all her skills. Thibault was grinning and shaking his head in amazement; he had heard the sequence as clearly as she. "We must be on to something," he whispered, "if it's hidden behind that complex a lock. That must have cost a tidy fortune to craft."

"And a tidy amount of skill to pick," Jen countered, stowing her tools. "But better that than a shield spell, which is hardly a shield at all when too many night watchmen know the code." Then, putting her hand to the knob and ignoring a heart that seemed inclined to pound its way straight out of her chest, she eased the door open and peered inside.

Darkness; thick and unrelenting.

"Ready?" she whispered to Thibault.

He nodded, and she drew a darkened globe of hand-held magelight from a pouch at her waist, passing it back to her partner. "Then let's do it."

She pushed the door wider and slipped inside, with Thibault close at her heels. When he shut the portal behind him, blackness enveloped them. Blackness and silence, broken only by the frantic pounding of her heart—which seemed to reach into every corner of the warehouse like the echo of jungle drums.

She was amazed Thibault couldn't hear it. Or perhaps he could, and was only being polite.

"Hullabaloo," he whispered.

A cool, verdant magelight leaked from between his fingers, oozing into the corners of the vast warehouse, casting her shadow grotesquely out in front of her. As she pivoted, surveying the cavernous space, it writhed on the floor, twisting like a spitted beast.

She let out a breath she hadn't been aware she was holding, feeling a vague slackening of the tension inside her. Not a trap, then. At least, not yet. She dared a step forward, and then another, and her shadow lurched with her as Thibault adjusted his grip on the magelight. Crate after unidentifiable wooden crate were stacked high against the walls, and in regular rows down the length of the warehouse floor, with wide aisles between them. A corner office was dark and empty, its door half ajar. As she watched, she could swear it swung imperceptibly wider, but perhaps that was only a trick of the wavering magelight.

You have to stop jumping at nothing, she told herself firmly. *Gideon is not here. He's safe in the Cauldron, doing Saul's filthy bidding—whatever the blazes that is. So what in perdition did Aubrey send us here for?*

"What *is* this place?" breathed Thibault, echoing her sentiments. "What is Saul up to?"

"I don't know," she answered, in the same breathless thread of a whisper. "But maybe we should check the crates. Something has to be . . ."

"What?" Thibault demanded, as her voice trailed off.

She motioned him frantically to silence, every sense screaming. There; that creak of boards. The natural shifting of wood in the evening chill, or . . . *footsteps*? A creak, another, a ripple in the shadows like heat rising from desert sands, and then . . . An audible gasp, and two dark-clad figures where there was only air before. And, unbelievably, her name leaking incredulously from the lips of one.

"Jen . . ."

Trap! her panicked mind shrilled. Without pausing to think, she drew her garroting cord and leaped, looping the wire around the slenderer of the two necks and yanking. The fury of her attack, fueled by fear and adrenaline, surprised even herself. But she might as well have attacked a tree. The cord jerked taut against an impenetrable barrier and snapped, dumping her ignominiously to the floor.

She was scrambling to her feet and opening her mouth to wail for Thibault when the figure turned. Reality jerked and shattered, and Jen sat back down with a bump, her mouth hanging open but her cry aborted.

All she could manage was a strangled peep.

Vera was staring down at her, rubbing her neck ruefully. "Great shades of oblivion," she muttered. "Good save, Absalom."

The second figure grinned and bowed, resolving into the mage. His very gestures, at once foppish and filled with a sinister purpose, were unmistakable. "And a near one it was, too," he drawled. "I had no idea you could move so fast, young Jen." Extending a hand, he helped her to her feet.

"Vera, what the blazes are you doing here?" Thibault demanded furiously, while Jen was still mentally fumbling her way through apologies and denials.

"I might ask the same of you," her aunt snapped. A globe of magelight twin to Thibault's own flared to life in her hands, casting a twisted landscape of double-edge shadows. "Do you have any idea what this place is, or how dangerous it is for you to be here?"

"And it's all right for you?" he countered. "I hardly think . . ."

Jen gathered her tumbled thoughts and very slowly, very deliberately, interrupted, saying, "Vera, what are you doing in Ephanon? Are you spying on me?"

Silence fell like a load of bricks. Thibault gasped, and Vera turned her killing gaze on Jen. "Why must everything always be about you, Jenifleur? I may have come to keep an eye on you at first, just to make sure you were all right, but I haven't been near you or your target in a long time. I've been too involved in a job of my own, and you're perfectly capable of taking care of yoursel . . ." Vera's voice trailed off as she caught her first clear glimpse of Jen's face. Brisk but far from unkindly fingers grasped her chin, and tilted her face to the light. "Scarlet sentinels of doom, girl! What have you done to yourself?"

To Jen's infinite horror, she felt tears pricking at her eyelids. She blinked them back furiously and jerked her face away. "I don't want to talk about it," she said. When Vera showed signs of protest, she added, "What is this place? And why are you here?"

Vera sighed heavily, and looked from Jen to Thibault to Absalom. "I'd prefer not to explain right now. The longer we stay in this place—and in an observable form—the more

danger we are in. But just briefly . . . Absalom, will you
do the honors?''

Jen didn't feel anything happen, but Vera nodded with
satisfaction, so she could only assume that the mage had
placed them all under an invisibility spell.

"Now, follow me," Vera added. "But quickly. And
quietly!''

Jen exchanged a puzzled glance with her partner, then
followed Vera to an isolated corner of the warehouse where
two guards were slumped in magically induced slumber,
snoring softly. Beside them was a half-open crate, filled
with what looked like brownish dust or ash.

"What . . ." Jen began, but it was Thibault who made
the intuitive leap.

"Dreamsmoke," he breathed. "Bloody shades of oblivion! That bastard . . .''

Jen gasped, Aubrey's bitter voice echoing in her head: *If
you want to really know what is going on, pay a visit to
Number 17 Veridien Street.* And, *Saul, of course. Who else
do you think gave the order?*

She felt abruptly sick. Her knees buckled, and she collapsed on a nearby crate, resting her head in her hands.

Vera knelt down beside her, shaking her. "What is it,
Jenny? What do you know? Why are you here?''

She looked up, blindly extending a hand. Thibault took
it and held it tightly, as she had known he would. She
clutched at him convulsively.

"This is the master supplier's warehouse, isn't it?" she
asked dully.

Vera nodded. "That it is. Jenny . . . *who owns it*?''

Thibault was cursing a blue streak.

"I'm not sure," she temporized. "But I think . . . Saul.''

The Hawk's face went grey. "Bloody shades of perdition.
That poor old man!''

No one had to ask whom she meant; Owen's face loomed
large in all their minds.

An hour later, the four of them were sitting in the back
garden of Vera's rooming house, sipping tea and watching
the lights dance over the harbor. Their hostess had roused
herself when they entered and tried to make tea, but Absa-

lom had sent her kindly but firmly back to bed and taken over that duty himself. So now Thibault clutched his mug, gazing about at the benign neglect of the garden.

He still felt numb. A cool breeze was blowing off the water, but it wasn't that which chilled him—especially since Absalom had laid a mild heating spell on the stones beneath their feet. Under any other circumstances, there would have been something sensual in the fluctuating contrast between heat and cool. Just as there would have been in the warmth of Jen's body, pressed close against him. But though he had an arm around her and her cheek was pillowed on his chest, one hand curled unconsciously high on his thigh, he felt nothing. Just the numb chill of unwanted knowledge.

It seemed that Saul Soleneides, their charming employer and Owen's best friend—that philanthropist extraordinaire who had seduced them all so utterly—was nothing but a common criminal. Or rather the most uncommon of criminals: the master Dreamsmoke supplier of all of Ephanon and most of Konasta. The man who single-handedly held his country in a financial choke-hold.

Jen had been right. There had been more to Saul's story than a peeved petty dealer and a greedy grandson, and it was no wonder Gideon had reacted so violently to Jen's violation of Saul's office. If the Guild had determined Saul's true activities . . .

But the Guild had determined it, he reminded himself—though not without help. They had all compared their stories. Vera, alone, would never have solved it; Saul had covered his tracks too well and for too long. And Thibault and Jen would never have been able to provide the missing piece of the puzzle without Aubrey's startling defection. The man *hadn't* set them up. Whatever his reasons, Aubrey had given them the only gift he had: the truth.

They still had no proof—nothing concrete to tie Saul to his treacherous warehouse—but Aubrey wouldn't have set them on the trail if there wasn't some evidence to be found. Of that, Thibault was certain.

"What?" Vera asked him, as she watched his face harden.

"We'll find proof," he said grimly. "That much I promise."

There was another long moment of silence—an event which had been occurring all too frequently in this terse discussion. Beside him, Jen shivered and nestled closer. Did she really think he hadn't noticed her shaking as she entered that warehouse? Almost absently, he dropped a kiss on her forehead, then looked up to find Vera watching him curiously.

He grimaced, then raised his eyebrows in a shrug. "It's not what you think," he said.

She grinned.

"What's not?" Jen asked.

"Nothing," he responded.

Another pause.

"But where?" he continued intently. "Where do we start?"

"For proof?" Vera asked.

Thibault nodded.

More silence. Vera exchanged a glance with Absalom, and the mage rose without a word to fetch more tea and a plate piled high with tiny cakes and biscuits. He laid a brief hand on her shoulder as he refilled her mug and handed her a biscuit before he turned away to serve the others.

Vera took a bite of her biscuit, then looked up to find Thibault watching.

"It's not what you think, either," she said, and Thibault laughed—though he wasn't quite sure he believed her. There seemed an odd, weighty intimacy between Vera and her mage, and he wasn't quite sure what he thought about it. He had enough problems envisioning Vera with any man, let alone a mage. How could she trust him?

"What's so funny?" Jen demanded, poking him. Thibault looked down, relieved to see a semblance of life returning to her eyes. She abruptly seemed to become aware of her position, curled up so intimately in his arms, and stiffened. He let her go before she could pull away.

"Nothing," he said again. "Vera was making faces."

"Vera never makes faces," she returned, but seemed

willing enough to drop the subject. "So, what now? Return
to Saul's, knowing what we know?"

"What other choice do we have? He'll just get suspicious
if we sneak away in the night. Besides, we're supposed to
be leaving for Phykoros tomorrow. If we pretend to board a
ship, he'll never know we've not gone. We can lurk around
Ephanon all we like then, searching for clues. Hannah can
put us up here. It might mean sharing another room,
but . . ."

"No," she said abruptly, and his heart sank. Was the idea
that repellent to her? But all she said was, "We're not
staying in Ephanon. We're going to Phykoros." She turned
a sudden stern gaze on her aunt and Absalom. "You, too."

"Jen," Thibault protested. "You can't tell me you're just
running away! Not after everything that's happened . . ."

"Is that all you think of me?" she flared. "That I'm a
quitter? Use your head, Thib! The Dreamsmoke's got to
come from somewhere; Vera told you about the shipments.
Where else does Saul have a free landing port and an entire
island to exploit? I'm willing to bet that if it's proof you
want, you'll find it on . . ."

"Phykoros," he finished. "Bloody blazes, Jen, you're brilliant!" And, despite her bruises, he wrapped her in both
arms and hugged her until she squeaked.

"We'll book the ship in the morning," she continued, her
voice half-muffled in his chest, "and Saul will never suspect
a thing." Then she pushed at him to free herself, turning
her gaze to Vera and Absalom. "I think you should be on
our ship, too."

Absalom grinned. "Consider it done. But don't expect to
recognize us until after we've docked on Phykoros."

"Fair enough." She looked up at the sky, where the
moon was setting and a faint light was beginning to bleed
over the horizon from the east. "We should get back before
we're missed."

"Missed by whom?" a new voice asked, its tones slightly
slurred. A fifth figure sauntered into the garden, smelling
faintly of Dreamsmoke and looking like a rather dissipated
version of Absalom. He had also, Thibault suspected,
been drinking.

Vera scowled at him. "Are you just getting home?"

"Well, as you didn't seem to have need of me . . ." The stranger shrugged slightly, which made him sway, but he recovered himself quickly enough. "Who are these people, Vi? More partners?" There was a faint bitterness in his voice.

Jen was scowling. "You know this man?"

Vera heaved a great sigh. "Well, I suppose this was bound to happen eventually," she muttered, half under her breath. Then, louder, she added, "Nick, these are the two newest members of the Guild: my niece, Jenifleur Radineaux, and her partner, Thibault Lescevre. Otherwise known as the Cloak and the Dagger."

Nick chuckled. "Clever," he opined.

"Vera!" Jen was horrified. "How could you just tell him . . ."

"And this," Vera continued heavily, ignoring her, "is Nick. Nikolaos Constantin Navarin, once known as the Lammergeier. And my former fiancé."

43

Jen was still in a state of shock as she progressed back to Saul's manor with Thibault; what a night of surprises this was proving to be. First the revelation of Saul's identity, and then Vera's erstwhile fiancé, a former Guild member and current drug addict, rehabilitated off the Ephanon streets. She didn't know which surprised her more—although, to be honest, it was probably the latter.

Vera, engaged? It just didn't seem possible, even if it was sixteen years ago, when Jen herself was three. And Vera married? Impossible. Vera was too . . . Vera. Too independent; too self-sufficient. Too complete unto herself. She had been Jen's inspiration for more years than Jen cared to mention, and from her Jen had learned that male companionship was a pleasant diversion rather than a requirement.

Was she going to have to rethink her whole philosophy now?

"Blast it . . ."

"What?" Thibault had wisely remained silent until she had spoken.

"Vera?" she exclaimed. *"Engaged?"*

He chuckled. "I had a feeling that was bothering you more than the revelation about our employer."

"Well, of course. I mean, this is *Vera* we are talking about!"

"So?"

She searched for an answer, but was unable to articulate it more than just repeating, "Vera!" in somewhat scandalized tones, waving her arms about for emphasis.

"Then what of Absalom?"

"Absalom? What about him?" And at his look, she added, "They're just friends, Thibault."

Annoyingly, he shrugged.

"They are!" she insisted. "I mean, they aren't . . . That is . . . Oh, never mind; it's not important."

But Thibault's eyes seemed to refute the lie.

Still, apart from the issue of Vera's personal life, the revelation did make one or two things frighteningly apparent. For one, it was no wonder Vera hated the drug trade so greatly. Jen had known of her aunt's prejudice for years, but she had never imagined it had such personal origins. She supposed she would hate it, too, if it had destroyed Thibault's life. Not that Thibault and her relationship was anything like Vera's and Nick's had been.

And why did *that* make her feel particularly maudlin?

Worse, it cast Vera's carefree independence into a whole different light. What if Jen had been wrong and Vera had been avoiding permanent relationships not because she deemed them unnecessary, but rather because she never wanted to be hurt that badly again?

No, all around it had been an evening too full of surprises and near-miss accidents. By Varia, Jen had almost killed her aunt, and how would she have been able to live with that? If Absalom hadn't interceded, throwing up that magical barrier, Vera would have been deader than dirt. And all thanks to Jen's usual heedless impulsiveness.

And yet . . . A tiny corner of her reveled in the action. It had proved that she was still capable of action—that she had not frozen—even though it could have been Gideon hiding in those shadows. And that reassured her more than she liked to admit.

Perhaps she had not been broken irreparably, after all.

"Ready to climb?" Thibault asked eventually, interrupting the tangle of her thoughts.

She looked up in confusion, not realizing they had reached the back of Saul's manor already. "That was fast."

"Well, it helps when you actually know where you're going," Thibault said, with a self-deprecating laugh. He reached behind the drainpipe and drew out the coiled mass of rope and grapple, which he then proceeded to unwind.

His toss was flawless, the grapple catching against the second floor window ledge with barely a click.

"Is your shoulder up to this?" Jen inquired.

"Are your ribs?" he answered.

She grimaced. "I suppose they will have to be."

"Well, the same applies for me. Want a boost?"

She measured the distance with her eyes. It was not far but still a climb for a person whose body ached just standing. She held a brief debate with her pride and almost refused the offer—just on the sheer principle of the thing—but Thibault was her partner. And if you couldn't trust your partner with your weaknesses, then who could you trust?

So, "If you wouldn't mind . . ." she said.

"My pleasure." He knelt down in the alley and helped her onto his shoulders. Then, when she was seated, her legs straddling his neck, he advised, "Hang on." And stood.

She clutched at his hair as the world tipped and straightened. Then, with one hand braced against the manor's wall for balance, she levered herself cautiously up to a stand. He grunted slightly as she shifted her weight on his injured shoulder, but the position left her only slightly below the level of the window. She grasped the rope and, ignoring the twinges of pain, transferred her weight to the grapple. A few steps brought her to the window ledge and she pulled herself up and over, trying not to gasp.

Then she watched Thibault grasp the rope in turn and pull himself, virtually one-handed, up the wall, somehow managing to make the ascent look effortless.

She helped him through the window, then stood with him in the leaking dawn, gazing about the room they had shared for the past month. It looked oddly desolate in the growing half-light, with their possessions packed neatly away. Now it was merely a barren chamber, bereft of all their pains and passions, and that seemed the strangest thing of all. That after all that had happened, they had left so little impression on their surroundings.

Would future denizens ever know that she and Thibault had shared this chamber? That here the Cloak had bedded the Dagger for the first—and what might now be the only—time? And in that very bed which, neatly made, now seemed so impersonal?

More than anything, she longed for him to share it again, if only for one last time. But she couldn't bear another rejection—not after all that had happened.

"We should get some sleep," Thibault said at last, as if reading her mind. "It's almost dawn."

"Yes," she said, but made no move toward the bed. Instead, she found herself seized by a sudden, brittle anticipation, waiting to see what he would do.

For a long moment, he didn't move either. She had a feeling he was looking at her, but couldn't bring herself to look back, not wanting to see a vague pity or sympathy in his eyes. After all, she couldn't keep running to him every time she felt fragile and vulnerable.

But as the silence continued to stretch out, suddenly awkward and weighted, she raised her head. She needn't have worried about deciphering his expression. His eyes were heavily lidded and swallowed in shadow; she couldn't read their import.

For a moment, he seemed like he was on the verge of speech, but then he sighed and turned away, pulling the pallet from under the bed.

Well, that settles that, she thought, letting a sigh of her own trickle from her lips. She was back on her own against the world.

The *Phykoros Queen* was a trim three-master, with clean, elegant lines and a plethora of passenger cabins at the expense of the cargo holds. Moreover, Saul had done them proud, finagling them a first-class cabin with two wide berths and three portholes, refusing all payment. He had even seen them onto the ship himself, keeping up a stream of cheerful chatter as he walked them to the quay, his anecdotes interspersed with thanks for their service and promises to sing their praises to Owen. And despite everything Jen knew, she was still under his spell.

It was almost as if everything that had transpired the previous evening had been a dream. And why not? It all felt dim and unreal in this crisp, effulgent morning. The sun dazzled though a cloudless sky the color and clarity of a finely cut sapphire. The sea was aquamarine, and stitched with darting schools of silver fishes; the islands soared from its surface like fairy castles. How, in all this glory, could Saul be the master Dreamsmoke supplier of all of Ephanon and most of Konasta? How could this man who laughed so amiably at their side, his dimples popping, be responsible for the deaths of hundreds? And the ruin of thousands more?

It simply didn't seem possible. Which was why Jen was able to bid him farewell with an unstrained ease, and a promise to keep in touch. It had nothing to do with acting; it was disbelief, pure and simple.

And so, with Thibault at her side—masking only her lack of sleep behind a cheerful demeanor—she stood on the deck in the brilliant morning light, leaning her elbows against the rail and waving at the gathered crowds as the ship eased out of the quay, unfurling its sails to the winds.

When they were finally underway, running smartly before a stiff breeze, Jen turned and leaned her back against the rail, gazing over at her partner.

He smiled back, his hair blowing rakishly into his eyes. She hadn't realized he had golden lights in his mousy locks, or amber flecks in his eyes.

"You did well back there," he told her. "I would never have guessed you knew the truth about Saul."

"That's because I didn't—not in the light of day. He's too blasted good. I believe him, even when I know I shouldn't. What if Aubrey was wrong?"

"That's what we're going to Phykoros to determine. And, I admit, he is a master; it's no wonder Owen was fooled. But, either way, we're going to get to the bottom of this. With Vera's help, of course."

"Yes, Vera. I'm still annoyed that she felt I needed supervision . . ."

"As if our past history is anything to be proud of? No, even Vera admits we did a credible job on this one."

"Well, thank Varia for small favors." Jen scanned the deck and the milling passengers. "I wonder which ones they are," she added.

The possibilities were endless. Was it the elderly couple occupying the deck chairs, he leaning solicitously over to tuck in her blanket? Or the laughing young woman with the auburn hair and her dark-eyed suitor, pointing at the dolphins that frolicked off the stern? Or the two young men who strolled leisurely up the deck? No one said Absalom had to preserve their sexes along with their identities, and the taller of the two did have a walk that seemed a little fey . . .

If she were Vera, how would she be hiding?

Well, it wasn't the couple with the three rambunctious children, that was certain; Vera would never have survived that. Jen didn't know how the woman did, either. If the family weathered the overnight voyage without one of the children falling overboard, it would be a wonder! Nor could it be the two elderly ladies complaining vociferously at the bow; even Vera wasn't that good an actress. How did people like that function, Jen wondered, seeing nothing but the unpleasant side of life? How could they be unaffected by the jubilant swell of the ship; the cool, brisk breeze and balmy sunshine; the darting schools of rainbow fish and the sleek-bodied dolphins who raced beside the vessel then leaped before it in taunting triumph?

Well, there was one young man not unaffected by the ship's motion. Green-faced and miserable, he leaned out over the ship's railing, gifting his breakfast to the fishes. *That* would certainly not be Vera. Nor the young couple lounging a few feet down the railing. And not because of their youth or their obvious affection for each other—a quiet caring that was not in the least demonstrative, but still profoundly apparent—but more because they lacked a certain vibrancy. And Jen could not imagine either Vera or Absalom falling that much into the background—no matter what disguise they were in.

Certain things showed through, illusion or no.

She continued to scan the passengers. What of the young man lounging against the forecastle wall, staring at her so intensely? No, that sort of thing happened all the time; Vera wouldn't be that obvious.

And then an elegant matron walked by, her suhdabhar at her side, and Jen knew instantly. Feeling inordinately pleased with herself, she poked Thibault and pointed. There was the flare she associated with Vera—and an almost overly dramatic verve that let her know the Hawk was relishing the absurdity of her current disguise.

Absalom, too; that hunched and dark-eyed suhdabhar could not possibly be real. He was more a caricature of a caricature than a proper person, indicative of Absalom's bizarre and often whimsical sense of humor. Jen had seen him in his scruffy guise in the Nhuras bazaar; she knew the levels of absurdity to which he could sink.

Coming off the rail with a grin, she intercepted her aunt, grabbing her by the arm. "So, there you are," she crowed. "And you thought I wouldn't recognize you!"

The woman stared at her in consternation and yanked her arm away. "Am I supposed to know you?" she demanded.

Jen grinned, and punched her lightly on the shoulder. "Good one, Vera, but the joke's over." She turned toward the suhdabhar. "Absalom, take it off, won't you? We're out of sight of the harbor."

There was no recognition in either pair of eyes, and Jen felt a sudden flicker of doubt. She was aware of Thibault behind her, frantically waving her off.

"Take what off?" the woman persisted, scandalized. "What improper suggestions are you making to my suhdabhar, hussy?"

Jen's mouth dropped open. "You're not Vera?"

"I am most certainly not, and moreover I think I resent the implication! If you attempt to come near me again, I shall have the captain confine you to quarters." And she whirled irately and stalked away, muttering imprecations.

Thibault had his head down on the ship's railing, shaking with silent laughter.

Jen's face flamed crimson and she grabbed her partner by the arm, dragging him from the rail. "Let's get out of here," she said. "We have to unpack anyway."

Still laughing, he suffered himself to be led.

"She doesn't have a clue, does she?" Vera said to Absalom, as Jen and her partner passed within inches of them on their way back to their cabin. She had been watching the pair in amusement for the past several minutes, leaning against the railing and letting the ship's motion carry her.

Absalom chuckled. "Not even a tiny one. I could have sworn that woman was going to hit her."

Vera grinned and studied her companion. She liked him in this guise. He had put aside the dark-haired glamour that always left her subtly on edge, and instead had adopted a quiet demeanor without an ounce of flair or sparkle. His eyes were still impenetrably dark, but his hair was lost in that no-man's land between brown and blond. His features were unspectacular yet oddly harmonious, and she felt a strong attraction to him that had nothing to do with the years he had apparently lost in transition.

He now appeared somewhere in his mid-thirties, settled and stable, as if he had nothing to prove. Actually, he reminded her somewhat of Thibault. She wondered what she herself looked like, and how well he had matched them.

"We are both plain as dirt, my dear," he said, as if reading her mind. His dark eyes twinkled. "I told you they wouldn't recognize us. Except . . . I begin to think the boy suspects. He smiled at me quite pointedly as he went past."

"Perhaps he was just being polite."

"Perhaps."

There was a moment of silence, then they both looked at each other and laughed, shaking heir heads.

"No," Absalom said. "He knew."

"He's too smart for his own good, that one," Vera agreed.

Her companion grinned. "They're in love with each other, you know."

She shook her head. "No, he's in love with her. Tragically. Poor Jen could do a lot worse than marry Thibault—but, of course, she never will. The girl doesn't have the sense to see what she's got in that boy."

"Don't be so certain."

"Oh, honestly," she scoffed. "Next you'll be telling me that *we're* destined to be lovers!"

Absalom just smiled and said, "Stranger things have happened."

44

Dusk was falling when a knock came on their cabin door. Jen looked up from the wreckage of their meal and began hastily piling the debris back on the tray, assuming it was the porter returning for the dishes. In deference to her bruises, she and Thibault had elected not to join the others in the dining room, instead ordering a tray brought to their stateroom.

"A moment," she shouted at the door, then glared over at her partner who was lounging indolently on his bunk, sharpening his dagger. "You could help, you know."

"Why?" He flashed her a lazy grin. "You seem to be doing an exemplary job on your own."

She growled at him, momentarily regretting the lack of seasickness which had so incapacitated him on their first ocean voyage. At least then he had an excuse for loafing.

As if reading her thoughts, he blew her a teasing kiss, which caused her to scowl anew for the sudden way it made her stomach flutter. He was lounging atop the covers like a panther, looking smugly pleased with himself. Torn between an urge to hit him and a desire to leap atop him and kiss him until she relented, she threw the last pieces of cutlery onto the tray, balanced it in one hand, and wrenched open the cabin door with the other.

Vera grinned back at her. "Are you going to throw that at me, or can I come in?"

Thibault chuckled from behind her; Jen could hear the rustle of movement as he sat and tossed the dagger aside.

"Be my guest," she said, thrusting the tray at Vera and moving out of the doorway.

Her aunt laid the tray on the floor outside the cabin, then entered, shutting the portal behind her. She surveyed their quarters in amusement, her eyes flicking over the generous berths and gracious furnishings, then took a seat in a well-stuffed armchair across from Thibault's bunk. Jen claimed its twin.

"Duplicitous he may be," she said, "but you can hardly call our Saul stingy."

"I doubt the cost of this cabin will break him," Thibault replied.

"Still," she answered. "It's often the richest men who are the most miserly. You should see the little hole that Absalom and I have been granted in the name of second class passengers. It almost makes me wish we'd rethought our disguises."

"Yes, who *are* you?" Jen demanded. "I almost assaulted a stranger this afternoon, thinking it was you!"

"I know, I witnessed it. Quite a performance—on both sides!"

Thibault laughed, and Jen transferred her scowl to him again, wondering idly what had put her in so foul a mood.

Vera seemed to notice it too, saying, "Don't pout, Jenny. It's not attractive."

Which only made it worse.

"Who are you?" she persisted.

"Figure it out," her aunt challenged.

"I can't. It's impossible."

"Quite the contrary. Thibault knows."

Jen whirled on him. "You do?"

He had the grace to look embarrassed. "I suspected. It seems I was right."

"How?"

He smiled. "I think I recognized the model." He arched an eyebrow at Vera. "Did I?"

She smiled back. "I can't be certain—who can fathom the workings of that man's mind?—but I strongly suspect that you might have. I'd consider it a compliment."

"What?" Jen demanded, feeling absurdly isolated.

Her partner looked over at her. "Do you really want me to tell you?"

"No; I'll figure it out myself." She turned back to Vera. "What are you doing here, anyway? And where's your faithful shadow?"

"Still at dinner. It seems Absalom's developed an inexplicable passion for brandy and cigars."

"Meaning?"

"That he's up to something—Varia knows what. I suppose I'll find out soon enough. Meanwhile, I came to make sure you are up to this. We dock at Phykoros tomorrow." She turned her gaze to Jen. "I saw the way you looked at Saul as he was seeing you off. If you're having second thoughts . . ."

"I'm not!"

"Are you sure?"

Thibault picked up his dagger and gave it a few more passes with the whetstone before sheathing it at his side. Then he crossed to Jen's chair, perching on its arm. He laid a hand on her shoulder—a deliberate gesture, cementing the camps. *See where my loyalties lie?* it seemed to say. *No matter how prickly she's being.* Jen was infinitely aware of the meaning of that gesture—and the heat of his hand though her shirt. She felt profoundly grateful for his support, and suddenly knew what had been bothering her all along.

Somehow, against all hope, she had expected this to be the night that changed everything between herself and Thibault. After all, here they were, in this luxurious cabin, in the middle of the Belapharion, bound for one of Konasta's most romantic islands. There were no demands on their time—at least not for this evening—and with Vera and Absalom in disguise, it was almost as if they weren't present at all. And for a brief moment, with the falling dark, Jen had possessed the heady illusion of isolation. A sense that, for once, no one knew where they were or what they were doing. That no one was depending on them. That they were not the Cloak and the Dagger, but merely Jen and Thibault, thrown together on a lonely stretch of ocean. And that, without the world to intervene, they could merely be themselves as they wished to be.

And she could once more lie safe in Thibault's arms, surrounded by that indescribable passion that was at once so soft and gentle, and yet unbearably deep.

But that was all it was: illusion. Vera's presence had shattered the bubble, letting the world and its responsibilities intrude. And Thibault's hand on her shoulder, strong yet impersonal, promised nothing more than he had ever been able to give her: deep and abiding friendship.

Her partner; that was all.

And maybe that was as it should be. Maybe her sudden awareness of him was built out of no more than insecurity and an incessant questioning of her own abilities. After all, she had been through unimaginable upsets in the past few weeks—not the least of which was bedding the very last man on Varia she should have trusted. And if what she craved now was stability, who better to give her that than Thibault? He had always been her rock, from the earliest days of her misadventures. Reliable, safe, steady, and boring; that was her Thibault.

Wasn't it?

No, she wasn't in love with Thibault. She was merely seduced by what he represented: temporary safety and stability in a world where all sense and meaning seemed to have eroded. And imagine what might have happened had she acted on those impulses—beyond that one ill-advised night—forcing their relationship into paths it was never meant to travel. Imagine the endless years stretching out before her with only Thibault at her side, and only Thibault in her bed. She'd be bored stiff within months.

Wouldn't she?

Deliberately she laid her hand over Thibault's, which still rested on her shoulder, employing the same impersonal pressure, confirming their alliance, and resolutely masked the small twinge of regret she felt at the motion. "We're ready," she promised. "Honestly. I'll admit, Saul is compelling, but if he is guilty, I want to take him down. I owe Owen that much."

"I see." Vera's eyes were hard. "And you?" she demanded of Thibault.

"I'm with Jen, as always. You know that."

"Good. And I'm sorry to pressure you, Jenny, but I had to know. You've been through a lot lately, and I had to be sure I could still rely on you."

"You can," Jen said firmly. "Always. My life is the Guild, Vera; you know that. And while the Gideons of this world may shake me, they will never sink me."

"I'm glad." The Hawk and her niece shared a grin that did more than all the words in the world to strengthen her. And in that instant, Jen believed her own resolve whole-heartedly. She wouldn't drown; not because of one person. And for the first time since Gideon's beating, she began to believe she might actually heal, given time.

Absalom returned to their cabin two hours after Vera had left him, stinking of cigars and brandy. She looked up from her book as he entered, his somehow larger-than-life presence—even in disguise—instantly making the cramped, narrow quarters seem smaller. He shook himself, shedding his nondescript looks much as a dog sheds water, until he was back in his familiar, glamourous, slightly rough-hewn guise.

"Hot in here, isn't it?" he said, crossing to the far side of the cabin in two long strides and flinging open the port-hole glass. A cool wind immediately skirled though the cabin, probing cold fingers into the corners.

Vera sat up in her bunk, wrapping a blanket around her shoulders, and almost banged her head against the low overhang of Absalom's bunk. "By Varia," she swore, "what did we do to deserve this? You should see Jenny and Thi-bault's cabin!"

"Comparison is odious," Absalom observed, taking a seat beside her with considerably more aplomb. He pulled a bottle of brandy and two glasses from the air with a flourish.

She raised an eyebrow. "And how long have you been carrying *that* around?"

"Not long. I swiped it from the bartender when he wasn't looking."

"Absalom . . ."

"Not to worry. I spirited a little something into his pocket in recompense. It's a twenty-five-year-old Lusanian from the Vilandry vineyards; very fine. Just what I need to get the taste of that awful, cheap brandy out of my mouth. Can I tempt you?" And he waved the bottle invitingly.

She gazed at him suspiciously, aware of a heightened glitter in his eyes. "Are you drunk?"

"Not anymore," he answered, looking abruptly lucid.

"Ah; one of the little advantages of magerie. Brandy, my dear?"

She grinned and relented, drawing the blanket more closely around her. "Decant away. But"—she wrinkled her nose—"can your magerie do anything about that stench as well? You reek of cigars."

"Alas, I cannot change the smell itself. But I can alter your perception of it a little. There; is that an improvement?" And the mage exuded a sudden, ridiculous scent of roses.

Vera laughed and accepted the glass of liquor he handed her. "Don't go overboard. Neutral will do."

The odor of roses abruptly vanished, but she didn't think he had quite followed her instructions. A scent still existed: heady and indefinable, lurking beneath the chill sea air. She knew better than to call attention to it, however. He would merely smile his catlike smile and look innocent. He was too blasted good at that.

"Satisfactory?" he asked.

"Infinitely. So"—she masked a shiver—"were you really smoking cigars for two hours?"

"Regrettably. It's a filthy habit, but such are my sacrifices in the face of necessity." He peered at her expectantly as she lifted the snifter of brandy and took a sip. "Well?"

"Absalom, this is excellent!" And indeed it was, like smoky velvet. Rich, and smooth as sin going down. It almost offset the chill. "But then, I rarely have questioned your taste—which is impeccable for a street rat who apparently made his fortunes in the Nhuras bazaar." He just chuckled, looking annoyingly innocent again. "So what compelled you to spend two hours in the ship's bar drinking bad brandy and smoking cheap cigars?"

"What makes you think they were cheap cigars?"

"I am not entirely without refinements myself," she countered, and he touched her glass with his.

"Touché. Well, then, to answer your question: information."

"What sort of information?"

"Guild sort of information."

"Specifically?"

He grinned. "You're relentless, aren't you?"

"Always. It's why you love me."

He chuckled appreciatively.

"Spill it, Absalom."

He floated his glass of brandy ostentatiously in the air and cracked his knuckles, leaning back in the bunk and appropriating Vera's pillow. Then, crossing one leg casually over the other, he brought the brandy bobbing back. She pulled the blanket tighter and turned to sit cross-legged, facing him. He looked smug. "What would you say to a disgruntled former employee of the Kettle?"

"You found one?"

"Indubitably."

"And?"

"He had some rather interesting things to say. Mysterious dawn visitors, odd comings and goings. Rumors of ghosts in the hills."

Vera arched an eyebrow. "Ghosts?"

"Bobbing lights, echoes of voices . . . you interpret it."

"By Varia. The factory!"

"That was my thought. I say we take to the hills while your pair investigate the Kettle. Jen's already robbed one club to date."

"With disastrous consequences."

"Nonetheless . . . Are you cold?" Absalom inquired at last, seeing her shiver.

"Yes, you dolt!"

"Then why didn't you say anything?"

"Trust me; I was about to. But you seemed so happy . . ."

"Well, fresh air is always welcome, especially on shipboard. These tiny cabins can be so confining . . ." He raised an arm, inviting her closer.

"Why don't you just shut the window?" she said, around chattering teeth.

"Easier this way," he responded. "Not to mention nicer."

She regarded him in silence for a moment. "Are you trying to seduce me?"

"Varia forfend," he replied mildly, and looked innocent again.

Another long, pointed look, and then she slid beside him, tucking herself, blanket and all, beneath his arm. She had to admit it was comforting. He radiated his usual mageheat, like a banked furnace. His breath smelled of fine Lusanian brandy.

Idly, he touched the ends of her hair, now hanging a little past her shoulders.

"I'm thinking of cutting it again," she said.

"Why? I like it this length."

"You do?"

"Mmm. It accents your eyes. You have remarkable eyes."

"No, *you* have remarkable eyes." She was getting unaccountably sleepy, well-plied with brandy and caught in that peaceful midland between heat and cold. Or maybe Absalom himself was exuding some sort of soporific. She wouldn't put it past him, the sneaky bastard. She chuckled.

"What?"

"You *are* trying to seduce me," she accused.

She sensed more than saw him smile. "Is it working?"

"Not even close." And yet, after a few more minutes of desultory conversation, with her eyelids sinking lower and lulled by the low rumble of his voice within his chest, she was aware of him drawing her down to lie beside him, pulling the covers up over their bodies. She was tempted to object—solely on principle—but she was too comfortable to bother. And besides, if he had intended anything more, he had defeated his own purpose, for she was asleep within minutes, a faint smile on her lips.

45

Vera awoke the next morning to a flood of sunlight pouring in through the porthole. The glass was still open, carrying in a fresh breeze. She could hear the creaking of the masts and the cries of the sailors as they went about their morning business. But, despite it, she was still toasty warm. Absalom, or . . .

No, he must have done something to the blankets, for she was alone in the bed—naked, she noticed; he must have done something with her clothes as well—and the mage was snoring gently in the berth above her.

She grinned and reached up with one fist, pounding on the bunk. "Absalom!"

He muttered something incoherent and rolled over.

"Absalom," she repeated, with another series of bangs. "What time is it?"

"An hour past dawn," he responded, with his usual, impeccable sense of timing—and in a voice that sounded only marginally more awake. "Go back to sleep, Vera."

"Nonsense. It's a beautiful morning, so rise and shine! Time's a-wasting."

"Time for what?" he muttered.

"Things," she responded, feeling frighteningly alert and chipper for such an early hour; it must be the prospect of finally nearing the end of a sixteen-year journey. "You know."

"No, I don't."

Another long silence, then she pounded on the bottom of his bunk again.

"What?" This time he sounded more irate than sleepy. "You are a very annoying woman. Go away and leave me alone."

"Gladly, if you will see fit to return my clothing. Where is it?"

A weight materialized on her stomach: her clothes, wadded in a haphazard ball.

"There. Are you happy?" the mage grumbled.

"Infinitely. Thank you, Absalom."

Another grunt was his sole response. Chuckling, she bounced from the bunk, still naked and shivering in the cool breeze. But, as usual in Konasta, the air was warming with the rising sun and the chill was almost tolerable, so she rested her elbows on the edge of Absalom's bunk and grinned down at him.

The mage's dark hair was tousled with sleep, and he seemed to have lost about five years off his age. She wondered curiously if he resorted to his true appearance when he slept, or if this was simply some vague reflection of his dreams. She had never shared a chamber with him before.

As if aware of her regard, he rolled over and opened his eyes, still infinitely dark and deep—though now shadowed with sleep. He rubbed at them with one fist, and then suddenly seemed to become aware of her breasts, peeking pertly over the edge of his bunk. His gaze sharpened reflexively, and he gazed down the length of her lean, bare body before burying his head under the covers.

"For Varia's sake," came his muffled voice, from below the blankets. "Please don't assault my incipient virtue any further. I gave you back your clothes for a reason."

"Prudish, darling?"

"Not hardly. Now get dressed and leave me in peace."

She laughed and complied, gaining the deck and trusting that the mage had restored her appearance along with her clothing.

Few of the passengers were up at this early hour, so she found herself chatting with several of the younger sailors as she leaned on the deck rail and gazed out across the cerulean water—implying that she was, indeed, still in disguise. Even she had to admit that, in her own skin, she could be a rather intimidating package.

It was a lovely morning, the breeze still fresh and cool but no longer chill, the sunlight dancing off the water. A group of laughing sailors were throwing fish to a pod of dolphins that raced alongside the ship, their silver-grey bodies gleaming as they leaped and cavorted. Shadow smudges on the horizon indicated the islands; the largest was Phykoros, she was informed as she joined the group. Yes, the sailors made this run often; from Phykoros, they'd be on to Krissos, and ultimately to Sandoval, the farthest-flung of the Konastan islands. And then the whole voyage in reverse, carrying passengers and supplies.

She had her hand in the fish bucket and was tossing mackerel to the dolphins when Absalom joined her on deck, back in his guise as Nondescript Young Man. Barely a half an hour had passed since her own emergence—and despite his previous grouchiness, the mage looked composed and rested, as if he had been awake for hours instead of minutes. He greeted her with an easy smile and a chaste kiss, making no reference to their earlier encounter. She grinned back at him, and saw a rueful amusement twinkling deep in his eyes.

"Fish?" she said, handing him a mackerel.

The sailors hooted and cheered as he accepted it with a grimace, then flung it wide in a spiraling arc that brought a dolphin leaping from the depths to intercept it. It was a move as beautiful as if it had been choreographed, and Vera wondered again just how much control Absalom really had over his environment. And how the bloody blazes he had learned so much as a bastard mage on the streets of Nhuras. Sometimes she despaired of ever deciphering his secrets.

Eventually, the sailors drifted off to other tasks; Vera remained with Absalom at the rail.

"When do we dock?" he said.

"Shortly before noon." She pointed. "That's Phykoros there."

"Indeed." He gauged the distance with his eyes. "With this wind, I suspect we'll be in about an hour before that. But then"— he grinned—"I could be wrong."

"Doubtful. I don't know how you . . ."

"Good morning, Vera; Absalom," Thibault said, coming up behind them. "Do we have a plan?"

"A shell of one, at any rate," Vera responded. "Where's Jen?"

"Still asleep. She hasn't been getting that much rest of late, the poor girl. If I ever find that bastard, Gideon, I'm going to kill him . . ."

"I don't doubt it; it sounds as if he deserves it. Well, according to Absalom, we'll be docked in a few hours. And as soon as we gather all the evidence we need, we can go back and settle the score."

"It won't be soon enough for me," Thibault vowed. "Should I wake Jen?"

"No, let her sleep," Absalom said. "Meanwhile, why don't you take breakfast with us, and I'll tell you everything I discovered in the bar last night."

"And are you sure our sudden friendship won't be questioned?" Thibault replied, looking suspiciously about the deck. But as near as Vera could figure, they were alone— save for a young man taking his morning constitutional. He smiled and nodded affably as he passed.

The mage just grinned. "Well, if it is, you can always claim we're brothers. Especially since I suspect my subtle attempt at tribute has escaped neither of your attentions. Now, are you coming?" And leaving Thibault and Vera to stare after him in consternation, the mage sauntered toward the dining hall.

As Absalom had predicted, the *Phykoros Queen* dropped her sails and bumped gently against the dock almost an hour before noon, and Thibault suddenly understood what made these islands such a popular haven. The white houses sparkled like jewels in the sun, adorned with door and shutters of the same brilliant blue as the sea and sky. Sunlight washed the rocks and paving stones a silver-gilt, and the beaches unfurled like bolts of rippled silk.

"Beautiful, isn't it?" said Jen at his side.

He turned to her with a smile that was only partly forced. "That it is. And a hotbed of corruption to boot, I suspect."

"Oh, Thibault." She grinned. "Such negativity. What would Vera and Absalom say?"

"No doubt they'd agree," Vera replied, strolling past them in her average guise, arm in arm with Absalom. Thibault had the pleasure of seeing Jen's jaw drop open in surprise.

"Those two?" she whispered, and when he nodded, added, "How did you guess?"

"Too average in all respects. How better to not be noticed? Plus, as I said, I recognized the model."

"What model?"

"Absalom. Doesn't he remind you of someone?"

Quite clearly he didn't, which pleased Thibault no end. At least Jen didn't see him as boring—even if she did see him as no more than a friend; that much had been made amply clear last night. He had wondered what new equilibrium their relationship might reach, and now it seemed he had his answer.

He had almost literally felt the change in her, as he sat with his hand on her shoulder the night before. He had felt her hardening, and the return of her resolve. And not the brittle hardening of the past few days either, but a true return of strength, like a putting down of roots. And he was glad for her; he really was. Only . . .

He had gone to her in that moment seeking unity, and had found only division. For as viscerally as the resolution had flowed into her, so too had she pulled away from his support, erecting a wall of friendship and duty between them. That safe and familiar wall which he would probably never breach again.

He had reflected on that late into the night, after Jen had extinguished the magelights in their cabin and settled into her bunk with a whisper of sheets. In that silence, Thibault had stared into a darkness broken only by the rippled dance of moonlight on waves, reflected from the portholes onto the cabin's ceiling. And in the shifting, impermanent light—accentuated by the gentle rocking of the ship—he had an odd sense of his world breaking and reforming.

He wasn't entirely sure he liked it, but at least he was familiar with the pattern.

"Who was the model?" she persisted.

"Me. Can't you tell? Unassuming peasant stock and all?"

She surveyed Absalom critically for a moment, her brow furrowed. "No, I don't see it. He's not half so imposing."

Thibault almost laughed. He would have preferred "handsome," but "imposing" would do.

He cast his eyes about the deck, surveying the disembarking passengers. Another young man was staring at his partner, and Thibault let loose a thread of a sigh. No wonder she would never notice him when she was constantly at the center of attention this way. He was quite a good-looking young man, too—not that Jen even seemed aware of his regard. This sort of thing must happen to her far too often.

And then the gangplank dropped and they descended onto a dock mobbed with eager throngs of hoteliers and innkeeps, each hawking the virtues of their residence in carrying voices. Thibault collected their luggage, and in the confusion noted that Vera and Absalom had reverted to their normal guises—if, indeed, the mage's appearance could ever be called normal.

"So, where to?" Vera asked, strolling up to them as Thibault shouldered the last of the trunks.

"We defer to you, of course," Absalom said. "Don't we?"

Jen shrugged. "Your guess is as good as mine, but pick it quickly, before Thibault collapses under the weight of my luggage."

"Well, if you would only learn not to overpack," Vera retorted, "you wouldn't have that problem . . . Oof!" She grunted slightly as an older man brushed rudely past her, obviously on his way somewhere. "Blast him, that hurt." She rubbed absently at her neck and returned that attention to Jen. "As I was saying . . ."

"And as I've told you before," Jen retorted, "I need everything I brought. Besides, I've used all of it once, already. Or I intend to, before the week is out. So . . ."

Exchanging an amused glance with Thibault, Absalom left them to it, and quietly contracted for two rooms, each with two beds; Thibault wasn't sure whether to be annoyed or grateful at that specification. Then, interrupting the discussion—which was showing every sign of developing into a fair-sized argument—Absalom ushered Vera and Jen toward their host, who set off at a brisk pace for his establishment.

Thibault readjusted his grip on the trunks—and almost staggered when they suddenly lightened by half, floating partway off his shoulders. He shot a sudden glance at Absalom, who just grinned and winked—though his expression did seem a little strained. He also, Thibault noticed, as they wound up the narrow, twisting streets, was puffing and sweating a little more than the terrain seemed to warrant.

He eased up beside the mage. "Give them back. I can manage."

"Nonsense," Absalom wheezed. He took a deep breath, then said in a more even tone, "It doesn't seem fair to let you take all the weight."

"At least let me take most of it. At the risk of being blunt, I'm younger and stronger than you are."

The mage just chuckled. "That's what you think." But Thibault did notice the weight of the trunks increase a fraction, and some of the hectic flush left Absalom's face. "Thanks. You must have ox blood in you, lad, and no mistake!"

"Yes, that's me," Thibault answered, not without a hint of bitterness. "Sturdy peasant stock to the end."

"Oh, I don't know," Absalom temporized. "You might be surprised."

"By what?"

"Fate."

Thibault arched an eyebrow. "Are you a fortune-teller as well?"

The mage chuckled but said no more, for they had arrived at the inn. It was as blindingly white as all the other houses, with broad balconies that overlooked the sea. They were, Thibault noted, quite high up the island slope, on a busy street only slightly lower than a vast structure domed in gold and winking with magelights.

"Let me guess," Vera said. "The Kettle?"

"Yes," their innkeep said proudly. "That's our Kettle, the most famous illusion club on the islands—although the Sailor's Rest, two doors down, is not bad, either. I have deals with both clubs. If you mention my name, they'll let you in for two marks off the cover price—and you'll get a free drink to boot."

"Sounds like quite a deal," Vera said neutrally. "We'll have to visit."

Vera and Absalom received a large room to the front,

with one of the wide balconies overlooking the harbor and the water. Jen and Thibault received a smaller one to the back, fronting an alley. As they split off to their separate chambers, Absalom returned the full weight of the trunks to Thibault's shoulders, and he almost staggered again. He hadn't been aware of how much weight the mage had still been carrying. Perhaps he was both younger and stronger than he looked.

"What's the matter?" Jen asked.

"Nothing," he wheezed, pushing open the door and dropping the trunks inside with an audible thump. "But perhaps you should listen to Vera's advice about packing, in future. Or hire another suhdabhar."

"Nonsense," she scoffed, then frowned, peering about her. "Well, it's better than the room at Saul's," she opined, "but not by much."

Thibault couldn't have cared less. At least it was clean and comfortable, if not exactly bright, and had its own attached bath. And he wouldn't have to sleep on the floor. He threw open the outer doors and stepped onto the tiny balcony, stretching out his back and rotating the kinks from his shoulders. Above the rooftops, he could see a corner of the Kettle's ornate dome.

After a moment, Jen joined him at the rail. "Does your shoulder still hurt?"

"A bit. And your ribs?"

"I've been better." She followed his gaze to the Kettle. "I know I have to go raiding later, but . . . After dinner, and before my duties begin, can I treat you to a night on the town? Just for fun? We'll have a drink or two, do some dancing, gawk at the illusions?"

He looked down at her, her face oddly tentative in the shadowed half-light of the alley, brushed with the fading purple remnants of bruises and that one, wide swathe of scab. He felt a sudden surge of tenderness for her. The poor girl hadn't had much fun lately. Besides, he wanted to go. Wanted to have a night with her, free from expectations.

He glanced at the corner of the Kettle's dome, then back at Jen. "Why not? I'd hate to leave Konasta without seeing the inside of an illusion club. Let's hope the display's a good one."

She brightened, flashing a grin. "It should be, if Saul has anything to say about it. Bastard he may be, but he's a bloody good showman for all that."

"Indeed. Well, then, we'll drink and gawk, and I'll endeavor not to tromp all over your feet when we dance."

"You'd better not." She smiled at him, tucking her hand into the crook of his arm and resting her cheek against his shoulder. "I've already got more than my fair share of bruises as it is."

His shout of laughter brought Vera at a run, but she left again in disgust when neither of them could explain why they were collapsed against the balcony railing, laughing until the tears ran down their faces in giddy release.

46

Dusk was falling over Ephanon harbor when the little crystal shard Saul had implanted in his wrist flared with a sudden heat. He looked up from his papers and pulled one of his desk drawers open, withdrawing a crystal ball.

The shard in his wrist pulsed insistently.

"Patience; patience," he muttered under his breath, cuing the large crystal on. Gideon stared back at him, looking almost smug.

Saul felt a pinch of doom. "What is it?"

"I was right," Gideon said. "They are up to something."

"Are you certain?"

"As certain as I can be with no evidence. I followed them throughout the ship. They were clearly traveling with another couple in disguise. A rather nondescript couple at first, but when they docked, they changed—and the woman looked remarkably like an older version of Jen."

"The Hawk?"

"My thoughts exactly. And her companion's clearly a mage. And why would the Cloak and the Dagger be arriving on Phykoros with the Hawk and a mage unless they suspect something?"

Saul cursed bitterly, then added, "Well, I'll leave it in your capable hands, as usual. Do whatever it takes to stop them. And I do mean whatever."

The Golden Boy smiled. "That goes without saying. Jen and Thibault are planning an excursion to the Kettle tonight; I overheard them when I was lurking beneath their window under an invisibility spell. And I've already tagged the Hawk. But there's something else you should be worried about."

"Which is?"

"Who tipped them off. There is no way anything they found in your Cauldron office would have done it, and we both know someone was snooping around the warehouse. That means there's a leak in your security. If I were you, I would keep close tabs on Aubrey."

"Aubrey?" Saul exclaimed, but Gideon had already blanked the crystal. With another curse, Saul threw the orb back into the drawer and slammed it shut. Then he rose and stormed across the room, already planning what he would say to Aubrey Dunning when he reached the Cauldron.

His hand was on the knob when a knock came on his office door.

He yanked it open, revealing the startled face of one of the club's mages.

"What is it, Eledon?" he barked.

"Excuse me, sir," the man faltered, "but have you seen Aubrey? He never showed up for work this morning."

"You're going *where*?" Vera exclaimed after dinner, pushing her chair away from the table in consternation.

"The Kettle," Jen said defiantly. "Just for fun. And a little pre-mission reconnaissance."

"Then you'd better get Absalom to do you. How do you want to look?"

"Why do we have to look like anything? Why can't we just go as Jen and Thibault?"

Thibault felt obscurely pleased that she wanted him in his native guise, but wisely remained silent in the face of Vera's scowl.

"Because the Kettle is Saul's club! And while Saul may not be on Phykoros, someone in his organization may recognize you and report!"

"And what if they do?" Jen flared. "We're on Phykoros with Saul's express permission—and knowledge. It would be more suspicious for us *not* to visit the Kettle. It's only the cloak and dagger stuff, so to speak, that needs to happen in disguise."

"She's right, you know," Thibault supplied. "You might almost say it's our duty to go. To present a public appearance that will detract from the private endeavors."

Vera snorted, then threw up her hands in resignation. "On your heads be it. But you will accept Absalom's help for later?"

"I'm not invisible, you know," the mage commented, with a certain amusement.

"Of course; we're not stupid," Jen said almost simultaneously, then smiled apologetically at Absalom. "Um, we'll need a new amulet against illusion, though."

"Why?" he asked, with a puckish smile. "What happened to the first one?"

"*You* took it?" Vera exclaimed.

Jen nodded sheepishly. "I swiped it from your box right before we left Bergaetta. I figured I needed it more than you, since you had its creator."

Vera shook her head in disgust, but couldn't quite mask a smile. "I keep forgetting my boxes are no longer safe from your meddling. So what did happen to the first one?"

Jen colored. "Well, what with one thing and another, I just did not feel like sifting through the chamber pot the morning it came out. Rather painfully, I might add."

"Came out?" Vera exclaimed.

"She didn't want Gideon to find it," Thibault supplied, "so she swallowed it."

Jen scowled at him.

"Jen, didn't you even consider whether or not that might have any adverse effects?" Vera began, but Absalom interrupted, asking curiously, "And it worked?"

"It did, indeed. Like the proverbial charm."

The mage grinned, rubbing his hands together. "Now that gives me an idea. If you will excuse me . . ." And without another word, he rose from the table and hurried in the direction of the inn's tiny back garden, mumbling excitedly to himself.

Vera raised an eyebrow. "I'd better go after him before he incinerates every plant in the vicinity. Or something worse." And she, too, quit the table.

Thibault grinned over at his partner. They were alone now in the tiny dining room, with its stuccoed walls and low, rough-hewn ceiling beams. The balcony doors were thrown open, revealing a dusky sky with the lights just winking on in the harbor. A single candle in a cut-brass holder danced and flickered on their table, its flame stirred by the breeze. Thibault could almost feel the peace settling over him.

It seemed unreal that a little past midnight they would be breaking into yet another illusion club.

"Well," he said. "That went well, don't you think?"

Jen gave a little snort of laughter, and poured them each another glass of the very fine brandy which Absalom had somehow materialized in the wake of dinner. "Sometimes I don't know how Vera puts up with that mage," she said, and raised her glass to Thibault in a toast. "To success."

"To success," he echoed, and took another sip of the rich, smoky liquor. He could get used to this, he reflected, the spoils of wealth and good living.

He and Jen sipped their brandy in companionable silence, then she leaned over and blew out the candle. The smoke drifted up in lazy spirals. "Now, I think we should get ready to visit the Kettle," she said. "It's too lovely an evening to waste."

No sooner had they crested the stairs, however, than Absalom appeared from around the corner, herding them into their chamber.

"Brilliant idea!" he declared, closing the door behind them and displaying what looked like four small, polished pebbles from the inn's back garden: two white, and two dark. "Don't worry, I cleaned them first. The dark ones are for invisibility, the white for penetrating illusion. And they shouldn't hurt too much coming out."

Thibault raised an eyebrow. "That was fast."

"Well, it's not the spell that's the problem, it's the carrier," Absalom said, handing them one of each. "Once I found the pebbles . . . It was nothing to cue them. They're each coded on and off by the same phrases: 'Great purple lumpfish'—what you don't want to see—for illusions; 'nighted minions of doom'—what you want to be—for invisibility. That way, they shouldn't get triggered involuntarily."

"Not unless you are standing in a room with Vera in a temper," Jen said dryly, and Absalom laughed.

"Yes, I thought you would recognize the author of the

codes. Truly, though, it's merely a precaution. I'm not sure if other people's voices *can* trigger them once they're inside; it's something we'll have to experiment with. Now, swallow up."

Jen opened her hand and gave a faint squeak, for while she clearly felt the two pebbles in her palm, only the white one was actually present. "Absalom," she exclaimed, "what did you do with it?"

Thibault chuckled. "Involuntarily triggered its invisibility spell, I assume, by telling us the code. Shall I?"

Absalom nodded, his eyes twinkling.

"Nighted minions of doom," Thibault intoned, and the black pebble winked back into view.

"Fine, then," Jen said, grabbing a glass of water from the bedside table. She popped the pebbles into her mouth and promptly dispatched them with two large swallows, then passed the glass to Thibault.

"Is the anti-illusion device still activated?" Thibault inquired, as he, too, swallowed the amulets.

"Most likely," Absalom said, and Jen gazed curiously at the mage.

He grinned. "Nice try, but my amulets won't work against my own illusions. In fact, comfortingly enough, I don't think an amulet exists that can work against a mage's illusion on himself." She masked a surge of disappointment. "Look at something else."

"Such as?"

"Great purple lumpfish," Thibault said.

Nothing changed.

"Well?" she asked the mage.

"Try going invisible," he said to Thibault.

"Nighted minions of doom," Thibault said, gamely.

"He's still there," Jen said.

The door to their chamber opened. "How's the experiment going?" Vera inquired. "And where's Thibault?" She looked about curiously.

Absalom grinned. "Well, at least that answers one question. Once inside, the amulets can only be triggered by the carrier's voice—which means that in future, I can cue them to much simpler phrases . . . no offense, my dear," he added to Vera.

"None taken. Where *is* Thibault?"

"Here," he said, tapping Vera on the arm. She jumped as if goosed. "Nighted minions of doom," he added, apparently winking back into view—although, from Jen's perspective, nothing had changed.

"It also," Absalom continued happily, "solves the whole problem of linked invisibility spells: no more dead areas between linked partners. Hmm; I should have thought of this whole spell synergy thing a lot earlier. I wonder . . ." His voice trailed off.

"Now you've done it," Vera said. "I'm not going to get a coherent sentence out of him for hours."

"I'm confused," Jen complained. "Am I still foiling illusions?"

"I think so," Thibault said. "You certainly saw me. Try recuing."

"Nighted minions of doom," she said.

"Wrong one." He chuckled. "You've disappeared now. Which I guess clarifies my condition."

She was tempted to take advantage of her invisibility and hit him, but instead she said, "Great purple lumpfish. I mean . . . nighted minions of doom. No, great purple lumpfish . . . Oh, blast, I'm completely confused. Can you see me?"

"Yes," Thibault and Vera replied simultaneously.

Absalom was still muttering to himself, his eyes half-lidded.

"Do you want me to go invisible?" Thibault offered.

"No, too confusing. I think I'll just go look at something outside."

"Such as?"

"The Kettle's dome. That should have some sort of illusion cast over it, now that night has fallen." And so saying, she threw open the balcony doors and glanced up over the rooftops.

The corner of the Kettle's dome was wreathed with magelights, but nothing more. She must be blocking illusions, then. Curious to see what else might have changed, she glanced down at the alley . . . and froze.

Lounging against the alley wall and staring up at her— large as life, and twice as handsome—was Gideon.

Her mind raced in a panic. She forced her eyes away—slowly, casually—as if she hadn't seen him. And indeed, though it felt like an eternity had passed while she sat frozen and staring, it must have been only seconds, for he didn't seem to have noticed her regard.

He knows, she thought. *He followed us from Ephanon because he knows what we suspect. Which means it must be true . . .*

Tentatively, in the merest thread of a whisper, she said, "Great purple lumpfish?" and forced her eyes back down the alley. No Gideon, and the Kettle's dome was happily spewing forth red-tinted steam, much like its sister club, the Cauldron.

Slowly, carefully—the precision of her movements the only thing that kept her from bolting—she backed from the balcony and into the safety of her chamber, closing the doors behind her.

"Jenny?" Thibault seized her by both shoulders. His voice was sharp with concern. And no wonder; she must be as white as a ghost, for surely her blood had all congealed in her veins. She was shaking, badly. "What is it? What's the matter?"

She forced her eyes to his face, her hands clamping hard about his wrists; he winced at her grip. She made herself say the words, around a lump in her throat the size of Arrhyndon. "Gideon. In the alley. He must have followed us here under illusion. I don't think he knew that I saw him, but . . ."

She abruptly ran out of words. Thibault gathered her close and she huddled into his embrace, hating herself anew. *Just when I think I can handle it, one sight of that bastard . . .*

"Gideon?" Vera exclaimed.

The mage looked up from his muttering.

"This changes everything." Thibault's commanding voice echoed from somewhere deep within his chest. "We can't go to the Kettle tonight."

"No." Jen forced the words out, pushing herself erect. She willed her teeth not to chatter. "We can't let him know we suspect. He has to have heard our intentions, earlier. We'll go to the Kettle as promised, and then . . ." A plan.

She needed a plan. She'd be cursed if she let Gideon best her again. "And then"—inspiration struck—"we'll do a switch. Earlier than intended. Thibault, you'll pick up some woman. A prostitute; something. Absalom, you'll decoy her to look like me. Your illusions are proof against most standard amulets, are they not?"

"Indubitably."

"Good. Then, Thibault, you'll continue to entertain this woman as if she were me—and make sure Gideon is watching. Meanwhile, I'll sneak back here, get into disguise, and search the Kettle while he's otherwise occupied. That'll still give Absalom and Vera plenty of time to search the hills."

"No!" Thibault protested. "I'm not going to let you search another club alone; it's too dangerous. Let Absalom create a fake Thibault for you to entertain while I conduct the search. You're better at being charming, anyway."

The offer was so tempting that Jen knew she had to refuse it. "No. I have to do this. If I don't, I . . ." Her voice trailed off, but she knew that Thibault understood. If she backed down now, she'd never be able to trust herself again.

And he did understand—she could see it in his eyes—though he didn't look happy about it. "Promise me you'll be careful?"

She nodded. "And promise me you'll keep Gideon away?"

"Of course."

"Oh, and Thibault," she added.

"Yes?"

"Don't sell yourself short. You can be perfectly charming when you set your mind to it."

47

Full dark had fallen when the lights in Jen's chamber were extinguished and Gideon left the alley, circling around to intercept them at the front door. He was still under an invisibility guise, and confident that whatever talismans Jen had couldn't penetrate *his* illusions. She hadn't seen him in the alley, and wouldn't see him now—stupid girl—as she took her oversized oaf of a partner out on what she no doubt fervently hoped was a romantic evening. When not a fortnight ago she had been bedding Gideon.

He felt a certain satisfaction at the thought as he trailed them through the winding Phykoros streets. Arm in arm with her partner, Jen was uncharacteristically silent—but then she had probably said everything she needed to that boy ten thousand times before. And, really, how scintillating could his conversation be?

She was also, Gideon noticed, still moving stiffly—a continued result of his beating. He grinned. The last time he had encountered her, she had frozen like a rabbit. Bold assassin, member of the vaunted Guild, and he had conquered her. Just by looking.

There was no way she would stand up to him tonight.

It was one of those perfect Phykoros evenings, the kind that made Gideon feel glad to be alive. A warm sea wind was blowing, sweeping over the stacked town like a caress, scented with flowers from the many pots still blooming on the window ledges. A slender crescent moon soared, its silvery light dancing off the harbor waters, vying with the magelights for ascendancy. And those latter, glowing from lightposts and the windows and awnings of the still-open shops, seemed to issue a challenge to the glowing dome of the Kettle, rising high overhead. And, above it all, the approving twinkle of the stars, as bright and punctate as the laughing voices of both natives and visitors as they prepared to unload their hard-earned money into the Kettle's deep coffers.

While the Cauldron was more imposing, there were many things Gideon preferred about the Kettle. There was a greater decadence to the islands, more of a sense of vacation, festival, the erosion of boundaries. Meaning the Kettle carried more of an edge than the Cauldron—though maybe that was just a factor of the Acaeus, the depraved genius who ran it. Gideon had always liked the man—he had imagination and talent. Eschewing the weekly rotating displays of his sister club, Acaeus kept the Kettle a-simmer with a common theme that nonetheless varied from night to night, like some vast, unending Smoke Dream, skirting the narrow borders of psychosis. In fact, there were times Gideon suspected it was no more than that: a nightly vision vomited forth from the minds of Dreamsmoke-soaked mages, lying in a stupor in some back room. But it worked. It made his patrons more reckless, Acaeus claimed, and loosened their purse-strings. That it also made many eager to recapture those same sensations outside the Kettle was, of course, only a fringe benefit.

Yes, Gideon reflected, Acaeus was a visionary—and the only one in Saul's employ he trusted as greatly as himself.

Tonight's display was no exception: a swirling, surrealistic haze dominated by purples and yellows. The music was louder, rawer, than at the Cauldron; and the spirits dispensed at the bar harsher and more potent than Ephanon's smooth liqueurs. The in-house stable of hookers and catamites were blatantly obvious, and the lures of fetishistic sex more apparent. Patrons were clad—or unclad, as the case might be—with greater abandon, from the two foppish young men wearing nothing but fishnets and spangles to the male/female/female trio decked in chains and hard leather.

In many ways, it was the ultimate illusion club, Gideon reflected. Nothing was what it seemed, for everything was in a constant state of flux. Even such staple dependables as chairs and tables occasionally forsook their boundaries, warping into weirdly fantastical forms that seemed to swallow their denizens whole. Your dance partner could be handsome one minute, and an eight-tentacled creature from the depths of nightmare the next. Illusions layered on top of illusions, until reality slipped and became fluid, then trickled from your fingers. Gideon wondered how Jen and Thibault were enjoying this particular manifestation of the mages' power.

Briefly, he scanned the crowded club until he located them perched on two barstools—hers traditional, his just morphing into a distorted mushroom, glabrous and pale. She looked both sallow and exotically alien in the swirling purple and yellow light, an illumination which matched her bruises to perfection. And what she no doubt expected was a risqué outfit looked stultifyingly conservative and out of place.

Seeing as they were busy sampling glasses of the local Huitoxa spirits which, when diluted with water, swirled into a cloudy, unappetizing concoction, Gideon left them to it, figuring they weren't going anywhere for a while. Instead, he sought out the back reaches of the club, where he knew he could find Acaeus surveying his domain from an office that was mage-spelled for sound and vision. And, indeed, Acaeus rose as he entered, his face breaking into a delighted smile.

"Gideon!" he exclaimed, crossing the room to embrace him. "What brings you to the Kettle?"

"Apart from seeing your charming self, you mean?" They regarded each other, eye to eye, from a handspan apart, and Gideon felt a familiar shiver go through him. He hadn't had a man in a while, and especially not one such as Acaeus, whose inclinations so closely mirrored his own. His heart pumped a little faster, and he could tell from the glitter in Acaeus's dark eyes that the Kettle's manager was entertaining similarly enticing thoughts.

For an instant, he forgot about Jen and Thibault as he breathed the breath of his breath and wondered why he had stayed away from Phykoros so long.

"I have a new pair," Acaeus informed him, with a slow, lazy grin. "Man and a woman; quite a high pain threshold. In fact, they almost seem to enjoy it. Can I offer you their services? Or perhaps . . . something else?"

With the thread of a sigh, Gideon detached himself from

Acaeus' grasp. "Business first," he said, indicating one of the spare chairs. "May I?"

"Of course." With catlike grace, Acaeus settled himself across from Gideon, regarding him expectantly. He was a handsome bastard, saved from prettiness only by his shrewdly calculating expression and the whip-thin slice of scar across one cheek, legacy of a misspent youth. In fact, there was such a strong shadow of Saul in his face—with its fine bones and whisper of dimples, surmounted by a crop of thick, dark curls—that Gideon often suspected him of being Saul's son, although firmly on the wrong side of the blanket. Acaeus had grown up in his mother's brothel, which was undoubtedly where he had gleaned most of his superlative repertoire.

"And after?" Acaeus added.

Gideon permitted himself a smile. "The latter, I think. Definitely . . . something else."

Acaeus grinned. "Then dispense with your business quickly. It's been too long."

Gideon wouldn't give him the satisfaction of a response. Instead he rose, crossing to one of the room's many crystals—the one that reflected the bar. "See these two?" he said, tapping its surface to indicate Jen and Thibault.

Acaeus uttered a brief command, and the image expanded until the assassins' faces filled the crystal. He regarded them with a polite interest which Gideon knew did not mask the sharp workings of his mind. "What about them?"

"The Cloak and Dagger," Gideon said. "Guild."

A brief expression of alarm lit Acaeus' face. "Are they wise to our operation?"

"I think they suspect, but they have no direct evidence. And I intend to keep it that way."

"Tell me," Acaeus said, sharply.

"Saul hired them—virtually untrained, mind you—from the Guild, to fill in for Avram and Lucinda while we were having certain problems with a dissatisfied dealer who had tried to strike out on his own. Are Avram and Lucinda still around?"

Acaeus nodded. "Up in the caves, last I heard, supervising the production. They had an idea for making the

Dreamsmoke more addictive that they wanted to explore. But finish your story. I'm all ears."

"Not from where I'm sitting," Gideon leered. Acaeus chuckled. "So anyway, this dealer—Sauron Telos—defied Saul. Saul turned him over to the Guild, and the Stiletto took him down." Acaeus smiled appreciatively. "Yes, I see you can understand just what that means. Exemplary woman, the Stiletto." Gideon reflected for a moment, a faint smile on his lips, then shook his head, banishing the memories. "Unfortunately, Telos' family declared a vendetta against Saul. Hired a rogue assassin. So Saul brought in the Cloak and Dagger to neutralize the situation. Unfortunately, they proved far more persistent that any of us suspected—coupled with the fact that someone, I suspect Aubrey, leaked information about our operation. At any rate, someone found the warehouse, and rigorously questioned one of the caretakers—not that the man knew anything, of course. But just to be safe, I had him replaced. A few days later, those two set sail for Phykoros, accompanied by the Hawk and a mage."

Acaeus whistled. "So what do you want me to do?"

"Keep an eye on them from back here; I'll be out on the floor doing the same. I overheard them planning to infiltrate the back rooms later tonight, and you know how vulnerable we are here—mainly because no one was ever supposed to get this far. Do you still remember the summoning signal for the crystal in my wrist?" Acaeus nodded, and Gideon handed him a crystal shard. "Then if the two show up here, say the word, and I'll come. I've got the girl cowed, at least."

Acaeus cued his viewing crystal to expand Jen's image, regarding the fading remnants of her bruises. "Your work?"

Gideon nodded.

"Well, I see you haven't lost your touch." Then his companion laughed and added, "Sleeping your way through the Guild?"

"I assure you, this one wasn't worth the effort. Utterly, bloody prosaic. Unlike some people I could mention . . ."

They exchanged a knowing smile. "Well, then," Acaeus

concluded. "I'll be warned. And expecting you, after we've got this business all wrapped up."

"Merely sauce for the main dish," Gideon commented off-handedly, and left Acaeus laughing as he quit the chamber.

So much for the perfect romantic evening, Jen thought ruefully. The night was beautiful, and the club possessed a raw edge that discouraged inhibitions even more than the Cauldron. And while the mages' displays weren't as impressive for sheer artistry, they were more insidious, as if they snuck beneath your skin and took up residence. It reminded her vaguely of the time she had shared Gideon's Dreamsmoke-laced cigarette—only stronger. Under any other circumstances in such an environment, she would have thrown caution to the winds, flung herself at Thibault, and hang the consequences.

But tonight . . . tonight she could not relax. It felt like a key was buried somewhere in her guts, winding her tighter and tighter. Even the Huitoxa, strong as it was, couldn't quite cut the fear.

For that's what it was. Sheer, overwhelming terror at the prospect that she might have to face Gideon alone again. Worse, everything was depending on her tonight, and she didn't know if she was strong enough to complete her mission. And yet, to admit that—to abrogate her responsibilities—would be infinitely worse. Because if she didn't even try, she might never be able to function as a Guildmember again. And being a Guildmember was all she had ever wanted from her life.

Which, the more she thought of it, was ridiculously self-indulgent of her. Here she was, risking everything to provide herself with a test she wasn't even sure she could pass. And if she failed, Saul went free, and Gideon went free, and generations more would lose their lives to Dreamsmoke.

After all, wasn't the mission the most important thing? Shouldn't she be placing that first, letting someone less fragile complete its final stages? And yet she couldn't—and that made her hate herself all the more, leaving her with a constant dull ache of shame that swirled nauseously amidst the fear.

In fact, the only time she managed to relax, just marginally, was when Thibault tempted her out onto the dance floor. And far from tromping all over her toes as he had threatened, he moved with an astonishing grace and surety, with no wasted motion. He danced like he made love: with passion and gentleness combined—and for a moment she was too fascinated to recall her troubles.

Thibault was deceptively competent—had been, ever since he was young. It was one of the reasons she had sought him out. Not because he was the only companion available—Jen had no illusions about the powers of her own tolerance, even tempered by desperation—but more because he had never managed to disappoint. It had almost become a private game over the years, to see how far she could push him before he broke. But perhaps the game was still on-going, because he never had broken and she had yet to discover his limits.

And wasn't that an intimidating thought when she had so clearly located her own.

Nonetheless, she reveled in the dance and the feeling of Thibault's hands at her waist, that large, graceful body pressed close to her own—and had almost managed to forget her fears when she felt an invisible tap on her arm.

"Time for the switch," Absalom's cheerful voice declared, from the seemingly empty space near her right shoulder.

She masked a shiver, and Thibault momentarily bent his head closer. "Are you sure you want to go through with this? You can still serve as the decoy . . ."

She was tempted to accept his offer when Absalom's cheerful voice added, "Too late for that, now; I've already hired your replacement."

"You . . . *What*?"

She could almost hear the grin in his voice as he answered. "Some things, I figured, were best not to leave to chance. I hired a woman for the night; she won't leave until Thibault tells her to."

"What, didn't you trust my power to charm?" Thibault replied, somewhat sourly.

"As I said," Absalom answered. "Best not to tempt fate. Now, into the lavatory with you, my girl. Your replacement's waiting. And be careful; Gideon's at the end of the bar."

Masking a renewed sense of panic, Jen excused herself from Thibault's company, muttering, "Great purple lumpfish," as she went. And in the dull grey light of the illusionless club, she saw that Absalom was right. Gideon was indeed perched on the terminal stool, watching her progress. She tried not to react as she passed and he stood to follow. He trailed her all the way to the bathroom door, then snorted in quiet derision and let her enter on her own.

She heaved a huge sigh of relief as the door shut behind her, and leaned momentarily against the portal, closing her eyes and forcing her panicked heartbeat to still. Then, opening her eyes again, she took in the chipped enamel and stained tile of the restroom, the mildewed mirrors in which a woman was reflected, her back toward Jen.

Depressed by the squalor, Jen rescued the amulet, revealing a luxurious vision in marble and gilt. The mirrors, unclouded now, reflected the woman's face clearly. *Blast her, she's beautiful,* Jen thought, suddenly feeling scruffy and unwanted. And then, *By Varia, she's me!* with a sluggish stirring of guilt.

She had never seen herself objectively before—certainly never seen herself outside her self—and she drew in a disbelieving breath as the woman turned, Jen's own awe and discomfort mirrored in her face. They were alike as two peas in a pod, even down to the faint shadowing of bruises on their cheeks.

"Jen, meet Jen," Absalom said smugly, popping into being from behind one of the stall doors.

Neither one spoke.

"Do you know what to do, my dear?" Absalom added, addressing the fake Jen.

"Bloody right I do. And I get my other fifty after this is over?" At least her voice, with its lower class accents, was nothing like Jen's, which helped. There was something disturbing about feeling yourself stretched between two bodies, as if you no longer had enough substance for either.

"Yes, the other fifty after. So get out there and have fun. And remember . . ."

"I know. Don't speak too loudly." She turned briefly to Jen, and nodded. "I don't know what this is," she said, "but good luck with it, whatever."

Jen cleared her throat. "Thank you."

Absalom raised an eyebrow at her and held out his arm. When she took it, she could tell by the widening of the other Jen's eyes that they had both disappeared.

The fake Jen opened the door and exited, the real Jen and Absalom behind her. Jen triggered her amulet again to reveal Gideon still waiting in the corridor, and his lips curved in a superior smile as he followed the fake Jen back into the club, settling again on his stool as she returned to Thibault's arms for another dance.

She brought the illusion back, and seeing them together, her partner's head bent solicitously over her own false one, she felt a surge of anger even though she knew it was only part of the act.

"Shall we?" Absalom said.

Jen nodded with some reluctance and followed him from the club, gazing back at Thibault and her double to the last.

"Well, that was disconcerting," she said, when they emerged onto the still busy streets.

The mage chuckled. "I had a feeling it might be. So, do you want my help for the next part?"

She shook her head. "No offense, Absalom, but sometimes the best illusion is no illusion at all. So while Vera might have ridiculed me for bringing my disguises, I will do what I have to with paint and powder. And don't worry; not even Thibault himself will know me when I'm finished."

"I have no doubt. Well, then." He gestured to the inn. "Shall we?"

"Lead on," she replied, and hoped she wasn't progressing toward her doom.

48

"Are we all set?" Vera asked, as Absalom returned to their chambers.

"All set. We passed off the switch without a hitch, and the girl is now in her chamber, busy with pots and paints and no doubt feeling smug for having brought her disguise kit against your express wishes."

Vera smiled. "Well, don't tell her I said so, but I am occasionally known to be wrong. But only occasionally, mind you."

He chuckled, but still she was aware of him watching as she tucked the last of her tools and weapons away, and gathered what hair she had into a stubby tail.

"Ready when you are," she added.

"Well, then, esteemed lady. Are you ready to vanish?" He broke off abruptly, his brow furrowing.

"What is it?" she asked, in some alarm. As long as she had known Absalom, she had never seen him at a loss when it came to magerie. She was even more alarmed when he started running his fingers questingly across her skin; she slapped at him irritably.

"What is this? Some bizarre sort of seduction?"

"Don't imagine that you are that irresistible," he said, then added with a grin, "When I seduce you, you will most certainly know it."

She snorted at his presumption, but felt an obscure relief—whether for the fact that he was not seducing her, or that he felt he would be more expert when he did, she didn't know. His careful fingers ran across every inch of exposed skin, sending a faint shiver up her spine for all that the caress was brisk and impersonal.

"What are you doing?" she repeated.

"Ah, ha!" he exclaimed triumphantly, his fingers halted at the back of her neck. "Found it."

"Found what?"

"You've been tagged, my dove." And he guided her fingers to her neck, where she felt a rough patch of pebbling beneath her hairline.

"The bastard!" she exclaimed. "Gideon?"

"One can only assume. Fortunately, rival magic systems tend to send out a few . . . conflicting impulses, so I found this before it was too late. Hang on, this may hurt."

"Hurt" was an understatement. Vera yelped as the patch ripped free—along with a sizable portion of her skin, she imagined. She held out her hand. "Give me that."

Absalom grinned and passed her a small, clear disk salted with fine crystal powder, which must have been glued to her neck. The underside, when she tested it, was still tacky.

"Want me to destroy it?" Absalom asked.

"Gracious, no! I have a much better idea. Give me fifteen minutes."

She was back in ten, enormously pleased with herself.

"Well?" the image demanded. "What did you do?"

"I have always had an affinity for dogs," she said obliquely, by way of answer. Two could play at the obscurity game, and she knew it would annoy him.

Indeed, his fine brows pinched into a scowl. "That's not an answer."

"Nor are half of what you give me." Then, taking pity on him, she added, "There are many strays in this town, some of them quite skittish. No doubt the creature I found will lead him a merry chase—and I doubt he'll be able to catch him as easily."

The mage laughed, then offered his arm. "Shall we, then?"

"Indubitably."

Ensconced before her mirror, Jen wielded tubes and brushes, all the while reviling the circumstances that had led her to this extreme. Normally, she would have reveled in the task—at the art of becoming other, which even she had to admit she excelled at—but tonight she was painfully aware that any mistake she made might lead to her capture. Of course, there was always Absalom's invisibility spell, but—ultimately—vanishing would not help.

No, if she was going to do this, she would have to do it right—for, invisible or not, they would know who she was and what she wanted from the minute she was captured. And if Gideon had had her beaten once in an attempt to stop her from discovering the truth, what would he do now that she was so close? For this was it; she could feel it. Not all of her assassin's instincts were gone, and she knew that whatever answers existed lay inside that club. She had never been more certain of anything in her life.

Glad, at least, that she had been able to familiarize herself with the club's surroundings and patrons, she dressed with care, choosing an outfit that no one would question. Tall boots and tight trousers. A blousy shirt, opened an inch or two beyond propriety. Subtle shadings in the hollows of her throat, collarbones, cheeks and wrists, to make her look gaunt. Eyes heavily lidded and shadowed into pits, such that their color was completely camouflaged. Bruises not masked but enhanced, and subtlely complemented by the purple streaks she created in her long, white wig.

When she finished, she looked nothing like herself, but rather a creature one step from the grave—and a short step at that.

Satisfied, she almost smiled, then slipped from the room, extinguishing the magelights behind her.

Back in the Kettle, Gideon remained entrenched on his barstool, watching Thibault and her double—whom she had to admit were making a decent go of it. He didn't even blink when she walked past him, momentarily obscuring his vision. So she no longer existed as Jen—only her double did—and the fact that that they had actually fooled him gave her the first hope she had had all evening.

By Varia, she thought, *this might actually work!*

The club still looked dull and dingy without its illusory trappings, but it was smaller than the Cauldron, and thus not hard to penetrate its back ways unseen. Once there, in a long hallway behind the kitchens, she briefly invoked Absalom's invisibility spell and began systematically opening door after door all down the long hallway, employing her lockpicks as necessary. They were storerooms, mostly, until she came to the door at the end of the corridor.

There, the knob turned to reveal a startlingly handsome young man, like a youthful version of Saul, seated behind a desk. He was surrounded by a welter of crystals and other surveillance equipment.

"I believe I've been expecting you," he said, as the door shut behind her.

She cued off the invisibility spell and faced him, her heart pounding a furious cadence. "Oh? And how is that?" she asked, forcing her voice to a semblance of calm.

"*Gideon* told me you'd be coming." The word was oddly accented, and spiked her panic. "No doubt he'll be here, soon."

"And what makes you so certain?"

"Because I just summoned him."

A sudden wave of fury surged through her. Twice, blast it. *Twice* he had thwarted her! But it would not happen again. Not this time, when she was so close.

With a formless growl, Jen launched herself across the desk, grabbing the stranger by the neck and squeezing. Caught off guard, he batted at her, choking, "Gideon, help! *Gideon*!" a few more times before he struck back, throwing them both off balance.

They went down in a crash of splintered chair, Jen gasping aloud as his elbow rebounded off one of her bruised ribs. But a red rage gripped her—part fury, and part panic that Thibault would not live up to his part of the bargain and stop Gideon; she didn't want to discover his limits to-night—so she reasserted her grip on the stranger's chin, banging his head emphatically against one of the desk drawers as she fumbled, one handed, for her bag of tranquilizer darts.

Confidence reasserted; she could take this one. She could.

Blood was leaking sluggishly down the back of his head from her repeated blows, but still he managed to fling her off. She used the opportunity to palm the bag and extract one of the darts before he was on her again.

He grabbed for her mouth, as if to silence the screams she wouldn't utter. She bit down hard, her teeth sinking into his palm. Blood flowed, sweet and metallic, across her tongue. He yelped, and smashed his dripping fist across her face.

She ducked and whirled, catching the blow only glancingly across her jaw, and used the confusion to flip the cap off the dart. She shifted the barb to her left hand, and with her right struck out in turn. Her fist collided with his nose. There was a sickening crunch, and more blood bloomed. He reeled back—straight into the point of the dart she had positioned behind him.

His eyes widened in surprise. One heartbeat; two . . . and then he crumpled, falling to a limp heap at her feet.

She fell back herself, panting heavily.

But she had done it. She had actually done it!

Of course, Gideon could be here at any minute. She had to hurry.

She rose and locked the office door, knowing that would only hold him for seconds.

Please, Thibault, she urged, wishing harder than she had ever wished in her life. *Keep him away. Please. Don't fail me now.*

The night was turning into an exercise in futility, Gideon thought bitterly, as he perched beside the bar and sipped his third purloined Ghedrin. He had always known Jen was prosaic, but now she was proving downright dull as she simpered and flirted with her partner, joining him in dance after dance with no apparent thought for their more nefarious purposes.

It was getting close to midnight now, and neither had so much as made a move away from the crowded common area. Had they become so absorbed in each other that they had forgotten their plans to rob the club? Blast it all, they were wasting his time. Why couldn't they just end their flirtation and get on with their thievery so he could proceed with his night with Acaeus? If this continued much longer, he'd be too tired to do anything useful.

Then the crystal in his wrist flared, and he grinned. That Acaeus; it seemed they were linked even now. But did the man really expect him to give up his observation for a little misbehavior, tempting as that was? He hadn't gotten where he was by putting pleasure ahead of duty.

And then the crystal flared again—once, twice—with the rapid rhythm of panic, and Gideon started. A sensualist Acaeus might be, but an alarmist he was not. And this smacked suspiciously of fright.

He gazed sharply at his targets, trying to determine the cause of Acaeus' summons. Nothing unusual there; still besottedly normal. Thibault bent his head to whisper something to Jen. Her laughter drifted back, harsh and strident . . .

Gideon stiffened, a sudden fury blowing through him. Blast it all to perdition, they had tricked him! That wasn't Jen. She didn't sound like Jen. Nor, now that he noticed it, did she move like Jen. They had magicked someone up to look like the girl, and he had fallen for it.

He had *fallen* for it!

He had no idea how they had managed to out-illusion him, but with another muffled curse, he flung his glass down on the bar and darted from the room, flying toward his compatriot's office.

Thibault had kept his anti-illusion spell active since the moment Jen had abandoned him with her double, and while the club admittedly lacked a certain glamor without it, at least it enabled him to keep an eye on Gideon. Which he did, with a canny indirectness he had developed from years of gazing at Jen without her knowledge.

And his long practice must have paid off, for Gideon seemed unaware of his notice. The man merely fidgeted on his stool, clearly bored by his subjects' exploits. Not that Thibault could entirely blame him; he was growing a little restless himself. His companion was nice enough, but he was rapidly running out of things to say. And he was growing weary of keeping the amused and affectionate smile affixed to his face.

Which was why, in that first second after Gideon vaulted from his stool, Thibault was almost grateful for the distraction. Then a wave of panic spiked through him.

"Stay here," he hissed at his companion. "I'll be back as soon as I can."

He raced off after Gideon, waiting until he had skidded around a less populous corner to breathlessly cue his invisibility spell.

Gideon was racing down the corridor ahead of him, but with Thibault's longer stride it was no problem to intercept him. He tackled Jen's nemesis from behind, pouring all his jealousy, anger, and frustration into that blow.

Gideon went down hard, grunting as Thibault's full weight landed atop him, pinning him to the floor.

"Who . . . ? What . . . ?" he exclaimed furiously.

"Never mind that," Thibault grated. "You're coming with me."

He grabbed Gideon by his collar and hauled him to his feet. Then testing the handle of a nearby door and finding it unlocked, he pushed Gideon inside. It was a storeroom, with boxes piled high against the walls and a barren expanse of cracked stone floor. Moonlight filtered in through two high-set windows.

"Who are you?" Gideon repeated, as Thibault shut and locked the door behind him, then took up guard with his back to the portal.

Thibault cued off the spell.

"Oh. You." Gideon frowned, then added, "And how long have you been able to see me?"

"I don't think you want to know the answer to that one."

Gideon looked briefly disconcerted. Then he crossed his arms over his chest, saying, "So? What now?"

Thibault regarded him in silence for a moment. In the faint moonlight, Gideon's hair gleamed silver-gilt; his eyes were pale and brilliant. No wonder Jen had found him so devastating. He was beautiful and deadly—a jeweled killer. And Thibault didn't intend to let him leave this room alive.

"I suppose," he responded, crossing his arms in turn, "we wait. Unless you have a better suggestion?"

49

Vera could almost understand why the hills were rumored to be haunted. At an hour past midnight, when all should have been still and quiet, random glints of light flashed from the bushes, and snatches of voices floated on the shifting breeze.

She turned to Absalom. "Industrious, aren't they?"

The mage shrugged. "It's a million-mark-a-year industry, if not more. I'm not surprised they throw so much energy into it. For many, I imagine, such work represents the difference between life and death."

"And for others," Vera responded bitterly, "the difference between death and life. But I know what you mean. It's not exactly a country suited to alternate pursuits, is it?"

And indeed, looking along the dark ribbon of the road to the land beyond, dimly lit beneath the thin sliver of the moon, Vera could understand—intellectually, at least—the importance of the Dreamsmoke trade to the people of Konasta. It was a barren country at best, rich only in a stark, natural beauty. But those scrubby, rock-strewn fields, picturesque as they were, would not support crops; they barely seemed able to harbor the few goats and sheep that foraged there by day. Moreover, what few cottages existed outside the clutter of the city were poor, ramshackle affairs that looked as if the slightest wind might topple them. Scoured by the constant soughing of the wind off the sea, even those rocky hills seemed desolate—an impression only accentuated by the ghostly flickers of light and voices that occasionally emanated from their depths.

"Well, shall we?" she said to Absalom.

The mage bowed and gestured her forward, beautiful and courtly in the silvery light.

Vera quit the roadway and began forging across the rough country, attempting to skirt the thorny bushes and the jagged stones that thrust up treacherously from the soil. But the light was uncertain, the obstacles masquerading as shadows, and the third time she barked her shin against a lurking rock and bit back a muffled curse, Absalom took pity on her and magicked her boots to emit a faint glow, assuring her that the illumination was likewise hidden behind his invisible shield. She felt almost like one of the ghosts herself, creeping along on her luminescent feet, but the eerie, verdant light did help, and before long they had reached the hillside, pocked with its multiplicity of caves.

"Where to now?" she whispered to Absalom, who was radiating a full-body nimbus of pale light. "Which entrance would you prefer?"

"I imagine any one of them would serve equally well. Unless I miss my guess, this whole hillside has been hollowed out into one vast laboratory."

She arched one eyebrow sardonically. "And how did you reach that conclusion?"

"By the pattern of the lights, of course," he said, as if the solution were perfectly obvious. "Most of those flickers we saw progressed across the hillside at a steady pace, although on slightly different levels. Likely the result of two patrolling guards with lanterns."

So what she had seen as chaos, a pattern of illumination that had seemed to dance from top to bottom of the hillside without cause or logic, he had perceived as order. Blast him. Swallowing another curse, she pointed to a nearby darkness, looming out of the hillside. "That one, then?"

"Good as any."

But it wasn't—or perhaps it was; she didn't know what the other entrances contained. She only knew that, around one corner, this one was blocked by an impressively large rockslide.

"Absalom . . ." she began.

The mage was striding forward, unconcerned. "What?"

"Um . . . rockslide," she counseled, then broke off in consternation as her companion walked straight into the pile of boulders and vanished.

"Illusion," his voice came cheerfully from behind the rocks. "Come along."

Nonetheless, she found herself drawing a deep breath and holding it as she passed through the perceived impediment. She let it out with a grunt on the other side, and almost walked straight into a grated wall instead. Thick iron bars rose from floor to ceiling, driven deep into the rock to either end; the same applied to the crossbars, woven in between the main struts. In the center of the cage, a locked gate cut out a man-sized arch.

"That," Absalom cautioned, putting a hand to her elbow to halt her, "is very real. Care to do the honors?"

"Why, can't you magic it?" she asked tartly.

"Contrary to popular expectations, my powers are finite; no sense exhausting them on something you could do equally well. Besides," he added, with a wicked twinkle in his eyes, "I like to make you feel useful."

Vera snorted and drew out her picks, finessing the lock open within seconds. She pushed at the gate, and it swung open on smoothly oiled hinges.

There were no further impediments to their progress, and around two more bends a series of dim magelights set into the rock walls provided a watery illumination; Absalom extinguished her boots, and his spectral glow.

As they wound up a narrow, sloping tunnel, the sound of voices gradually grew louder until they emerged into a large room hollowed out of the hill, with wooden shipping crates stacked in neat piles against the walls. The light was brighter here, and two teams of laborers were hard at work—one loading the boxes from the near wall onto a wheeled cart, and the other unloading similar boxes onto the pile on the far wall. Vera shrank back instinctively until one of the worker's eyes passed right over her and she realized Absalom's spell was still in effect.

She turned briefly to regard the mage, who grinned and waggled his eyebrows. She stuck out her tongue in response, then returned her attention to the chamber, wondering how she could pry open a crate to examine the contents, even though she had no doubt what they contained.

The scope of Saul's empire struck her anew. Each one

of these crates, even halfway full, would bring a fortune on the streets. And there were more crates than she could count in this chamber alone; she had no doubt that similar chambers, further on, held equivalent numbers of boxes.

"Where to?" one the workers asked another.

"There's a ship bound for Kymini and the outer islands tomorrow," the second replied. "Twenty crates are needed aboard. So shift your lazy ass; it sails on the morning tide, and we need to get it loaded before first light."

The first man grunted and heaved another crate onto the wheeled cart. "Didn't we just send a shipment to Kymini?"

"That was last week."

"Oh. Greedy bastards," he observed, and his companion chuckled.

Realizing she was unlikely to learn anything more, Vera gestured to Absalom and they moved on, trying to keep their footfalls silent in the echoing stone cavern. More crates were piled haphazardly along a winding hallway leading from the storeroom and, as no one was present, Vera used the tines of her grappling hook to pry up one of the lids.

As expected, nested amidst a bed of fragrant grasses to disguise the odor, were a dozen large packets of dried and cured Dreamsmoke.

Absalom let out a low, impressed whistle. "Well, if this isn't the source, I don't know what is. There must be a bloody fortune here."

"Yes. No wonder Saul will go to almost any lengths to protect his empire. The profits from this room alone would support him like a king."

"Makes the Guild and its profits look positively paltry, does it not?" the mage added. "Poor Owen."

"Poor Owen, indeed. Now, let's get some more proof so we can firmly destroy all the rest of poor Owen's illusions."

Two more corridors and intermediate storage chambers, where dried leaves were stacked in piles like cordwood and vats of crumbled leaves awaited packing, and they entered what had to be the main chamber. It was a vast room, obviously the terminus of about three caverns combined. The rock walls had been whitewashed to about twelve feet up, and the rest rose into measureless darkness. But within that lower extremity, large stone laboratory benches stretched out in ordered rows, surmounted by bubbling crucibles heated by spouts of flame.

A man and a woman, clearly in some position of authority, were talking to a white-coated scientist in one corner. Vera drifted closer to observe.

"Are you certain you have the formula right?" the woman was saying. There was a hard edge to her, and the scientist swallowed nervously.

"As near as I can get it," he assured her. "It's a bit of a tricky procedure, getting the proportions right. And refining the substance is not exactly cheap. But . . . while it has no obvious hallucinogenic effects on its own, the substance does seem to be quite addictive."

"And you are certain that curing the Dreamsmoke as you have will cause this substance to permeate the leaves without adversely affecting the Dreamsmoke's properties?"

The man seemed almost offended. "You asked me to double the Dreamsmoke's addictive qualities," he said, drawing himself up indignantly, "and I have done so."

"The bastards!" Vera hissed involuntarily.

The woman's companion, who had previously been propped nonchalantly against the wall, now came erect, saying, "Did you hear something?"

Vera stopped breathing.

"What are you talking about, Avram?" the woman responded.

Avram's eyes darted about the room, and then he shook his head. "Nothing. I thought I heard an intruder, but there's no one here."

"Are you're sure your amulet is properly activated?"

Avram frowned. "I didn't get where I am by being careless, Lucinda."

Vera let her breath trickle out in relief.

"Of course not." Lucinda turned back to the scientist, adding, "Our employer will be pleased, I'm sure. But he'll be even more pleased if you can manage to find a cheaper way to produce your substance."

"I'll work on it."

"Very good. Well, I'd say it's been a highly successful

month, all around. We'll recommend you for a raise when we get back to Ephanon."

"That would be welcome. Working with addictive substances is a mixed blessing, at best, as I'm sure you appreciate."

"Indeed. As does our employer. You can be assured you will be suitably rewarded."

Avram and Lucinda, Vera thought as the scientist moved off. *Now why does that sound so blasted familiar?*

She was about to ask Absalom when the woman turned to her companion and remarked, "What do you think?"

"I think you were right. It's been a most profitable month, all told. Saul will be pleased."

"Pleased enough to promote us over that psychopath, Gideon?"

Vera felt a surge of anger at the mention of the man who had so abused her niece, and willfully suppressed an involuntary exclamation. Absalom was watching her knowingly.

"Look who's talking," Avram said, grinning.

Lucinda pouted. "I am *not* a psychopath."

"Not quite of the same flower, I admit. But you know I love you, anyway."

"Anyway? You love me because of it, you old reprobate!"

He chuckled. "Guilty as charged. But it's going to take more than this for Saul to oust his Golden Boy. He's uncommonly attached to the creature."

"One almost wonders if he isn't fucking the lad—along with half of the known universe. Gideon's not exactly shy with his favors when he thinks it will gain him something."

"Which is doubtless why Aubrey has been left moping so long; he's not valuable enough for the Golden Boy to waste his attention on."

"And Acaeus is?" Lucinda countered.

Avram laughed. "You have a point. I admit, I have wondered if Gideon really came here chasing those assassins as he claimed, or if was more the appeal of Acaeus' tight little ass that drew him."

Lucinda chuckled nastily. "Well, either way, it's his business to sort out. We have to get back to Ephanon on the morrow, and see what kind of a reward we can coax out of Saul for our efforts."

And then Vera remembered where she had heard their names. Avram and Lucinda were the vacationing body-guards that Jen and Thibault had replaced. Vacationing, indeed.

As Avram put an arm around his companion and led her away, Vera turned to Absalom in disgust. "Blast it all to perdition, now wasn't *that* an intriguing little conversation! I only wish we had had the foresight to record it . . ."

The mage looked smug; he withdrew a crystal from his pocket. "Fortunately," he responded, "you have me around. And 'Foresight' just happens to be my middle name."

"You annoying, delightful man, I forgive you all your faults! Did you get it all?"

"Every last word. Every first word, too."

"Brilliant! Well, then, let's poke around a little more to see if we can find any further evidence against Saul. But if not, I think that what we have will be sufficient."

"Providing that your niece doesn't find anything in the Kettle."

"Yes, Jen. Honestly, Absalom, I only let her go because her confidence needed boosting. I don't expect she's going to find anything of note."

"You might be surprised," the mage countered, and annoyingly refused to say anything further when pressed.

50

Contrary to Vera's beliefs, Jen had found something of note in the back offices of the Kettle. Something very definitely of note. And while she still jumped at every shadow, she was beginning to believe that Thibault had indeed kept his part of the bargain and taken care of Gideon. For as she tore apart the offices in an increasing frenzy, keeping one eye always on her latest victim, slumped unconscious in his corner, the expected interruption never occurred.

And she found the accounting books.

Every last one of them.

Leather-bound and dated, they contained everything she needed. Shipments and payments, the dealers dealt and the sums exchanged. Nothing to tie it to Saul, of course, but the rest was all there. And the amounts of money involved were nothing short of staggering. In fact, when she first saw the tallies in the "profits" column, she had to sit down for a minute just to catch her breath.

She doubted Vera even earned in a year what Saul collected in a month. And Vera was the highest paid assassin in the Guild.

It was no wonder Gideon had gone to such lengths to preserve Saul's secret. If she controlled an empire this vast, she would . . . Well, she didn't know just how far she would go to preserve it, but it would probably test limits she didn't even know she had. Were she the type of person who cared about such things.

And then another sensation gradually overcame the awe: triumph. By all that was precious, she had done it! She had found the prize, despite Vera and Thibault. Despite herself.

Despite Gideon.

By all that was precious, she had actually beaten Gideon at his game!

She began to laugh then, ignoring the twinging pain in her jaw. He had beaten her, he had broken her, and still she had won.

She drew out a carryall and stuffed the books inside. Then she glanced down at the man—likely the Kettle's manager—slumped unconscious on the floor.

What to do with him? Kill him?

Or did he have some other purpose?

Could she use him to tie this whole mess in to Saul?

Well, she decided, it was foolish to waste a resource even when you weren't entirely sure of its value, so she grabbed his limp arms and gave a mighty heave, dragging the body up over her shoulder. Although the man was no more than her own height, and slightly built, she still staggered under his weight. The carryall threatened to slip off her other shoulder, and there was a tricky moment when she thought she was going to lose them both, but eventually she achieved a precarious balance and considered her next move.

She didn't know how long Thibault would be able to hold Gideon off, which meant she had to leave as soon as possible. But how? Was there a back door? For she couldn't very well carry the club's manager over her shoulder through the crowded front room, no matter how well disguised she was.

Or could she?

The man's head hung at her waist, his visage smeared with blood and swollen from her blows. She would barely have recognized him herself, and that was provided anyone could see his face. From the front, all that was visible was the back of his head, and many men in Konasta possessed a similar crop of tight dark curls. He could be almost anyone. And, besides, half the battle of not being stopped was to act like you knew precisely what you were doing. People usually saw what they wanted or expected to see. And how many would expect to see the Kettle's manager carried out unconscious over some assassin's shoulder?

It just might work. Besides, she stood as much chance getting caught while sneaking about looking for the back door as she did going out the front. So, gathering up the shreds of her courage, she cracked the door open and peered out into the hall. No one. She quickly scooted out, and emerged back into the main room without incident.

She cued off her anti-illusion amulet and let the swirling madness claim her. Immediately, she found herself the target of incredulous stares, but she merely winked back boldly, and strode for the door as if her knees were not shaking and her pulse not racing loudly enough to drown out the music.

"Here, what's going on?" one of the door guards demanded. She forced herself not to flinch, meeting his eyes directly.

"I might ask the same of you," she countered, donning an accent her double might have envied. "Aren't you supposed to be protecting us innocent patrons?"

The second guard eyed her with a barely disguised prurience. "You don't look all that innocent to me."

She masked a grin. By Varia, it was actually working! The knowledge brought more of a swagger to her voice and manner. "Be that as I may, I shouldn't have to find myself pawed by one of your drunken sot patrons after I have paid perfectly good money for entry. This one got a little above himself, so . . . I taught him a lesson. What else is a girl supposed to do?"

The first guard's eyes narrowed. "Then why didn't we hear the commotion?"

Blast it! Vera was right; always keep the story simple. The more details you added, the more likely you were to get caught in a lie. Clamping down on her panic, she managed a coy smile and endeavored to rectify the situation. "Because a girl deserves a little fun on her night off. I let him buy us a room—more fool me. But what he proposed went a good deal beyond fun. You should thank me for eliminating him before he harmed anyone less able to take care of themselves. Now, if you will excuse me, I want to dump this trash in the alley with the rest of the garbage. And then come back and find myself a real man!"

Her increasingly loud tirade had drawn stares from the nearby patrons, and her final words drew a rousing chorus of catcalls and cheers, and many shouted offers. The two guards began to grin and motioned her gallantly through the door. She passed between them with her head held high and the applause ringing loudly in her ears. With a dramatic flourish, she retreated into a nearby alley and dumped her load, careful to keep her victim's face toward the alley wall. The bag of record books she deposited half under his body and half under a pile of refuse, invisible save to anyone who knew they were there. Then, swiftly, she checked the pulse in his neck.

Slow and sluggish. He wouldn't shake off the drug for another hour, at least.

Plenty of time. She hoped.

She reemerged from the alley, making a show of dusting off her hands, and the two guards laughed. They let her back into the club amidst more hoots and cheers, and she shakily accepted drinks and laughing offers, giddy from actually having succeeded with the first part of her plan. But still she couldn't help wondering just how soon she could complete her charade as offended patron and legitimately make her escape.

In the locked storeroom of the Kettle, Thibault and Gideon regarded each other in a frozen silence, at an impasse of sorts. Then Gideon said, "I know what you're doing here. And I know where your partner is. She won't find anything. Acaeus is waiting for her. And Acaeus is almost as twisted as I am."

Thibault masked a sudden surge of panic. He didn't know if Jen could survive another Gideon. But she was his partner, and he had to trust her. So, "I wouldn't underestimate her, if I were you," he replied. "This Acaeus may be twisted, but Jen can be quite vicious herself. Especially when her judgment isn't impaired by having slept with her victim."

But he couldn't quite keep the bitterness from his voice, and Gideon heard it. He laughed. "Don't think I haven't seen the expression in your eyes when you look at her. Doesn't it annoy you, knowing that I had what you desire? And so often? And that it meant nothing to me?"

But I did have her, you bastard, Thibault thought, although the words rankled, because in a way Gideon was right. Jen had turned to Thibault for comfort, in response to Gideon's actions; she had not chosen him spontaneously, as she had Gideon, and as she would no doubt choose many others in the future. She had made that amply clear. So in that sense, Gideon had received something that Thibault never would. And he had treated it like trash.

A red rage gripped him even as a small corner of his mind told him that Gideon was goading him, forcing him to lose his temper and thus his control. Well, two could play at that game, he thought, resolutely clamping down on his anger.

"She will find it, you know."

"Find what?"

"Whatever evidence you're hiding. It must be here, for why else would you be trying so hard to stop her?"

Gideon arched an eyebrow. "That's specious reasoning. I punished her for breaking into Saul's office, and there was not a scrap of evidence there."

A vision of Jen as she had appeared the evening he found her in the closet rose in Thibault's mind, filling his throat with bile. "So why did you do it?"

"For the sheer principle of the thing. And because I enjoyed it. Isn't that enough?"

Thibault scowled. "She will take down your Acaeus," he flared, "and she will find what you and Saul have been hiding. And she will use it to bring your whole bloody empire to the ground!"

Gideon just grinned. "It's not my empire. And, besides, the most she can do is topple Saul."

"And that doesn't bother you?"

"Why should it? Saul is not bad as bosses go, but if he is removed, someone else will take his place."

"You are a cold bastard, aren't you?"

"So I've been told. But think about it. The empire is greater than the man. And the empire will never fall."

"And what makes you so certain it won't?"

"What makes you so certain it will?"

"You bastard! Don't you have any emotions? Isn't there anything in this world that matters?"

"Not much. I don't regard consequences as you do; I'm gifted that way. Emotions are a curse. They tie you down;

they limit you. Look at you. Stupidly content to play second fiddle to your pathetic little Jen, and just because you're hopelessly in love with her. And I do mean hopelessly. She'll never reciprocate that feeling; she's too shallow to recognize quality when she sees it. And you are quality. You're fundamentally stronger and smarter than she will ever be. Without her, who knows how far you could go? And yet you limit yourself, And for what? A love that will never be returned? Pardon me if I feel contempt for you and most of *emotional* humanity."

"And I feel nothing but pity for you," Thibault returned, despite the doubt that niggled at the back of his mind. What *was* he doing hanging his life on a hope that might never be achieved? "You'll never know the nobility of sacrifice . . ."

Gideon broke into a peal of contemptuous laughter. "The nobility of sacrifice? Oh, spare me! That's the same pathetic excuse all you weaklings use to justify your weakness. There is nothing remotely noble about sacrifice. In life—in *persistence*—there is always hope. In giving up—in *death*—there is nothing. But if you want to throw your life away on a dream, be my guest. Now, if you'll excuse me, I have business outside."

But Thibault wouldn't budge. Gideon's coldly logical words were punching holes in all he believed, yet one fact remained clear. He had promised Jen he would not let Gideon escape him, and he intended to keep that promise, no matter the cost. Even if it did mean sacrificing himself. And maybe that made him as much a fool as Gideon believed. But it also felt right, in a part of him that went beyond logic and emotion. In that part of him that made him uniquely Thibault.

So he scrambled to find a hole among Gideon's words, some flaw he could exploit. "Then if that's the way you feel, there is one thing you value. Life. Or, more specifically, your life. That means something to you, doesn't it?"

Gideon didn't seem disconcerted by his insight, but Thibault was coming to expect that. Instead, the Golden Boy laughed and applauded. "How clever of you, to discern my one weakness. You see what I mean? Never in a million years would Jen have reached that conclusion. And you know why? Because she is a creature of instinct and impulse. She acts. She would have tried to kill me for my comments, and she would have failed. The weakness of emotion, as I was saying. But you . . . You think. You consider before you act. And that is why you will succeed. Providing you are smart enough never to get overruled by your emotions."

"And if I, coldly and logically, attempt to kill you? Will I succeed?"

Gideon laughed. "You may have discerned my weakness, but you are far from discovering the way around it. If you do try to kill me, it will not be coolly and logically. And you, too, will fail."

"You're certain of that?"

"As certain as I've ever been of anything in my life. I cannot be killed by such as you. At least not in a fit of passion and emotion. And there; now you have all the answers you need. If you really were smart, you would have me."

"So you don't believe I can kill you?"

Gideon shook his head reproachfully. "Oh, dear; this will never do. You're getting all emotional again. What did I tell you? I do believe you can kill me, in the right frame of mind. But whether you can get there . . . It's hard to kill in true cold blood—at least for those burdened by emotion."

"I've killed before," Thibault flared.

"A fine bluff, my friend. And a noble try. But"—Gideon shook his head—"no. You're a virgin in more than just sex. Oh, I know you had Jen after I discarded her; that's no great secret. And moreover, I know she was your first."

"How . . . Who . . ."

"No one told me, if that's what you're concerned about. I can just read people like a book. So, tell me, what was it like, learning that reality can never quite measure up to the fantasy? A bitter lesson, no?"

Thibault winced, recognizing the truth of the words. Nice as the experience had been, he had repeatedly tried to impart a transcendence to the act that it simply hadn't possessed. Bedding Jen hadn't been the answer to all his dreams; it hadn't changed his world. At the base of it, it was only sex—wonderful in its way, but also awkward and messy. There was no magical bond, no sense of the two becoming one which he had always been promised. But still, it had contained a sweetness that almost compensated. So, "What do you know?" he grated. "It was . . ."

"Perfection? That's all right; go ahead and lie to me, if that's what you require. But don't lie to yourself. Reality never matches the fantasy; it's one of life's bitterest truths. The triumph is learning not to care."

"Or not to have fantasies," Thibault growled.

Gideon laughed. "I like you. I truly do. You have spirit."

"I wish I could say the feeling is mutual."

"No, you don't. You wish you could kill me. You, who have never taken knife to flesh; who have never felt life leaking out over your hands in a rush of hot, bitter blood. I take it all back. I no longer believe you can kill me."

"Oh?" And without pausing to think, Thibault drew his stag's head dagger and plunged it into Gideon's breast, driving it up through the ribs to the heart. He hadn't expected there to be so little resistance—or so much. And the blood did, indeed, rush hot and bitter over his hands.

Gideon's jade-green eyes widened in surprise and reproach.

Thibault almost retched and dropped the dagger, but he forced himself to stand, clamping down on a rising nausea as Gideon slowly slipped from the point of the blade and crumpled to the floor.

Not so difficult to kill, after all, the Golden Boy.

Thibault stood, shaking slightly, as he gazed down at the crumpled form of what was, mere moments ago, a living person. And then he turned and threw up noisily in the corner.

51

Thibault didn't know how long he sat there on the cold stone floor of the storeroom, his arms wrapped around his legs and his chin on his knees, the stench of his vomit sharp and acrid in his nose, and tried to stop shaking. He didn't really even know what he was waiting for. To be able to face himself and the world again as a murderer? Or simply to be sure that Gideon, for all his insane claims, was dead? The crumpled body seemed to accuse him.

He was now an assassin, in truth, and he wasn't certain he liked it.

There was some sort of commotion in the larger club, a riot of hoots, catcalls and applause; ironically, he imagined it was for him. For he had done a wonderful thing, hadn't he? He'd rid the world of a monster. But if killing monsters left him this shaken, then what would the others be like? Those that weren't monsters but simply guilty of bad judgment? Could he, like Vera, have killed Guy Istarbion? Iaon Pehndon? Men whose only crime was an excess of ambition and a certain lack of caring for those they exploited on their way up?

Or were these just the weak emotions Gideon had cautioned him about? By suppressing them, could he rise to the top of his profession? Did he want to?

Eventually, he managed to push himself to his feet. The blood had spread in a wide puddle around Gideon's body, soaking into the porous stone. Who would have thought a human body could contain that much liquid? There would be a stain on the floor for life.

He probably should arrange the body, close Gideon's wide-staring eyes, but he couldn't bring himself to touch the corpse.

Why was he feeling so guilty? Gideon had deserved his death, for everything he had done to Jen. Amply deserved it.

Justification, Gideon's voice seemed to whisper in his ear. *By killing me, you have become no better than me. An eye for an eye. Now you are a killer, too.*

Thibault turned hastily to the door, unlocking it and wrenching it open. He wiped his hands on his pants and thrust the dagger blindly into its sheath. The club looked grim and cheerless; he had forgotten he had the anti-illusion spell still active. He hastily cued it off, losing himself momentarily in the swirling, colorful riot, then stumbled from the Kettle, thankful the guards appeared not to see the blood on his clothing.

Jen was drunk. Not badly drunk; not drunk enough to forget her victim's body, crumpled in the alley. He would be waking soon, and she had to be there. But drunk enough to be able to tolerate the attentions of strangers, any one of whom could be the equivalent of Gideon. Drunk enough not to care if one of them tried the same trick on her and she killed him in return.

She was, she realized, flirting with them, egging them on, recklessly daring one of them to hurt her so she could prove, again, that she could hold her own. Hurt him back, gifting pain for pain. And, oddly, this recklessness only seemed to attract more of them, each bearing drinks. Which she accepted, and so became more drunk.

A throbbing urgency was growing in her loins, fueled half by alcohol and half by a mad desire for revenge. She had to act fast—and soon—or her victim would awake and flee with the record books, and she would lose everything.

Then, there was the question of Gideon. She had seen Thibault stumble from the club, looking like death warmed over. What, then, had happened to the Golden Boy?

Abruptly, she singled out one of her many suitors—a rough-cut, handsome brute who looked as if he could take as good as he got. "You'll do," she informed him curtly. "Get us a room."

He complied, and she followed him there, the throbbing pulse growing in her loins. She would fuck him hard and then leave, she decided—though a part of her realized she was spinning rather badly out of control. But when he got her upstairs and turned slobbily sentimental, trying to shower her with kisses, the hot, relentless ache in her loins suddenly vanished and she found herself heartily sick of the whole ordeal. So she pricked him with the same type of dart she had used on the club manager and left him crumpled, half-naked, on the floor. Then she activated her invisibility spell, and this time without the manager's body to give her away, slipped noiselessly past the door guards and returned to the alley.

Her victim was just beginning to stir. She extracted some rope from the coil around her waist and tied his hands, then hauled him to his feet.

"Wha . . . ?" he mumbled.

"You're coming with me," she informed him, then slung the bag of record books over her shoulder.

He swayed against her, stumbling and barely able to walk, but at least she didn't have his full weight over her shoulder this time. She maneuvered him through the streets in silence while his head cleared and his gait improved. "You drugged me," he accused.

"And you were trying to summon Gideon to assault me," she returned.

"Gideon," he said, desperately.

"Don't bother; you're too late. He can't hear you." She hoped fervently that it was true. But still, that brought up a point. If Gideon could hear him, he might be able to track him down; she couldn't just stash him in her rooms as she planned. So where could she keep him? And then she remembered the root cellar below the inn, with its padlocked entrance off the garden. She would stash him down there, drugged to ensure he remained silent—at least until Vera and Absalom returned and they could figure out what to do with him.

Still groggy from the drugs, he barely resisted as she picked the cellar lock and pushed him down the steps, pricking him again with another thorn at the bottom. He crumpled and she dragged him into the darkest corner. She tested the bonds on his wrists, then bound his legs as well before retreating up the steps and repadlocking the cellar door.

She looked around the silent gardens and, suddenly unwilling to deal with the hassles of keys and front doors, retreated to the alley where she had first seen Gideon. There she extracted her rope and grapple. Dawn was breaking, lightening the sky to a gauzy periwinkle as she tossed the grapple skywards, watching it catch the balcony rail with a clink. Then, backlit by the swelling light, she began to climb.

Thibault was asleep when Jen first crested the balcony rail, but he woke when he heard her fumbling with the window catch. She threw open the doors, and his first, sleep-drugged thought upon seeing the outrageous figure with its purple-streaked white hair and its white face shadowed with violet bruises, was: *Oh, no; not again!* And then the events of the night came flooding back and he heaved a sigh.

He hadn't bothered to change when he returned to the inn. Instead, he had merely collapsed atop the blankets and fallen into a weary slumber. Now, he was infinitely aware of his filthy and bedraggled condition, and even more so as she settled beside him, her eyes sunken into deep, exhausted pits that had nothing to do with make-up or artifice.

"Well?" he demanded, when she didn't speak.

"It's over," she said. "I have the club manager drugged in the cellar, awaiting questioning. And I found these." She emptied the contents of her carrysack across the bed. "It's all there. Dates, names, prices."

Thibault picked up one of the thick, leather-bound volumes and flipped through it in silence. It was, indeed, all there. All but Saul's name—and at this point, that shouldn't be hard to add.

Gideon had been wrong again. She had found what they needed.

And now the empire would fall.

"You're awfully quiet," she said at last. "What happened to my double?"

His hand flew to his mouth. "By Varia, I forgot all about her! I hope Absalom takes care of everything . . ."

"No doubt he will. Absalom's awfully good with details."

More silence, and then, "Gideon?" she asked at last—the question he knew she had been thinking since she entered.

He drew a deep breath. "Dead."

"How?" Her voice was almost inaudible.

"I killed him." He choked back a sob, fighting for composure.

She stared at him in incomprehension.

"Is it always this hard, the first time?" he asked, his voice thick and plaintive.

In that same, tiny voice, she admitted, "I wouldn't know. I've never killed anyone before. But Thibault . . ."

"What?"

"Thank you."

When he said nothing, she reached for him—and he flinched away. He had killed for her, after all. If not for her, he would never have been in this mess in the first place. Which, he knew objectively, was not a fair accusation. But he had the sudden urge to blame someone, and he had already borne enough of his own recrimination this evening.

Then, seeing the hurt flaring in her eyes, he added, "Don't," trying to justify his reaction. "I'm covered with blood."

Another pause, and then she said, her voice puzzled, "No you're not."

Startled momentarily out of his self-pity, he looked down at himself. She was right. There was no blood, either on his hands or on his clothing. With a shaking hand, he drew his dagger. He had thrust it into his belt without cleaning it, but now it was as pristine and shiny as if freshly cleaned.

What the blazes . . . ?

In his confusion, Gideon's voice seemed to mock at him.

I cannot be killed by such as you. At least not in a fit of passion and emotion. And there; now you have all the answers you need. If you really were smart, you would have me.

Passion and emotion. He had killed in a fit of passion

and emotion, and now for the first time he began to wonder. Had he even killed at all?

"Thibault?" Jen's voice was high and panicked. "Is Gideon dead or not?"

He stared back at her in consternation. She looked oddly vulnerable beneath that ridiculous purple and white wig. "I . . . I don't know," he admitted.

52

The voyage back to Ephanon was almost an anticlimax, the four of them crammed into a tiny third class cabin that had been the only thing available when they booked passage at the last minute. It was a situation made all the more difficult by the fact that none of them seemed much inclined to be sociable. Vera was quietly contemplative and faintly incredulous, as if she couldn't believe her sixteen-year quest was over. Jen had withdrawn into herself and would barely speak. Absalom, blast him, was as bright-eyed and garrulous as ever, only he couldn't get anyone to talk to him. And as for Thibault . . .

He was simply confused, his mind spinning among a million probabilities that he hadn't even considered until yesterday.

Events had come fast and furious after his discovery that he might not have killed Gideon. For even as he sat staring at his pristine dagger, Vera and Absalom had entered the chamber, bearing news about the secret laboratory in the hills. They hadn't been able to find any concrete evidence implicating Saul, but Absalom did have a recording of one rather intriguing conversation, which he obligingly played back. Then Jen had brought out her account books, and revealed the presence of Gideon's accomplice Acaeus in the cellars. Vera and Absalom had spirited him back to the room, and Absalom had summarily removed and destroyed the summoning crystal in his wrist. Then, bringing him out of his drugged torpor, the mage had placed the man under a brutal truth spell and recorded the results of that as well.

And though he clearly hadn't wanted to, Acaeus had sung like a canary under Absalom's spell, truth after truth spilling out of him, implicating Saul in heinous act after heinous act. And all the while, tears of rage and betrayal had spilled down his cheeks, and he had chewed his lips to a bloody pulp in a futile effort to keep from talking.

The testimony was compelling, and would have convinced even the most trusting of Guildmasters. And so with Acaeus' physical presence now superfluous, Vera had taken him off somewhere and put him out of his misery. Thibault would have almost been thankful for this reprieve if the whole act had not sickened him so greatly.

He still remembered what it felt like to kill Gideon. If he had indeed killed Gideon. How many virginities was he to lose on this assignment?

But now they had everything, and as a bonus Saul's faithful bodyguards were dead as well. Avram and Lucinda, Vera eventually admitted, were food for vultures somewhere in the barren Phykoros hills. So nothing now stood in the way of their revenge—except perhaps their own resolve. For as Vera and Absalom had gone to the docks to book their berth on the first outgoing ship and Jen had haphazardly thrown their possessions back into their trunks, Thibault, seized by a consuming curiosity, had activated his invisibility spell one final time and broken into the Kettle.

He didn't know what he most wanted to see—the visceral remains of Gideon's death, or the lack thereof—but he was somehow unsurprised to see the stone floor clean of blood, no body in sight.

So Gideon had been right: he wasn't able to be killed by one such as Thibault. Unless someone had removed the corpse and somehow managed to clean up the bloodstains.

Thibault supposed he would never know the truth, but he did have his suspicions.

The news had sent Jen into an even deeper funk.

And so, each locked into his own private misery, sleep on shipboard took them early, and held them hard. And before they had even fully processed the events on Phykoros, they had docked at Ephanon again, better rested but no more cheerful.

Incredibly enough, Thibault realized, it had been barely a month since they had first docked at Konasta's main port, unaware of the depth of darkness into which this assignment would carry them. What a child he had been back then—an innocent, unsuspecting boy. He couldn't help wondering if every assassin had assignments like this, from which they emerged a different person than they had gone in. Was this one of the casualties of the job? Was this why their pay scale was so inflated? If so, it didn't even begin to compensate.

"It seems an eternity ago, doesn't it?" Jen said, approaching the railing where he stood, incongruously gloomy in the bright morning. Her face was pinched and strained, still shadowed by bruises. Parts of the scab on her cheek had begun to flake off, revealing the faint pink tracery of scar. Seeing her, a little of the tension drained out of him. He wasn't the only one who had paid. And despite all of Gideon's words, she sometimes still knew his mind better than he knew it himself.

For the first time since he had sunk his knife into Gideon's breast, he felt a faint, genuine smile curve his lips. "An eon and a half," he agreed. "Who would have guessed it?"

"Not Owen," she said, and they were abruptly gloomy again.

This time it was Thibault who attempted to restart the conversation. "Do you remember how Saul came to greet us at the docks?"

"Who could forget? How handsome he looked; how cheerful. Who would have guessed he would turn out to be such a monster?"

"Well, I guess monsters can come in all guises," Thibault replied.

"Even golden-haired, green-eyed ones." She was silent for a long moment, then added, "Thibault, I can't pretend to know what it cost you to take Gideon down, but I just wanted to tell you that what you did . . . It meant the world to me, even if it didn't succeed. That you even tried . . . Well, thank you. From the bottom of my heart. I mean that."

Which almost made it better. But only almost. Still, he didn't back away when she leaned her head against his shoulder, and that was how Vera found them several minutes later, his arm around her, both gazing with long faces out over the Ephanon harbor.

To Jen, it seemed inconceivable that Ephanon should have altered so little in the past few days, while her own life had altered so greatly. But the streets were unchanged, and as she and Thibault wound their way up to Saul's Ephanon mansion, with Vera and Absalom ghosting invisibly behind them, she could almost imagine that the whole crazy week—from her beating to the revelation of Saul's true identity—had never transpired. In many ways, it made more sense for it to be a dream, or the conjuring of some particularly talented mage.

But as they crossed Sentenniel Street and saw the smoking dome of the Cauldron rising over the city, she knew it had been no illusion. And, moreover, she understood that someone had to pay.

With a new resolve, she emerged into the square that fronted Saul's mansion, noting that the fallen chunk of masonry still gaped in the roof like a missing tooth. Thibault noted it, too; she could tell by the way his gaze traveled upward.

A hysterical spurt of laughter escaped her.

"What?" he demanded.

"If only Patroch had known what he *really* stood to inherit, he might not have stopped with his club!"

Thibault actually smiled at that. "And can you see Patroch as the head of a Dreamsmoke empire?"

"Complete with satin dress?" She giggled. "Not hardly."

When they reached the front door, she hesitated, then led her party around to the back and knocked.

Jahnee answered the door.

The girl's brown eyes widened. "Gilyan; Ty! What are you doing back?"

"Emergency," Thibault said shortly. "Is Saul around? We need to talk to him."

"Hold on a minute; let me check. Kore, look who's here!"

Kore emerged from the pantry with a load of bread in her arms. She dropped the loaves on the table, despite a shriek from Beroe, and rushed to embrace them.

"Such excitement," she crowed. "You'll never guess what has happened in your absence! Aubrey was caught stealing from Saul, and has vanished. And that just goes to show you what you get for trusting *him*," she added pointedly to Jahnee, who flushed and departed.

"Actually," Jen admitted, "it's not quite that simple. Aubrey discovered something he wasn't supposed to know, and disappeared in fear for his life. So Jahnee was right; he was the good guy, after all."

"Really? What did he find out?"

"Later," Jen promised. "But for now . . ."

Jahnee returned, saying coolly, "Alcina says he's in his study. You might as well go in. You know the way."

Jen sighed and followed Thibault down the hall. She could sense Vera and Absalom behind her, still wrapped in their invisibility spell. When they reached Saul's study, Thibault knocked on the door.

"Come." Saul's familiar, cheerful voice echoed from behind the portal. But he looked less than pleased when Thibault pushed open the door and entered the chamber, with Jen a half step behind him.

In fact, his face congealed. But, "Back from Phykoros already?" he inquired with a false solicitousness. "What's the matter? Were the islands not to your liking?"

"You could say that," Thibault said tightly. "Or perhaps you could say we were not to the island's liking. But before we get into specifics, I would like to introduce some associates of ours."

On cue, Vera and Absalom materialized, and Saul's face went the color of curdled milk.

"May I introduce the Hawk and her mage?" Thibault continued, with certain deadly courtesy.

Saul looked about to choke, so Vera kindly unstoppered the decanter of brandy on his desk and poured him a generous glass. She handed it across to him and he gulped it greedily. And as Jen saw the catlike smile that curved her aunt's lips, she knew what had just transpired.

Well, it was fitting. It had started as Vera's quest, after all.

Still, "We know everything," Jen said. "Veridien Street,

and the Kettle. The secret lab on Phykoros. Acaeus, Avram and Lucinda. We even have proof. Absalom?"

Wordlessly, the mage withdrew his crystal and projected its stored conversations into the air.

Saul seemed to shrink. "My son?" he choked.

"Dead," Jen informed him.

"Mercifully," Thibault added.

"And we also have these," Jen continued, pulling out the log books. She had studied them on the voyage back, and had discovered one or two other things of interest. "How do you think your dealers would react to the knowledge that you have been systematically cheating them for years?"

Thibault started slightly, and she permitted herself a smile. She, too, was learning to keep her secrets.

"I . . ." Saul began.

"We can, of course, go public with this," Vera declared. "I think our evidence is quite compelling. And would stand up in any court of law."

Saul laughed. "What do you want from me? Money? Is that it? I'm quite rich, you know. I can pay."

"Oh," Vera purred. "What I want is a good deal more esoteric than money."

Saul looked blank.

"I have been hunting for you for sixteen years," she said. "What I want is for you to suffer now as much as you have made me and mine suffer in the past."

"Why? What have I ever done to you?"

"Do remember your vendetta against the Navarin family?"

"I have vendettas against many families. What made this one special?"

"Because I almost married into it. Nick Navarin was my fiancé. When you destroyed his family, you destroyed him as well. And set me on a sixteen-year quest to bring you and your empire down. And now I have done it."

Saul was suddenly contemptuous. "How, by going public with your knowledge? I am well beloved in Konasta. Many will not believe you. Besides, I am wealthy enough to buy off the courts several times over. This will never come to trial, and you know it."

"But still," she continued, equally placidly, "many of the dealers will believe it, and it will be interesting to see them all conspiring to kill you and take over your empire. Ever seen rats in a feeding frenzy? I imagine it will be somewhat equivalent around the back alleys of Ephanon for a while."

Saul seemed unimpressed. "So? I'll just hire more and better assassins. And better bodyguards. Have you also killed Avram and Lucinda?" When she nodded, he added, "A pity. But more can be found. I've weathered vendettas before; I can weather this."

"Perhaps," she said. "But there's one thing you can't weather."

"And that is?"

"Poison. I hope you enjoyed that brandy, because it will be your last. You'll be dead before evening."

He squawked and flung the glass from him. "You're bluffing!"

"Believe that if you want," she said. "It doesn't matter."

"But . . . You didn't have time to poison it!"

She flipped the hinge on one of her rings open and shut with an almost invisible flash of fingers. "They teach you certain things in the Guild. Especially when you're Owen's hand-picked successor."

"But my empire . . ."

"I don't want your empire," she said simply. "I just wanted you. And now I've got you. Come on, everyone. We're done here."

And one by one they trooped out of the study, leaving Saul gaping stupidly behind them.

53

Night was falling over Hannah's garden as Vera sat with Nick and looked out over the lights of the Ephanon harbor.

"Well, I did it," she said softly. "I found the master supplier. And the man who killed your family. And I took your revenge."

"And now?"

"The Dreamsmoke trade comes tumbling down," she said, deliberately misunderstanding his question.

"Ultimately? I doubt it. The Dreamsmoke trade is too well established. Killing the master supplier may throw things into temporary chaos—great temporary chaos, I grant you—but someone will eventually take his place. The empire will continue."

She sighed deeply, shivering slightly in the cool breeze. "I know. But I did what I said I would, sixteen years ago. I revenged your family like I promised."

"And how do you feel?"

"Strangely empty," she admitted. "I wonder if it even matters anymore."

"Sometimes I wonder the same thing. Not that I don't appreciate your actions. You always did believe in keeping your word, and in that you are a better person than I could ever be. But the reason I became what I am now seems so distant that it is all but irrelevant. I think I forgave them—and myself—years ago. Almost without knowing it. But that still doesn't change my life."

"Mmm. I suppose fate works in mysterious ways. But I still wish . . ."

"What?"

Vera paused and then said, "That I'd been able to forgive you as easily as you've forgiven yourself."

They were both silent for a long moment, and then he added, "So, what now?"

"We catch the next ship back to Ceylonde. Jen and Thibault's second term at the University is about to begin."

He grinned faintly. "I remember. They ease you though the first term, and then . . ."

"Bang," she agreed, with a smile of her own. "They're going to be impossible to live with for the next year and a half, you know."

"So? Go back to Nova Castria with Absalom and leave them in Ceylonde."

They regarded each other in silence for a moment, then burst out laughing.

"Not a chance!" she said. "Would you have left us alone when we were second termers?"

"Not hardly." Another silence, and then, "Aren't you even going to ask me to come back with you?" he said.

"No." Then, regretting the stark word, she added, "It's been over between us for a long time, Nick. I'm only sorry it took me so long to realize it. And even if I had asked you, would you have come?"

"No," he agreed, almost sheepishly. "You're right. I'm no longer a part of your world. My life, such as it is, is here."

She could smell the Ghedrin on his breath, the Dreamsmoke in his clothes; he was no longer even trying to hide it from her.

"You'll be dead in a year, you know," she told him.

He almost smiled. "Who knows? I've surprised you before; I may surprise you again. I can be amazingly stubborn, remember?"

"I remember. And you may just surprise me. For your sake, I hope so."

Another silence, and then she said, "I'm glad I found you again, Nikki. I think I can finally remember all the good times without having them poisoned by the bad."

"I'm glad," he said simply. "And I'm sorry I never could be the man you deserved, Vi . . . I mean, Vera."

She gave a strangled laugh. "Vi will do."

"Vi, then." He smiled at her, a ghost of the old Nick. "And what of Absalom?"

"What of him?"

"Don't get prickly, Vi; I'm no longer in competition. I like him. He'll be good for you."

"Don't be silly. We're just friends."

"Of course you are," he said, in such a neutral tone that she glared at him.

"Besides," she added, "can you see me with a mage and a passel of little magelings?"

She intended it as a joke, but he merely said, in all seriousness, "I can't see you with anything less. Face it, Vivi, you always liked a challenge."

"That's one way of putting it. Another might be: a stubborn tendency to bite off more than I can chew. But you might be right, at that. I'll have to think it over."

"Fair enough. But don't think it over too long. You deserve a little happiness after all the years I sabotaged."

She chuckled ruefully. "Whatever damage I did to myself, Nikki, was solely my fault. Maybe it has taken me this trip to realize that, too."

"Never too old to learn?"

"Something like that," she replied. "It just goes to show, even old dogs like me can sometimes learn new tricks."

He grinned. "So where's Absalom, now?"

"Keeping tactfully out of the way, no doubt."

"Then . . ." He paused. "A kiss for the road? For old time's sake?"

"For old times," she agreed, meeting his lips with hers.

It was infinitely the same, and yet utterly different, gaining in sweetness what it lacked in passion. And she knew she would never break her heart over Nick again.

And for that alone, maybe the whole trip had been worthwhile.

"So where are we going?" Thibault demanded.

"You'll see," Jen declared, leading a stiff pace through the streets.

"We're going back to Saul's, aren't we? What's wrong; do you doubt Vera's resolve?"

"Of course not. And we're not going back to Saul's; not precisely. I just intend to keep a promise. And I need to feel that one good thing has come out of this whole experience . . . Ah, here we are."

It was a café she had occasionally dined at with Jahnee and Kore. And indeed, as she had specified in the note she had delivered to the house earlier, the two were sitting at their usual table, awaiting her.

"Such news!" Kore exclaimed as they approached. "Saul is dead. A heart attack." But her eyes on Jen's were sharp and probing. "What did Aubrey know?"

Jahnee flushed.

"Are you going to tell them *everything*?" Thibault said, wearily.

Ignoring them both, Jen grinned at Kore. "How would you like to be rich?"

"Blackmail?"

"No. Rather call it a reward for a job well done. You're right to suspect me—not that I administered the poison myself. A higher-placed Guild assassin than I did that job."

"A higher placed . . ." Kore's eyes almost went as round as Jahnee's, and she clapped her hands together excitedly. "You're Guild? Both of you?"

Jen bowed slightly. "The Cloak and the Dagger at your service."

"Who's who?"

"Honestly." Jen grinned. "Do you really need to ask?"

"Of course not. So what was Saul up to?"

"The master Dreamsmoke supplier of all of Konasta," Jahnee said quietly.

Jen gaped at her. "How did you know that?" she demanded.

Thibault chuckled.

Jahnee went red. "Aubrey told me," she admitted softly.

"Aubrey?" Kore exclaimed.

"I told you he was one of the good ones. He came to me last night and confessed everything. We're leaving the city together as soon as he takes care of one final task."

Now what on Varia could that be? Jen wondered.

"Well, I'll be hanged," Kore exclaimed. "You sly boots! How long have you and Aubrey . . ."

"For several months now," Jahnee admitted, with another blush.

"Well, I guess *you* don't want a job, then," Jen said. She turned toward Kore. "How would you like to outdo Jahnee and marry an aristocrat?"

"An aristocrat?" The girl's eyes twinkled.

"It would mean working for me for five years. But you'd be paid handsomely for your services, and educated to boot. And when your term of service is up . . . My aunt and I will fix you up with whatever situation you want. It's a system she's used very effectively in the past with her own servants, and I think it's time I had a household of my own."

"Any situation I want?" Kore repeated with a grin, clearly still processing the information. "What if I want the Guild?"

"That may be the easiest of all, if that's truly what you desire."

"I'll have to think on it. But in the meantime . . . You have yourself a servant!"

"Excellent. Here's my address in Ceylonde. The minute you free yourself from service here, come to me. I'll be waiting. Oh, and you might want to start calling me Jen. And he's Thibault. We're not married, either."

"You're not?" Kore's eyes became keener, and Jen masked a sudden surge of anger. It wasn't any of her business. If Thibault wanted Kore . . . she'd kill him!

She turned to Jahnee. "I owe your Aubrey a big favor, myself. I can understand if neither of you want to be in service anymore, but if you ever need any help . . . Come to me."

"Thank you. We will."

"And thank you for everything," Kore added, reaching out to embrace Jen impulsively. "And if Thibault is off limits," she whispered, "you just tell me. I owe you too much to quibble over details."

Jen grinned, hugging her in return. "Off limits," she whispered. "And thanks."

"You're welcome. And I wish you luck. Not that you'll need it." And Kore's eyes sparkled as she released her.

Jen only wished she could share the girl's optimism.

"Did you really mean that?" Absalom said to Vera much

later, when he found her alone in the garden. Nick had long since retreated, and she was enmeshed in a web of thought that twisted she knew not where; she almost didn't hear the mage approach.

She smiled at him ruefully and shifted on the bench to make room. He was wrapped in that hideous dressing gown again, and was radiating his usual welcoming heat, staving off a cold she hadn't realized she felt.

"Did I mean what?" she asked.

"What you said to Saul. That it was only getting him that mattered, not bringing down the Dreamsmoke trade. Was it true? I've been curious about that all day."

"And such remarkable restraint you have shown in not asking me about it until now."

"I am, of course, the soul of tact and discretion," he agreed.

"You are, you know. Thank you for leaving me and Nick some moments alone."

"It's the least I could do. Is he gone now?"

"In all ways. At least, all the bad things are. I don't think he will ever haunt me again."

"I'm glad. But . . ." He waggled an eyebrow at her. "You are, as usual, evading the issue. Did you mean it, or not?"

She smiled. "I'm getting to be rather a good liar, am I not? No, I didn't mean it. The Dreamsmoke trade matters. And I know that the death of one man won't destroy the empire. But at least I can shake it up a little. With your help, of course?"

"Of course. What do you need."

"Your recordings. Magecast, far and wide. Can you do it?"

He appeared to ponder. "It'll be a challenge, but . . . Yes, I believe I can. For a price."

"A price?" She had never known Absalom to stipulate payment before. But when she stared at him, he grinned.

"I have grown irrationally attached to this dressing gown. I know you despise it, but I should hate to part with it. Therefore, in the name of future domestic tranquility . . . I will magecast your recordings if you will promise not to disparage it again."

Vera's shout of laughter echoed over the garden. And

when Absalom grinned back at her, she added, "I have to admit I've grown rather attached to the thing myself; you simply wouldn't seem like Absalom without it. It shall henceforth be safe from my barbs."

"Then all of Konasta will know the identity of the master supplier," he promised. And, however he managed it, she had no doubt it would be so.

54

And, with that, everything was over. Gideon might or might not be dead; Saul was definitely deceased; and the Dreamsmoke empire was, at least temporarily, in tatters.

No one knew quite how Absalom had done it—and the mage was being characteristically mum on the subject—but somehow the word had gone out. By morning, all of Ephanon was buzzing with the revelation. The great philanthropist, exposed for the fraud he was. They were even ruling his poison-induced death a suicide. Stavros had inherited several clubs he reviled, and the threads of Saul's secret fortune had disappeared into who knew what void. Thibault could only imagine Lydea's consternation, both at the knowledge of her father-in-law's duplicity and the loss of all those additional marks.

That alone made the revelation worthwhile.

And in a climate of chaos that threatened to engulf the country for months, they departed Konasta on a modest passenger ship. Vera had secured for each pair a moderately sized cabin, but still Thibault felt a growing claustrophobia that had little to do with the walls of the ship and more to do with the increasing confusion in his mind. Gideon's words continued to eat at him, growing into a festering wound that made him increasingly short-tempered. But he didn't know how to break the cycle until the morning Vera and Absalom came to find him on the deck.

He had been spending more and more time above decks, for out in the wind and the waves was the only time he felt the walls in his mind looming less oppressively. This particular morning was uncharacteristically grey, and the heavy, leaden sky matched his mood, for the questions that plagued him were weighty.

If Gideon had been right about his death, how much else had he been right about? Was Thibault forever doomed to sacrifice his potential for foolish love of Jen? Was it time he accepted that nothing would ever happen between them beyond what had already transpired? Was it time he grew up and moved on? Became the Cloak in truth, to the best of his abilities? Or maybe just abandoned that foolish dream, which had always been more Jen's than his, and went back to the Carpenter's Guild in Gavrone where life had been simpler if less exciting?

He was still mulling over these possibilities when he sensed Vera and Absalom behind him.

"You've been awfully quiet these past few days," Vera said gently. "What ails?"

He felt a betraying prickle of tears in his eyes, and suddenly found himself spilling the whole sordid story of his confrontation with Gideon. There was a long moment of silence when he had finished, and then Absalom said, "It sounds like you've been well and truly mind-fucked, my boy. And by an expert. Let's start with Gideon's death itself. What can you tell me about it?"

Thibault was suddenly grateful for the presence of these two quiet, nonjudgmental souls that bracketed him, one to either side, as if their very essence could bolster and protect him.

He struggled to find an answer to Absalom's question.

I cannot be killed by such as you, he thought. *At least not in a fit of passion and emotion. And there; now you have all the answers you need. If you really were smart, you would have me.*

Logic. Divorce the emotion, and somehow the answer was there. But how?

"I felt the knife go in," he said. "There was blood all over. I felt it, hot on my hands. It was all over the floor, soaking into the stone. And then . . . it was not. No blood. No body."

What else was it that Gideon had said? *It's hard to kill in true cold blood—at least for those burdened by emotion.* Something . . .

Thibault almost had it, but then it skittered away, as elusive as Gideon himself.

"It's almost as if it were all illusion," he exclaimed bitterly. "But I had my amulet activated the whole time. It wasn't as if . . ."

His voice trailed off.

"What is it, lad?" The mage sounded almost amused.

He remembered Jen, the first time they had tried Absalom's new amulets, gazing curiously at the mage. And the mage's own words in reply: *Nice try, but my amulets won't work against my own illusions. In fact, comfortingly enough, I don't think an amulet exists that can work against a mage's illusion on himself.*

"You've worked it out, haven't you?" Absalom added.

"By Varia," Thibault breathed, his jaw falling open. "How long have you known?"

"Since your confusion over his death. There was only one explanation that could fit all the facts. Once you worked that out . . . the rest was obvious."

"What is obvious?" Vera demanded. "What are you talking about?"

Thibault almost smiled.

"Do you want to tell her, or shall I?" Absalom queried.

"I will. Vera, Gideon is a bastard mage. He tricked me with a body shield and a detailed illusion of death. And a whole bunch of things suddenly start to make sense!"

"A bastard mage?" She whistled. "Absalom's kin . . ."

"Except that I am not a sociopath, to boot. Which I strongly suspect our boy might be. All his talk about lack of emotion . . . Never fool yourself, my lad. The lack of emotion is a liability, not a strength. I would have been more worried if you had felt nothing at Gideon's death."

"But . . ." Thibault felt a plaintive note creep into his voice. "Should I have had such an extreme reaction? Is the first time always so hard? I mean, how can I be an assassin—a real assassin—when I can't even kill the bad ones? The ones who really deserve it?"

"I can't answer that, my boy," Absalom said. "But I think I know someone who can. Vera?"

Thibault turned pleading eyes to his mentor.

She smiled ruefully. "Do you think it's ever easy? I've killed more people than I can number, and every one of them deserved it. And the day I stop questioning the necessity will be the day I cease to be an assassin. Don't you see? The only real danger is that it will *cease* to bother you; that it will *cease* to become a problem. Only by having a conscience can you be a true Guild assassin. Otherwise you are just a killer."

"But still, if it troubled me this much this time around—for someone I didn't even kill—will I ever be able to do it again? When it really counts?"

"Let me ask you this," Vera replied. "This time, when it counted, did you hesitate?"

"No . . ."

"Why?"

"Because it was the right thing to do. Because Jen was depending on me to keep Gideon away from her. Because I gave my word. Because he was a monster."

"Just so. And, trust me on this—though I know it doesn't seem possible right now—the next time it really matters, your decision will be the same. No matter how hard it is. In fact, maybe *because* of how hard it is. Taking a life is a serious matter, Thibault, and nothing that serious should ever be easy. It's how you know what's truly important."

He thought about that for a moment; it made an obscure kind of sense. "But Vera . . ."

"What?"

"Your first time. What was it like?"

"Miserable." She chuckled. "I threw up three ways to tomorrow, and wouldn't talk to anyone for a week. Nick had to work hard to cajole me out of it. So, you see, you're doing better than me, already."

"Gideon was right about two things," Absalom added. "You underestimate yourself shockingly, my boy, and you are too content to accept a supporting role. Start discovering who you are, and for yourself—not for me, or Vera, or Jen. I guarantee you'll be pleasantly surprised."

Thibault felt the tears threaten again, but this time out of gratitude. With a few simple words, Absalom had put everything Gideon had said—every ugly truth that had resonated—into a context that made sense. And a context of hope, not despair.

It wasn't just Jen's dream, Thibault suddenly realized. He wanted to be a Guild assassin; he always had. He just hadn't had the confidence in his ability to succeed. So he had accepted the inferior position, letting her lead. Letting her take the blame for his failures. And he had clung to the presumed safety of the Carpenters' Guild like a lifeline, but he didn't want to be safe. He didn't want his life to be boring and predictable.

Jen wasn't the only one who craved challenges.

Things would be different in their partnership from now on, he resolved. He would start holding his own, making demands, expressing his opinion, and if she didn't like it . . . Well, she would just have to learn to. It might even be good for her, in the long run.

He turned suddenly, embracing both Vera and Absalom. "Thank you both; I mean that. What you've done for me . . ."

"Don't be foolish, Thib." Vera cuffed him. "And don't go all sentimental; you'll embarrass me. Now, get back to your partner. She needs a spot of cheering, too."

As Thibault vanished, Absalom leaned back against the ship's railing and said, "Now there's a lad with a considerable weight lifted from his shoulders."

"And all due to you. You're a good man, Absalom."

He grinned at her sardonically. "Don't go all sentimental; you'll embarrass me."

She laughed despite herself, and swatted him. "Must you deflate every serious moment?"

"Only those not of my initiation." He turned to face her then, moving subtly closer, and she felt a panicked pulse leap high in her throat.

"What are you doing?" she squeaked.

"I told you once that when I tried to seduce you, you would know it. Consider yourself forewarned."

She didn't know whether to step closer or bolt, but he soon solved the problem, pulling her to him. He dipped his head and kissed her, long and expertly, until her knees went weak and she had to clutch at him just to remain standing.

And then, just when she thought she couldn't abide any more—that a body could die from such sensations—he released her and stepped away.

She staggered and grabbed at the ship's rail.

"Well?" he said, with a grin. "How was that?"

She wasn't sure whether to kick him overboard or somehow make him kiss her again, so all she said was, tartly, "How can you be so infernally smug about it?"

His lazy grin widened. "That good, huh?"

"What do you think?"

He took her hand and pressed it to his neck; she was startled to find his pulse racing as strongly as her own, for all his calm demeanor.

"I think we all have our own forms of protection," he replied.

"Oh." She paused a moment, still feeling his pulse racing strongly under her fingers. "So what do we do now?"

He leered at her.

"Besides that, I mean."

In response, he took her hand from his neck, and kissed her fingertips instead. "I think, maybe, we just see what life brings us."

"It will be complicated," she cautioned.

"You don't know the half of it! But, as you just said to Thibault, what's worth it that isn't?" And when she didn't reply, he added, cajolingly, "Nick approves . . ."

"Oh," she said dryly. "That makes it all right, then."

He grinned.

"So tell me why I feel like I'm either about to enter into the greatest thing ever, or make the single biggest mistake of my life."

"Probably because you are," he responded. "To both. But, as I have come to realize, you are a women who revels in a good challenge."

"And you can provide that?"

"In abundance. It's the one constant I can guarantee."

She began to laugh. "Well, then, how can I pass on such an offer?"

"I was rather hoping you'd say that. But . . ."

"What?"

He smiled and stepped closer. "I don't think I want to talk anymore, just now."

*   *   *

Thibault found Jen lying face down on her bunk, staring disconsolately out the porthole.

"What's the matter?" he asked.

She turned. "You sound disgustingly chipper. What happened?"

"Vera and Absalom just reminded me of a few very important truths."

"I could use a few of those," she admitted. "Such as?"

"Such as the fact that we've both been had by an expert manipulator. Gideon may not have touched me physically, but he did a tidy number on my mind. I'm kind of glad I killed him. Even though I didn't."

She laughed at that, as he had intended, but it was a sort of strangled laugh. "Sometimes I wonder," she said, after a moment, "if this job was a screaming success or a colossal failure."

He smiled and sat down beside her on the bunk. "Maybe it was a bit of both. You know, I am gradually coming to realize that the world is not rendered in black and white, and that mutually contradictory possibilities can sometimes coexist."

"And what led to this startling revelation?"

He forced himself to say it. "I've lost all sorts of virginities on this job. It kind of makes you think."

Another strangled laugh, but she was regarding him more directly now. "Was it really that hard to kill someone?" she asked. "Even though you didn't?"

He emitted a strangled laugh of his own. "The hardest thing in the world, and don't let anyone tell you differently. But I now know I can do it again, if need be. And so can you."

"Are you sure of that?"

"More sure than I've ever been of anything in my life." And when she didn't answer, he added, "Jen, don't think you're alone in collecting scars. We all have our wounds from this one. Even Vera."

"I suppose. But I sometimes wonder if this isn't why they pay us so highly. Because every now and then a job comes along that changes you at some fundamental level you don't even recognize."

"I was thinking the same thing."

"Really?"

"Yes. Great minds think alike."

"Or great partners. Thibault . . ."

"What?"

"Is it worth it? The money, I mean?"

They regarded each other in silence for a moment. Not all of her scars were physical, he knew, yet that legacy remained, and probably would for life.

"Not even close," they said, simultaneously, and both started laughing.

"Great minds do think alike," she said. "But I still wonder . . . How long is it going to take us to get over this?"

"Or realize we are never going to, and just get on with our lives?"

She stared at him in consternation for a moment. "Is that any way to cheer a girl up?" she demanded, and he shrugged.

"It won't do either of us any good to sugar coat the truth."

"I suppose not. Thank you, though, Thibault. For all you did for me. I wouldn't have made it through this one without you."

"Ditto, ditto," he replied lightly, reaching out to embrace her. "Even if you did try to poison me with rancid fishcake."

She gave a little snort of laughter, but didn't shift or pull away. They just sat that way in silence for long moments, her cheek against his chest and his arm about her shoulders.

And, for once, it was enough.

EPILOGUE

"Well, to what do I owe this unexpected pleasure?" Owen said cheerfully as the four of them trooped glumly into his offices. It wasn't a confrontation any of them relished, and Vera least of all. She had known Owen too long; she knew what this revelation would do to him.

So, "I'm not sure it's going to be a pleasure," she said, and took a seat. The rest followed suit: Jen beside her, and Thibault behind them, with Absalom perched on the window ledge.

Owen studied each of their faces in turn. "This does not look good," he said. No one spoke. "Did you finish your jobs?"

"Yes," Jen said.

"Yes," Vera echoed.

The Guildmaster stared at her in consternation. "Yours, too?"

She nodded.

"Then you found the master supplier? But . . . that's wonderful!" He paused, suddenly uncertain. "Isn't it?"

"It all depends how you define your terms. What is more important? Saving one life, or saving millions?"

"Saving millions, of course, but . . ."

"Then I suppose you could say that our job was a screaming success. At least until a new supplier takes over. For now, though, Ephanon is in chaos. And Nick is still alive."

"He is?" The old man's face brightened; it nearly broke Vera's heart. "How is he?"

"Beyond redemption."

"Oh." His bright expression dimmed, and suddenly the Guildmaster looked every one of his sixty-odd years—and more. "That explains the long faces. But first things first. Is my old friend Saul now safe from assassins?"

"You could say that," Thibault temporized.

"Permanently," Jen added.

"At least from the rogue variety," Vera answered.

"What do you mean?" The old man's voice was plaintive. "I don't understand. You bring me good news, but clothe it in dire words and faces. The lot of you look as if you've just come from a funeral. What ails?"

They all exchanged glances, but Vera knew the task was hers. Owen was practically a father to her; it would kill him if the news came from anyone else.

It would kill him if it came from her.

She steeled herself. "You said that lives of millions outweighed the lives of one. Do you really believe that, no matter the circumstances?"

"Yes, of course. I . . . What do you mean?" His voice was sharp.

She sighed, and gazed out over the courtyard. It was strange to see snow again, after her time in Bergaetta and Konasta. But the quad was thick with it, white, drifted mounds obscuring walls and bushes alike.

"If the one was a friend whom you believe you trusted, would that outweigh the needs of millions?"

Blast the man, he wasn't slow. He was beginning to comprehend it; she could see the hurt blooming like blood in his eyes. "The one being the master supplier?"

She nodded, reluctantly.

"Who is it?" he demanded.

"Who was it," she corrected.

"Very well. Who was it, then?"

"Saul." Her voice was stark as the snow.

He had suspected, yes—but hearing it confirmed was another thing, entirely. His face seemed to crumple, folding in on itself like so much old paper. "No," he moaned. Then more firmly, "No. There has to be a mistake."

Jen was looking like she wanted to vanish. Vera couldn't see Thibault's face from this angle, and she wasn't sure she wanted to see Absalom's. Ever since they had become lovers, the mage's visage did odd things to her at unexpected moments.

"No mistake," she said. "Absalom?"

She did look at him, then, and there were no distractions. His face was as grave as her own.

"I'm sorry," the mage murmured, and activated his device. "I truly am."

Owen sat, stony-faced, through the revelations. Through Avram and Lucinda's conversation; through Acaeus' tormented ramblings. He seemed to be trembling by the end of it.

When it all was over, Absalom deactivated the crystal and handed it across to the Guildmaster. "You can validate it with any mage you want. It's genuine."

Owen clutched it in his palm, hard enough to draw blood. "No need. I believe you. I've met Avram and Lucinda. And I knew about Acaeus. At least . . . that he existed." He seemed to gather himself with an effort. "Is there anything more?"

"Just these." Jen passed the record books across the table.

The Guildmaster studied them in silence. "Been an industrious little traitor, hasn't he?" he said at last. "And all while busily pulling the wool over one foolish old man's eyes."

"Owen . . ." Vera began.

He studied the four of them in turn. "None of you seems to have gotten off lightly." His eyes lingered on Jen's scars and bruises; he seemed to sense the darkness in Thibault's gaze. No doubt he had seen it all, a million times, the subtle flaying of the spirit. "Who killed him?"

Vera could barely speak past the constriction in her throat. "I did. But, Owen, I promise you . . . He didn't suffer."

"That goes without saying. You are not the Stiletto, nor would I wish you to be. Now, how much do I owe you? What did we say? Two thousand for the search, five thousand for locating the master supplier, six thousand for his head?"

"Owen!" She was horrified. "I won't take your money."

"Yes, you will. I didn't become Guildmaster by reneging on deals with my assassins. No matter how distasteful they might be to me personally. I will deposit the six thousand into your account tomorrow."

"I . . ."

"Don't argue with me, Vera; we both know I'm right. Or you will know, when you become Guildmaster after me. Now if you'll excuse me . . ." And he shuffled out, looking old and broken, and she wondered why she had the impression that she had just hastened her advancement to his position by years.

A long silence fell.

"He didn't even ask us what we learned," Jen said at last, her voice small.

Vera heaved a sigh. "Then I suppose that task belongs to me, as his chosen successor." She turned briefly to Jen. The gash on her niece's cheek was finally fading to a pale line of scar. "What did you learn?"

"I don't want to talk about it," Jen answered with a scowl.

She rotated in her seat. "And you, Thibault?"

"I don't want to talk about it, either. Maybe someday, but . . . Not yet."

"Can we go now?" Jen added.

Vera measured them a moment. Then, "Yes; go," she said, wearily.

She turned to Absalom when the two had quit the chamber. "Well, that went extraordinarily badly. Fine Guildmaster *I'm* going to make when I can't even get answers out of my two favorite assassins."

He smiled his slow smile and crossed the room, kneeling down before her chair. He rested one hand on its arm, and the other on her knee. All the distraction was back in force, churning her insides into knots.

She was too old for this, curse it.

"It's always hard to be firm with those we love," he said. "Well . . . under most circumstances."

His wicked grin made his meaning clear, and she hit him.

"Ouch," he said. "I'm filing for mage abuse by upstart Guildmasters-to-be."

"Be serious, Absalom."

"I am being serious. There have been enough long faces

around here to last us a lifetime. Bad things happen. People die, friends betray you, and somehow life goes on."

She almost smiled, and reached out a hand to touch his cheek. "Philosophy from a bastard mage?"

He turned his head, pressing his lips into her palm for a long moment, sending odd little tremors through her before saying cheerfully, "Oh, I'm not precisely a *bastard* mage . . . Didn't I mention?"

If he had intended it as a ploy to distract her, it succeeded. Her startled yelp could be heard halfway across the college.

It was not a pleasant job. It was not even how he had expected to spend his last days in Konasta. But Aubrey could not bring himself to leave the country without this one final revelation.

He knew it was coming, from the moment the news broke, from the moment Saul's star began to fade. The master supplier had fallen, and his illusion clubs with him. Stavros was frantically trying to find a new owner for the Cauldron and its subsidiaries, but in the meantime chaos reigned. And amidst it, Aubrey knew, the murderer who had plagued the Cauldron would be back for one final fling before the club changed hands.

It was too tempting an opportunity to pass up. Especially as no one was likely to catch him.

No one except Aubrey, that is.

Though, to be honest, Aubrey still didn't know exactly what he would do once he unmasked the culprit; that remained in fate's hands. But he had to know, had to confirm that his suspicions were correct, if only for his own peace of mind.

So he haunted the Cauldron, swathed in an illusory disguise. And a week after Jen and Thibault had quit Ephanon, his hunch paid off. He apprehended the murderer in the act, knife poised over the still twitching body.

"Hello," he said.

Gideon looked up. "You," he responded, unsurprised. "You have a lot of gall, showing up here after what you did."

"I might say the same for you," Aubrey replied. "What does this make it? Seven? Eight?"

"That you know of," Gideon countered. "Countless more that you don't."

"Why?" Aubrey asked, almost plaintively.

The Golden Boy shrugged. "Why not? The opportunity was here, so I took it. How long have you suspected?"

"The rumors of your death have been greatly exaggerated," Aubrey responded obliquely, knowing the man would understand.

"So you put two and two together, and made five."

Aubrey nodded. "It wasn't that hard, once I had all the information. I had wondered how the killer kept penetrating our defenses. It didn't seem possible, unless he was part of our defenses. And then I heard that Thibault had killed you, and that you lived. That's when I knew. You're a mage, aren't you?"

Gideon bowed. "Guilty as charged."

"And a psychopath to boot."

"Now, that's uncharitable. I paid my money, the same as everybody."

"And that makes it all right?" Aubrey could barely look at the flayed and twitching body. "To take a life like this?"

"He was a criminal, doomed to die in any case. And isn't it better I sate my urges among the guilty rather than preying on the innocent?"

"I no longer buy that argument. Innocent or guilty, it all means the same to you."

"So?" Gideon said, raising his bloody hands. "What are you going to do?"

"I don't know," Aubrey admitted.

"I'll tell you what you are going to do. You are going to leave me in peace, to go about my business."

"And why would I do that?" It was the moment when fate hung in the balance, when Aubrey could choose between being a hero and being a coward. He only hoped he could make the right decision.

But Gideon knew better. "Because you have have one fatal weakness," he said.

"And what's that?"

Gideon leaned close and, bloody hands to either side of Aubrey's face, kissed him, hard and deep. "That you can't resist me," he said. "Have a good life, Aubrey, though I'm sure we'll meet again. Who knows? I may even feel that I owe you a debt."

"For what?" Aubrey managed.

"For freeing me an empire."

And he quit the room, leaving Aubrey with the corpse and a nagging feeling that, no matter how hard he tried, his life would always feel incomplete without a golden sociopath in it.

Some people, he decided, were just not cut out to be heroes.

Jen shuffled along the hidden paths in the blanketed courtyard, kicking snow up in sparkling drifts. More often than not, it filtered back down, sifting into the tops of her boots and chilling her feet, but she no longer cared. Everything was different, and she wasn't certain if any of it was for the best. She and Thibault had an oddly fraught history between them, her aunt and Absalom were lovers, and they had just killed the Guildmaster's best friend. What was a little snow in her boots to that?

"You're going to catch cold," Thibault said.

She just shrugged.

"So, what are we going to do, now?" he added. "Now that we have defied a soon-to-be Guildmaster and hastened her ascension by almost destroying her predecessor?"

She stared at him in consternation; he sounded almost cheerful. "I don't know. What do you suggest?"

"Well, if I were being sensible and being the old Thibault, I would say we see if the library's open and start studying; I've heard that second term's a nightmare."

"Boring . . ." she began, reflexively.

"I agree. So, as the new Thibault, I suggest we go celebrate my belated majority in style. On your expense. And minus the fish-cake."

That caught her attention. "The *new* Thibault?"

He grinned. "Welcome to a whole new world, my dear. Vera and Absalom—not to mention that bastard Gideon— have opened my eyes about some things, and I'm going to start giving you a run for your money in future. So you'd better step lively if you want to keep up. Now, where are you going to take me?"

Jen's jaw dropped, and it took her a moment to gather her thoughts. Then, "Remi?" she suggested.

"No, not expensive enough; I deserve better. Menot's."

She gaped at him, stopping dead in a snowdrift that mired her to the knees.

He laughed, and fished her out. "See?" he continued. "I have opinions now, too—and I'm not afraid to express them! So what are you going to buy me to drink at Menot's?"

"Champagne?" she hazarded.

"A start. What type?"

"Heinzer?" she began, and then corrected herself with a chuckle. "No, wait; I know. Not expensive enough. Joilliet."

"That'll do. For a start."

She began to grin, feeling the light of a challenge coming on inside her. She could get to like this new Thibault; it certainly would keep her life interesting.

"And what will you get me for *my* majority?" she challenged.

"I don't know; it depends how good you are. If you're very good . . . I may get you two quite nice—and only slightly used—Mepharstan carpets. I happen to know where some good ones are. Along with a lovely crystal chandelier, the perfect receptacle for a little magerie . . ."

He held out an arm and she took it, her delighted laughter carrying them out of the quadrangle and into the wider streets of Ceylonde, sparkling and brilliant under the new-fallen snow.